THE WORLD'S CLASSICS

THE LAW AND THE LADY

WILKIE COLLINS was born in London in 1824, the son of a popular landscape painter. In 1846 he entered Lincoln's Inn as a law student; in 1851 he was called to the bar, and in the same year met Dickens for the first time. Adopting literature as a profession and collaborating with Dickens, he contributed to *Household Words* and *All the Year Round. Basil*, his second novel, was published in 1852. Among his best-known works are *The Woman in White* (1860) and *The Moonstone* (1868). The 'original' of the woman in white was Mrs Caroline Graves with whom Wilkie Collins lived for most of his life from 1859 until his death, though he had three children by Martha Rudd. He died in 1889.

JENNY BOURNE TAYLOR is a lecturer in English at Sussex University. She is the author of *In the Secret Theatre of Home: Wilkie Collins, Sensation Narrative and Nineteenth-Century Psychology* (London, 1988).

THE WORLD'S CLASSICS

WILKIE COLLINS

The Law and the Lady

Edited with an Introduction by
JENNY BOURNE TAYLOR

Oxford · New York
OXFORD UNIVERSITY PRESS

Oxford University Press, Walton Street, Oxford OX2 6DP

Oxford New York

Athens Auckland Bangkok Bogota Bombay
Buenos Aires Calcutta Cape Town Dar es Salaam
Delhi Florence Hong Kong Istanbul Karachi
Kuala Lumpur Madras Madrid Melbourne
Mexico City Nairobi Paris Singapore
Taipei Tokyo Toronto

and associated companies in
Berlin Ibadan

Oxford is a trade mark of Oxford University Press

Editorial material © Jenny Bourne Taylor 1992

First published as a World's Classics paperback 1992

British Library Cataloguing in Publication Data
Data available

Library of Congress Cataloging in Publication Data
Collins, Wilkie, 1824-1889.
The law and the lady / Wilkie Collins; edited with an introduction by
Jenny Bourne Taylor.
p.   cm.—(The World's classics)
Includes bibliographical references.
I. Taylor, Jenny, 1949-   . II. Title.   III. Series.
PR4494.L39   1992   823'8—dc20   91-42961
ISBN 0-19-282847-9

5 7 9 10 8 6

Printed in Great Britain by
BPC Paperbacks Ltd.
Aylesbury, Bucks

CONTENTS

CONTENTS

INTRODUCTION

ALTHOUGH Wilkie Collins wrote over thirty books during a writing career which lasted from 1848 to 1889, until recently his reputation rested on only two—*The Woman in White* and *The Moonstone*. Seldom if ever out of print since they first appeared in 1860 and 1868, these novels became established as classic examples of mid-nineteenth-century mystery and detective fiction—as early specimens of a genre that was to come of age in the 1890s and the 1920s. As interest in Victorian sensation fiction has grown, however, other novels have come back into view. *No Name* (1862) and *Armadale* (1866) have both been republished in the last few years, and together the four novels confirm Collins's place as a writer who, as he put it in the Preface to *Armadale*, often 'oversteps, in more than one direction, the narrow limits within which [critics] are disposed to restrict the development of modern fiction'.[1]

The sensation novels of the 1860s owed their contemporary notoriety to the ways in which they blurred the boundaries between the strange and the familiar—exploring what Henry James described as 'those most mysterious of mysteries, the mysteries that are at our own doors'.[2] They transposed the disturbing and exotic elements of Gothic fiction, the sinister city underworlds of the crime, or 'Newgate', novel, and the excesses of high melodrama into the everyday, domestic, familiar world of the majority of their readers, exploiting the undercurrents of anxiety that lurked behind the doors of the apparently secure middle-class home. Sensation fiction continually played on its central narrative features of disguise and secrecy in order to emphasize the instability of identity, and to display the means

---

[1] Wilkie Collins, Preface to *Armadale* (London, 1866), p. i.
[2] Henry James, 'Miss Braddon', *The Nation*, 9 Nov. 1865, p. 594.

by which social roles (particularly feminine ones) are shaped through the manipulation of cultural perceptions and codes. They formed, in the words of a contemporary critic, 'a host of cleverly complicated stories, the whole interest of which consists in the gradual unravelling of some carefully prepared enigma'.[3] But that pleasurable process of unravelling often revealed not a solution, but another set of questions and secrets that hinged on the protagonist's position within the family. Sensation fiction is concerned with crime and deviance, but it doesn't work by simply tearing off a mask and revealing the criminal. It deploys intricate narrative structures to scrutinize how deviance is perceived and defined. It does not merely exploit the thrill offered by the image of the safe home being threatened from within or without; it breaks down the boundaries between those inner and outer, public and private, worlds.

We are now beginning to recognize the complexity of Collins's fiction, but the emphasis still tends to be confined to the novels of the 1860s. The consensus about his work as a whole is that the last twenty years of his life represented a steady decline, in quality if not in quantity (he published nineteen novels and volumes of stories after 1870). Various factors are held responsible for this decline. His close friend Dickens died in 1870. His health started to deteriorate rapidly after the publication of *The Moonstone* in 1868, and this was accompanied by his growing dependence on opium. His novels in general became much more explicit in their social commitment, dealing with topics as wide-ranging as domestic violence and the lack of control married women had over their property (*Man and Wife*), the condition of 'the fallen woman' (*The New Magdalen*), Christian Socialism (*The Fallen Leaves*), and vivisection (*Heart and Science*). But Collins didn't investigate these issues by turning to recognizably naturalistic modes—he often exaggerated Gothic and melodramatic conventions,

[3] 'The Enigma Novel', *Spectator*, 28 Dec. 1861, p. 1428.

producing novels that appeared dissonant, heavy-handed, bizarre. Yet while his post-1870 work frequently lacks the sophistication of the earlier novels, this process of decline is less relentless than is often assumed. Much of his later work shows an attempt to write socially committed popular literature using the resources of the sensation novel, and illustrates the problems such a project encounters. And while his critical reputation had certainly declined by the mid-1870s, his mass popularity in both Britain and America continued till his death. As far as Collins was concerned he was able to sustain and develop his writing, despite increasingly poor health, throughout the 1870s and 1880s—indeed the early 1870s were, financially, the most successful and stable years of his life.

The Law and the Lady, serialized in the *Graphic* and published in three volumes by Chatto & Windus in 1875, is an intriguing example of Collins's later fiction. An early instance of a novel with a woman investigator as its heroine, it mingles and amplifies, often bizarrely and disturbingly, the concerns and conventions of the novels of the 1860s— 'his new book is an outrageous burlesque upon himself', a reviewer in the *Athenaeum* noted.[4] It focuses on the contest over meaning and power that is bound up with the reconstruction and representation of the past. It investigates the significance of marriage as a legitimation of feminine identity that is founded, essentially, on masquerade. It explores unconscious processes as a key to the workings of the conscious mind, demonstrating, as the prefatory Note points out, 'that the actions of human beings are not invariably governed by the laws of pure reason'. It presents the insane and the abnormal as, in effect, exaggerated versions of the codes that they transgress and as a clue to the workings of the unconscious. *The Law and the Lady*, moreover, is not just a kaleidoscopic replay of the concerns and narrative conventions of the 1860s' novels. By some criteria it is

[4] *Athenaeum*, 20 Feb. 1875, p. 258.

certainly a less successful book than any of these, lacking
the labyrinthine threads of interwoven narrative found in
Armadale or *The Moonstone*. But it also takes greater risks
than did many of the earlier novels, and pushes their central
themes far beyond their previous limits. This occurs both
in its self-conscious recourse to Gothic conventions and in
the central theme of the story: the quest of the heroine to
discover the truth of her husband's first marriage in order
to save her own. In a way that twists round elements of
Charlotte Brontë's *Jane Eyre* and anticipates aspects of
Daphne du Maurier's *Rebecca*, *The Law and the Lady* is
about not one marriage but two: the marriage in the past
embedded within the marriage in the present.

The Law and the Lady marks a significant development of
Collins's career as a popular novelist who appealed primar-
ily to a middle-class readership, but who was also able to
reach beyond it at a time when popular fiction itself was
undergoing complex changes. It was the capacity of sensation novelists to cut across class boundaries, pleasing the
inhabitants of the kitchen as much as those of the drawing
room, that prompted many critics to see them as symptomatic of contemporary cultural crisis and decline. Collins
saw himself above all as a professional writer, and this strict
professionalism was closely bound up with his determination never to remain satisfied with a familiar community of
readers but to extend the boundaries of his audience: to try
to reach that 'Unknown Public' '*beyond the pale of literary
civilization* . . . a public unknown, as an audience, to the
distinguished writers of our time . . . [which] is, in a literary
sense, hardly beginning, as yet, to learn to read'; the 'un-
fathomable' public of the penny novel-journals, or yellow-
backs.[5] Though this readership lay ultimately beyond his
grasp, throughout his working life Collins consistently
attempted to break into new markets both in the magazine

---

[5] Wilkie Collins, 'The Unknown Public', *My Miscellanies* (London,
1863; 2-vol. edn., 1875), 251, 263.

serializations of his novels and in their published form, and *The Law and the Lady* is important in this process.

During the second half of the nineteenth century novel-writing remained dominated by two interconnected methods of publication: journal and magazine serialization, and book publication in the form of the three-volume novel. Collins had built up and consolidated his career and narrative method during the late 1850s and early 1860s, above all through working with Dickens on the weekly journals *Household Words* and *All the Year Round*, journals which actively attempted to develop and address a lower-middle-class family audience. Collins's extraordinary success with *The Woman in White* helped establish him in a position from which he could bargain with publishers; he was lured away from *All the Year Round* by Smith, Elder, owners of the solidly middle-brow *Cornhill*, who paid him the impressive sum of £5,000 for the serialization and publishing rights of *Armadale*. After 1870 his novels were serialized in widely differing kinds of publication, from the well-established, middle-class *Temple Bar* to the proliferating illustrated newspapers such as the *Graphic* and the *Illustrated London News*; he also placed work in *Arrowsmith's Christmas Annual* and in the newspapers syndicated by Tillotson & Co., who owned a newspaper chain in the North of England.

Collins's willingness to publish in a range of different newspapers and journals sprang from the need to hold his own in an expanding world of markets and readers. By 1875 he was in a strong position to set the terms for the publication of his work and to withstand all editorial attempts to tamper with it—his insistence that the editor of the *Graphic* restore the cuts made to the episode in *The Law and the Lady* in which Dexter makes a pass at Valeria demonstrates this. (See the Note on the Text and Appendix.) This publishing flexibility was also an aspect of Collins's ambitious strategy to be at the forefront of new modes of book and journal publication which were becoming possible by the 1870s, and which built on the enormous

expansion of middle-range publishing inaugurated in the
previous decade by the sensation novel. A key part of this
plan was his longer-term aim to bypass the stranglehold of
the three-volume novel format and of the circulating libraries, which maintained a tired hegemony over novel-pro-
duction throughout the second half of the nineteenth
century (as Hardy, Moore, and Gissing were to bear witness). Collins saw these as being both morally and cultu-
rally restrictive—Mudie, the circulating library magnate, a
pious Evangelical, on more than one occasion censored
Collins's work, including *The New Magdalen* (1872). Moreover, for many years Collins had wanted to work with
publishers who were willing to challenge the monopoly of
the exorbitantly priced three-decker, a first edition of which
was extremely expensive—£1. 10s. 6d.[6] In 1853 *Basil* was
one of the novels chosen by Richard Bentley, one of his
most loyal publishers, in an early attempt to lower the price
of first editions. Collins warmly supported the move, although the venture was not to prove successful.[7]

By 1875 Collins was in a position to negotiate a deal with
Andrew Chatto, agreeing that the copyright of all his past
and future books be transferred to the newly established
firm of Chatto & Windus, who would bring out 2s. editions
of his novels within the year, and in some cases 6d. editions.
The Law and the Lady was the first title to appear in this
series, and the scheme was advantageous to both Collins
and Chatto for several reasons. Andrew Chatto was in the
vanguard of a new generation of publishers bringing out
cheap editions in the middle and upper ranges of 'mass'
publishing—the normal price of similar editions was 6s. He
was responding to mid-nineteenth-century developments in
mass-marketing, such as the proliferation of railway
bookstalls selling cheap 'yellowback' editions (often pir-

---

[6] See G. Griest, *Mudie's Circulating Library and the Victorian Novel*
(Bloomington, Ind., 1971).
[7] Ibid. 68.

ated) to a fluid and mobile modern readership. Publishing during the 1870s was thus marked by mutually sustaining tendencies: the expansion of cheap editions at the lower end of the market, and at the upper, the increasingly ossified dominance of the three-volume form. Collins's arrangement with Chatto was shaped by both aspects of this complex process. While his work remained structurally dominated by the need to fill three volumes, he was given the opportunity to expand the market for his earlier work and a stable economic base from which to continue to produce his fiction—he was paid £1,000 for *The Law and the Lady*.[8] The novel that resulted from this, with its web of cultural and literary allusions, cuts right across conventional distinctions between high and popular literary forms.

The plot of *The Law and the Lady* revolves around the gradual disclosure of a series of secrets, each one leading to another set of questions and problems. Valeria Woodville's discovery that her husband Eustace Macallan has been tried for the murder of his first wife Sara is traced in the first volume. The transcript of the trial is embedded in the main body of the story and is organized around another set of questions. Did the woman die poisoned? Who poisoned her? What was his (or her) motive? The finding of the Not Proven verdict leaves Eustace, and Valeria herself, in an unresolved state of limbo. Valeria's circuitous path to 'the truth' is strewn with false clues and misleading signs. As in all detective fiction, two orders of narrative are at work here—the hidden story of the past that emerges through the process of detection and the process of reconstruction through which identities in the present are shaped and confirmed. The ideological meanings of detective stories often hinge on the ways in which the tensions and connections between these two kinds of narrating are con-

[8] Letter from Andrew Chatto to Collins, 5 Feb. 1875; Chatto & Windus Archive, University of Reading.

trolled. What forms of authority are invested in the history that is disinterred and the voice that reconstructs it? What forms of psychic identity are being explored in the drive to disclose the past?

Valeria's reopening of the unresolved trial of her husband is prompted both by the desire to clear his name, and by the need to establish her own position as his legitimate wife—to provide herself with a full selfhood within a given set of symbolic meanings and social conventions—in other words, within the Law. The double story of the marriages in the present and the past act as inverted reflections of each other, each deconstructing the meaning of the other. The vindication of Eustace rests on decoding Sara's ambiguous identity; yet this, and indeed Eustace's innocence of indirectly prompting her death, remain 'not proven'. Valeria's unravelling of the past in order to give herself a place demonstrates how tenuous and indeterminate both her own and her predecessor's selves really are. *The Law and the Lady* thus revolves around the questioning of the two concepts embodied in its title—What is the Law? What is a Lady?—and taking them to pieces. In the process it emerges, not exactly as a feminist detective story, more as a book organized around ambivalence, which is the source of much of its narrative tension. Valeria herself is an ambivalent figure, transgressing wifely roles to give her husband back his name; Eustace is unable to uphold the codes of patriarchal authority, indeed collapses into a ridiculous parody of masculinity in attempting to do so. Moreover, the story hinges on the tacit connections it draws between the process of disclosure through the reading of clues, the exploration of the tangled workings of the mind, and the investigation of the elusive meaning of femininity.

Detective fiction works above all by appealing to a very basic psychic drive: the desire to know. In psychoanalytic terms it can be described as an 'Oedipal' form *par excellence*; indeed the myth of Oedipus itself is, in a sense, the first detective story. This fundamental drive to disclose origins, to discover and control the past, has prompted some to see detective fiction as an implicitly 'masculine' form; but the genre cannot be slotted into neatly gendered categories in this way. In the first place, both women writers and the figure of the female sleuth have always played a crucial, if not canonical role in its development. The female investigator does not make her very first appearance with Valeria, although she is probably the first detective heroine in a full-length novel. The adventures of Mrs Paschell, the 'lady detective' in the anonymous short stories of the 1860s, and the heroine of Anna Katherine Green's *The Levenworth Case* (1878) anticipate the women sleuths of the 'Golden Age' of the 1920s and 1930s.[9]

Secondly, detective fiction is an inherently double-edged form. On the one hand, its central narrative drive is to re-establish order, either to restore the firmly coded social hierarchy of a limited community or to impose coherence on the frightening unknowableness of the city streets (deciphering the mysterious figure of a woman is often a key to this investigation). It can proceed through rational induction and recourse to scientifically proven evidence—the genre developed throughout the latter part of the nineteenth century alongside the establishment of the Metropolitan police and the growth of forensic science.[10] But detective fiction also evolved alongside and as part of the fascination of nineteenth-century culture with the investigation of the unconscious and with irrational states of mind, prior to and culminating with the development of psychoanalysis. It is not surprising that Freud's case histories in the 1890s, with their reading of symptomatic meanings and their decoding of clues, often read like de-

[9] See Michele B. Slung, *Crime On Her Mind* (New York, 1976), 14–20.
[10] See Dennis Porter, *The Pursuit of Crime: Art and Ideology in Detective Fiction* (New Haven, Conn. 1981), and Stephen Knight, *Form and Ideology in Detective Fiction* (London, 1980) for overall accounts of this.

tective stories. Detective fiction might finally be concerned with establishing knowledge of the past and restoring order, but the mysteries which generate them are concerned with overturning established evidence, undermining received truth. Above all they appeal to curiosity, to a kind of inquisitiveness which has distinctly feminine connotations. If the genre owes something to the story of Oedipus, it owes as much to the myth of Pandora.

Connections between Valeria's curiosity, her resolution, her femininity, and her transgression are set down in the opening few chapters of the novel, as 'a strange condition—capricious, idle, inquisitive'.[11] *The Law and the Lady* begins with the final words of the Protestant marriage service in the Book of Common Prayer—words which unambiguously define the legal state of marriage as the wife's subjection to the will of her husband. Valeria's defiance of that rule by disobeying Eustace's wishes thus puts her initially outside the law. And although she voluntarily relinquishes control at the penultimate stage of the investigation, leaving it to the lawyer Mr Playmore and returning to her husband on the discovery of her pregnancy, it is Valeria who throughout reveals the limitations of the lawyer's legal training, showing his perceptions to be built on prejudice and speculation. Thus 'The Law and the Lady begin to understand one another' as Valeria gradually gains ascendancy, not only over her husband and the narrative, but also over the fragmentary texts and visual images around which it revolves. Valeria is, paradoxically, both resolute and indeterminate, both the narrator of the story and a figure in it, and in this she is set against a range of images of femininity that continually shift and flicker. Her first act in the story is to sign the marriage register incorrectly, suggesting that she is in control of neither writing nor identity. She first presents herself to the reader as a reflection in the mirror and through a set of cultural constructions: as the recognizable

[11] *The Law and the Lady*, p. 24.

'strong-minded woman' (her dark hair and heavy eyebrows recall Marian Halcombe in *The Woman in White*), as *not* exhibiting 'the popular yellow hair and the popular painted cheeks', as modelling her hairstyle on that of the Venus de' Medici—an allusion to the most provocative of classical representations of Venus which is picked up later. The partially lame, vacillating Eustace is also described against prevailing masculine stereotypes—indeed he bears an unmistakable physical resemblance to Collins himself.

Valeria's ambiguous position as both narrator of and figure in the story is created in part by the shifting position of the reader, who is encouraged to view and identify with different characters in a range of ways. And Valeria in turn needs to become various kinds of reader or interpreter herself as she attempts to decipher the clues, stories, and images around her. She does not, like her male amateur detective counterparts, depend on rational induction or scientific evidence, but is more likely to follow a different kind of logic, to act impulsively, to pursue random associations, to move in a dream- or trance-like state. In pursuing Valeria's quest, Collins is exploring a range of kinds of mental activity, developing the current debates on the unconscious and its relation to the workings of the conscious mind, and continually exceeding them.[12] In this way the novel does not simply embody a range of processes of projection and fantasy that can be decoded symptomatically—it incorporates that process of decoding into the narrative itself. The episodes that illustrate this exploration most clearly are the scene in Major Fitz-David's study where Valeria is left to discover the clue to her husband's past; the trial, where the past is re-narrated as courtroom drama; and, above all, the appearances of Miserrimus Dexter.

---

[12] For a fuller analysis of this process in Collins's work, see Jenny Bourne Taylor, *In the Secret Theatre of Home: Wilkie Collins, Sensation Narrative and Nineteenth-Century Psychology* (London, 1988).

The Major, an ageing Don Juan, functions as an exaggerated romantic caricature, and recognizing this, Valeria im-
personates an ideal version of herself by applying make-up
before her visit. His study is composed of a set of frag-
mented reflections—a hall of mirrors of fetished femininity.
An aria from Bellini's opera *La Sonnambula* is being sung
as Valeria begins her exploration (somnambulism was often
seen as a key to the workings of the unconscious in contemporary psychological debates), and the search itself
takes on a dream-like aura, as every object in the room
becomes saturated with potential significance. The reader
is placed in the position of voyeur—reinforced when Valeria
discovers that the Major has been watching her unseen
through a chink in the door, as she works her way through
a variety of objects looking for the key to organize them
into a coherent narrative. Valeria makes two traumatic discoveries—that her husband has been married and that he
has been tried for murder; the shock of the second discovery initially obliterates and represses the trauma of the
first. The photograph of Sara and Eustace together is disclosed through a chain of apparently random associations
linked by mementoes or representations of female figures.
The miniature statues that Valeria encounters at the outset,
the Venus de Milo and the Callipygean Venus, not only have
phallic connotations, but also more precisely suggest respec-
tively controlled sexuality and provocative excess; together
they refer back to the Venus de' Medici to which Valeria had
earlier compared herself. These are set against the frag-
mented images on the broken vase, in the water-colours on
the walls, in the locks of women's hair hidden in the Major's
drawer. In the background sounds the dissonant singing of
Fitz-David's protégée prima donna, who unwittingly leads
her to the text of her husband's trial by presenting it as a
sensation drama—as indeed the reader reads it, in a
'Chinese box' structure of reflections and replications.

The 'Story of the Trial' is embedded in the main body
of the narrative, and the reader, like Valeria herself, is

positioned as part of a 'public gallery' of spectators. Reports of trials, both in the press and in book form, were enormously popular in Britain in the mid-nineteenth century. As Anthea Trodd has argued, their fascination, like that of the sensation novel itself, sprang from the pleasurable tension generated by the secrets of domestic life displayed on the public stage.[13] Collins exploits widely in his work both this fascination and his own knowledge of the law; here he may well have drawn in part on a case in J. H. Burton's *Narratives from Criminal Trials in Scotland* (1852) (he owned a copy of this, and other accounts of trials).[14] But the case of Eustace Macallan in *The Law and the Lady* bears a much more obvious resemblance to the celebrated Scottish case of Madeleine Smith of 1857, much reported in the press, which continued to reverberate across England and Scotland for many years to come.[15]

Madeleine Smith was a young middle-class woman, the daughter of a prosperous Glasgow architect, who was tried for murdering her lover, a Jersey shipping-clerk with whom she had conducted a passionate liaison and whom she wished to leave in order to marry into respectable society. Despite overwhelming evidence of her guilt the jury found a verdict of Not Proven, unable to reconcile her apparent display of ladylike refinement with the cunning and resource she must have shown to commit the murder.[16] The

[13] Anthea Trodd, *Domestic Crime in the Victorian Novel* (London, 1989).

[14] See M. L. Bennett, *Catalogue Sale of Books in Wilkie Collins's Library* (London, 1890).

[15] D. MacEachen, 'Wilkie Collins and British Law', *Nineteenth-Century Fiction*, 5 (Sept. 1950), 121–36, and Julian Symons, *Bloody Murder: From the Detective Story to the Crime Novel* (Harmondsworth, 1974), 54 both note the correspondence to the Smith case.

[16] See Richard Altick, *Victorian Studies in Scarlet* (London, 1970), 175–90; Mary Hartman, *Victorian Murderesses* (London, 1985); id., 'Madeleine Smith: Murder for Respectability', *Victorian Studies*, 16 (1973), 381–400; and F. Tennyson Jesse (ed.), *The Trial of Madeleine Smith* (Edinburgh, 1927).

fictional Macallan trial to some extent operates as the inverted replication of the Madeleine Smith affair, replaying its central themes in a different key. Madeleine Smith's explicit letters were read out in court to everyone's prurient fascination; the contents of Eustace Macallan's diary are put on public display. Madeleine Smith was accused of killing her lover with arsenic, concealed in a beverage, the excuse used to obtain the poison being to get rid of rats; Eustace Macallan was accused of doing the same. Both juries arrived at Not Proven verdicts. The case for the defence of Eustace Macallan rested on the argument that Sara Macallan asked Eustace to obtain the arsenic to improve a bad complexion—the same explanation is provided by Madeleine Smith's defence counsel. Both *Chambers's Journal* and *Blackwood's Magazine* had carried articles on the practice of arsenic-eating to improve the complexion (including the discussion of the habits of the Styrian peasantry) in 1851 and 1853, articles which had vastly improved their circulations.[17] Collins inverts the sexes of the accused (the person corresponding most closely to Madeleine Smith is the enigmatic Mrs Beauly, Valeria's real rival). But in tacitly referring back to the earlier case he is both obliquely implying Eustace's moral if not actual responsibility, and drawing on these earlier resonances to suggest that the central question of the trial is somehow bound up with perceptions and anxieties surrounding femininity as masquerade, or impersonation.

Moreover, in replaying the story of the trial in such detail Collins is drawing on and elaborating a well-established set of fictional conventions in which a woman, often middle-class, is the object of the fascinated public gaze. As Anthea Trodd points out, this tradition can be traced back to Scott, whom Collins once described as 'the Prince, the King, the

---

[17] 'The Poison-Eaters', *Chambers's Edinburgh Journal*, 16 (1851), 389–91; 'The Beverages We Infuse', *Blackwood's Edinburgh Magazine*, 74 (1853), 687–9. See also Altick, *Victorian Studies in Scarlet*.

Emperor, the God Almighty of novelists'.[18] *The Heart of
Midlothian* (1818) devotes several chapters to the trial of
Effie Deans. Collins himself uses the trial form as an extended metaphor to organize the narrative of *The Woman
in White*, in which the narrators give testimony to the
readers, who sit in the place of the jury. Other mid-nineteenth-century novels which incorporate trial scenes in-
clude Elizabeth Gaskell's *Mary Barton* (1848), Mrs Henry
Wood's *Mrs Halliburton's Troubles* (1862), Anthony Trollope's *Orley Farm* (1862) and *The Eustace Diamonds* (1873),
George Eliot's *Felix Holt* (1866), and Charles Reade's *Grif-
fith Gaunt* (1866). Collins indirectly alludes to this tradition, particularly to the *frisson* of excitement in the crowd
at the entry of a beautiful woman into the witness-box: 'An
interest of a new kind was excited by the appearance of the
next witness. . . . The Report describes her as a remarkably
attractive person; modest and ladylike in her manner, and,
to all appearance, feeling sensitively the public position in
which she was placed.'[19] Indeed, Helena Beauly is
presented here as another deeply puzzling character, mistress of the codes of femininity and of disguise: a *femme
fatale*. She is indeed revealed to be a mistress of dissem-
blance, but for her own pleasure. She engages in a substitu-
tion plot worthy 'of a French play' to attend a masked ball
full of 'ladies of doubtful virtue . . . and gentlemen on the
outlying limits of society'.[20] Her disguise is shown to be
playfully transgressive, her suspicious behaviour another
false clue, interpreted through Valeria's own jealous projec-
tions.

It is Sara Macallan whose ambiguous character is resolved neither in the trial nor in the story as a whole; she
is the underside of all the images of 'the lady', including

---

[18] Trodd, *Domestic Crime in the Victorian Novel*, 135; Kenneth Robinson, *Wilkie Collins: A Biography* (London, 1951), 298.
[19] *The Law and the Lady*, 169.
[20] p. 267.

that of Valeria, that play across the novel. Like Rosanna Spearman in *The Moonstone*, Sara is disturbing because she represents passionate female sexuality that is not the object of male desire. Her shifting identity as it emerges during the trial reveals the unreliability of perception and testimony: the one constant feature she displays is her refusal to keep within the proper limits. Helena Beauly and Sara Macallan are polarized figures in many ways but they share certain characteristics—impulsiveness, unpredictability, the desire to transform themselves—characteristics shared too, of course, by Valeria herself.

Valeria's resemblance to Helena is emphasized by Eustace's desire for them both, but Valeria and Sara merge together in the imagination of Miserrimus Dexter. 'Where is the resemblance which has brought her back to me? . . . In the pose of the figure, perhaps?' he asks himself.[21] With the appearance of Dexter *The Law and the Lady* radically changes key, ironically and self-reflexively mingling the conventions of detective fiction with Gothic and fantastic modes. Critics consistently found Dexter the most unacceptable figure in the book, not simply macabre but impossible to make sense of at all. He overturns all rational and coherent ways of making sense of him, and thus acts out the investigation of the boundaries of consciousness at work in the novel in his continual transformations. He is weird but never monstrous, never completely 'other', even if he is made so by others's ignorance and fear. His character and behaviour are presented as exaggerations of familiar cultural stereotypes, taken to pieces and juxtaposed in startling combinations. At the same time he provides a self-conscious commentary on the processes of representation and story-telling that are at work throughout, starting with his analysis of his own name, and undermining the notion of objective evidence by retelling all versions of events as yet another kind of story.

[21] p. 215.

Dexter thus appears not simply as a fantastic image but as a figure who works on different registers directly analogous to both the dreaming and the creative process. In many ways he embodies the activity that a contemporary critic, E. S. Dallas, described as characterizing the working of the 'Hidden Soul' or the unconscious, particularly in artistic activity: 'It is reason out for a holiday; it is perception in a hurry; it is memory gone wild; it is the dalliance of desire.'[22] He is a 'strange and startling creature—literally the half of a man', whose truncated body displaces the 'lower half' that he lacks.[23] He challenges the notion of a coherent self by crossing human boundaries—he is described as a 'new Centaur', hybrid or cyborg: part human, part machine, part animal; he is finally fetished into a 'Thing', an 'Indian idol'. He enacts and subverts different Romantic and post-Romantic styles, periods, and genres, from creative genius to orientalized exotic to decadent aesthete. His house is a pastiche of high Gothic set in a bleak landscape of modernity—a half-built suburb. He is first seen in an apparent state of high mania, impersonating Nelson, Napoleon, Shakespeare. But this soon turns into a performance of a performance, presented as a 'fantastic and frightful apparition' and concluding with the performance of a playwright. His painting could be a parody of Fuseli or of Richard Dadd's 'Sketches to Illustrate the Passions'; his dress, his poetry, his music display an exaggerated decadence. The views of Dexter in his different roles as agent in the story continually shift, but the most sustained account of him is provided by Valeria herself:

It seems to me that he openly expresses—I admit in a very reckless and boisterous way—thoughts and feelings which most of us are ashamed of as weaknesses, and which we keep to ourselves accordingly. I confess I have often fancied myself transformed into some other person, and have felt a certain

---

[22] E. S. Dallas, *The Gay Science* (London, 1866), i. 182.
[23] *The Law and the Lady*, 173.

pleasure in seeing myself in my new character. . . . Mr Dexter lets out the secret, just as the children do . . . I must say I have enjoyed my visit; and, worse still, Miserrimus Dexter really interests me![24]

Dexter's final demise is explained by implicit reference to two contemporary psychological paradigms. The complete breakdown of his consciousness, brought about by his 'morbid sensitivity' and his limited environment, corresponds with more liberal notions of 'moral management' that were current in the mid-nineteenth century. At the same time, however, his collapse in the form of an inevitable process of degeneration, in which his latent insanity is on a direct continuum with his eccentricity, draws on later, social Darwinist theories of mental decay.[25] But his 'advancing eclipse of the brain', when his consciousness finally disintegrates and the clue to the past emerges, takes place as he is composing a story. Memory takes the place of narrative and finally usurps it—but as another story of displaced and transformed identities, which at first 'seemed to set interpretation at defiance'.[26] The truth that is finally revealed turns out to be no mystery at all, but to be at once both the simplest and the most difficult of resolutions, arrived at via a tortuous route.

[24] pp. 221-2.
[25] See Taylor, *In the Secret Theatre of Home*, 223–7, for a more detailed account of this.
[26] *The Law and the Lady*, p. 349.

NOTE ON THE TEXT

The Law and the Lady was first issued in serial form in twenty-six episodes in the *Graphic* between 26 September 1874 and 13 March 1875. The *Graphic* newspaper was composed almost entirely of engraved illustrations, the weekly serial being the longest piece of continuous prose. Each episode began with a full-page illustration, a selection of which were used as illustrations for the one-volume editions of the novel. A significant, if small, intervention by the editor of the *Graphic* occurs at the end of Chapter XXXV. The description of Miserrimus Dexter's advances to Valeria appears in the manuscript and the one- and three-volume editions as 'He caught my hand in his, and devoured it with kisses. His lips burnt me like fire. He twisted himself suddenly in the chair, and wound his arm round my waist. In the terror and indignation of the moment, vainly struggling with him, I cried out for help.' (p. 299.) This is modified in the *Graphic* to 'He caught my hand in his and covered it with kisses. In the indignation of the moment I cried out for help.' (26 January 1875, p. 83.) A note is appended to the end of the following episode, quoting Collins's full version and adding: 'The editor of this journal suppressed a portion of the paragraph on the grounds that the description originally given was objectionable. Mr Wilkie Collins having since informed us, through his legal advisors, that, according to the terms of his agreement with the proprieters of *The Graphic* his proofs are to be published *verbatim* from his MS, the passage in question is here given in its original form.' (30 January, p. 107.) A further editorial note, expressing disapproval of *The Law and the Lady*, follows the final episode on 13 March 1875 (p. 251). For details of this and the correspondence in the *World* that followed (including Collins's lengthy defence), see Appendix.

Apart from minor changes of punctuation the serial version was not revised for the three-volume edition, which was published by Chatto & Windus in February 1875. Collins was paid £1,000 by Chatto & Windus for the novel, £500 in August 1875 and £500 in February 1876. With the publication of *The Law and the Lady*, copyright for all Collins's past and future work transferred to Chatto & Windus, who agreed to bring out one-volume editions of his novels within the year. The first issue of the one-volume edition of *The Law and the Lady* was duly published later in 1875, with only slight revisions of punctuation, and subsequent editions (what we would now call impressions) were published in 1876, 1885, and in various Chatto collected editions from 1890 onwards, including the 'Piccadilly', 6d. edition of 1890. It was also published in volume form for the European market by Tauchnitz in Leipzig almost simultaneously with the Chatto three-volume edition, and a French edition, *La Piste du crime*, was published by the Librairie Hachette et Cie. It was published in New York by Harper Brothers, with some minor cuts and American spelling, in the Harper's Illustrated Library edition in 1875, and in Canada by Hunter, Rose & Co, Toronto, in the same year.

The text of this edition of the novel is based on the 1876 one-volume edition. It has been compared with the *Graphic* serialization, the Chatto three-volume edition, the Tauchnitz edition, and the Harper's Illustrated Library edition. I should like to thank Andrew Gasson, of the Wilkie Collins Society, for making his impressive Collins collection (possibly the finest that exists in private hands) available to me. The only corrections made to this edition are the silent emendation of printers' errors.

The manuscript, originally owned by Dorothy Sayers, is now held at the Harry Ransom Humanities Research Center at the University of Texas, Austin, and I should like to thank the librarians for sending me photocopies of sections of it. It consists of 281 pages and, like most of Collins's manuscripts, is much revised and overscored but still marked up as printer's copy.

SELECT BIBLIOGRAPHY

BIBLIOGRAPHIES

ANDREW, R. V., 'A Wilkie Collins Check-List', *English Studies in Africa* (March 1960), 79–98.

ASHLEY, ROBERT P., 'Wilkie Collins', in *Victorian Fiction: A Second Guide to Research*, ed. George H. Ford, (New York 1978).

BEETZ, KIRK H., *Wilkie Collins: An Annotated Bibliography, 1889–1976* (Metuchen, NJ, and London, 1976).

GASSON, ANDREW, 'Wilkie Collins: A Collector's and Bibliographer's Challenge', *Private Library*, Third Ser., 3/2 (Summer 1980), 51–77.

PARRISH, M. L., *Wilkie Collins and Charles Reade: First Editions, with a Few Exceptions, in the Library at Dormy House* (London, 1940).

WOLFF, ROBERT L., 'Wilkie Collins', in *Nineteenth-Century Fiction: A Bibliographical Catalogue* (New York, 1981–6), i. 254–72.

BIOGRAPHIES

CLARKE, WILLIAM, *The Secret Life of Wilkie Collins* (London, 1988).

PETERS, CATHERINE, *The King of Inventors: A Life of Wilkie Collins* (London, 1991).

ROBINSON, KENNETH, *Wilkie Collins: A Biography* (London, 1951; repr. 1974).

SAYERS, DOROTHY L., *Wilkie Collins: A Biographical and Critical Study*, ed. E. R. Gregory (uncompleted) (Toledo, 1977).

CRITICAL STUDIES

ANDREW, R. V., *Wilkie Collins: A Critical Survey of his Prose Fiction* (New York, 1979).

ASHLEY, ROBERT P., *Wilkie Collins* (London, 1952).

BARICKMAN, R., MacDONALD, S., and STARK, M.,

Corrupt Relations: Dickens, Thackeray, Trollope, Wilkie Collins and the Victorian Sexual System (New York, 1982).

FAHNESTOCK, JEANNE, 'The Heroine of Irregular Features: Physiognomy and Conventions of Heroine Description', *Victorian Studies*, 24 (Spring 1981), 325–50.

HUGHES, WINNIFRED, *The Maniac in the Cellar: The Sensation Novel of the 1860s* (Princeton, NJ, 1980).

LONOFF, SUE, *Wilkie Collins and His Victorian Readers: A Study in the Rhetoric of Authorship* (New York, 1982).

MACEACHEN, D., 'Wilkie Collins and British Law', *Nineteenth-Century Fiction*, 5 (Sept. 1950), 121–36.

MARSHALL, WILLIAM, *Wilkie Collins* (New York, 1970).

O'NEILL, PHILLIP, *Wilkie Collins: Women, Property and Propriety* (London, 1988).

RANCE, NICHOLAS, *Wilkie Collins and Other Sensation Novelists: Walking the Moral Hospital* (London, 1991).

TAYLOR, JENNY BOURNE, *In the Secret Theatre of Home: Wilkie Collins, Sensation Narrative and Nineteenth-Century Psychology* (London, 1988).

GENERAL STUDIES

CADOGAN, MARY, and CRAIG, PATRICIA, *The Lady Investigates* (London, 1981).

OUSBY, IAN, *Bloodhounds of Heaven: The Detective in English Fiction from Godwin to Doyle* (Cambridge, Mass., 1976).

PORTER, DENNIS, *The Pursuit of Crime: Art and Ideology in Detective Fiction* (New Haven, Conn., 1981).

PRIESTMAN, MARTIN, *Detective Fiction and Literature: The Figure on the Carpet* (New York, 1991).

SLUNG, MICHELE B., *Crime on Her Mind* (New York, 1976; repr. Harmondsworth, 1977).

SYMONS, JULIAN, *Bloody Murder: From the Detective Story to the Crime Novel* (London, 1972; repr. Harmondsworth, 1974).

TODOROV, T., 'The Typology of Detective Fiction', trans. Richard Howard, in *The Poetics of Prose* (Oxford, 1977).

TRODD, ANTHEA, *Domestic Crime in the Victorian Novel* (London, 1989).

A CHRONOLOGY OF WILLIAM WILKIE COLLINS

1824   (8 January) Born at 11 New Cavendish Street, St Marylebone, London, elder son of William Collins, RA (1788–1848), artist, and Harriet Collins *née* Geddes (1790–1868).

1826   (Spring) Family moves to Pond Street, Hampstead.

1828   (25 January) Brother, Charles Allston Collins, born.

1829   (Autumn) Family moves to Hampstead Square.

1830   Family moves to Porchester Terrace, Bayswater.

1835   (January) Starts school, the Maida Hill Academy.

1836   (19 September–15 August 1838) Family visits France and Italy, then settles at 20 Avenue Road, Regent's Park.

1838–40 Attends Mr Cole's private boarding-school in Highbury.

1840   (Summer) Family moves to 85 Oxford Terrace, Bayswater.

1841   (January) Apprenticed to Antrobus & Co., tea merchants, The Strand.

1842   (June–July) Trip to the Highlands of Scotland and Shetland with his father.

1843   (August) First signed publication, 'The Last Stage Coachman', in the *Illuminated Magazine*.

1845   (January) First novel, set in Tahiti, submitted to Chapman & Hall. Rejected.

1846   (May) Admitted to Lincoln's Inn as law student.

1847   (17 February) Death of William Collins.

1848   (Summer) Family moves to 38 Blandford Square; (November) first book, *Memoirs of the Life of William Collins, Esq., R.A.*, published.

1850   (February) First novel, *Antonina*, published; (Summer) family moves to 17 Hanover Terrace.

1851   (January) Travel book on Cornwall, *Rambles Beyond Railways*, published; (March) meets Dickens for the first time; (May) acts with Dickens in Bulwer-Lytton's *Not So Bad As We Seem*.

1852   (January) *Mr Wray's Cash Box* published; (24 April) 'A Terribly Strange Bed', first contribution to *Household Words*; (November) *Basil* published.

1853   (October–December) Tours Switzerland and Italy with Dickens and Augustus Egg.

1854   (June) *Hide and Seek* published.

1855   (16 June) First play, *The Lighthouse*, performed by Dickens's theatrical company at Tavistock House.

1856   (February) *After Dark* published; (March) *A Rogue's Life* serialized in *Household Words*; (March–April) visit to Paris with Dickens; (October) joins staff of *Household Words*.

1857   (January–June) *The Dead Secret* serialized in *Household Words* (published in volume form in June); (6 January) *The Frozen Deep* performed by Dickens's theatrical company at Tavistock House; (August) *The Lighthouse* performed at the Olympic Theatre; (October) *The Lazy Tour of Two Idle Apprentices* serialized in *Household Words*; collaborates with Dickens on *The Perils of Certain English Prisoners*.

1858   (October) *The Red Vial* produced at the Olympic Theatre.

1859   (January–February) Lives with Caroline Graves (with whom he lives for the rest of his life, with one interlude); (May–December) lives at 2a New Cavendish Street; (October) *The Queen of Hearts* published; (November–August 1860) *The Woman in White* serialized in *All the Year Round*; (December) Moves to 12 Harley Street.

1860   (August) *The Woman in White* published in volume form.

1861   (January) Resigns from *All the Year Round*.

1862   (March–January 1863) *No Name* serialized in *All the
            Year Round* (published in volume form in December).

1863   *My Miscellanies* published.

1864   (November–June 1866) *Armadale* serialized in the
            Cornhill; (December) moves to 9 Melcombe Place,
            Dorset Square.

1866   (May) *Armadale* published in volume form.

1867   (September) Moves to 90 Gloucester Place, Port-
            man Square; collaborates with Dickens on *No
            Thoroughfare*, published as Christmas number of *All
            the Year Round*; dramatic version performed at the
            Adelphi Theatre (Christmas Eve).

1868   (January–August) *The Moonstone* serialized in *All the
            Year Round* (published in volume form in July); (19
            March) mother, Harriet Collins, dies; Collins forms
            relationship with Martha Rudd (Mrs Dawson);
            (October) Caroline Graves marries Joseph Clow.

1869   (March) *Black and White*, written in collaboration
            with Charles Fechter, produced at the Adelphi
            Theatre; (4 July) daughter, Marian Dawson, by Mar-
            tha Rudd, born at 33 Bolsover Street, Portland Place.

1870   (June) *Man and Wife* published in volume form; (9
            June) Dickens dies.

1871   (14 May) Second daughter, Harriet Constance
            Dawson, by Martha Rudd, born at 33 Bolsover
            Street; (May) Caroline Graves again living with
            Collins; (October) dramatic version of *The Woman
            in White* performed at Olympic Theatre; (October–
            March 1872) *Poor Miss Finch* serialized in *Cassell's
            Magazine*.

1872   (January–December) *The New Magdalen* serialized
            in *Temple Bar*; (February) *Poor Miss Finch* published
            in volume form.

1873   (9 April) Brother, Charles Allston Collins, dies;
            (May) *The New Magdalen* published in volume
            form; dramatic version performed at the Olympic

Theatre; *Miss or Mrs? and Other Stories in Outline*
published; (September–March 1874) tours United
States and Canada, giving readings of his work.

1874   (September–March 1875) *The Law and the Lady*
serialised in the *Graphic*; (November) *The Frozen
Deep and Other Stories* published; (December) son,
by Martha Rudd, William Charles Collins Dawson
born, at 10 Taunton Place, Regent's Park.

1875   Copyrights in Collins's work transferred to Chatto
& Windus who become his main British publisher;
(February) *The Law and the Lady* published in vol-
ume form.

1876   (April) *Miss Gwilt* (dramatic version of *Armadale*)
performed at the Globe Theatre; (August) *The Two
Destinies* serialized in *Temple Bar*; published in volume form.

1877   (September) Dramatic version of *The Moonstone*
performed at the Olympic Theatre; (December)
'My Lady's Money' published in *Illustrated London
News*; published in volume form.

1878   *The Haunted Hotel* published in volume form; *The
Fallen Leaves—First Series* serialized in both *The
World* and *Canadian Monthly*.

1879   *The Fallen Leaves* published in volume form; *A
Rogue's Life* published in volume form; *Jezebel's
Daughter* syndicated by Tillotson's newspaper
chain, appearing in thirteen Northern newspapers.
Collins syndicates several of his later books with
Tillotson.

1880   *Jezebel's Daughter* published in volume form.

1881   *The Black Robe* serialized in *Canadian Monthly*; published in volume form.

1881   A. P. Watt becomes Collins's literary agent.

1883   *Heart and Science* published in volume form.

1884   'I Say No' published in volume form.

1886   *The Evil Genius* published in volume form; *The Guilty
River* published in *Arrowsmith's Christmas Annual*.

The Law and the Lady

Inscribed to

REGNIER*

(of the Théâtre Français, Paris),

*in token of admiration for the great actor
and of affection for the true friend*

NOTE

Addressed to the Reader[*]

IN offering this book to you, I have no Preface to write. I have only to request that you will bear in mind certain established truths, which occasionally escape your memory when you are reading a work of fiction. Be pleased, then, to remember (First): that the actions of human beings are not invariably governed by the laws of pure reason. (Secondly): that we are by no means always in the habit (especially when we happen to be women) of bestowing our love on the objects which are the most deserving of it, in the opinions of our friends. (Thirdly and Lastly): that Characters which may not have appeared, and Events which may not have taken place, within the limits of our own individual experience, may nevertheless be perfectly natural Characters and perfectly probable Events, for all that. Having said these few words, I have said all that seems to be necessary at the present time; and I bid you cordially farewell.

W.C.

London, February 1, 1875.

CONTENTS

THE LAW AND THE LADY

CHAPTER I*

The Bride's Mistake

'FOR after this manner in the old time the holy women also, who trusted in God, adorned themselves, being in subjection unto their own husbands; even as Sarah obeyed Abraham, calling him lord; whose daughters ye are, as long as ye do well, and are not afraid with any amazement.'

Concluding the Marriage Service of the Church of England* in those well-known words, my Uncle Starkweather shut up his book, and looked at me across the altar rails with a hearty expression of interest on his broad red face. At the same time my aunt, Mrs Starkweather, standing by my side, tapped me smartly on the shoulder, and said,

'Valeria,* you are married!'

Where were my thoughts? What had become of my attention? I was too bewildered to know. I started and looked at my new husband. He seemed to be almost as much bewildered as I was. The same thought had, as I believe, occurred to us both at the same moment. Was it really possible—in spite of his mother's opposition to our marriage—that we were Man and Wife? My Aunt Starkweather settled the question by a second tap on my shoulder.

'Take his arm!' she whispered in the tone of a woman who had lost all patience with me.

I took his arm.

'Follow your uncle.'

Holding fast by my husband's arm, I followed my uncle and the curate who had assisted him at the marriage.

The two clergymen led us into the vestry. The church was in one of the dreary quarters of London, situated between the City and the West End; the day was dull; the atmosphere was heavy and damp. We were a melancholy little wedding party, worthy of the dreary neighbourhood and the dull day. No relatives or friends of my husband's were present; his family, as I have already hinted, disapproved of his marriage. Except my uncle and my aunt, no other relations appeared on my side. I had lost both my parents, and I had but few friends. My dear father's faithful old clerk, Benjamin, attended the wedding to 'give me away,' as the phrase is. He had known me from a child, and, in my forlorn position, he was as good as a father to me.

The last ceremony left to be performed was, as usual, the signing of the marriage-register. In the confusion of the moment (and in the absence of any information to guide me) I committed a mistake—ominous, in my Aunt Starkweather's opinion, of evil to come. I signed my married instead of my maiden name.

'What!' cried my uncle, in his loudest and cheeriest tones, 'you have forgotten your own name already? Well! well! let us hope you will never repent parting with it so readily. Try again, Valeria—try again.'

With trembling fingers I struck the pen through my first effort and wrote my maiden name, very badly indeed, as follows:-

Valeria Brinton *

When it came to my husband's turn I noticed, with surprise, that *his* hand trembled too, and that *he* produced a very poor specimen of his customary signature:-

Eustace Woodville

My aunt, on being requested to sign, complied under protest. 'A bad beginning!' she said, pointing to my first unfortunate signature with the feather-end of her pen. 'I say with my husband—I hope you may not live to regret it.'

Even then, in the days of my ignorance and my innocence, that curious outbreak of my aunt's superstition produced a certain uneasy sensation in my mind. It was a consolation to me to feel the reassuring pressure of my husband's hand. It was an indescribable relief to hear my uncle's hearty voice wishing me a happy life at parting. The good man had left his north-country Vicarage (my home since the death of my parents) expressly to read the service at my marriage; and he and my aunt had arranged to return by the mid-day train. He folded me in his great strong arms, and he gave me a kiss which must certainly have been heard by the idlers waiting for the bride and bridegroom outside the church door.

'I wish you health and happiness, my love, with all my heart. You are old enough to choose for yourself, and—no offence, Mr Woodville, you and I are new friends—and I pray God, Valeria, it may turn out that you have chosen well. Our house will be dreary enough without you; but I don't complain, my dear. On the contrary, if this change in your life makes you happier, I rejoice. Come! come! don't cry, or you will set your aunt off—and it's no joke at her time of life. Besides, crying will spoil your beauty. Dry your eyes and look in the glass there, and you will see that I am right. Good-bye, child—and God bless you!'

He tucked my aunt under his arm, and hurried out. My heart sank a little, dearly as I loved my husband, when I had seen the last of the true friend and protector of my maiden days.

The parting with old Benjamin came next. 'I wish you well, my dear; don't forget me,' was all he said. But the old days at home came back on me at those few words. Benjamin always dined with us on Sundays in my father's time, and always brought some little present with him for his master's child. I was very near to 'spoiling my beauty' (as my uncle had put it) when I offered the old man my cheek to kiss, and heard him sigh to himself, as if he too was not quite hopeful about my future life.

My husband's voice roused me, and turned my mind to happier thoughts.

'Shall we go, Valeria?' he asked.

I stopped him on our way out, to take advantage of my uncle's advice. In other words, to see how I looked in the glass over the vestry fireplace.

What does the glass show me?

The glass shows a tall and slender young woman of three-and-twenty years of age. She is not at all the sort of person who attracts attention in the street, seeing that she fails to exhibit the popular yellow hair and the popular painted cheeks. Her hair is black; dressed, in these later days (as it was dressed years since to please her father), in broad ripples drawn back from the forehead, and gathered into a simple knot behind (like the hair of the Venus de' Medici*), so as to show the neck beneath. Her complexion is pale: except in moments of violent agitation there is no colour to be seen in her face. Her eyes are of so dark a blue that they are generally mistaken for black. Her eyebrows are well enough in form, but they are too dark, and too strongly marked. Her nose just inclines towards the aquiline bend, and is considered a little too large by persons difficult to please in the matter of noses. The mouth, her best feature, is very delicately shaped, and is capable of presenting great varieties of expression. As to the face in general, it is too narrow and too long at the lower part; too broad and too low in the higher regions of the eyes and the head. The whole picture, as reflected in the glass, represents a woman of some elegance, rather too pale, and rather too sedate and serious in her moments of silence and repose—in short, a person who fails to strike the ordinary observer at first sight; but who gains in general estimation, on a second, and sometimes even on a third, view. As for her dress, it studiously conceals, instead of proclaiming, that she has been married that morning. She wears a grey Cashmere tunic* trimmed with grey silk, and having a skirt of the same material and colour beneath it. On her head is a bonnet to match, relieved by a quilling of white muslin, with one deep red rose, as a morsel of positive colour, to complete the effect of the whole dress.

Have I succeeded or failed in describing the picture of myself which I see in the glass? It is not for me to say. I have done my best to keep clear of the two vanities—the vanity of depreciating, and the vanity of praising, my own personal appearance. For the rest, well written or badly written, thank Heaven it is done!

And whom do I see in the glass, standing by my side?

I see a man who is not quite so tall as I am, and who has the misfortune of looking older than his years. His forehead is prematurely bald. His big chestnut-coloured beard and his long overhanging moustache are already streaked with grey. He has the colour in his face which my face wants, and the firmness in his figure which my figure wants. He looks at me with the tenderest and gentlest eyes (of a light brown) that I ever saw in the countenance of a man. His smile is rare and sweet; his manner, perfectly quiet and retiring, has yet a latent persuasiveness in it, which is (to women) irresistibly winning. He just halts a little in his walk, from the effect of an injury received in past years, when he was a soldier serving in India, and he carries a thick bamboo cane, with a curious crutch handle (an old favourite), to help himself along whenever he gets on his feet, indoors or out. With this one little drawback (if it *is* a drawback), there is nothing infirm or old or awkward about him; his slight limp when he walks has (perhaps to my partial eyes) a certain quaint grace of its own, which is pleasanter to see than the unrestrained activity of other men. And last, and best of all, I love him! I love him! I love him! And there is an end of my portrait of my husband on our wedding-day.

The glass has told me all I want to know. We leave the vestry at last.

The sky, cloudy since the morning, has darkened while we have been in the church, and the rain is beginning to fall heavily. The idlers outside stare at us grimly under their umbrellas, as we pass through their ranks, and hasten into our carriage. No cheering; no sunshine; no flowers strewn in our path; no grand breakfast; no genial speeches; no bridesmaids; no father's or mother's blessing. A dreary wedding—there is no denying it—and (if Aunt Starkweather is right) a bad beginning as well!

A *coupé* has been reserved for us at the railway station. The attentive porter, on the look-out for his fee, pulls down the blinds over the side windows of the carriage, and shuts out all prying eyes in that way. After what seems to be an interminable delay the train starts. My husband winds his arm round me. 'At last!' he whispers, with love in his eyes that no words can utter, and presses me to him gently. My arm steals round his neck; my eyes answer his eyes. Our lips meet in the first long lingering kiss of our married life.

Oh, what recollections of that journey rise in me as I write! Let me dry my eyes, and shut up my paper for the day.

CHAPTER II

The Bride's Thoughts

WE had been travelling for a little more than an hour, when a change passed insensibly over us both.

Still sitting close together, with my hand in his, with my head on his shoulder, little by little we fell insensibly into silence. Had we already exhausted the narrow yet eloquent vocabulary of love? Or had we determined by unexpressed consent, after enjoying the luxury of passion that speaks, to try the deeper and finer rapture of passion that thinks? I can hardly determine; I only know that a time came when under some strange influence our lips were closed towards each other. We travelled along, each of us absorbed in our own reverie. Was he thinking exclusively of me—as I was thinking exclusively of him? Before the journey's end I had my doubts. At a little later time I knew for certain, that his thoughts, wandering far away from his young wife, were all turned inward on his own unhappy self.

For me, the secret pleasure of filling my mind with him while I felt him by my side, was a luxury in itself.

I pictured in my thoughts our first meeting in the neighbourhood of my uncle's house.

Our famous north-country trout-stream wound its flashing and foaming way through a ravine in the rocky moorland. It was a windy, shadowy evening. A heavily clouded sunset lay low and red in the west. A solitary angler stood casting his fly, at a turn in the stream, where the backwater lay still and deep under an overhanging bank. A girl (myself) standing on the bank, invisible to the fisherman beneath, waited eagerly to see the trout rise.

The moment came; the fish took the fly.

Sometimes on the little level strip of sand at the foot of

the bank; sometimes (when the stream turned again) in the shallower water rushing over its rocky bed, the angler followed the captured trout, now letting the line run out, and now winding it in again, in the difficult and delicate process of 'playing' the fish. Along the bank I followed, to watch the contest of skill and cunning between the man and the trout. I had lived long enough with my uncle Starkweather to catch some of his enthusiasm for field sports, and to learn something, especially, of the angler's art. Still following the stranger, with my eyes intently fixed on every movement of his rod and line, and with not so much as a chance fragment of my attention to spare for the rough path along which I was walking, I stepped by chance on the loose overhanging earth at the edge of the bank, and fell into the stream in an instant.

The distance was trifling; the water was shallow; the bed of the river was (fortunately for me) of sand. Beyond the fright and the wetting I had nothing to complain of. In a few moments I was out of the water and up again, very much ashamed of myself, on the firm ground. Short as the interval was, it proved long enough to favour the escape of the fish. The angler had heard my first instinctive cry of alarm, had turned, and had thrown aside his rod to help me. We confronted each other for the first time, I on the bank and he in the shallow water below. Our eyes encountered, and I verily believe our hearts encountered at the same moment. This I know for certain, we forgot our breeding as lady and gentleman; we looked at each other in barbarous silence.

I was the first to recover myself. What did I say to him?

I said something about my not being hurt, and then something more, urging him to run back, and try if he might not yet recover the fish.

He went back unwillingly. He returned to me—of course, without the fish. Knowing how bitterly disappointed my uncle would have been in his place, I apologized very earnestly. In my eagerness to make atonement I even offered to show him a spot where he might try again, lower down the stream.

He would not hear of it; he entreated me to go home and change my wet dress. I cared nothing for the wetting, but I obeyed him without knowing why.

He walked with me. My way back to the Vicarage was his way back to the inn. He had come to our parts, he told me, for the quiet and retirement as much as for the fishing. He had noticed me once or twice from the window of his room at the inn. He asked if I was not the Vicar's daughter.

I set him right. I told him that the Vicar had married my mother's sister, and that the two had been father and mother to me since the death of my parents. He asked if he might venture to call on Doctor Starkweather the next day: mentioning the name of a friend of his, with whom he believed the Vicar to be acquainted. I invited him to visit us, as if it had been my house; I was spell-bound under his eyes and under his voice. I had fancied, honestly fancied, myself to have been in love, often and often before this time. Never, in any other man's company, had I felt as I now felt in the presence of *this* man. Night seemed to fall suddenly over the evening landscape when he left me. I leaned against the Vicarage gate. I could not breathe; I could not think; my heart fluttered as if it would fly out of my bosom—and all this for a stranger! I burned with shame; but oh, in spite of it all, I was so happy!

And now, when little more than a few weeks had passed since that first meeting, I had him by my side; he was mine for life! I lifted my head from his bosom to look at him. I was like a child with a new toy—I wanted to make sure that he was really my own.

He never moved in his corner of the carriage. Was he deep in his own thoughts? and were they thoughts of Me?

I laid down my head again softly, so as not to disturb him. My mind wandered backward once more, and showed me another picture in the golden gallery of the past.

The garden of the Vicarage formed the new scene. The time was night. We had met together in secret. We were walking slowly to and fro, out of sight of the house; now in the shadowy paths of the shrubbery, now in the lovely moonlight on the open lawn.

We had long since owned our love, and devoted our lives to each other. Already our interests were one; already we shared the pleasures and the pains of life. I had gone out to meet him that night with a heavy heart, to seek comfort in his presence, and to find encouragement in his voice. He noticed that I sighed when he first took me in his arms, and he gently turned my head towards the moonlight, to read my trouble in my face. How often he had read my happiness there in the earlier days of our love!

'You bring bad news, my angel,' he said, lifting my hair tenderly from my forehead as he spoke. 'I see the lines here which tell me of anxiety and distress. I almost wish I loved you less dearly, Valeria.'

'Why?'

'I might give you back your freedom. I have only to leave this place, and your uncle would be satisfied, and you would be relieved from all the cares that are pressing on you now.'

'Don't speak of it, Eustace! If you want me to forget my cares, say you love me more dearly than ever.'

He said it in a kiss. We had a moment of exquisite forgetfulness of the hard ways of life—a moment of delicious absorption in each other. I came back to realities, fortified and composed, rewarded for all that I had gone through, ready to go through it all over again for another kiss. Only give a woman love, and there is nothing she will not venture, suffer, and do.

'Have they been raising fresh objections to our marriage?' he asked, as we slowly walked on again.

'No; they have done with objecting. They have remembered at last that I am of age, and that I can choose for myself. They have been pleading with me, Eustace, to give you up. My aunt, whom I thought rather a hard woman, has been crying—for the first time in my experience of her. My uncle, always kind and good to me, has been kinder and better than ever. He has told me that if I persist in becoming your wife I shall not be deserted on my wedding-day. Wherever we may marry he will be there to read the service, and my aunt will go to the church with me. But he entreats me to consider seriously what I am doing—to consent to a separation from you for a time—to consult other people on my position towards you, if I am not satisfied with his opinion. Oh, my darling, they are as anxious to part us, as if you were the worst, instead of the best, of men!'

'Has anything happened since yesterday to increase their distrust of me?' he asked.

'Yes.'

'What is it?'

'You remember referring my uncle to a friend of yours and of his?'

'Yes. To Major Fitz-David.'

'My uncle has written to Major Fitz-David.'

'Why?'

He pronounced that one word in a tone so utterly unlike his natural tone that his voice sounded quite strange to me.

'You won't be angry, Eustace, if I tell you?' I said. 'My uncle, as I understood him, had several motives for writing to the Major. One of them was to inquire if he knew your mother's address.'

Eustace suddenly stood still.

I paused at the same moment, feeling that I could venture no further without the risk of offending him.

To speak the truth, his conduct, when he first mentioned our engagement to my uncle, had been (so far as appearances went) a little flighty and strange. The Vicar had naturally questioned him about his family. He had answered that his father was dead; and he had consented, though not very readily, to announce his contemplated marriage to his mother. Informing us that she too lived in the country, he had gone to see her—without more particularly mentioning her address. In two days he had returned to the Vicarage with a very startling message. His mother intended no disrespect to me or my relatives; but she disapproved so absolutely of her son's marriage that she (and the members of her family, who all agreed with her) would refuse to be present at the ceremony, if Mr Woodville persisted in keeping his engagement with Doctor Starkweather's niece. Being asked to explain this extraordinary communication, Eustace had told us that his mother and his sisters were bent on his marrying another lady, and that they were bitterly mortified and disappointed by his choosing a stranger to the family. This explanation was enough for me; it implied, so far as I was concerned, a compliment to my superior influence over Eustace, which a woman always receives with pleasure. But it failed to satisfy my uncle and my aunt. The Vicar expressed to Mr Woodville a wish to write to his mother, or to see her, on the subject of her strange message. Eustace obstinately declined to mention his mother's address, on the ground that the Vicar's interference would be utterly useless. My uncle at once drew the conclusion that the mystery about the address indicated something wrong. He refused to favour Mr Woodville's renewed proposal for my hand; and he wrote the same day to make inquiries of Mr Woodville's reference, and of his own friend—Major Fitz-David.

Under such circumstances as these, to speak of my uncle's motives was to venture on very delicate ground. Eustace relieved me from further embarrassment by asking a question to which I could easily reply.

'Has your uncle received any answer from Major Fitz-David?' he inquired.

'Yes.'

'Were you allowed to read it?' His voice sank as he said those words; his face betrayed a sudden anxiety which it pained me to see.

'I have got the answer with me to show you,' I said.

He almost snatched the letter out of my hand; he turned his back on me to read it by the light of the moon. The letter was short enough to be soon read. I could have repeated it at the time. I can repeat it now.

'DEAR VICAR,—Mr Eustace Woodville is quite correct in stating to you that he is a gentleman by birth and position, and that he inherits (under his deceased father's will) an independent fortune of two thousand a year.

'Always yours,
'LAWRENCE FITZ-DAVID.'

'Can any one wish for a plainer answer than that?' Eustace asked, handing the letter back to me.

'If *I* had written for information about you,' I answered, 'it would have been plain enough for me.'

'Is it not plain enough for your uncle?'

'No.'

'What does he say?'

'Why need you care to know, my darling?'

'I want to know, Valeria. There must be no secret between us in this matter. Did your uncle say anything when he showed you the Major's letter?'

'Yes.'

'What was it?'

'My uncle told me that his letter of inquiry filled three pages, and he bade me observe that the Major's answer contained one sentence only. He said, "I volunteered to go to Major Fitz-David and talk the matter over. You see, he takes no notice of my proposal. I asked him for the address of Mr Woodville's mother. He passes over my request, as he has passed over my proposal—he studiously confines himself to the shortest possible statement of bare facts. Use your own common sense, Valeria. Isn't this rudeness rather remarkable on the part of a man who is a gentleman by birth and breeding, and who is also a friend of mine?'

Eustace stopped me there.

'Did you answer your uncle's question?' he asked.

'No,' I replied. 'I only said that I did not understand the Major's conduct.'

'And what did your uncle say next? If you love me, Valeria, tell me the truth.'

'He used very strong language, Eustace. He is an old man; you must not be offended with him.'

'I am not offended. What did he say?'

'He said, "Mark my words! There is something under the surface in connexion with Mr Woodville, or with his family, to which Major Fitz-David is not at liberty to allude. Properly interpreted, Valeria, that letter is a warning. Show it to Mr Woodville, and tell him (if you like) what I have just told you——"'

Eustace stopped me again.

'You are sure your uncle said those words?' he asked, scanning my face attentively in the moonlight.

'Quite sure. But I don't say what my uncle says. Pray don't think that!'

He suddenly pressed me to his bosom, and fixed his eyes on mine. His look frightened me.

'Good-bye, Valeria!' he said. 'Try and think kindly of me, my darling, when you are married to some happier man.'

He attempted to leave me. I clung to him in an agony of terror that shook me from head to foot.

'What do you mean?' I asked, as soon as I could speak. 'I am yours and yours only. What have I said, what have I done, to deserve those dreadful words?'

'We must part, my angel,' he answered, sadly. 'The fault is none of yours; the misfortune is all mine. My Valeria! how can you marry a man who is an object of suspicion to your nearest and dearest friends? I have led a dreary life. I have never found in any other woman the sympathy with me, the sweet comfort and companionship, that I find in you. Oh, it is hard to lose you! it is hard to go back again to my unfriended life! I must make the sacrifice, love, for

your sake. I know no more why that letter is what it is than
you do. Will your uncle believe me? Will your friends believe me? One last kiss, Valeria! Forgive me for having loved
you—passionately, devotedly loved you. Forgive me—and
let me go!'

I held him desperately, recklessly. His eyes put me beside
myself; his words filled me with a frenzy of despair.

'Go where you may,' I said, 'I go with you! Friends—
reputation—I care nothing who I lose, or what I lose. Oh,
Eustace, I am only a woman—don't madden me! I can't
live without you. I must and will be your wife!' Those wild
words were all I could say before the misery and madness
in me forced their way outward in a burst of sobs and tears.

He yielded. He soothed me with his charming voice; he
brought me back to myself with his tender caresses. He
called the bright heaven above us to witness that he devoted
his whole life to me. He vowed—oh, in such solemn, such
eloquent words!—that his one thought, night and day,
should be to prove himself worthy of such love as mine.
And had he not nobly redeemed the pledge? Had not the
betrothal of that memorable night been followed by the
betrothal at the altar, by the vows before God? Ah, what a
life was before me! What more than mortal happiness was
mine!

Again, I lifted my head from his bosom to taste the dear
delight of seeing him by my side—my life, my love, my
husband, my own!

Hardly awakened yet from the absorbing memories of the
past to the sweet realities of the present, I let my cheek
touch his cheek, I whispered to him softly, 'Oh, how I love
you! how I love you!'

The next instant I started back from him. My heart stood
still. I put my hand up to my face. What did I feel on my
cheek? (*I* had not been weeping—I was too happy.) What
did I feel on my cheek? A tear!

His face was still averted from me. I turned it towards
me, with my own hands, by main force.

I looked at him—and saw my husband, on our wedding day, with his eyes full of tears.

CHAPTER III

Ramsgate Sands

EUSTACE succeeded in quieting my alarm. But I can hardly say that he succeeded in satisfying my mind as well.

He had been thinking, he told me, of the contrast between his past and his present life. Bitter remembrances of the years that had gone had risen in his memory, and had filled him with melancholy misgivings of his capacity to make my life with him a happy one. He had asked himself if he had not met me too late? if he was not already a man soured and broken by the disappointments and disenchantments of the past? Doubts such as these, weighing more and more heavily on his mind, had filled his eyes with the tears which I had discovered—tears which he now entreated me, by my love for him, to dismiss from my memory for ever.

I forgave him, comforted him, revived him—but there were moments when the remembrance of what I had seen troubled me in secret, and when I asked myself if I really possessed my husband's full confidence as he possessed mine.

We left the train at Ramsgate.*

The favourite watering-place was empty; the season was just over. Our arrangements for the wedding-tour included a cruise to the Mediterranean in a yacht lent to Eustace by a friend. We were both fond of the sea, and we were equally desirous, considering the circumstances under which we had married, of escaping the notice of friends and acquaintances. With this object in view, having celebrated our marriage privately in London, we had decided on instructing the sailing-master of the yacht to join us at Ramsgate. At this port (when the season for visitors was at an end) we could embark far more privately than at the popular yachting stations situated in the Isle of Wight.

Three days passed—days of delicious solitude, of exquisite happiness, never to be forgotten, never to be lived over again, to the end of our lives.

Early on the morning of the fourth day, just before sunrise, a trifling incident happened, which was noticeable, nevertheless, as being strange to me in my experience of myself.

I awoke, suddenly and unaccountably, from a deep and dreamless sleep, with an all-pervading sensation of nervous uneasiness, which I had never felt before. In the old days at the Vicarage, my capacity as a sound sleeper had been the subject of many a little harmless joke. From the moment when my head was on the pillow I had never known what it was to wake until the maid knocked at my door. At all seasons and times the long and uninterrupted repose of a child was the repose that I enjoyed.

And now I had awakened, without any assignable cause, hours before my usual time. I tried to compose myself to sleep again. The effort was useless. Such a restlessness possessed me that I was not even able to lie still in the bed. My husband was sleeping soundly by my side. In the fear of disturbing him I rose, and put on my dressing gown and slippers.

I went to the window. The sun was just rising over the calm grey sea. For a while, the majestic spectacle before me exercised a tranquillising influence on the irritable condition of my nerves. But, ere long, the old restlessness returned upon me. I walked slowly to and fro in the room, until I was weary of the monotony of the exercise. I took up a book and laid it aside again. My attention wandered; the author was powerless to recall it. I got on my feet once more, and looked at Eustace, and admired him and loved him in his tranquil sleep. I went back to the window, and wearied of the beautiful morning. I sat down before the glass, and looked at myself. How haggard and worn I was already, through waking before my usual time! I rose again, not knowing what to do next. The confinement to the four walls of the room began to be intolerable to me. I opened the door that led into my husband's dressing-room, and entered it, to try if the change would relieve me.

The first object that I noticed was his dressing-case,* open on the toilette table.

I took out the bottles and pots and brushes and combs, the knives and scissors in one compartment, the writing materials in another. I smelt the perfumes and pomatums; I busily cleaned and dusted the bottles with my handker-chief as I took them out. Little by little I completely emp-tied the dressing-case. It was lined with blue velvet. In one corner I noticed a tiny strip of loose blue silk. Taking it between my finger and my thumb, and, drawing it upward, I discovered that there was a false bottom to the case, forming a secret compartment for letters and papers. In my strange condition—capricious, idle, inquisitive—it was an amusement to me to take out the papers, just as I had taken out everything else.

I found some receipted bills, which failed to interest me; some letters, which it is needless to say I laid aside, after only looking at the addresses; and, under all, a photograph, face downwards, with writing on the back of it. I looked at the writing, and saw these words:

'To my dear son, Eustace.'

His mother! the woman who had so obstinately and so mercilessly opposed herself to our marriage!

I eagerly turned the photograph, expecting to see a woman with a stern, ill-tempered, forbidding countenance. To my surprise, the face showed the remains of great beauty; the expression, though remarkably firm, was yet winning, tender, and kind. The grey hair was arranged in rows of little quaint old-fashioned curls on either side of the head, under a plain lace cap. At one corner of the mouth there was a mark, apparently a mole, which added to the characteristic peculiarity of the face. I looked and looked, fixing the portrait thoroughly in my mind. This woman, who had almost insulted me and my relatives, was, beyond all doubt or dispute, so far as appearances went, a person possessing unusual attractions—a person whom it would be a pleasure and a privilege to know.

I fell into deep thought. The discovery of the photograph quieted me as nothing had quieted me yet.

The striking of a clock downstairs in the hall warned me of the flight of time. I carefully put back all the objects in the dressing-case (beginning with the photograph) exactly as I had found them, and returned to the bedroom. As I looked at my husband still sleeping peacefully, the question forced itself into my mind, What had made that genial, gentle mother of his so sternly bent on parting us? so harshly and pitilessly resolute in asserting her disapproval of our marriage?

Could I put my question openly to Eustace when he woke? No; I was afraid to venture that length. It had been tacitly understood between us that we were not to speak of his mother—and, besides, he might be angry if he knew that I had opened the private compartment in his dressing-case.

After breakfast that morning we had news at last of the yacht. The vessel was safely moored in the inner harbour, and the sailing-master was waiting to receive my husband's orders on board.

Eustace hesitated at asking me to accompany him to the yacht. It would be necessary for him to examine the inventory of the vessel, and to decide questions, not very interesting to a woman, relating to charts and barometers, provisions and water. He asked me if I would wait for his return. The day was enticingly beautiful, and the tide was on the ebb. I pleaded for a walk on the sands; and the landlady at our lodgings, who happened to be in the room at the time, volunteered to accompany me and take care of me. It was agreed that we should walk as far as we felt inclined, in the direction of Broadstairs, and that Eustace should follow and meet us on the sands, after having completed his arrangements on board the yacht.

In half an hour more, the landlady and I were out on the beach.

The scene on that fine autumn morning was nothing less than enchanting. The brisk breeze, the brilliant sky, the flashing blue sea, the sun-bright cliffs and the tawny sands at their feet, the gliding procession of ships on the great marine highway of the English Channel—it was all so exhilarating, it was all so delightful, that I really believe if I had been by myself I could have danced for joy like a child. The one drawback to my happiness was the landlady's untiring tongue. She was a forward, good-natured, empty-headed woman, who persisted in talking, whether I listened or not; and who had a habit of perpetually addressing me as 'Mrs Woodville,' which I thought a little over-familiar as an assertion of equality from a person in her position to a person in mine.

We had been out, I should think, more than half-an-hour when we overtook a lady walking before us on the beach.

Just as we were about to pass the stranger she took her handkerchief from her pocket, and accidentally drew out with it a letter which fell, unnoticed by her, on the sand. I was nearest to the letter, and I picked it up and offered it to the lady.

The instant she turned to thank me, I stood rooted to the spot. There was the original of the photographic portrait in the dressing-case! there was my husband's mother, standing face to face with me! I recognised the quaint little grey curls, the gentle genial expression, the mole at the corner of the mouth. No mistake was possible. His mother herself!

The old lady, naturally enough, mistook my confusion for

shyness. With perfect tact and kindness she entered into conversation with me. In another minute I was walking side by side with the woman who had sternly repudiated me as a member of her family; feeling, I own, terribly discomposed, and not knowing in the least whether I ought, or ought not, to assume the responsibility, in my husband's absence, of telling her who I was.

In another minute my familiar landlady, walking on the other side of my mother-in-law, decided the question for me. I happened to say that I supposed we must by that time be near the end of our walk—the little watering-place called Broadstairs. 'Oh, no, Mrs Woodville!' cried the irrepressible woman, calling me by my name, as usual; 'nothing like so near as you think!'

I looked with a beating heart at the old lady.

To my unutterable amazement, not the faintest gleam of recognition appeared in her face. Old Mrs Woodville went on talking to young Mrs Woodville just as composedly as if she had never heard her own name before in her life!

My face and manner must have betrayed something of the agitation that I was suffering. Happening to look at me at the end of her next sentence, the old lady started, and said in her kindly way,—

'I am afraid you have over-exerted yourself. You are very pale—you are looking quite exhausted. Come and sit down here; let me lend you my smelling-bottle.'

I followed her, quite helplessly, to the base of the cliff. Some fallen fragments of chalk offered us a seat. I vaguely heard the voluble landlady's expressions of sympathy and regret; I mechanically took the smelling-bottle which my husband's mother offered to me, *after hearing my name*, as an act of kindness to a stranger.

If I had only had myself to think of, I believe I should have provoked an explanation on the spot. But I had Eustace to think of. I was entirely ignorant of the relations, hostile or friendly, which existed between his mother and himself. What could I do?

In the mean time, the old lady was still speaking to me with the most considerate sympathy. She too was fatigued, she said. She had passed a weary night at the bedside of a near relative, staying at Ramsgate. Only the day before, she had received a telegram announcing that one of her sisters was seriously ill. She was herself, thank God, still active and strong; and she had thought it her duty to start at once for Ramsgate. Towards the morning the state of the patient had improved. 'The doctor assures me, ma'am, that there is no immediate danger; and I thought it might revive me, after my long night at the bedside, if I took a little walk on the beach.'

I heard the words—I understood what they meant—but I was still too bewildered and too intimidated by my extraordinary position to be able to continue the conversation. The landlady had a sensible suggestion to make; the landlady was the next person who spoke.

'Here is a gentleman coming,' she said to me, pointing in the direction of Ramsgate. 'You can never walk back. Shall we ask him to send a chaise from Broadstairs to the gap in the cliff?'

The gentleman advanced a little nearer.

The landlady and I recognised him at the same moment. It was Eustace coming to meet us, as we had arranged. The irrepressible landlady gave the freest expression to her feelings. 'Oh, Mrs Woodville, ain't it lucky? here is Mr Woodville himself!'

Once more I looked at my mother-in-law. Once more the name failed to produce the slightest effect on her. Her sight was not so keen as ours; she had not recognised her son yet. *He* had young eyes like us, and he recognised his mother. For a moment he stopped like a man thunderstruck. Then he came on—his face white with suppressed emotion, his eyes fixed on his mother.

'You here?' he said to her.

'How do you do, Eustace?' she quietly rejoined. 'Have *you* heard of your aunt's illness, too? Did you know she was staying at Ramsgate?'

He made no answer. The landlady, drawing the inevitable inference from the words she had just heard, looked from me to my mother-in-law in a state of amazement, which paralysed even *her* tongue. I waited, with my eyes on my husband, to see what he would do. If he had delayed acknowledging me another moment, the whole future course of my life might have been altered—I should have despised him.

He did *not* delay. He came to my side and took my hand.

'Do you know who this is?' he said to his mother.

She answered, looking at me with a courteous bend of her head,—

'A lady I met on the beach, Eustace, who kindly restored to me a letter that I dropped. I think I heard the name' (she turned to the landlady): 'Mrs Woodville, was it not?'

My husband's fingers unconsciously closed on my hand with a grasp that hurt me. He set his mother right, it is only just to say, without one cowardly moment of hesitation.

'Mother,' he said to her, very quietly, 'this lady is my wife.'

She had hitherto kept her seat. She now rose slowly and faced her son in silence. The first expression of surprise passed from her face. It was succeeded by the most terrible look of mingled indignation and contempt that I ever saw in a woman's eyes.

'I pity your wife,' she said.

With those words, and no more, lifting her hand she waved him back from her, and went on her way again, as we had first found her, alone.

CHAPTER IV

On the Way Home

LEFT by ourselves, there was a moment of silence amongst us. Eustace spoke first.

'Are you able to walk back?' he said to me. 'Or shall we go on to Broadstairs, and return to Ramsgate by the railway?'

He put those questions as composedly, so far as his manner was concerned, as if nothing remarkable had happened. But his eyes and his lips betrayed him. They told me that he was suffering keenly in secret. The extraordinary scene that had just passed, far from depriving me of the last remains of my courage, had strung up my nerves and restored my self-possession. I must have been more or less than woman if my self-respect had not been wounded, if my curiosity had not been wrought to the highest pitch, by the extraordinary conduct of my husband's mother when Eustace presented me to her. What was the secret of her despising him, and pitying me? Where was the explanation of her incomprehensible apathy when my name was twice pronounced in her hearing? Why had she left us, as if the bare idea of remaining in our company was abhorrent to her? The foremost interest of my life was now the interest of penetrating these mysteries. Walk? I was in such a fever of expectation that I felt as if I could have walked to the world's end, if I could only keep my husband by my side, and question him on the way!

'I am quite recovered,' I said. 'Let us go back, as we came, on foot.'

Eustace glanced at the landlady. The landlady understood him.

'I won't intrude my company on you, sir,' she said,

sharply. 'I have some business to do at Broadstairs—and, now I am so near, I may as well go on. Good morning, Mrs Woodville.'

She laid a marked emphasis on my name; and she added one significant look at parting, which (in the preoccupied state of my mind at that moment) I entirely failed to comprehend. There was neither time nor opportunity to ask her what she meant. With a stiff little bow, addressed to Eustace, she left us as his mother had left us; taking the way to Broadstairs, and walking rapidly.

At last, we were alone.

I lost no time in beginning my inquiries; I wasted no words in prefatory phrases. In the plainest terms I put the question to him,—

'What does your mother's conduct mean?'

Instead of answering, he burst into a fit of laughter—loud, coarse, hard laughter, so utterly unlike any sound I had ever yet heard issue from his lips, so strangely and shockingly foreign to his character as I understood it, that I stood still on the sands, and openly remonstrated with him.

'Eustace! you are not like yourself,' I said. 'You almost frighten me.'

He took no notice. He seemed to be pursuing some pleasant train of thought just started in his mind.

'So like my mother!' he exclaimed, with the air of a man who felt irresistibly diverted by some humorous idea of his own. 'Tell me all about it, Valeria!'

'Tell *you?*' I repeated. 'After what has happened, surely it is your duty to enlighten *me*.'

'You don't see the joke?' he said.

'I not only fail to see the joke,' I rejoined, 'I see something in your mother's language and your mother's behaviour which justifies me in asking you for a serious explanation.'

'My dear Valeria! if you understood my mother as well as I do, a serious explanation of her conduct would be

the last thing in the world that you would expect from me.
The idea of taking my mother seriously!' He burst out
laughing again. 'My darling! you don't know how you
amuse me.'

It was all forced; it was all unnatural. He, the most
delicate, the most refined of men—a gentleman in the highest sense of the word—was coarse and loud and vulgar! My
heart sank under a sudden sense of misgiving which, with
all my love for him, it was impossible to resist. In unutterable distress and alarm I asked myself: 'Is my husband
beginning to deceive me? is he acting a part, and acting it
badly, before we have been married a week?'

I set myself to win his confidence in a new way. He was
evidently determined to force his own point of view on me.
I determined, on my side, to accept his point of view.

'You tell me I don't understand your mother,' I said,
gently. 'Will you help me to understand her?'

'It is not easy to help you to understand a woman who
doesn't understand herself,' he answered. 'But I will try.
The key to my poor dear mother's character is, in one
word—Eccentricity.'*

If he had picked out the most inappropriate word in the
whole Dictionary to describe the lady whom I had met on
the beach, 'Eccentricity' would have been that word. A
child who had seen what I saw, who had heard what I
heard, would have discovered that he was trifling—grossly,
recklessly trifling—with the truth.

'Bear in mind what I have said,' he proceeded; 'and, if
you want to understand my mother, do what I asked you
to do a minute since—tell me all about it. How came you
to speak to her, to begin with?'

'Your mother told you, Eustace. I was walking just behind
her, when she dropped a letter by accident——'

'No accident,' he interposed. 'The letter was dropped on
purpose.'

'Impossible!' I exclaimed. 'Why should your mother drop
the letter on purpose?'

'Use the key to her character, my dear. Eccentricity! My mother's odd way of making acquaintance with you.'

'Making acquaintance with me? I have just told you that I was walking behind her. She could not have known of the existence of such a person as myself until I spoke to her first.'

'So you suppose, Valeria.'

'I am certain of it.'

'Pardon me—you don't know my mother as I do.'

I began to lose all patience with him.

'Do you mean to tell me,' I said, 'that your mother was out on the sands to-day for the express purpose of making acquaintance with Me?'

'I have not the slightest doubt of it,' he answered, coolly.

'Why she didn't even recognise my name!' I burst out. 'Twice over, the landlady called me Mrs Woodville in your mother's hearing—and, twice over, I declare to you on my word of honour, it failed to produce the slightest impression on her. She looked, and acted, as if she had never heard her own name before in her life.'

' "Acted" is the right word,' he said, just as composedly as before. 'The women on the stage are not the only women who can act. My mother's object was to make herself thoroughly acquainted with you, and to throw you off your guard by speaking in the character of a stranger. It is so like her to take that roundabout way of satisfying her curiosity about a daughter-in-law whom she disapproves of! If I had not joined you when I did, you would have been examined and cross-examined about yourself and about me; and you would innocently have answered under the impression that you were speaking to a chance acquaintance. There is my mother all over! She is your enemy, remember—not your friend: she is not in search of your merits but of your faults. And you wonder why no impression was produced on her when she heard you addressed by your name! Poor innocent! I can tell you this—you only discovered my mother in her own character, when I put an end to the mystification by presenting you to each other. You saw how angry she was; and now you know why.'

I let him go on without saying a word. I listened—oh, with such a heavy heart! with such a crushing sense of disenchantment and despair! The idol of my worship; the companion, guide, protector of my life—had he fallen so low? could he stoop to such shameless prevarication as this?

Was there one word of truth in all that he had said to me? Yes! If I had not discovered his mother's portrait, it was certainly true that I should not have known, not even vaguely suspected, who she really was. Apart from this, the rest was lying; clumsy lying which said one thing at least for him, that he was not accustomed to falsehood and deceit. Good Heavens—if my husband was to be believed, his mother must have tracked us to London; tracked us to the church; tracked us to the railway station; tracked us to Ramsgate! To assert that she knew me by sight as the wife of Eustace, and that she had waited on the sands, and dropped her letter for the express purpose of making acquaintance with me, was also to assert every one of these monstrous improbabilities to be facts that had actually happened!

I could say no more. I walked by his side in silence feeling the miserable conviction that there was an abyss in the shape of a family secret between my husband and me. In the spirit, if not in the body, we were separated—after a married life of barely four days!

'Valeria,' he asked, 'have you nothing to say to me?'

'Nothing.'

'Are you not satisfied with my explanation?'

I detected a slight tremor in his voice as he put that question. The tone was, for the first time since we had spoken together, a tone that my experience associated with him in certain moods of his which I had already learnt to know well. Among the hundred thousand mysterious influences which a man exercises over the woman who loves him, I doubt if there is any more irresistible to her than the influence of his voice. I am not one of those women who shed tears on the smallest provocation: it is not in my temperament, I suppose. But when I heard that little natural change in his tone, my mind went back (I can't say why) to the happy day when I first owned that I loved him. I burst out crying.

He suddenly stood still, and took me by the hand. He tried to look at me.

I kept my head down and my eyes on the ground. I was ashamed of my weakness and my want of spirit. I was determined not to look at him.

In the silence that followed, he suddenly dropped on his knees at my feet, with a cry of despair that cut through me like a knife.

'Valeria! I am vile—I am false—I am unworthy of you. Don't believe a word of what I have been saying—lies, lies, cowardly contemptible lies! You don't know what I have gone through; you don't know how I have been tortured. Oh, my darling, try not to despise me! I must have been beside myself when I spoke to you as I did. You looked hurt; you looked offended; I didn't know what to do. I wanted to spare you even a moment's pain—I wanted to hush it up, and have done with it. For God's sake don't ask me to tell you any more! My love! my angel! it's something between my mother and me; it's nothing that need disturb you, it's nothing to anybody now. I love you, I adore you; my whole heart and soul are yours. Be satisfied with that. Forget what has happened. You shall never see my mother again. We will leave this place to-morrow. We will go away in the yacht. Does it matter where we live, so long as we live for each other? Forgive and forget! Oh, Valeria, Valeria, forgive and forget!'

Unutterable misery was in his face; unutterable misery was in his voice. Remember this. And remember that I loved him.

'It is easy to forgive,' I said sadly. 'For your sake, Eustace, I will try to forget.'

I raised him gently as I spoke. He kissed my hands, with the air of a man who was too humble to venture on any more familiar expression of his gratitude than that. The sense of embarrassment between us, as we slowly walked on again, was so unendurable that I actually cast about in my mind for a subject of conversation as if I had been in the company of a stranger! In mercy to *him*, I asked him to tell me about the yacht.

He seized on the subject as a drowning man seizes on the hand that rescues him.

On that one poor little topic of the yacht, he talked, talked, talked, as if his life depended upon his not being silent for an instant on the rest of his way back. To me, it was dreadful to hear him. I could estimate what he was suffering, by the violence which he—ordinarily a silent and thoughtful man—was now doing to his true nature and to the prejudices and habits of his life. With the greatest difficulty I preserved my self-control, until we reached the door of our lodgings. There, I was obliged to plead fatigue, and ask him to let me rest for a little while in the solitude of my own room.

'Shall we sail to-morrow?' he called after me suddenly, as I ascended the stairs.

Sail with him to the Mediterranean the next day? Pass weeks and weeks absolutely alone with him, in the narrow limits of a vessel, with his horrible secret parting us in sympathy further and further from each other day by day? I shuddered at the thought of it.

'To-morrow is rather a short notice,' I said. 'Will you give me a little longer time to prepare for the voyage?'

'Oh, yes—take any time you like,' he answered, not (as I thought) very willingly. 'While you are resting—there are still one or two little things to be settled—I think I will go back to the yacht. Is there anything I can do for you, Valeria, before I go?'

'Nothing—thank you, Eustace.'

He hastened away to the harbour. Was he afraid of his

own thoughts, if he were left by himself in the house? Was the company of the sailing-master and the steward better than no company at all?

It was useless to ask. What did I know about him or his thoughts? I locked myself into my room.

CHAPTER V

The Landlady's Discovery

I SAT DOWN, and tried to compose my spirits. Now, or never, was the time to decide what was my duty to my husband and my duty to myself to do next.

The effort was beyond me. Worn out in mind and body alike, I was perfectly incapable of pursuing any regular train of thought. I vaguely felt—if I left things as they were—that I could never hope to remove the shadow which now rested on the married life that had begun so brightly. We might live together, so as to save appearances. But to forget what had happened, or to feel satisfied with my position, was beyond the power of my will. My tranquillity as a woman— perhaps my dearest interests as a wife—depended absolutely on penetrating the mystery of my mother-in-law's conduct, and on discovering the true meaning of the wild words of penitence and self-reproach which my husband had addressed to me on our way home.

So far as I could advance towards realising my position— and no farther. When I asked myself what was to be done next, hopeless confusion, maddening doubt, filled my mind, and transformed me into the most listless and help- less of living women.

I gave up the struggle. In dull, stupid, obstinate despair, I threw myself on my bed, and fell, from sheer fatigue, into a broken, uneasy sleep.

I was awakened by a knock at the door of my room.

Was it my husband? I started to my feet as the idea occurred to me. Was some new trial of my patience and my fortitude at hand? Half nervously, half irritably, I asked who was there.

The landlady's voice answered me.

'Can I speak to you for a moment, if you please?'

I opened the door. There is no disguising it—though I loved him so dearly; though I had left home and friends for his sake—it was a relief to me, at that miserable time, to know that Eustace had not returned to the house.

The landlady came in, and took a seat, without waiting to be invited, close by my side. She was no longer satisfied with merely asserting herself as my equal. Ascending another step on the social ladder, she took her stand on the platform of patronage, and charitably looked down on me as an object of pity.

'I have just returned from Broadstairs,' she began. 'I hope you will do me the justice to believe that I sincerely regret what has happened?'

I bowed, and said nothing.

'As a gentlewoman myself,' proceeded the landlady—'reduced by family misfortunes to let lodgings, but still a gentlewoman—I feel sincere sympathy with you. I will even go further than that. I will take it on myself to say that I don't blame *you*. No, no. I noticed that you were as much shocked and surprised at your mother-in-law's conduct as I was; and that is saying a great deal, a great deal indeed. However, I have a duty to perform. It is disagreeable, but it is not the less a duty on that account. I am a single woman; not from want of opportunities of changing my condition—I beg you will understand that—but from choice. Situated as I am, I receive only the most respectable persons into my house. There must be no mystery about the positions of *my* lodgers. Mystery in the position of a lodger carries with it—what shall I say? I don't wish to offend you—I will say, a certain Taint. Very well. Now I put it to your own common sense. Can a person in my position be expected to expose herself to—Taint? I make these remarks in a sisterly and Christian spirit. As a lady yourself (I will even go the length of saying a cruelly-used lady) you will, I am sure, understand——'

I could endure it no longer. I stopped her there.

'I understand,' I said, 'that you wish to give us notice to quit your lodgings. When do you want us to go?'

The landlady held up a long, lean, red hand, in sorrowful and sisterly protest.

'No,' she said. 'Not that tone! not those looks! It's natural you should be annoyed; it's natural you should be angry. But do—now do please try and control yourself. I put it to your own common sense (we will say a week for the notice to quit)—why not treat me like a friend? You don't know what a sacrifice, what a cruel sacrifice I have made—entirely for your sake.'

'You!' I exclaimed. 'What sacrifice?'

'What sacrifice?' repeated the landlady. 'I have degraded myself as a gentlewoman. I have forfeited my own self-respect.' She paused for a moment, and suddenly seized me by the hand, in a perfect frenzy of friendship. 'Oh, my poor dear,' cried this intolerable person, 'I have discovered everything! A villain has deceived you. You are no more married than I am!'

I snatched my hand out of hers, and rose angrily from my chair.

'Are you mad?' I asked.

The landlady raised her eyes to the ceiling, with the air of a person who had deserved martyrdom, and who submitted to it cheerfully.

'Yes,' she said. 'I begin to think I *am* mad—mad to have devoted myself to an ungrateful woman, to a person who doesn't appreciate a sisterly and Christian sacrifice of self. Well! I won't do it again. Heaven forgive me—I won't do it again!'

'Do what again?' I asked.

'Follow your mother-in-law,' cried the landlady, suddenly

dropping the character of a martyr, and assuming the character of a vixen in its place. 'I blush when I think of it. I followed that most respectable person every step of the way to her own door.'

Thus far, my pride had held me up. It sustained me no longer. I dropped back again into my chair, in undisguised dread of what was coming next.

'I gave you a look when I left you on the beach,' pursued the landlady; growing louder and louder, and redder and redder as she went on. 'A grateful woman would have understood that look. Never mind! I won't do it again. I overtook your mother-in-law at the gap in the cliff. I followed her— oh, how I feel the disgrace of it *now!*—I followed her to the station at Broadstairs. She went back by train to Ramsgate. *I* went back by train to Ramsgate. She walked to her lodgings. *I* walked to her lodgings. Behind her. Like a dog. Oh, the disgrace of it! Providentially, as I then thought—I don't know what to think of it now—the landlord of the house happened to be a friend of mine, and happened to be at home. We have no secrets from each other, where lodgers are concerned. I am in a position to tell you, madam, what your mother-in-law's name really is. She knows nothing about any such person as Mrs Woodville, for an excellent reason. Her name is *not* Woodville. Her name (and consequently her son's name) is Macallan. Mrs Macallan, widow of the late General Macallan. Yes! your husband is *not* your husband. You are neither maid, wife, nor widow. You are worse than nothing, madam—and you leave my house.'

I stopped her as she opened the door to go out. She had roused *my* temper by this time. The doubt that she had cast on my marriage was more than mortal resignation could endure.

'Give me Mrs Macallan's address,' I said.

The landlady's anger receded into the background, and the landlady's astonishment appeared in its place.

'You don't mean to tell me you are going to the old lady yourself?' she said.

'Nobody but the old lady can tell me what I want to know,' I answered. 'Your discovery (as you call it) may be enough for *you*; it is not enough for *me*. How do we know that Mrs Macallan may not have been twice married; and that her first husband's name may not have been Woodville?'

The landlady's astonishment subsided in its turn, and the landlady's curiosity succeeded as the ruling influence of the moment. Substantially, as I have already said of her, she was a good-natured woman. Her fits of temper (as is usual with good-natured people) were of the hot and the short-lived sort; easily roused and easily appeased.

'Stop a bit!' she stipulated. 'If I give you the address, will you promise to tell me everything your mother-in-law says to you when you come back?'

I gave the required promise, and received the address in return.

'No malice,' said the landlady, suddenly resuming all her old familiarity with me.

'No malice,' I answered, with all possible cordiality on my side.

In ten minutes more I was at my mother-in-law's lodgings.

CHAPTER VI

My own Discovery

FORTUNATELY for me, the landlord did not open the door when I rang. A stupid maid-of-all-work, who never thought of asking me for my name, let me in. Mrs Macallan was at home, and had no visitors with her. Giving me this information, the maid led the way upstairs, and showed me into the drawing-room without a word of announcement.

My mother-in-law was sitting alone, near a work-table, knitting. The moment I appeared in the door-way, she laid aside her work; and, rising, signed to me with a commanding gesture of her hand to let her speak first.

'I know what you have come for,' she said. 'You have come here to ask questions. Spare yourself, and spare me. I warn you beforehand that I will not answer any questions relating to my son.'

It was firmly, but not harshly, said. I spoke firmly in my turn.

'I have not come here, madam, to ask questions about your son,' I answered. 'I have come—if you will excuse me—to ask you a question about yourself.'

She started, and looked at me keenly over her spectacles. I had evidently taken her by surprise.

'What is the question?' she inquired.

'I now know for the first time, madam, that your name is Macallan,' I said. 'Your son has married me under the name of Woodville. The only honourable explanation of this circumstance, so far as I know, is that my husband is your son by a first marriage. The happiness of my life is at stake. Will you kindly consider my position? Will you let me ask if you have been twice married, and if the name of your first husband was Woodville?'

She considered a little before she replied.

'The question is a perfectly natural one, in your position,' she said. 'But I think I had better not answer it.'

'May I ask why?'

'Certainly. If I answered you, I should only lead to other questions; and I should be obliged to decline replying to them. I am sorry to disappoint you. I repeat what I said on the beach—I have no other feeling than a feeling of sympathy towards *you*. If you had consulted me before your marriage, I should willingly have admitted you to my fullest confidence. It is now too late. You are married. I recommend you to make the best of your position, and to rest satisfied with things as they are.'

'Pardon me, madam,' I remonstrated. 'As things are, I don't know that I *am* married. All I know, unless you enlighten me, is that your son has married me under a name that is not his own. How can I be sure whether I am, or am not, his lawful wife?'

'I believe there can be no doubt that you are lawfully my son's wife,' Mrs Macallan answered. 'At any rate it is easy to take a legal opinion on the subject. If the opinion is that you are *not* lawfully married, my son (whatever his faults and failings may be) is a gentleman. He is incapable of wilfully deceiving a woman who loves and trusts him; he will do you justice. On my side, I will do you justice too. If the legal opinion is adverse to your rightful claims, I will promise to answer any questions which you may choose to put to me. As it is, I believe you to be lawfully my son's wife; and I say again, make the best of your position. Be satisfied with your husband's affectionate devotion to you. If you value your peace of mind, and the happiness of your life to come, abstain from attempting to know more than you know now.'

She sat down again with the air of a woman who had said her last word.

Further remonstrance would be useless—I could see it in her face; I could hear it in her voice. I turned round to open the drawing-room door.

'You are hard on me, madam,' I said, at parting. 'I am at your mercy, and I must submit.'

She suddenly looked up, and answered me with a flush on her kind and handsome old face.

'As God is my witness, child, I pity you from the bottom of my heart!'

After that extraordinary outburst of feeling, she took up her work with one hand, and signed to me with the other to leave her.

I bowed to her in silence, and went out.

I had entered the house, far from feeling sure of the course I ought to take in the future. I left the house, positively resolved, come what might of it, to discover the secret which the mother and son were hiding from me. As to the question of the name, I saw it now in the light in which I ought to have seen it from the first. If Mrs Macallan *had* been twice married (as I had rashly chosen to suppose) she would certainly have shown some signs of recognition, when she heard me addressed by her first husband's name. Where all else was mystery, there was no mystery here. Whatever his reasons might be, Eustace had assuredly married me under an assumed name.

Approaching the door of our lodgings, I saw my husband walking backwards and forwards before it, evidently waiting for my return. If he asked me the question, I decided to tell him frankly where I had been, and what had passed between his mother and myself.

He hurried to meet me with signs of disturbance in his face and manner.

'I have a favour to ask of you, Valeria,' he said. 'Do you mind returning with me to London by the next train?'

I looked at him. In the popular phrase, I could hardly believe my own ears.

'It's a matter of business,' he went on, 'of no interest to any one but myself; and it requires my presence in London. You don't wish to sail just yet, as I understand? I can't leave you here by yourself. Have you any objection to going to London for a day or two?'

I made no objection. I too was eager to go back.

In London, I could obtain the legal opinion which would tell me whether I was lawfully married to Eustace or not. In London, I should be within reach of the help and advice of my father's faithful old clerk. I could confide in Benjamin as I could confide in no one else. Dearly as I loved my uncle Starkweather, I shrank from communicating with him in my present need. His wife had told me that I had made a bad beginning, when I signed the wrong name in the marriage register. Shall I own it? My pride shrank from acknowledging, before the honeymoon was over, that his wife was right.

In two hours more we were on the railway again. Ah, what a contrast that second journey presented to the first!

On our way to Ramsgate, everybody could see that we were a newly-wedded couple. On our way to London, nobody noticed us; nobody would have doubted that we had been married for years.

We went to a private hotel in the neighbourhood of Portland Place.

After breakfast, the next morning, Eustace announced that he must leave me to attend to his business. I had previously mentioned to him that I had some purchases to make in London. He was quite willing to let me go out alone—on the condition that I should take a carriage provided by the hotel.

My heart was heavy that morning: I felt the unacknowledged estrangement that had grown up between us very keenly. My husband opened the door to go out—and came back to kiss me before he left me by myself. That little afterthought of tenderness touched me. Acting on the impulse of the moment, I put my arm round his neck, and held him to me gently.

'My darling,' I said, 'give me all your confidence. I know that you love me. Show that you can trust me too.'

He sighed bitterly, and drew back from me—in sorrow, not in anger.

'I thought we had agreed, Valeria, not to return to that subject again,' he said. 'You only distress yourself and distress me.'

He left the room abruptly, as if he dare not trust himself to say more. It is better not to dwell on what I felt after this last repulse. I ordered the carriage at once. I was eager to find a refuge from my own thoughts in movement and change.

I drove to the shops first, and made the purchases which I had mentioned to Eustace by way of giving a reason for going out. Then I devoted myself to the object which I really had at heart. I went to old Benjamin's little villa, in the by-ways of St. John's Wood.

As soon as he had got over the first surprise of seeing me, he noticed that I looked pale and careworn. I confessed at

once that I was in trouble. We sat down together by the
bright fireside in his little library (Benjamin, as far as his
means would allow, was a great collector of books), and
there I told my old friend, frankly and truly, all that I have
told here.

He was too distressed to say much. He fervently pressed
my hand; he fervently thanked God that my father had not
lived to hear what he had heard. Then, after a pause, he
repeated my mother-in-law's name to himself, in a doubting, questioning tone.

'Macallan?' he said. 'Macallan? Where have I heard that
name? Why does it sound as if it wasn't strange to me?'

He gave up pursuing the lost recollection, and asked, very
earnestly, what he could do for me. I answered that he
could help me in the first place to put an end to the
doubt—an unendurable doubt to *me*—whether I was lawfully married or not. His energy of the old days, when he
had conducted my father's business, showed itself again,
the moment I said those words.

'Your carriage is at the door, my dear,' he answered.
'Come with me to my own lawyer, without wasting another
moment.'

We drove to Lincoln's Inn Fields.*

At my request, Benjamin put my case to the lawyer, as
the case of a friend in whom I was interested. The answer
was given without hesitation. I had married, honestly believing my husband's name to be the name under which I
had known him. The witnesses to my marriage—my uncle,
my aunt, and Benjamin—had acted, as I had acted, in
perfect good faith. Under those circumstances, there was
no doubt about the law. I was legally married. Macallan or
Woodville, I was his wife.*

This decisive answer relieved me of a heavy anxiety. I accepted my old friend's invitation to return with him to St.
John's Wood, and to make my luncheon at his early dinner.

On our way back I reverted to the one other subject which
was now uppermost in my mind. I reiterated my resolution

to discover why Eustace had not married me under the name that was really his own.

My companion shook his head, and entreated me to consider well beforehand what I proposed doing. His advice to me—so strangely do extremes meet!—was my mother-in-law's advice, repeated almost word for word. 'Leave things as they are, my dear. In the interest of your own peace of mind, be satisfied with your husband's affection. You know that you are his wife, and you know that he loves you. Surely that is enough?'

I had but one answer to this. Life, on such conditions as my good friend had just stated, would be simply unendurable to me. Nothing could alter my resolution—for this plain reason, that nothing could reconcile me to living with my husband on the terms on which we were living now. It only rested with Benjamin to say whether he would give a helping hand to his master's daughter or not.

The old man's answer was thoroughly characteristic of him.

'Mention what you want of me, my dear,' was all he said.

We were then passing a street in the neighbourhood of Portman Square.* I was on the point of speaking again, when the words were suspended on my lips. I saw my husband.

He was just descending the steps of a house—as if leaving it after a visit. His eyes were on the ground: he did not look up when the carriage passed. As the servant closed the door behind him, I noticed that the number of the house was sixteen. At the next corner I saw the name of the street. It was Vivian Place.

'Do you happen to know who lives at number sixteen, Vivian Place?' I inquired of my companion.

Benjamin started. My question was certainly a strange one, after what he had just said to me.

'No,' he replied. 'Why do you ask?'

'I have just seen Eustace leaving that house.'

'Well, my dear, and what of that?'

'My mind is in a bad way, Benjamin. Everything my husband does that I don't understand, rouses my suspicion now.'

Benjamin lifted his withered old hands, and let them drop on his knees again in mute lamentation over me.

'I tell you again,' I went on, 'my life is unendurable to me. I won't answer for what I may do, if I am left much longer to live in doubt of the one man on earth whom I love. You have had experience of the world. Suppose you were shut out from Eustace's confidence, as I am? Suppose you were as fond of him as I am, and felt your position as bitterly as I feel it—what would you do?'

The question was plain. Benjamin met it with a plain answer.

'I think I should find my way, my dear, to some intimate friend of your husband's,' he said, 'and make a few discreet inquiries in that quarter first.'

Some intimate friend of my husband's? I considered with myself. There was but one friend of his whom I knew of—my uncle's correspondent, Major Fitz-David. My heart beat fast as the name recurred to my memory. Suppose I followed Benjamin's advice? Suppose I applied to Major Fitz-David? Even if he too refused to answer my questions, my position would not be more helpless than it was now. I determined to make the attempt. The only difficulty in the way, so far, was to discover the Major's address. I had given back his letter to Doctor Starkweather, at my uncle's own request; I remembered that the address from which the Major wrote was somewhere in London; and I remembered no more.

'Thank you, old friend; you have given me an idea already,' I said to Benjamin. 'Have you got a Directory in your house?'

'No, my dear,' he rejoined, looking very much puzzled. 'But I can easily send out and borrow one.'

We returned to the Villa. The servant was sent at once to the nearest stationer's to borrow a Directory.* She returned with the book, just as we sat down to dinner. Searching for the Major's name, under the letter F, I was startled by a new discovery.

'Benjamin!' I said. 'This is a strange coincidence. Look here!'

He looked where I pointed. Major Fitz-David's address was Number Sixteen, Vivian Place—the very house which I had seen my husband leaving as we passed in the carriage!

CHAPTER VII

On the Way to the Major

'YES,' said Benjamin. 'It *is* a coincidence certainly. Still——'

He stopped and looked at me. He seemed a little doubtful how I might receive what he had it in his mind to say to me next.

'Go on,' I said.

'Still, my dear, I see nothing suspicious in what has happened,' he resumed. 'To my mind, it is quite natural that your husband, being in London, should pay a visit to one of his friends. And it's equally natural that we should pass through Vivian Place, on our way back here. This seems to be the reasonable view. What do *you* say?'

'I have told you already that my mind is in a bad way about Eustace,' I answered. '*I* say there is some motive at the bottom of his visit to Major Fitz-David. It is not an ordinary call. I am firmly convinced it is not an ordinary call!'

'Suppose we get on with our dinner?' said Benjamin, resignedly. 'Here is a loin of mutton, my dear—an ordinary loin of mutton. Is there anything suspicious in *that*? Very well, then. Show me you have confidence in the mutton; please eat. There's the wine, again. No mystery, Valeria, in that claret—I'll take my oath it's nothing but innocent juice of the grape. If we can't believe in anything else, let's believe in juice of the grape. Your good health, my dear.'

I adapted myself to the old man's genial humour as readily as I could. We ate and we drank, and we talked of bygone days. For a little while I was almost happy in the company of my fatherly old friend. Why was I not old too? Why had I not done with love—with its certain miseries; its transient delights; its cruel losses; its bitterly doubtful gains? The last autumn flowers in the window basked brightly in the last of the autumn sunlight. Benjamin's little dog digested his dinner in perfect comfort on the hearth. The parrot in the next house screeched his vocal accomplishments cheerfully. I don't doubt that it is a great privilege to be a human being. But may it not be the happier destiny to be an animal or a plant?

The brief respite was soon over; all my anxieties came back. I was once more a doubting, discontented, depressed creature, when I rose to say good-bye.

'Promise, my dear, you will do nothing rash,' said Benjamin, as he opened the door for me.

'Is it rash to go to Major Fitz-David?' I asked.

'Yes—If you go by yourself. You don't know what sort of man he is; you don't know how he may receive you. Let me try first, and pave the way, as the saying is. Trust my experience, my dear. In matters of this sort there is nothing like paving the way.'

I considered a moment. It was due to my good friend to consider before I said No.

Reflection decided me on taking the responsibility, whatever it might be, upon my own shoulders. Good or bad, compassionate or cruel, the Major was a man. A woman's influence was the safest influence to trust with him—where the end to be gained was such an end as I had in view. It was not easy to say this to Benjamin, without the danger of mortifying him. I made an appointment with the old man to call on me the next morning at the hotel, and talk the matter over again. Is it very disgraceful to me to add, that I privately determined (if the thing could be accomplished) to see Major Fitz-David in the interval?

'Do nothing rash, my dear. In your own interests, do nothing rash!'

Those were Benjamin's last words, when we parted for the day.

I found Eustace waiting for me in our sitting-room at the hotel. His spirits seemed to have revived since I had seen him last. He advanced to meet me cheerfully, with an open sheet of paper in his hand.

'My business is settled, Valeria, sooner than I had expected,' he began, gaily. 'Are your purchases all completed, fair lady? Are *you* free too?'

I had learnt already (God help me!) to distrust his fits of gaiety. I asked cautiously,

'Do you mean free for to-day?'

'Free for to-day, and to-morrow and next week, and next month—and next year, too, for all I know to the contrary,' he answered, putting his arm boisterously round my waist. 'Look here!'

He lifted the open sheet of paper which I had noticed in his hand, and held it for me to read. It was a telegram to the sailing master of the yacht, informing him that we had arranged to return to Ramsgate that evening, and that we should be ready to sail for the Mediterranean with the next tide.

'I only waited for your return,' said Eustace, 'to send the telegram to the office.'

He crossed the room, as he spoke, to ring the bell. I stopped him.

'I am afraid I can't go to Ramsgate to-day,' I said.

'Why not?' he asked, suddenly changing his tone and speaking sharply.

I dare say it will seem ridiculous to some people, but it is really true that he shook my resolution to go to Major Fitz-David, when he put his arm round me. Even a mere

passing caress, from *him*, stole away my heart, and softly
tempted me to yield. But the ominous alteration in his tone
made another woman of me. I felt once more, and felt more
strongly than ever, that, in my critical position, it was useless to stand still, and worse than useless to draw back.

'I am sorry to disappoint you,' I answered. 'It is impossible for me (as I told you at Ramsgate) to be ready to
sail at a moment's notice. I want time.'

'What for?'

Not only his tone, but his look, when he put that second
question, jarred on every nerve in me. He roused in my
mind—I can't tell how or why—an angry sense of the in-
dignity that he had put upon his wife in marrying her under
a false name. Fearing that I should answer rashly, that I
should say something which my better sense might regret,
if I spoke at that moment, I said nothing. Women alone can
estimate what it cost me to be silent. And men alone can
understand how irritating my silence must have been to my
husband.

'You want time?' he repeated. 'I ask you again—what
for?'

My self-control, pushed to its extremest limits, failed me
The rash reply flew out of my lips, like a bird set free from
a cage.

'I want time,' I said, 'to accustom myself to my right
name.'

He suddenly stepped up to me with a dark look.

'What do you mean by your "right name"?'

'Surely you know,' I answered. 'I once thought I was Mrs
Woodville. I have now discovered that I am Mrs Macallan.'

He started back at the sound of his own name, as if I had
struck him—he started back and turned so deadly pale that
I feared he was going to drop at my feet in a swoon. Oh,
my tongue! my tongue! Why had I not controlled my miserable, mischievous woman's tongue?

'I didn't mean to alarm you, Eustace,' I said. 'I spoke at
random. Pray forgive me.'

He waved his hand impatiently, as if my penitent words were tangible things—ruffling, worrying things like flies in summer—which he was putting away from him.

'What else have you discovered?' he asked, in low, stern tones.

'Nothing, Eustace.'

'Nothing?' He paused as he repeated the word, and passed his hand over his forehead in a weary way. 'Nothing, of course,' he resumed, speaking to himself, 'or she would not be here.'

He paused once more, and looked at me searchingly. 'Don't say again what you said just now,' he went on. 'For your own sake, Valeria, as well as for mine.' He dropped into the nearest chair, and said no more.

I certainly heard the warning; but the only words which really produced an impression on my mind were the words preceding it, which he had spoken to himself. He had said: 'Nothing, of course, *or she would not be here*.' If I had found out some other truth besides the truth about the name, would it have prevented me from ever returning to my husband? Was that what he meant? Did the sort of discovery that he contemplated, mean something so dreadful that it would have parted us at once and for ever? I stood by his chair in silence; and tried to find the answer to those terrible questions in his face. It used to speak to me so eloquently when it spoke of his love. It told me nothing now.

He sat for some time without looking at me, lost in his own thoughts. Then he rose on a sudden, and took his hat.

'The friend who lent me the yacht is in town,' he said. 'I suppose I had better see him, and say our plans are changed.' He tore up the telegram with an air of sullen resignation as he spoke. 'You are evidently determined not to go to sea with me,' he resumed. 'We had better give it up. I don't see what else is to be done. Do you?'

His tone was almost a tone of contempt. I was too depressed about myself, too alarmed about *him*, to resent it.

'Decide as you think best, Eustace,' I said, sadly. 'Every way, the prospect seems a hopeless one. As long as I am shut out from your confidence, it matters little whether we live on land or at sea—we cannot live happily.'

'If you could control your curiosity,' he answered, sternly, 'we might live happily enough. I thought I had married a woman who was superior to the vulgar failings of her sex. A good wife should know better than to pry into affairs of her husband's with which she has no concern.'

Surely it was hard to bear this? However, I bore it.

'Is it no concern of mine,' I asked, gently, 'when I find that my husband has not married me under his family name? Is it no concern of mine when I hear your mother say, in so many words, that she pities your wife? It is hard, Eustace, to accuse me of curiosity, because I cannot accept the unendurable position in which you have placed me. Your cruel silence is a blight on my happiness, and a threat to my future. Your cruel silence is estranging us from each other, at the beginning of our married life. And you blame me for feeling this? You tell me I am prying into affairs which are yours only? They are *not* yours only: I have my interest in them too. Oh, my darling, why do you trifle with our love and our confidence in each other? Why do you keep me in the dark?'

He answered with a stern and pitiless brevity,

'For your own good.'

I turned away from him in silence. He was treating me like a child.

He followed me. Putting one hand heavily on my shoulder, he forced me to face him once more.

'Listen to this,' he said. 'What I am now going to say to you, I say for the first, and last, time. Valeria! if you ever discover what I am now keeping from your knowledge— from that moment you live a life of torture; your tranquillity is gone. Your days will be days of terror; your nights will be full of horrid dreams—through no fault of mine, mind! through no fault of mine! Every day of your life, you will feel some new distrust, some growing fear of me—and you will be doing me the vilest injustice all the time. On my faith as a Christian, on my honour as a man, if you stir a step further in this matter there is an end of your happiness for the rest of your life! Think seriously of what I have said to you; you will have time to reflect. I am going to tell my friend that our plans for the Mediterranean are given up. I shall not be back before the evening.' He sighed, and looked at me with unutterable sadness. 'I love you, Valeria,' he said. 'In spite of all that has passed, as God is my witness, I love you more dearly than ever.'

So he spoke. So he left me.

I must write the truth about myself, however strange it may appear. I don't pretend to be able to analyse my own motives; I don't pretend even to guess how other women might have acted in my place. It is true of *me*, that my husband's terrible warning—all the more terrible in its mystery and its vagueness—produced no deterrent effect on my mind: it only stimulated my resolution to discover what he was hiding from me. He had not been gone two minutes before I rang the bell, and ordered the carriage to take me to Major Fitz-David's house in Vivian Place.

Walking to and fro while I was waiting—I was in such a fever of excitement that it was impossible for me to sit still—I accidentally caught sight of myself in the glass.

My own face startled me: it was so haggard and so wild. Could I present myself to a stranger, could I hope to produce the necessary impression in my favour, looking as I looked at that moment? For all I knew to the contrary, my whole future might depend upon the effect which I produced on Major Fitz-David at first sight. I rang the bell again, and sent a message to one of the chambermaids to follow me to my room.

I had no maid of my own with me: the stewardess of the yacht would have acted as my attendant, if we had held to our first arrangement. It mattered little, so long as I had a woman to help me. The chambermaid appeared. I can give no better idea of the disordered and desperate condition of my mind at that time, than by owning that I actually consulted this perfect stranger on the question of my personal appearance. She was a middle-aged woman, with a large experience of the world and its wickedness written legibly on her manner and on her face. I put money into the woman's hand, enough of it to surprise her. She thanked me with a cynical smile, evidently placing her own evil interpretation on my motive for bribing her.

'What can I do for you, ma'am?' she asked, in a confidential whisper. 'Don't speak loud! There is somebody in the next room.'

'I want to look my best,' I said; 'and I have sent for you to help me.'

'I understand, ma'am.'

'What do you understand?'

She nodded her head significantly, and whispered to me again.

'Lord bless you, I'm used to this!' she said. 'There is a gentleman in the case. Don't mind me, ma'am. It's a way I have, I mean no harm.' She stopped and looked at me critically. 'I wouldn't change my dress, if I were you,' she went on. 'The colour becomes you.'

It was too late to resent the woman's impertinence. There was no help for it but to make use of her. Besides, she was right about the dress. It was of a delicate maize colour, prettily trimmed with lace. I could wear nothing which suited me better. My hair, however, stood in need of some skilled attention. The chambermaid rearranged it, with a ready hand which showed that she was no beginner in the art of dressing hair. She laid down the combs and brushes, and looked at me—then looked at the toilette table, searching for something which she apparently failed to find.

'Where do you keep it?' she asked.

'What do you mean?'

'Look at your complexion, ma'am. You will frighten him if he sees you like that. A touch of colour you *must* have.

Where do you keep it? What! you haven't got it? you never use it? Dear, dear, dear me!'

For a moment, surprise fairly deprived her of her self-possession! Recovering herself, she begged permission to leave me for a minute. I let her go, knowing what her errand was. She came back with a box of paints and powders; and I said nothing to check her. I saw, in the glass, my skin take a false fairness, my cheeks a false colour, my eyes a false brightness—and I never shrank from it. No! I let the odious deceit go on; I even admired the extraordinary delicacy and dexterity with which it was all done. 'Anything' (I thought to myself, in the madness of that miserable time), 'so long as it helps me to win the Major's confidence! Anything so long as I discover what those last words of my husband's really mean!'

The transformation of my face was accomplished. The chambermaid pointed with her wicked forefinger in the direction of the glass.

'Bear in mind, ma'am, what you looked like when you sent for me,' she said. 'And just see for yourself how you look now. You're the prettiest woman (of your style) in London. Ah, what a thing pearl powder* is, when one knows how to use it!'

CHAPTER VIII

The Friend of the Women

I FIND it impossible to describe my sensations while the carriage was taking me to Major Fitz-David's house. I doubt, indeed, if I really felt or thought at all, in the true sense of those words.

From the moment when I had resigned myself into the hands of the chambermaid, I seemed in some strange way to have lost my ordinary identity—to have stepped out of my own character. At other times, my temperament was of the nervous and anxious sort, and my tendency was to exaggerate any difficulties that might place themselves in my way. At other times, having before me the prospect of a critical interview with a stranger, I should have considered with myself what it might be wise to pass over, and what it might be wise to say. Now, I never gave my coming interview with the Major a thought; I felt an unreasoning confidence in myself, and a blind faith in *him*. Now, neither the past nor the future troubled me; I lived unreflectingly in the present. I looked at the shops as we drove by them, and at the other carriages as they passed mine. I noticed—yes! and enjoyed—the glances of admiration which chance foot-passengers on the pavement cast at me. I said to myself, 'This looks well for my prospect of making a friend of the Major!' When we drew up at the door in Vivian Place, it is no exaggeration to say that I had but one anxiety—anxiety to find the Major at home.

The door was opened by a servant out of livery, an old man who looked as if he might have been a soldier in his earlier days. He eyed me with a grave attention, which relaxed little by little into sly approval. I asked for Major Fitz-David. The answer was not altogether encouraging; the man was not sure whether his master was at home or not.

I gave him my card. My cards, being part of my wedding outfit, necessarily had the false name printed on them—*Mrs Eustace Woodville*. The servant showed me into a front room on the ground floor, and disappeared with my card in his hand.

Looking about me, I noticed a door in the wall opposite the window, communicating with some inner room. The door was not of the ordinary kind. It fitted into the thickness of the partition wall, and worked in grooves. Looking a little nearer, I saw that it had not been pulled out so as completely to close the doorway. Only the merest chink was left; but it was enough to convey to my ears all that passed in the next room.

'What did you say, Oliver, when she asked for me?' inquired a man's voice, pitched cautiously in a low key.

'I said I was not sure you were at home, sir,' answered the voice of the servant who had let me in.

There was a pause. The first speaker was evidently Major Fitz-David himself. I waited to hear more.

'I think I had better not see her, Oliver,' the Major's voice resumed.

'Very good, sir.'

'Say I have gone out, and you don't know when I shall be back again. Beg the lady to write, if she has any business with me.'

'Yes, sir.'

'Stop, Oliver!'

Oliver stopped. There was another and longer pause. Then the master resumed the examination of the man.

'Is she young, Oliver?'

'Yes, sir.'

'And—pretty?'

'Better than pretty, sir, to my thinking.'

'Aye? aye? What you call a fine woman—eh, Oliver?'

'Certainly, sir.'

'Tall?'

'Nearly as tall as I am, Major.'

'Aye? aye? aye? A good figure?'

'As slim as a sapling, sir, and as upright as a dart.'

'On second thoughts, I am at home, Oliver. Show her in! show her in!'

So far, one thing at least seemed to be clear. I had done well in sending for the chambermaid. What would Oliver's report of me have been, if I had presented myself to him with my colourless cheeks and my ill-dressed hair?

The servant reappeared, and conducted me (by way of the hall) to the inner room. Major Fitz-David advanced to welcome me. What was the Major like?

Well—he was like a finely-preserved gentleman of (say) sixty years old; little and lean, and chiefly remarkable by

the extraordinary length of his nose. After this feature, I
noticed, next, his beautiful brown wig; his sparkling little
grey eyes; his rosy complexion; his short military whiskers,
dyed to match his wig; his white teeth and his winning smile;
his smart blue frock-coat, with a camellia in the button-hole;
and his splendid ring—a ruby, flashing on his little finger as
he courteously signed to me to take a chair.

'Dear Mrs Woodville, how very kind of you this is! I have
been longing to have the happiness of knowing you. Eustace
is an old friend of mine. I congratulated him when I heard
of his marriage. May I make a confession?—I envy him now
I have seen his wife.'

The future of my life was, perhaps, in this man's hands.
I studied him attentively; I tried to read his character in his
face.

The Major's sparkling little grey eyes softened as they
looked at me; the Major's strong and sturdy voice dropped
to its lowest and tenderest tones when he spoke to me; the
Major's manner expressed, from the moment when I entered the room, a happy mixture of admiration and respect.
He drew his chair close to mine, as if it was a privilege to
be near me. He took my hand, and lifted my glove to his
lips, as if that glove was the most delicious luxury the world
could produce. 'Dear Mrs Woodville,' he said, as he softly
laid my hand back on my lap, 'bear with an old fellow who
worships your enchanting sex. You really brighten this dull
house. It is *such* a pleasure to see you!'

There was no need for the old gentleman to make his
little confession. Women, children, and dogs proverbially
know by instinct who the people are who really like them.
The women had a warm friend—perhaps, at one time, a
dangerously warm friend—in Major Fitz-David. I knew as
much of him as that before I had settled myself in my chair
and opened my lips to answer him.

'Thank you, Major, for your kind reception and your
pretty compliment,' I said; matching my host's easy tone
as closely as the necessary restraints on my side would

permit. 'You have made your confession. May I make mine?'

Major Fitz-David lifted my hand again from my lap, and drew his chair as close as possible to mine. I looked at him gravely, and tried to release my hand. Major Fitz-David declined to let go of it, and proceeded to tell me why.

'I have just heard you speak for the first time,' he said. 'I am under the charm of your voice. Dear Mrs Woodville, bear with an old fellow who is under the charm! Don't grudge me my innocent little pleasures. Lend me—I wish I could say *give* me—this pretty hand. I am such an admirer of pretty hands; I can listen so much better with a pretty hand in mine. The ladies indulge my weakness. Please indulge me too. Yes? And what were you going to say?'

'I was going to say, Major, that I felt particularly sensible of your kind welcome, because, as it happens, I have a favour to ask of you.'

I was conscious, while I spoke, that I was approaching the object of my visit a little too abruptly. But Major Fitz-David's admiration rose from one climax to another with such alarming rapidity, that I felt the importance of administering a practical check to it. I trusted to those ominous words, 'a favour to ask of you,' to administer the check—and I did not trust in vain. My aged admirer gently dropped my hand, and (with all possible politeness) changed the subject.

'The favour is granted, of course!' he said. 'And now—tell me—how is our dear Eustace?'

'Anxious and out of spirits,' I answered.

'Anxious and out of spirits!' repeated the Major. 'The enviable man who is married to You, anxious and out of spirits? Monstrous! Eustace fairly disgusts me. I shall take him off the list of my friends.'

'In that case, take me off the list with him, Major. I am in wretched spirits too. You are my husband's old friend. I may acknowledge to *you* that our married life is—just now—not quite a happy one.'

Major Fitz-David lifted his eyebrows (dyed to match his whiskers) in polite surprise.

'Already!' he exclaimed. 'What can Eustace be made of? Has he no appreciation of beauty and grace? Is he the most insensible of living beings?'

'He is the best and dearest of men,' I answered. 'But there is some dreadful mystery in his past life—'

I could get no further: Major Fitz-David deliberately stopped me. He did it with the smoothest politeness, on the surface. But I saw a look in his bright little eyes, which said plainly, 'If you *will* venture on delicate ground, madam, don't ask me to accompany you.'

'My charming friend!' he exclaimed. 'May I call you my charming friend? You have—among a thousand other delightful qualities which I can see already—a vivid imagination. Don't let it get the upper hand! Take an old fellow's advice; don't let it get the upper hand! What can I offer you, dear Mrs Woodville? A cup of tea?'

'Call me by my right name, sir,' I answered boldly. 'I have made a discovery. I know, as well as you do, that my name is Macallan.'

The Major started, and looked at me very attentively. His manner became grave, his tone changed completely, when he spoke next.

'May I ask,' he said, 'if you have communicated to your husband the discovery which you have just mentioned to me?'

'Certainly!' I answered. 'I consider that my husband owes me an explanation. I have asked him to tell me what his extraordinary conduct means—and he has refused in language that frightens me. I have appealed to his mother—and *she* has refused to explain, in language that humiliates me. Dear Major Fitz-David, I have no friends to take my part; I have nobody to come to but you! Do me the greatest of all favours—tell me why your friend Eustace has married me under a false name!'

'Do *me* the greatest of all favours,' answered the Major. 'Don't ask me to say a word about it.'

He looked, in spite of his unsatisfactory reply, as if he really felt for me. I determined to try my utmost powers of persuasion; I resolved not to be beaten at the first repulse.

'I *must* ask you,' I said. 'Think of my position. How can I live, knowing what I know—and knowing no more? I would rather hear the most horrible thing you can tell me than be condemned (as I am now) to perpetual misgiving and perpetual suspense. I love my husband with all my heart; but I cannot live with him on these terms: the misery of it would drive me mad. I am only a woman, Major. I can only throw myself on your kindness. Don't—pray, pray don't keep me in the dark!'

I could say no more. In the reckless impulse of the moment, I snatched up his hand and raised it to my lips. The gallant old gentleman started as if I had given him an electric shock.

'My dear, dear lady!' he exclaimed, 'I can't tell you how I feel for you! You charm me, you overwhelm me, you touch me to the heart. What can I say? What can I do? I can only imitate your admirable frankness, your fearless candour. You have told me what your position is. Let me tell you, in my turn, how I am placed. Compose yourself—pray compose yourself! I have a smelling-bottle here, at the service of the ladies. Permit me to offer it.'

He brought me the smelling-bottle; he put a little stool under my feet; he entreated me to take time enough to compose myself. 'Infernal fool!' I heard him say to himself, as he considerately turned away from me for a few moments. 'If *I* had been her husband—come what might of it, I would have told her the truth!'

Was he referring to Eustace? And was he going to do what he would have done in my husband's place—was he really going to tell me the truth?

The idea had barely crossed my mind, when I was startled by a loud and peremptory knocking at the street-door. The Major stopped, and listened attentively. In a few moments the door was opened, and the rustling of a woman's dress was plainly audible in the hall. The Major hurried to the door of the room, with the activity of a young man. He was too late. The door was violently opened from the outer side, just as he got to it. The lady of the rustling dress burst into the room.

CHAPTER IX

The Defeat of the Major

MAJOR FITZ-DAVID'S visitor proved to be a plump, round-eyed, over-dressed girl, with a florid complexion and straw-coloured hair. After first fixing on me a broad stare of astonishment, she pointedly addressed her apologies for intruding on us to the Major alone. The creature evidently believed me to be the last new object of the old gentleman's idolatry; and she took no pains to disguise her jealous resentment on discovering us together. Major Fitz-David set matters right in his own irresistible way. He kissed the hand of the over-dressed girl, as devotedly as he had kissed mine; he told her she was looking charmingly. Then he led her, with his happy mixture of admiration and respect, back to the door by which she had entered—a second door communicating directly with the hall.

'No apology is necessary, my dear,' he said. 'This lady is with me on a matter of business. You will find your sing-ing-master waiting for you upstairs. Begin your lesson; and I will join you in a few minutes. *Au revoir*, my charming pupil—*au revoir*.'

The young lady answered this polite little speech in a whisper—with her round eyes fixed distrustfully on me while she spoke. The door closed on her. Major Fitz-David was at liberty to set matters right with me, in my turn.

'I call that young person one of my happy discoveries,' said the old gentleman, complacently. 'She possesses, I

don't hesitate to say, the finest soprano voice in Europe.
Would you believe it, I met with her at a railway station?
She was behind the counter in a refreshment-room, poor
innocent, rinsing wine-glasses, and singing over her work.
Good heavens, such singing! Her upper notes electrified
me. I said to myself, "Here is a born prima-donna—I will
bring her out!" She is the third I have brought out in my
time. I shall take her to Italy when her education is sufficiently advanced, and perfect her at Milan. In that unsoph-
isticated girl, my dear lady, you see one of the future
Queens of Song. Listen! she is beginning her scales. What
a voice! Brava! Brava! Bravissima!'

The high soprano notes of the future Queen of Song rang
through the house as he spoke. Of the loudness of the
young lady's voice there could be no sort of doubt. The
sweetness and the purity of it admitted, in my opinion, of
considerable dispute.

Having said the polite words which the occasion rendered
necessary, I ventured to recall Major Fitz-David to the
subject in discussion between us when his visitor had entered the room. The Major was very unwilling to return to
the perilous topic on which he had just touched when the
interruption occurred. He beat time with his forefinger to
the singing upstairs; he asked me about *my* voice, and
whether I sang; he remarked that life would be intolerable
to him without Love and Art. A man in my place would
have lost all patience, and would have given up the struggle
in disgust. Being a woman, and having my end in view, my
resolution was invincible. I fairly wore out the Major's
resistance, and compelled him to surrender at discretion.
It is only justice to add that, when he did make up his mind
to speak to me again of Eustace, he spoke frankly, and
spoke to the point.

'I have known your husband,' he began, 'since the time
when he was a boy. At a certain period of his past life,
a terrible misfortune fell upon him. The secret of that
misfortune is known to his friends, and is religiously kept

by his friends. It is the secret that he is keeping from You. He will never tell it to you as long as he lives. And he has bound *me* not to tell it, under a promise given on my word of honour. You wished, dear Mrs Woodville, to be made acquainted with my position towards Eustace. There it is!'

'You persist in calling me Mrs Woodville,' I said.

'Your husband wishes me to persist,' the Major answered. 'He assumed the name of Woodville, fearing to give his own name, when he first called at your uncle's house. He will now acknowledge no other. Remonstrance is useless. You must do, what we do—you must give way to an unreasonable man. The best fellow in the world in other respects: in this one matter, as obstinate and self-willed as he can be. If you ask me my opinion, I tell you honestly that I think he was wrong in courting and marrying you under his false name. He trusted his honour and his happiness to your keeping, in making you his wife. Why should he not trust the story of his troubles to you as well? His mother quite shares my opinion in this matter. You must not blame her for refusing to admit you into her confidence, after your marriage: it was then too late. Before your marriage, she did all she could do—without betraying secrets which, as a good mother, she was bound to respect—to induce her son to act justly towards you. I commit no indiscretion when I tell you that she refused to sanction your marriage, mainly for the reason that Eustace declined to follow her advice, and to tell you what his position really was. On my part, I did all I could to support Mrs Macallan in the course that she took. When Eustace wrote to tell me that he had engaged himself to marry a niece of my good friend Dr Starkweather, and that he had mentioned me as his reference, I wrote back to warn him that I would have nothing to do with the affair, unless he revealed the whole truth about himself to his future wife. He refused to listen to me, as he had refused to listen to his mother; and he held me, at the same time, to my promise to keep his secret. When Starkweather wrote to me, I had no choice but to involve myself in a deception of which I thoroughly disapproved—or to answer in a tone so guarded and so brief as to stop the correspondence at the outset. I chose the last alternative; and I fear I have offended my good old friend. You now see the painful position in which I am placed. To add to the difficulties of that situation, Eustace came here, this very day, to warn me to be on my guard, in case of your addressing to me the very request which you have just made! He told me that you had met with his mother, by an unlucky accident, and that you had discovered the family name. He declared that he had travelled to London for the express purpose of speaking to me personally on this serious subject. "I know your weakness", he said, "where women are concerned. Valeria is aware that you are my old friend. She will certainly write to you; she may even be bold enough to make her way into your house. Renew your promise to keep the great calamity of my life a secret, on your honour, and on your oath." Those were his words, as nearly as I can remember them. I tried to treat the thing lightly; I ridiculed the absurdly theatrical notion of "renewing my promise," and all the rest of it. Quite useless! He refused to leave me—he reminded me of his unmerited sufferings, poor fellow, in the past time. It ended in his bursting into tears. You love him, and so do I. Can you wonder that I let him have his way? The result is that I am doubly bound to tell you nothing, by the most sacred promise that a man can give. My dear lady, I cordially side with you in this matter; I long to relieve your anxieties. But what can I do?'

He stopped, and waited—gravely waited—to hear my reply.

I had listened from beginning to end, without interrupting him. The extraordinary change in his manner, and in his way of expressing himself, while he was speaking of Eustace, alarmed me as nothing had alarmed me yet. How terrible (I thought to myself) must this untold story be, if the mere act of referring to it makes light-hearted Major Fitz-David speak seriously and sadly—never smiling; never paying me a compliment; never even noticing the singing upstairs! My heart sank in me as I drew that startling conclusion. For the first time since I had entered the house, I was at the end of my resources; I knew neither what to say nor what to do next.

And yet, I kept my seat. Never had the resolution to discover what my husband was hiding from me been more firmly rooted in my mind than it was at that moment! I cannot account for the extraordinary inconsistency in my character which this confession implies. I can only describe the facts as they really were.

The singing went on upstairs. Major Fitz-David still waited impenetrably to hear what I had to say—to know what I resolved on doing next.

Before I had decided what to say or what to do, another domestic incident happened. In plain words, another knocking announced a new visitor at the house door. On this occasion, there was no rustling of a woman's dress in the hall. On this occasion, only the old servant entered the room carrying a magnificent nosegay in his hand. 'With Lady Clarinda's kind regards. To remind Major Fitz-David of his appointment.' Another lady! This time, a lady with a title. A great lady who sent her flowers and her messages without condescending to concealment. The Major—first apologising to me—wrote a few lines of acknowledgment, and sent them out to the messenger. When the door was closed again, he carefully selected one of the choicest flowers in the nosegay. 'May I ask,' he said, presenting the flower to me with his best grace, 'whether you now understand the delicate position in which I am placed between your husband and yourself?'

The little interruption caused by the appearance of the nosegay had given a new impulse to my thoughts, and had thus helped, in some degree, to restore me to myself. I was able at last to satisfy Major Fitz-David that his considerate and courteous explanation had not been thrown away upon me.

'I thank you, most sincerely, Major,' I said. 'You have convinced me that I must not ask you to forget, on my account, the promise which you have given to my husband. It is a sacred promise which I, too, am bound to respect—I quite understand that.'

The Major drew a long breath of relief, and patted me on the shoulder in high approval of what I had said to him.

'Admirably expressed!' he rejoined, recovering his light-hearted looks and his lover-like ways all in a moment. 'My dear lady, you have the gift of sympathy; you see exactly how I am situated. Do you know, you remind me of my charming Lady Clarinda? *She* has the gift of sympathy, and sees exactly how I am situated. I should so enjoy introducing you to each other,' said the Major, plunging his long nose ecstatically into Lady Clarinda's flowers.

I had my end still to gain; and being (as you will have discovered by this time) the most obstinate of living women, I still kept that end in view.

'I shall be delighted to meet Lady Clarinda,' I replied. 'In the mean time——'

'I will get up a little dinner,' proceeded the Major, with a burst of enthusiasm. 'You and I and Lady Clarinda. Our young prima-donna shall come in the evening, and sing to us. Suppose we draw out the *menu*? My sweet friend, what is your favourite autumn soup?'

'In the mean time,' I persisted, 'to return to what we were speaking of just now——'

The Major's smile vanished, the Major's hand dropped the pen, destined to immortalise the name of my favourite autumn soup.

'*Must* we return to that?' he asked, piteously.

'Only for a moment,' I said.

'You remind me,' pursued Major Fitz-David, shaking his head sadly, 'of another charming friend of mine—a French friend—Madame Mirliflore. You are a person of prodigious tenacity of purpose. Madame Mirliflore is a person of prodigious tenacity of purpose. She happens to be in London. Shall we have her at our little dinner?' The Major brightened at the idea, and took up the pen again. 'Do tell me,' he said, 'what *is* your favourite autumn soup?'

'Pardon me,' I began; 'we were speaking just now——'

'Oh, dear me!' cried Major Fitz-David. 'Is this the other subject?'

'Yes—this is the other subject.'

The Major put down his pen for the second time, and regretfully dismissed from his mind Madame Mirliflore and the autumn soup.

'Yes?' he said with a patient bow, and a submissive smile. 'You were going to say——?'

'I was going to say,' I rejoined, 'that your promise only pledges you not to tell the secret which my husband is keeping from me. You have given no promise not to answer me, if I venture to ask you one or two questions.'

Major Fitz-David held up his hand warningly, and cast a sly look at me out of his bright little grey eyes.

'Stop!' he said. 'My sweet friend, stop there! I know where your questions will lead me, and what the result will be if I once begin to answer them. When your husband was here to-day, he took occasion to remind me that I was as weak as water in the hands of a pretty woman. He is quite right. I *am* as weak as water; I can refuse nothing to a pretty woman. Dear and admirable lady, don't abuse your influence! don't make an old soldier false to his word of honour!'

I tried to say something here in defence of my motives. The Major clasped his hands entreatingly, and looked at me with a pleading simplicity wonderful to see.

'Why press it?' he asked. 'I offer no resistance. I am a lamb—why sacrifice me? I acknowledge your power; I throw myself on your mercy. All the misfortunes of my youth and my manhood have come to me through women. I am not a bit better in my age—I am just as fond of the women, and just as ready to be misled by them as ever, with one foot in the grave. Shocking, isn't it? But how true! Look at this mark.' He lifted a curl of his beautiful brown wig, and showed me a terrible scar at the side of his head. 'That wound (supposed to be mortal at the time) was made by a pistol bullet,' he proceeded. 'Not received in the service of my country—oh, dear no! Received in the service of a much-injured lady, at the hands of her scoundrel of a husband, in a duel abroad. Well, she was worth it!' He kissed his hand affectionately to the memory of the dead, or absent, lady, and pointed to a water-colour drawing of a pretty country house, hanging on the opposite wall. 'That fine estate,' he proceeded, 'once belonged to me. It was sold years and years since. And who had the money? The women—God bless them all!—the women. I don't regret it. If I had another estate, I have no doubt it would go the same way. Your adorable sex has made its pretty playthings of my life, my time, and my money—and welcome! The one thing I have kept to myself, is my honour. And now, *that* is in danger! Yes; if you put your clever little questions, with those lovely eyes and with that gentle voice, I know what will happen! You will deprive me of the last and best of all my possessions. Have I deserved to be treated in that way—and by you, my charming friend? by you of all people in the world? Oh, fie! fie!'

He paused, and looked at me as before—the picture of artless entreaty, with his head a little on one side. I made another attempt to speak of the matter in dispute between us, from my own point of view. Major Fitz-David instantly threw himself prostrate on my mercy more innocently than ever.

'Ask of me anything else in the wide world,' he said; 'but don't ask me to be false to my friend. Spare me *that*—and there is nothing I will not do to satisfy you. I mean what I say, mind!' he went on, bending closer to me, and speaking more seriously than he had spoken yet. 'I think you are very hardly used. It is monstrous to expect that a woman placed in your situation will consent to be left for the rest of her life in the dark. No! no! if I saw you, at this moment, on the point of finding out for yourself what Eustace persists in hiding from you, I should remember that my promise, like all other promises, has its limits and reserves. I should consider myself bound in honour not to help you—but I would not lift a finger to prevent you from discovering the truth for yourself.'

At last he was speaking in good earnest; he laid a strong emphasis on his closing words. I laid a stronger emphasis on them still, by suddenly leaving my chair. The impulse to spring to my feet was irresistible. Major Fitz-David had started a new idea in my head.

'Now we understand each other!' I said. 'I will accept your own terms, Major. I will ask nothing of you but what you have just offered to me of your own accord.'

'What have I offered?' he inquired, looking a little alarmed.

'Nothing that you need repent of,' I answered; 'nothing which it is not easy for you to grant. May I ask a bold question? Suppose this house were mine instead of yours?'

'Consider it yours,' cried the gallant old gentleman. 'From the garrets to the kitchen, consider it yours!'

'A thousand thanks, Major; I will consider it mine, for the moment. You know—everybody knows—that one of a woman's many weaknesses is curiosity. Suppose my curiosity led me to examine everything in my new house?'

'Yes?'

'Suppose I went from room to room, and searched everything, and peeped in everywhere? Do you think there would be any chance——?'

The quick-witted Major anticipated the nature of my question. He followed my example; he, too, started to his feet, with a new idea in his mind.

'Would there be any chance,' I went on, 'of my finding my own way to my husband's secret, in this house? One word of reply, Major Fitz-David! Only one word—Yes, or No?'

'Don't excite yourself!' cried the Major.

'Yes, or No?' I repeated, more vehemently than ever.

'Yes,' said the Major—after a moment's consideration.

It was the reply I had asked for; but it was not explicit enough—now I had got it—to satisfy me. I felt the necessity of leading him (if possible) into details.

'Does "Yes" mean that there is some sort of clue to the mystery?' I asked. 'Something, for instance, which my eyes might see, and my hands might touch, if I could only find it?'

He considered again. I saw that I had succeeded in interesting him, in some way unknown to myself; and I waited patiently until he was prepared to answer me.

'The thing you mention,' he said; 'the clue (as you call it) might be seen and might be touched—supposing you could find it.'

'In this house?' I asked.

The Major advanced a step nearer to me, and answered,—

'In this room.'

My head began to swim; my heart throbbed violently. I tried to speak; it was in vain; the effort almost choked me. In the silence, I could hear the music lesson still going on in the room above. The future prima-donna had done practising her scales, and was trying her voice now in selections from Italian operas. At the moment when I first heard her, she was singing the lovely air from the *Sonnambula*; 'Come per me sereno.'* I never hear that delicious melody, to this day, without being instantly transported in imagination to the fatal back room in Vivian Place.

The Major—strongly affected himself, by this time—was the first to break the silence.

'Sit down again,' he said; 'and pray take the easy chair. You are very much agitated; you want rest.'

He was right. I could stand no longer; I dropped into the chair. Major Fitz-David rang the bell, and spoke a few words to the servant at the door.

'I have been here a long time,' I said, faintly. 'Tell me if I am in the way.'

'In the way?' he repeated, with his irresistible smile. 'You forget that you are in your own house!'

The servant returned to us, bringing with him a tiny bottle of champagne, and a plate-full of delicate little sugared biscuits.

'I have had this wine bottled expressly for the ladies,' said the Major. 'The biscuits come to me direct from Paris. As a favour to *me* you must take some refreshment. And then——' he stopped, and looked at me very attentively. 'And then, he resumed, 'shall I go to my young primadonna upstairs, and leave you here alone?'

It was impossible to hint more delicately at the one request which I now had it in my mind to make to him. I took his hand and pressed it gratefully.

'The tranquillity of my whole life to come is at stake,' I said. 'When I am left here by myself, does your generous sympathy permit me to examine everything in the room?'

He signed to me to drink the champagne, and to eat a biscuit, before he gave his answer.

'This is serious,' he said. 'I wish you to be in perfect possession of yourself. Restore your strength—and then I will speak to you.'

I did as he bade me. In a minute from the time when I drank it, the delicious sparkling wine had begun to revive me.

'Is it your express wish,' he resumed, 'that I should leave you here by yourself, to search the room?'

'It is my express wish,' I answered.

'I take a heavy responsibility on myself in granting your request. But I grant it for all that, because I sincerely believe— as you believe—that the tranquillity of your life to come depends on your discovering the truth.' Saying those words, he took two keys from his pocket, 'You will naturally feel a suspicion,' he went on, 'of any locked doors that you may find here. The only locked places in the room are the doors of the cupboards under the long bookcase, and the door of the Italian cabinet in that corner. The small key opens the bookcase cupboards; the long key opens the cabinet door.'

With that explanation, he laid the keys before me on the table.

'Thus far,' he said, 'I have rigidly respected the promise which I made to your husband. I shall continue to be faithful to my promise, whatever may be the result of your examination of the room. I am bound in honour not to assist you, by word or deed. I am not even at liberty to offer you the slightest hint. Is that understood?'

'Certainly!'

'Very good. I have now a last word of warning to give you—and then I have done. If you do by any chance succeed in laying your hand on the clue, remember this—*the discovery which follows will be a terrible one.* If you have any doubt about your capacity to sustain a shock which will strike you to the soul, for God's sake give up the idea of finding out your husband's secret, at once and for ever!'

'I thank you for your warning, Major. I must face the consequences of making the discovery, whatever they may be.'

'You are positively resolved?'

'Positively.'

'Very well. Take any time you please. The house, and every person in it, is at your disposal. Ring the bell once, if you want the man servant. Ring twice, if you wish the housemaid to wait on you. From time to time, I shall just look in myself to see how you are going on. I am responsible for your comfort and security, you know, while you honour me by remaining under my roof.'

He lifted my hand to his lips, and fixed a last attentive look on me.

'I hope I am not running too great a risk,' he said—more to himself than to me. 'The women have led me into many a rash action in my time. Have *you* led me, I wonder, into the rashest action of all?'

With those ominous last words he bowed gravely, and left me alone in the room.

CHAPTER X

The Search

THE fire burning in the grate was not a very large one; and the outer air (as I had noticed on my way to the house) had something of a wintry sharpness in it that day.

Still, my first feeling when Major Fitz-David left me, was a feeling of heat and oppression—with its natural result, a difficulty of breathing freely. The nervous agitation of the time was, I suppose, answerable for these sensations. I took off my bonnet and mantle and gloves, and opened the window for a little while. Nothing was to be seen outside but a paved courtyard (with a skylight in the middle), closed at the farther end by the wall of the Major's stables. A few minutes at the window cooled and refreshed me. I shut it down again, and took my first step on the way to discovery. In other words, I began my first examination of the four walls round me, and of all that they enclosed.

I was amazed at my own calmness. My interview with Major Fitz-David had, perhaps, exhausted my capacity for feeling any strong emotion—for the time at least. It was a relief to me to be alone; it was a relief to me to begin the search. Those were my only sensations, so far.

The shape of the room was oblong. Of the two shorter walls, one contained the door in grooves which I have already mentioned as communicating with the front room; the other was almost entirely occupied by the broad window which looked out on the courtyard.

Taking the doorway wall first, what was there, in the shape of furniture, on either side of it? There was a card-table on either side. Above each card-table stood a magnificent china bowl, placed on a gilt and carved bracket fixed to the wall.

I opened the card-tables. The drawers beneath contained nothing but cards, and the usual counters and markers. With the exception of one pack, the cards in both tables were still wrapped in their paper covers exactly as they had come from the shop. I examined the loose pack, card by card. No writing—no mark of any kind—was visible on any one of them. Assisted by a library ladder which stood against the bookcase, I looked next into the two china bowls. Both were perfectly empty. Was there anything more to examine on that side of the room? In the two corners there were two little chairs of inlaid wood, with red silk cushions. I turned them up, and looked under the cushions; and still I made no discoveries. When I had put the chairs back in their places, my search on one side of the room was complete. So far, I had found nothing.

I crossed to the opposite wall—the wall which contained the window.

The window (occupying, as I have said, almost the entire length and height of the wall) was divided into three compartments, and was adorned at either extremity by handsome curtains of dark red velvet. The ample, heavy folds of the velvet, left just room at the two corners of the wall, for two antique upright cabinets in buhl;* containing rows of drawers, and supporting two fine bronze reproductions (reduced in size) of the Venus Milo and the Venus Callipyge.* I had Major Fitz-David's permission to do just what I pleased. I opened the six drawers in each cabinet, and examined their contents without hesitation.

Beginning with the cabinet in the right hand corner, my investigations were soon completed. All the six drawers were alike occupied by a collection of fossils, which (judging by the curious paper inscriptions fixed on some of them) were associated with a past period of the Major's life when he had speculated, not very successfully, in mines. After satisfying myself that the drawers contained nothing but the fossils and their inscriptions, I turned to the cabinet in the left hand corner next.

Here, a variety of objects was revealed to view; and the examination accordingly occupied a much longer time.

The top drawer contained a complete collection of carpenter's tools in miniature; relics, probably, of the far distant time when the Major was a boy, and when parents or friends had made him a present of a set of toy-tools. The second drawer was filled with toys of another sort—presents made to Major Fitz-David by his fair friends. Embroidered braces, smart smoking-caps, quaint pincushions, gorgeous slippers, glittering purses, all bore witness to the popularity of the friend of the women. The contents of the third drawer were of a less interesting sort: the entire space was filled with old account books, ranging over a period of many years. After looking into each book, and opening and shaking it uselessly, in search of any loose papers which might be hidden between the leaves, I came to the fourth drawer, and found more relics of past pecuniary transactions in the shape of receipted bills, neatly tied together, and each inscribed at the back. Among the bills, I found nearly a dozen loose papers, all equally unimportant. The fifth drawer was in sad confusion. I took out first a loose bundle of ornamental cards, each containing the list of dishes at past banquets given, or attended, by the Major, in London and Paris—next, a box full of delicately tinted quill pens (evidently a lady's gift)—next, a quantity of old invitation cards—next, some dog's-eared French plays and books of the opera—next, a pocket-corkscrew, a bundle of cigarettes, and a bunch of rusty keys—lastly, a passport, a set of luggage labels, a broken silver snuff-box, two cigar-cases, and a torn map of Rome. 'Nothing anywhere to interest *me*,' I thought, as I closed the fifth, and opened the sixth, and last, drawer.

The sixth drawer was at once a surprise and a disappointment. It literally contained nothing but the fragments of a broken vase.

I was sitting, at the time, opposite to the cabinet, in a low chair. In the momentary irritation caused by my discovery

of the emptiness of the last drawer, I had just lifted my foot
to push it back into its place—when the door communicating with the hall opened; and Major Fitz-David stood before me.

His eyes, after first meeting mine, travelled downwards
to my foot. The instant he noticed the open drawer, I saw
a change in his face. It was only for a moment; but, in that
moment, he looked at me with a sudden suspicion and
surprise—looked as if he had caught me with my hand on
the clue.

'Pray don't let me disturb you,' he said. 'I have only
looked in for a moment to ask you a question.'

'What is it, Major?'

'Have you met with any letters of mine, in the course of
your investigations?'

'I have found none yet,' I answered. 'If I do discover any
letters, I shall of course not take the liberty of examining
them.'

'I wanted to speak to you about that,' he rejoined. 'It only
struck me a moment since, upstairs, that my letters might
embarrass you. In your place, I should feel some distrust of
anything which I was not at liberty to examine. I think I can
set this matter right, however, with very little trouble to
either of us. It is no violation of any promises or pledges on
my part, if I simply tell you that my letters will not assist the
discovery which you are trying to make. You can safely pass
them over as objects that are not worth examining from your
point of view. You understand me, I am sure?'

'I am much obliged to you, Major—I quite understand.'

'Are you feeling any fatigue?'

'None whatever—thank you.'

'And you still hope to succeed? You are not beginning to
be discouraged already?'

'I am not in the least discouraged. With your kind leave,
I mean to persevere for some time yet.'

I had not closed the drawer of the cabinet, while we were
talking; and I glanced carelessly, as I answered him, at the

fragments of the broken vase. By this time he had got his feelings under perfect command. He, too, glanced at the fragments of the vase, with an appearance of perfect indifference. I remembered the look of suspicion and surprise that had escaped him on entering the room; and I thought his indifference a little over-acted.

'*That* doesn't look very encouraging,' he said, with a smile, pointing to the shattered pieces of china in the drawer.

'Appearances are not always to be trusted,' I replied. 'The wisest thing I can do, in my present situation, is to suspect everything—even down to a broken vase.'

I looked hard at him as I spoke. He changed the subject.

'Does the music upstairs annoy you?' he asked.

'Not in the least, Major.'

'It will soon be over now. The singing master is going; and the Italian master has just arrived. I am sparing no pains to make my young prima-donna a most accomplished person. In learning to sing, she must also learn the language which is especially the language of music. I shall perfect her in the accent when I take her to Italy. It is the height of my ambition to have her mistaken for an Italian when she sings in public. Is there anything I can do before I leave you again? May I send you some more champagne? Please say yes!'

'A thousand thanks, Major. No more champagne for the present.'

He turned at the door to kiss his hand to me at parting. At the same moment I saw his eyes wander slily towards the bookcase. It was only for an instant. I had barely detected him before he was out of the room.

Left by myself again, I looked at the bookcase—looked at it attentively for the first time.

It was a handsome piece of furniture in ancient carved oak; and it stood against the wall which ran parallel with the hall of the house. Excepting the space occupied, in the upper corner of the room, by the second door which opened into the hall, the bookcase filled the whole length of the wall down to the window. The top was ornamented by vases, candelabra, and statuettes, in pairs, placed in a row. Looking along the row, I noticed a vacant space on the top of the bookcase, at the extremity of it which was nearest to the window. The opposite extremity, nearest to the door, was occupied by a handsome painted vase of a very peculiar pattern. Where was the corresponding vase, which ought to have been placed at the corresponding extremity of the bookcase? I returned to the open sixth drawer of the cabinet, and looked in again. There was no mistaking the pattern on the fragments, when I examined them now. The vase which had been broken was the vase which had stood in the place now vacant on the top of the bookcase, at the end nearest to the window.

Making this discovery, I took out the fragments, down to the smallest morsel of the shattered china, and examined them carefully one after another.

I was too ignorant of the subject to be able to estimate the value of the vase, or the antiquity of the vase—or even to know whether it was of British or of foreign manufacture. The ground was of a delicate cream-colour. The ornaments traced on this were wreaths of flowers and cupids, surrounding a medallion on either side of the vase. Upon the space within one of the medallions was painted with exquisite delicacy a woman's head; representing a nymph, or a goddess, or perhaps a portrait of some celebrated person—I was not learned enough to say which. The other medallion enclosed the head of a man, also treated in the classical style. Reclining shepherds and shepherdesses, in Watteau costume,* with their dogs and their sheep, formed the adornments of the pedestal. Such had the vase been in the days of its prosperity, when it stood on the top of the bookcase. By what accident had it become broken? And why had Major Fitz-David's face changed when he found that I had discovered the remains of his shattered work of Art in the cabinet drawer?

The remains left those serious questions unanswered—
the remains told me absolutely nothing. And yet, if my own
observation of the Major was to be trusted, the way to the
clue of which I was in search, lay—directly or indirectly—
through the broken vase!

It was useless to pursue the question, knowing no more
than I knew now. I returned to the bookcase.

Thus far, I had assumed (without any sufficient reason)
that the clue of which I was in search must necessarily
reveal itself through a written paper of some sort. It now
occurred to me—after the movement which I had detected
on the part of the Major—that the clue might quite as
probably present itself in the form of a book.

I looked along the lower rows of shelves; standing just
near enough to them to read the titles on the backs of the
volumes. I saw Voltaire* in red morocco; Shakespeare in
blue; Walter Scott in green; the History of England* in
brown; the Annual Register* in yellow calf. There I paused,
wearied and discouraged already by the long rows of volumes. How (I thought to myself) am I to examine all these
books? And what am I to look for, even if I do examine
them all?

Major Fitz-David had spoken of a terrible misfortune
which had darkened my husband's past life. In what
possible way could any trace of that misfortune, or any
suggestive hint of something resembling it, exist in the
archives of the Annual Register, or in the pages of Voltaire?
The bare idea of such a thing seemed absurd. The mere
attempt to make a serious examination in this direction was
surely a wanton waste of time?

And yet, the Major had certainly stolen a look at the
bookcase. And again, the broken vase had once stood on
the bookcase. Did these circumstances justify me in con-
necting the vase and the bookcase as twin landmarks on the
way that led to discovery? The question was not an easy
one to decide on the spur of the moment.

I looked up at the higher shelves.

Here the collection of books exhibited a greater variety. The volumes were smaller, and were not so carefully arranged as on the lower shelves. Some were bound in cloth; some were only protected by paper covers. One or two had fallen, and lay flat on the shelves. Here and there I saw empty spaces from which books had been removed and not replaced. In short, there was no discouraging uniformity in these higher regions of the bookcase. The untidy top shelves looked suggestive of some lucky accident which might unexpectedly lead the way to success. I decided, if I did examine the bookcase at all, to begin at the top.

Where was the library ladder?

I had left it against the partition wall which divided the back room from the room in front. Looking that way, I necessarily looked also towards the door that ran in grooves—the imperfectly-closed door through which I had heard Major Fitz-David question his servant on the subject of my personal appearance, when I first entered the house. No one had moved this door, during the time of my visit. Everybody entering or leaving the room had used the other door which led into the hall.

At the moment when I looked round, something stirred in the front room. The movement let the light in suddenly through the small open space left by the partially-closed door. Had somebody been watching me through the chink? I stepped softly to the door, and pushed it back until it was wide open. There was the Major, discovered in the front room! I saw it in his face—he had been watching me at the bookcase!

His hat was in his hand. He was evidently going out; and he dexterously took advantage of that circumstance to give a plausible reason for being so near the door.

'I hope I didn't frighten you,' he said.

'You startled me a little, Major.'

'I am so sorry, and so ashamed! I was just going to open the door, and tell you that I am obliged to go out. I have received a pressing message from a lady. A charming per-

son—I should so like you to know her! She is in sad trouble,
poor thing. Little bills, you know, and nasty trades people
who want their money, and a husband—oh, dear me, a
husband who is quite unworthy of her! A most interesting
creature. You remind me of her a little—you both have the
same carriage of the head. I shall not be more than half-
an-hour gone. Can I do anything for you? You are looking
fatigued. Pray let me send for some more champagne. No?
Promise to ring when you want it. That's right! *Au revoir*,
my charming friend—*au revoir!*'

I pulled the door to again, the moment his back was
turned; and sat down for awhile to compose myself.

He had been watching me at the bookcase! The man who
was in my husband's confidence, the man who knew where
the clue was to be found, had been watching me at the
bookcase! There was no doubt of it now. Major Fitz-David
had shown me the hiding-place of the secret, in spite of
himself!

I looked with indifference at the other pieces of furniture,
ranged against the fourth wall, which I had not examined
yet. I surveyed, without the slightest feeling of curiosity, all
the little elegant trifles scattered on the tables and on the
chimney-piece; each one of which might have been an object of suspicion to me under other circumstances. Even the
water-colour drawings failed to interest me, in my present
frame of mind. I observed languidly that they were most of
them portraits of ladies—fair idols, no doubt, of the Major's
facile adoration—and I cared to notice no more. *My* business in that room (I was certain of it now!) began and ended
with the bookcase. I left my seat to fetch the library ladder;
determining to begin the work of investigation on the top
shelves.

On my way to the ladder I passed one of the tables, and
saw the keys lying on it which Major Fitz-David had left at
my disposal.

The smaller of the two keys instantly reminded me of
the cupboards under the bookcase. I had strangely over-

looked these. A vague distrust of the locked doors, a vague doubt of what they might be hiding from me, stole into my mind. I left the ladder in its place against the wall, and set myself to examine the contents of the cupboards first.

The cupboards were three in number. As I opened the first of them, the singing upstairs ceased. For a moment there was something almost oppressive in the sudden change from noise to silence. I suppose my nerves must have been over-wrought. The next sound in the house—nothing more remarkable than the creaking of a man's boots, descending the stairs—made me shudder all over. The man was no doubt the singing master, going away after giving his lesson. I heard the house door close on him—and started at the familiar sound as if it was something terrible which I had never heard before! Then there was silence again. I roused myself as well as I could, and began my examination of the first cupboard.

It was divided into two compartments.

The top compartment contained nothing but boxes of cigars, ranged in rows one on another. The under compartment was devoted to a collection of shells. They were all huddled together anyhow—the Major evidently setting a far higher value on his cigars than on his shells. I searched this lower compartment carefully for any object interesting to me which might be hidden in it. Nothing was to be found in any part of it, besides the shells.

As I opened the second cupboard, it struck me that the light was beginning to fail.

I looked at the window. It was hardly evening yet. The darkening of the light was produced by gathering clouds. Rain-drops pattered against the glass; the autumn wind whistled mournfully in the corners of the courtyard. I mended the fire before I renewed my search. My nerves were in fault again, I suppose. I shivered when I went back to the bookcase. My hands trembled: I wondered what was the matter with me.

The second cupboard revealed (in the upper division of it) some really beautiful cameos; not mounted, but laid on cotton wool, in neat cardboard trays. In one corner, half hidden under one of the trays, there peeped out the white leaves of a little manuscript. The manuscript proved to be a descriptive catalogue of the cameos—nothing more!

Turning to the lower division of the cupboard, I found more costly curiosities, in the shape of ivory carvings from Japan, and specimens of rare silk from China. I began to feel weary of disinterring the Major's treasures. The longer I searched, the farther I seemed to remove myself from the one object that I had it at heart to attain. After closing the door of the second cupboard, I almost doubted whether it would be worth my while to proceed farther, and open the third and last door.

A little reflection convinced me that it would be as well, now that I had begun my examination of the lower regions of the bookcase, to go on with it to the end. I opened the last cupboard.

On the upper shelf there appeared, in solitary grandeur, one object only—a gorgeously-bound book.

It was of a larger size than usual, judging of it by comparison with the dimensions of modern volumes. The binding was of blue velvet, with clasps of silver worked in beautiful arabesque patterns, and with a lock of the same precious metal to protect the book from prying eyes. When I took it up, I found that the lock was not closed.

Had I any right to take advantage of this accident, and open the book? I have put the question, since, to some of my friends, of both sexes. The women all agree that I was perfectly justified—considering the serious interests that I had at stake—in taking any advantage of any book in the Major's house. The men differ from this view, and declare that I ought to have put back the volume in blue velvet, unopened; carefully guarding myself from any after-temptation to look at it again, by locking the cupboard door. I dare say the men are right.

Being a woman, however, I opened the book, without a moment's hesitation.

The leaves were of the finest vellum, with tastefully-designed illuminations all round them. And what did these highly ornamented pages contain? To my unutterable amazement and disgust, they contained locks of hair let neatly into the centre of each page—with inscriptions beneath, which proved them to be love-tokens from various ladies, who had touched the Major's susceptible heart at different periods of his life. The inscriptions were written in other languages besides English; but they appeared to be equally devoted to the same curious purpose—namely, to reminding the Major of the dates at which his various attachments had come to an untimely end. Thus, the first page exhibited a lock of the lightest flaxen hair, with these lines beneath: 'My adored Madeline. Eternal constancy. Alas: July 22nd, 1839!' The next page was adorned by a darker shade of hair, with a French inscription under it: 'Clémence. Idole de mon âme. Toujours fidèle. Hélas: 2me Avril, 1840!'* A lock of red hair followed—with a lamentation in Latin under it; a note being attached to the date of dissolution of partnership, in this case, stating that the lady was descended from the ancient Romans, and was therefore mourned appropriately in Latin by her devoted Fitz-David. More shades of hair, and more inscriptions followed, until I was weary of looking at them. I put down the book disgusted with the creatures who had assisted in filling it—and then took it up again, by an after-thought. Thus far, I had thoroughly searched everything that had presented itself to my notice. Agreeable or not agreeable, it was plainly of serious importance to my own interests to go on as I had begun, and thoroughly to search the book.

I turned over the pages until I came to the first blank leaf. Seeing that they were all blank leaves from this place to the end, I lifted the volume by the back, and, as a last measure of precaution, shook it so as to dislodge any loose papers or cards which might have escaped my notice between the leaves.

This time, my patience was rewarded by a discovery which indescribably irritated and distressed me.

A small photograph, mounted on a card, fell out of the book. A first glance showed me that it represented the portraits of two persons.

One of the persons I recognised as my husband.

The other person was a woman.

Her face was entirely unknown to me. She was not young. The picture represented her seated on a chair, with my husband standing behind, and bending over her, holding one of her hands in his. The woman's face was hard-featured and ugly, with the marking lines of strong passions and resolute self-will plainly written on it. Still, ugly as she was, I felt a pang of jealousy as I noticed the familiarly-affectionate action by which the artist (with the permission of his sitters, of course) had connected the two figures in a group. Eustace had briefly told me, in the days of our courtship, that he had more than once fancied himself to be in love, before he met with me. Could this very unattractive woman have been one of the objects of his admiration? Had she been near enough and dear enough to him, to be photographed with her hand in his? I looked and looked at the portraits, until I could endure them no longer. Women are strange creatures; mysteries even to themselves. I threw the photograph from me into a corner of the cupboard. I was savagely angry with my husband; I hated—yes, hated with all my heart and soul!—the woman who had got his hand in hers; the unknown woman with the self-willed hard-featured face.

All this time the lower shelf of the cupboard was still waiting to be looked over.

I knelt down to examine it—eager to clear my mind, if I could, of the degrading jealousy that had got possession of me.

Unfortunately the lower shelf contained nothing but relics of the Major's military life; comprising his sword and pistols, his epaulettes, his sash, and other minor accoutrements. None of these objects excited the slightest interest in me. My eyes wandered back to the upper shelf; and, like the fool I was (there is no milder word that can fitly describe me at that moment), I took the photograph out again, and enraged myself uselessly by another look at it. This time I observed, what I had not noticed before, that there were some lines of writing (in a woman's hand) at the back of the portraits. The lines ran thus:—

'To Major Fitz-David, with two vases. From his friends S. and E. M.'

Was one of those two vases the vase that had been broken? And was the change that I had noticed in Major Fitz-David's face produced by some past association in connexion with it, which in some way affected me? It might or might not be so. I was little disposed to indulge in speculation on this topic, while the far more serious question of the initials confronted me on the back of the photograph.

'S. and E. M.'? Those last two letters might stand for the initials of my husband's name—his true name—Eustace Macallan. In this case, the first letter ('S.'), in all probability, indicated *her* name. What right had she to associate herself with him in that manner? I considered a little—my memory exerted itself—I suddenly called to mind that Eustace had sisters. He had spoken of them more than once, in the time before our marriage. Had I been mad enough to torture myself with jealousy of my husband's sister? It might well be so; 'S.' might stand for his sister's Christian name. I felt heartily ashamed of myself, as this new view of the matter dawned on me. What a wrong I had done to them both, in my thoughts! I turned the photograph, sadly and penitently, to examine the portraits again with a kinder and truer appreciation of them.

I naturally looked now for a family likeness between the two faces. There was no family likeness: on the contrary, they were as unlike each other in form and expression as faces could be. *Was* she his sister after all? I looked at her hands, as represented in the portrait. Her right hand was clasped by Eustace: her left hand lay on her lap. On the third finger—distinctly visible—there was a wedding-ring. Were any of my husband's sisters married? I had myself asked him the question when he mentioned them to me; and I perfectly remembered that he had replied in the negative.

Was it possible that my first jealous instinct had led me to the right conclusion after all? If it had, what did the association of the three initial letters mean? What did the wedding-ring mean? Good Heavens! was I looking at the portrait of a rival in my husband's affections—and was that rival his Wife?

I threw the photograph from me with a cry of horror. For one terrible moment, I felt as if my reason was giving way. I don't know what would have happened—or what I should have done next—if my love for Eustace had not taken the uppermost place among the contending emotions that tortured me. That faithful love steadied my brain. That faithful love roused the reviving influences of my better and nobler sense. Was the man whom I had enshrined in my heart of hearts capable of such base wickedness as the bare idea of his marriage to another woman implied? No!—mine was the baseness, mine the wickedness, in having even for a moment thought it of him!

I picked up the detestable photograph from the floor, and put it back in the book. I hastily closed the cupboard door, fetched the library ladder, and set it against the bookcase. My one idea, now, was the idea of taking refuge in employment of any sort from my own thoughts. I felt the hateful suspicion that had degraded me coming back again in spite of my efforts to repel it. The books! the books! my only hope was to absorb myself, body and soul, in the books.

I had one foot on the ladder, when I heard the door of the room open—the door which communicated with the hall.

I looked round, expecting to see the Major. I saw instead

the Major's future prima-donna, standing just inside the door, with her round eyes steadily fixed on me.

'I can stand a good deal,' the girl began, coolly; 'but I can't stand *this* any longer.'

'What is it that you can't stand any longer?' I asked.

'If you have been here a minute, you have been here two good hours,' she went on. 'All by yourself, in the Major's study. I am of a jealous disposition—*I* am. And I want to know what it means.' She advanced a few steps nearer to me, with a heightening colour and a threatening look. 'Is he going to bring *you* out on the stage?' she asked, sharply.

'Certainly not.'

'He ain't in love with you—is he?'

Under other circumstances, I might have told her to leave the room. In my position, at that critical moment, the mere presence of a human creature was a positive relief to me. Even this girl, with her coarse questions and her uncultivated manners, was a welcome intruder on my solitude: she offered me a refuge from myself.

'Your question is not very civilly put,' I said. 'However, I excuse you. You are probably not aware that I am a married woman.'

'What has that got to do with it?' she retorted. 'Married, or single, it's all one to the Major. The brazed-faced hussey who calls herself Lady Clarinda is married—and she sends him nosegays three times a week! Not that I care, mind you, about the old fool. But I've lost my situation at the railway, and I've got my own interests to look after, and I don't know what may happen if I let other women come between him and me. That's where the shoe pinches— don't you see? I'm not easy in my mind, when I see him leaving you mistress here to do just what you like. No offence! I speak out—*I* do. I want to know what you are about, all by yourself, in this room? How did you pick up with the Major? I never heard him speak of you before to-day.'

Under all the surface selfishness and coarseness of this
strange girl, there was a certain frankness and freedom
which pleaded in her favour—to my mind at any rate. I
answered frankly and freely, on my side.

'Major Fitz-David is an old friend of my husband's,' I
said; 'and he is kind to me for my husband's sake. He has
given me permission to look about in this room——'

I stopped, at a loss how to describe my employment in
terms which should tell her nothing, and which should at
the same time successfully set her distrust of me at rest.

'To look about in this room—for what?' she asked. Her
eye fell on the library ladder, beside which I was still standing. 'For a book?' she resumed.

'Yes,' I said, taking the hint. 'For a book.'

'Haven't you found it yet?'

'No.'

She looked hard at me; undisguisedly considering with
herself whether I was, or was not, speaking the truth.

'You seem to be a good sort,' she said, making up her
mind at last. 'There's nothing stuck-up about you. I'll help
you if I can. I have rummaged among the books here over
and over again, and I know more about them than you do.
What book do you want?'

As she put that awkward question, she noticed for the
first time Lady Clarinda's nosegay lying on the side table
where the Major had left it. Instantly forgetting me and my
book, this curious girl pounced like a fury on the flowers,
and actually trampled them under her feet!

'There!' she cried. 'If I had Lady Clarinda here, I'd serve
her in the same way.'

'What will the Major say?' I asked.

'What do I care? Do you suppose I'm afraid of *him*? Only
last week I broke one of his fine gimcracks up there, and
all through Lady Clarinda and her flowers!'

She pointed to the top of the bookcase—to the empty
space on it, close by the window. My heart gave a sudden
bound, as my eyes took the direction indicated by her

finger. *She* had broken the vase! Was the way to discovery about to reveal itself to me through this girl? Not a word would pass my lips; I could only look at her.

'Yes!' she said. 'The thing stood there. He knows how I hate her flowers, and he put her nosegay in the vase out of my way. There was a woman's face painted on the china; and he told me it was the living image of *her* face. It was no more like her than I am. I was in such a rage that I up with the book I was reading at the time, and shied it at the painted face. Over the vase went, bless your heart—crash to the floor. Stop a bit! I wonder whether *that's* the book you have been looking after? Are you like me? Do you like reading Trials?'*

Trials? Had I heard her aright? Yes: she had said, Trials.

I answered by an affirmative motion of my head. I was still speechless. The girl sauntered in her cool way to the fireplace, and taking up the tongs, returned with them to the bookcase.

'Here's where the book fell,' she said—'in the space between the bookcase and the wall. I'll have it out in no time.'

I waited without moving a muscle, without uttering a word.

She approached me, with the tongs in one hand, and with a plainly-bound volume in the other.

'Is that the book?' she said. 'Open it, and see.'

I took the book from her.

'It's tremendously interesting,' she went on. 'I've read it twice over—I have. Mind you, *I* believe he did it, after all.'

Did it? Did what? What was she talking about? I tried to put the question to her. I struggled—quite vainly—to say only those words: 'What are you talking about?'

She seemed to lose all patience with me. She snatched the book out of my hand, and opened it before me on the table by which we were standing side by side.

'I declare you're as helpless as a baby!' she said, contemptuously. 'There! *Is* that the book?'

I read the first lines on the title-page:—

A COMPLETE REPORT OF

THE TRIAL OF

EUSTACE MACALLAN

I stopped, and looked up at her. She started back from
me with a scream of terror. I looked down again at the
title-page, and read the next lines:—

FOR THE ALLEGED POISONING

OF

HIS WIFE.

There, God's mercy remembered me. There, the black
blank of a swoon swallowed me up.

CHAPTER XI

The Return to Life

MY FIRST remembrance, when I began to recover my
senses, was the remembrance of Pain—agonising pain, as if
every nerve in my body was being twisted and torn out of
me. My whole being writhed and quivered under the dumb
and dreadful protest of Nature against the effort to recall me
to life. I would have given worlds to be able to cry out—to
entreat the unseen creatures about me to give me back to
death. How long that speechless agony held me, I never
knew. In a longer or a shorter time there stole over me
slowly, a sleepy sense of relief. I heard my own laboured
breathing. I felt my hands moving feebly and mechanically like the hands of a baby. I faintly opened my eyes, and

looked round me—as if I had passed through the ordeal of death, and had awakened to new senses, in a new world.

The first person I saw was a man—a stranger. He moved quietly out of my sight; beckoning, as he disappeared, to some other person in the room.

Slowly and unwillingly, the other person advanced to the sofa on which I lay. A faint cry of joy escaped me; I tried to hold out my feeble hands. The other person who was approaching me was my husband!

I looked at him eagerly. He never looked at me in return. With his eyes on the ground, with a strange appearance of confusion and distress in his face, he, too, moved away out of my sight. The unknown man whom I had first noticed, followed him out of the room. I called after him faintly, 'Eustace!' He never answered; he never returned. With an effort I moved my head on the pillow, so as to look round on the other side of the sofa. Another familiar face appeared before me as if in a dream. My good old Benjamin was sitting watching me, with the tears in his eyes.

He rose and took my hand silently, in his simple, kindly way.

'Where is Eustace?' I asked. 'Why has he gone away and left me?'

I was still miserably weak. My eyes wandered mechanically round the room as I put the question. I saw Major Fitz-David. I saw the table on which the singing-girl had opened the book to show it to me. I saw the girl herself sitting alone in a corner, with her handkerchief to her eyes as if she was crying. In one mysterious moment my memory recovered its powers. The recollection of that fatal title page came back to me in all its horror. The one feeling that it roused in me now, was a longing to see my husband—to throw myself into his arms, and tell him how firmly I believed in his innocence, how truly and dearly I loved him. I seized on Benjamin with feeble, trembling hands. 'Bring him back to me!' I cried, wildly. 'Where is he? Help me to get up.'

A strange voice answered, firmly and kindly,—

'Compose yourself, madam. Mr Woodville is waiting until you have recovered, in a room close by.'

I looked at him, and recognized the stranger who had followed my husband out of the room. Why had he returned alone? Why was Eustace not with me, like the rest of them! I tried to raise myself, and get on my feet. The stranger gently pressed me back again on the pillow. I attempted to resist him; quite uselessly of course. His firm hand held me, as gently as ever, in my place.

'You must rest a little,' he said. 'You must take some wine. If you exert yourself now, you will faint again.'

Old Benjamin stooped over me, and whispered a word of explanation.

'It's the doctor, my dear. You must do as he tells you.'

The doctor? They had called the doctor in to help them! I began dimly to understand that my fainting-fit must have presented symptoms far more serious than the fainting-fits of women in general. I appealed to the doctor, in a helpless, querulous way, to account to me for my husband's extraordinary absence.

'Why did you let him leave the room?' I asked. 'If I can't go to him, why don't you bring him here to me?'

The doctor appeared to be at a loss how to reply to me. He looked at Benjamin, and said, 'Will you speak to Mrs Woodville?'

Benjamin, in his turn, looked at Major Fitz-David, and said, 'Will *you*?' The Major signed to them both to leave us. They rose together, and went into the front room; pulling the door to after them in its grooves. As they left us, the girl who had so strangely revealed my husband's secret to me rose in her corner and approached the sofa.

'I suppose I had better go too?' she said, addressing Major Fitz-David.

'If you please,' the Major answered.

He spoke (as I thought) rather coldly. She tossed her head, and turned her back on him in high indignation. 'I must say a word for myself!' cried this strange creature, with an hysterical outbreak of energy. 'I must say a word, or I shall burst!'

With that extraordinary preface, she suddenly turned my way, and poured out a perfect torrent of words on me.

'You hear how the Major speaks to me?' she began. 'He blames me—poor Me—for everything that has happened. I am as innocent as the new-born babe. I acted for the best. I thought you wanted the book. I don't know now what made you faint dead away when I opened it. And the Major blames Me! As if it was my fault! I am not one of the fainting sort myself; but I feel it, I can tell you. Yes! I feel it, though I don't faint about it. I come of respectable parents—*I* do. My name is Hoighty—Miss Hoighty. I have my own self-respect; and it's wounded. I say my self-respect is wounded, when I find myself blamed without deserving it. You deserve it, if anybody does. Didn't you tell me you were looking for a book? And didn't I present it to you promiscuously, with the best intentions? I think you might say so yourself, now the doctor has brought you to again. I think you might speak up for a poor girl who is worked to death with singing and languages and what not—a poor girl who has nobody else to speak for her. I am as respectable as you are, if you come to that. My name is Hoighty. My parents are in business, and my mamma has seen better days, and mixed in the best of company.'

There, Miss Hoighty lifted her handkerchief again to her face, and burst modestly into tears behind it.

It was certainly hard to hold *her* responsible for what had happened. I answered as kindly as I could; and I attempted to speak to Major Fitz-David in her defence. He knew what terrible anxieties were oppressing me at that moment; and considerately refusing to hear a word, he took the task of consoling his young prima-donna entirely on himself. What he said to her I neither heard nor cared to hear; he spoke in a whisper. It ended in his pacifying Miss Hoighty, by kissing her hand, and leading her (as he might have led a duchess) out of the room.

'I hope that foolish girl has not annoyed you—at such a time as this?' he said, very earnestly, when he returned to the sofa. 'I can't tell you how grieved I am at what has happened. I was careful to warn you, as you may remember. Still, if I could only have foreseen——'

I let him proceed no farther. No human forethought could have provided against what had happened. Besides, dreadful as the discovery had been, I would rather have made it, and suffer under it, as I was suffering now, than have been kept in the dark. I told him this. And then I turned to the one subject that was now of any interest to me—the subject of my unhappy husband.

'How did he come to this house?' I asked.

'He came here with Mr Benjamin, shortly after I returned,' the Major replied.

'Long after I was taken ill?'

'No. I had just sent for the doctor—feeling seriously alarmed about you.'

'What brought him here? Did he return to the hotel, and miss me?'

'Yes. He returned earlier than he had anticipated; and he felt uneasy at not finding you at the hotel.'

'Did he suspect me of being with you? Did he come here from the hotel?'

'No. He appears to have gone first to Mr Benjamin, to inquire about you. What he heard from your old friend, I cannot say. I only know that Mr Benjamin accompanied him when he came here.'

This brief explanation was quite enough for me—I understood what had happened. Eustace would easily frighten simple old Benjamin about my absence from the hotel; and, once alarmed, Benjamin would be persuaded without difficulty to repeat the few words which had passed between us, on the subject of Major Fitz-David. My husband's presence in the Major's house was perfectly explained. But his extraordinary conduct in leaving the room, at the very time when I was just recovering my senses, still remained to be accounted for. Major Fitz-David looked seriously embarrassed when I put the question to him.

'I hardly know how to explain it to you,' he said. 'Eustace has surprised and disappointed me.'

He spoke very gravely. His looks told me more than his words: his looks alarmed me.

'Eustace has not quarrelled with you?' I said.

'Oh, no!'

'He understands that you have not broken your promise to him?'

'Certainly. My young vocalist (Miss Hoighty) told the doctor exactly what had happened; and the doctor in her presence repeated the statement to your husband.'

'Did the doctor see the "Trial"?'

'Neither the doctor nor Mr Benjamin has seen the "Trial." I have locked it up; and I have carefully kept the terrible story of your connexion with the prisoner a secret from all of them. Mr Benjamin evidently has his suspicions. But the doctor has no idea, and Miss Hoighty has no idea, of the true cause of your fainting fit. They both believe that you are subject to serious nervous attacks; and that your husband's name is really Woodville. All that the truest friend could do to spare Eustace, I have done. He persists, nevertheless, in blaming me for letting you enter my house. And worse, far worse than this, he persists in declaring that the event of to-day has fatally estranged you from him. "There is an end of our married life," he said to me, "now she knows that I am the man who was tried at Edinburgh for poisoning my wife!" '

I rose from the sofa in horror.

'Good God!' I cried; 'does Eustace suppose that I doubt his innocence?'

'He denies that it is possible for you, or for anybody, to believe in his innocence,' the Major replied.

'Help me to the door,' I said. 'Where is he? I must and will see him!'

I dropped back exhausted on the sofa as I said the words.

Major Fitz-David poured out a glass of wine from the bottle on the table, and insisted on my drinking it.

'You shall see him,' said the Major. 'I promise you that. The doctor has forbidden him to leave the house, until you have seen him. Only wait a little! My poor dear lady, wait, if it is only for a few minutes, until you are stronger!'

I had no choice but to obey him. Oh, those miserable helpless minutes on the sofa! I cannot write of them without shuddering at the recollection—even at this distance of time.

'Bring him here!' I said. 'Pray, pray, bring him here!'

'Who is to persuade him to come back?' asked the Major, sadly. 'How can I, how can anybody, prevail with a man—a madman I had almost said!—who could leave you at the moment when you first opened your eyes on him? I saw Eustace alone, in the next room, while the doctor was in attendance on you. I tried to shake his obstinate distrust of your belief in his innocence, and of my belief in his innocence, by every argument and every appeal that an old friend could address to him. He had but one answer to give me. Reason as I might, and plead as I might, he still persisted in referring me to the Scotch Verdict.'

'The Scotch Verdict?' I repeated. 'What is that?'

The Major looked surprised at the question.

'Have you really never heard of the Trial?' he said.

'Never.'

'I thought it strange,' he went on, 'when you told me you had found out your husband's true name, that the discovery appeared to have suggested no painful association to your mind. It is not more than three years since all England was talking of your husband. One can hardly wonder at his taking refuge, poor fellow, in an assumed name! Where could you have been at the time?'

'Did you say it was three years ago?' I asked.

'Yes.'

I understood my strange ignorance of what appeared to be so well known to other people. Three years since, my father was alive. I was living with him, in a country house in Italy—up in the mountains, near Siena. We never saw an English newspaper, or met with an English traveller, for weeks and weeks together. There might certainly have been some reference made to the famous Scotch Trial in my father's letters from England. If there was, he never told me of it. Or, if he did mention the case, I must have forgotten it in course of time. 'Tell me,' I said to the Major, 'what has the Verdict to do with my husband's horrible doubt of us? Eustace is a free man. The verdict was Not Guilty, of course?'

Major Fitz-David shook his head sadly.

'Eustace was tried in Scotland,' he said. 'There is a verdict allowed by the Scotch law, which (so far as I know) is not permitted by the laws of any other civilized country on the face of the earth. When the jury are in doubt whether to condemn or acquit the prisoner brought before them, they are permitted, in Scotland, to express that doubt by a form of compromise. If there is not evidence enough, on the one hand, to justify them in finding a prisoner guilty, and not evidence enough, on the other hand, to thoroughly convince them that a prisoner is innocent, they extricate themselves from the difficulty by finding a verdict of Not Proven.'*

'Was that the verdict when Eustace was tried?' I asked.

'Yes.'

'The jury were not quite satisfied that my husband was guilty? and not quite satisfied that my husband was innocent? Is that what the Scotch Verdict means?'

'That is what the Scotch Verdict means. For three years that doubt about him in the minds of the jury who tried him has stood on public record.'

Oh, my poor darling! my innocent martyr! I understood it at last. The false name in which he had married me; the terrible words he had spoken when he had warned me to respect his secret; the still more terrible doubt that he felt of me at that moment—it was all intelligible to my sympathies; it was all clear to my understanding, now. I got up again from the sofa, strong in a daring resolution which the Scotch Verdict had suddenly kindled in me—a resolution, at once too sacred and too desperate to be confided, in the first instance, to any other than my husband's ear.

'Take me to Eustace,' I said. 'I am strong enough to bear anything now.'

After one searching look at me, the Major silently offered me his arm. We left the room together.

CHAPTER XII

The Scotch Verdict

WE walked to the far end of the hall. Major Fitz-David opened the door of a long narrow room, built out at the back of the house as a smoking-room, and extending along one side of the courtyard as far as the stable wall.

My husband was alone in the room; seated at the farther end of it, near the fireplace. He started to his feet, and faced me in silence as I entered. The Major softly closed the door on us, and retired. Eustace never stirred a step to meet me. I ran to him, and threw my arms round his neck, and kissed him. The embrace was not returned; the kiss was not returned. He passively submitted—nothing more.

'Eustace,' I said, 'I never loved you more dearly than I love you at this moment! I never felt for you as I feel for you now!'

He released himself deliberately from my arms. He signed to me, with the mechanical courtesy of a stranger, to take a chair.

'Thank you, Valeria,' he answered, in cold measured tones. 'You could say no less to me after what has happened; and you could say no more. Thank you.'

We were standing before the fireplace. He left me, and

walked away slowly with his head down; apparently intending to leave the room. I followed him—I got before him—I placed myself between him and the door.

'Why do you leave me?' I said. 'Why do you speak to me in this cruel way? Are you angry, Eustace? My darling,—you *are* angry, I ask you to forgive me.'

'It is I who ought to ask *your* pardon,' he replied. 'I beg you to forgive me, Valeria, for having made you my wife.'

He pronounced those words with a hopeless, heart-broken humility, dreadful to see. I laid my hand on his bosom. I said, 'Eustace, look at me.'

He slowly lifted his eyes to my face—eyes cold and clear and tearless, looking at me in steady resignation, in immovable despair. In the utter wretchedness of that moment, I was like him; I was as quiet and as cold as my husband. He chilled, he froze me.

'Is it possible,' I said, 'that you doubt my belief in your innocence?'

He left the question unanswered. He sighed bitterly to himself. 'Poor woman!' he said, as a stranger might have said, pitying me. 'Poor woman!'

My heart swelled in me as if it would burst. I lifted my hand from his bosom, and laid it on his shoulder to support myself.

'I don't ask you to pity me, Eustace; I ask you to do me justice. You are not doing me justice. If you had trusted me with the truth in the days when we first knew that we loved each other—if you had told me all, and more than all, that I know now—as God is my witness, I would still have married you! *Now* do you doubt that I believe you are an innocent man?'

'I don't doubt it,' he said. 'All your impulses are generous. You are speaking generously, and feeling generously. Don't blame me, my poor child, if I look on farther than you do; if I see what is to come—too surely to come—in the cruel future.'

'The cruel future!' I repeated. 'What do you mean?'

'You believe in my innocence, Valeria. The Jury who tried me doubted it—and have left that doubt on record. What reason have *you* for believing, in the face of the Verdict, that I am an innocent man?'

'I want no reason! I believe, in spite of the Verdict.'

'Will your friends agree with you? When your uncle and aunt know what has happened—and sooner or later they must know it—what will they say? They will say, "He began badly; he concealed from our niece that he had been a prisoner on his trial; he married our niece under a false name. He may say he is innocent; but we have only his word for it. When he was put on his trial, the verdict was Not Proven. Not Proven won't do for us. If the Jury have done him an injustice—if he *is* innocent—let him prove it." That is what the world thinks and says of me. That is what your friends will think and say of me. The time is coming, Valeria, when you—even You—will feel that your friends have reason to appeal to on their side, and that you have no reason on yours.'

'That time will never come!' I answered, warmly. 'You wrong me, you insult me, in thinking it possible!'

He put down my hand from him, and drew back a step, with a bitter smile.

'We have only been married a few days, Valeria. Your love for me is new and young. Time, which wears away all things, will wear away the first fervour of that love.'

'Never! never!'

He drew back from me a little farther still.

'Look at the world round you,' he said. 'The happiest husbands and wives have their occasional misunderstandings and disagreements; the brightest married life has its passing clouds. When those days come for *us*, the doubts and fears that you don't feel now, will find their way to you then. When the clouds rise on *our* married life—when I say my first harsh word, when you make your first hasty reply—then, in the solitude of your own room, in the stillness of the wakeful night, you will think of my first wife's miserable death. You will remember that I was held responsible for it, and that my innocence was never proved. You will say to yourself, "Did it begin, in *her* time, with a harsh word from him, and with a hasty reply from her? Will it one day end with me, as the Jury half feared that it ended with her?" Hideous questions for a wife to ask herself! You will stifle them; you will recoil from them, like a good woman, with horror. But, when we meet the next morning, you will be on your guard, and I shall see it, and know in my heart of hearts what it means. Embittered by that knowledge, my next harsh word may be harsher still. Your next thoughts of me may remind you, more vividly and more boldly, that your husband was once tried as a poisoner, and that the question of his first wife's death was never properly cleared up. Do you see what materials for a domestic hell are mingling for us here? Was it for nothing that I warned you, solemnly warned you, to draw back, when I found you bent on discovering the truth? Can I ever be at your bedside now, when you are ill, and not remind you, in the most innocent things I do, of what happened at that other bedside, in the time of that other woman whom I married first? If I pour out your medicine, I commit a suspicious action—they said I poisoned *her* in her medicine. If I bring you a cup of tea, I revive the remembrance of a horrid doubt—they said I put the arsenic in *her* cup of tea. If I kiss you when I leave the room—I remind you that the prosecution accused me of kissing *her*, to save appearances and produce an effect on the nurse. Can we live together on such terms as these? No mortal creatures could support the misery of it. This very day I said to you, "If you stir a step farther in this matter, there is an end of your happiness for the rest of your life." You have taken that step—and the end has come to your happiness and to mine. The doubt that kills love has cast its blight on you and on me for the rest of our lives!'

So far I had forced myself to listen to him. At those last words, the picture of the future that he was placing before

me became too hideous to be endured. I refused to hear
more.

'You are talking horribly,' I said. 'At your age and at
mine, have we done with love, and done with hope? It is
blasphemy to love and hope to say it!'

'Wait till you have read the Trial,' he answered. 'You
mean to read it, I suppose?'

'Every word of it! With a motive, Eustace, which you have
yet to know.'

'No motive of yours, Valeria, no love and hope of yours
can alter the inexorable facts. My first wife died poisoned;
and the verdict of the Jury has not absolutely acquitted me
of the guilt of causing her death. As long as you were
ignorant of that, the possibilities of happiness were always
within our reach. Now you know it, I say again—our married life is at an end.'

'No,' I said. 'Now I know it our married life has begun—
begun with a new object for your wife's devotion, with a
new reason for your wife's love!'

'What do you mean?'

I went near to him again, and took his hand.

'What did you tell me the world has said of you?' I asked.
'What did you tell me my friends would say of you? "Not
Proven won't do for us. If the Jury have done him an
injustice—if he *is* innocent—let him prove it." Those were
the words you put into the mouths of my friends. I adopt
them for mine! *I* say, Not Proven won't do for *me*. Prove
your right, Eustace, to a verdict of Not Guilty. Why have
you let three years pass without doing it? Shall I guess why?
You have waited for your wife to help you. Here she is, my
darling, ready to help you with all her heart and soul. Here
she is, with one object in life—to show the world, and to
show the Scotch Jury, that her husband is an innocent
man!'

I had roused myself; my pulses were throbbing, my voice
rang through the room. Had I roused *him*? What was his
answer?

'Read the Trial.' That was his answer.

I seized his arm. In my indignation and my despair, I shook him with all my strength. God forgive me, I could almost have struck him, for the tone in which he had spoken, and the look that he had cast on me!

'I have told you that I mean to read the Trial,' I said. 'I mean to read it, line by line, with you. Some inexcusable mistake has been made. Evidence in your favour, that might have been found, has not been found. Suspicious circumstances have not been investigated. Crafty people have not been watched. Eustace! the conviction of some dreadful oversight, committed by you or by the persons who helped you, is firmly settled in my mind. The resolution to set that vile Verdict right was the first resolution that came to me, when I first heard of it in the next room. We *will* set it right! We *must* set it right—for your sake, for my sake, for the sake of our children if we are blest with children. Oh, my own love, don't look at me with those cold eyes! Don't answer me in those hard tones! Don't treat me as if I was talking ignorantly and madly of something that can never be!'

Still, I failed to rouse him. His next words were spoken compassionately rather than coldly—that was all.

'My defence was undertaken by the greatest lawyers in the land,' he said. 'After such men have done their utmost, and have failed—my poor Valeria, what can you, what can I, do? We can only submit.'

'Never!' I cried. 'The greatest lawyers are mortal men; the greatest lawyers have made mistakes before now. You can't deny that.'

'Read the Trial.' For the third time, he said those cruel words, and said no more.

In utter despair of moving him—feeling keenly, bitterly (if I must own it), his merciless superiority to all that I had said to him in the honest fervour of my devotion and my love—I thought of Major Fitz-David as a last resort. In the disordered state of my mind, at that moment, it made no difference to me that the Major had already tried to reason with him, and had failed. In the face of the facts, I had a blind belief in the influence of his old friend, if his old friend could only be prevailed upon to support my view.

'Is there no persuading you?' I said. He looked away without answering. 'At least you can wait for me a moment,' I went on. 'I want you to hear another opinion, besides mine.'

I left him, and returned to the study. Major Fitz-David was not there. I knocked at the door of communication with the front room. It was opened instantly by the Major himself. The doctor had gone away. Benjamin still remained in the room.

'Will you come and speak to Eustace?' I began. 'If you will only say what I want you to say——'

Before I could add a word more, I heard the house door opened and closed. Major Fitz-David and Benjamin heard it too. They looked at each other in silence.

I ran back, before the Major could stop me, to the room in which I had seen Eustace. It was empty. My husband had left the house.

CHAPTER XIII

The Man's Decision

MY first impulse was the reckless impulse to follow Eustace—openly, through the streets.

The Major and Benjamin both opposed this hasty resolution on my part. They appealed to my own sense of self-respect, without (so far as I remember it) producing the slightest effect on my mind. They were more successful when they entreated me next to be patient, for my husband's sake. In mercy to Eustace, they begged me to wait half an hour. If he failed to return in that time, they pledged themselves to accompany me in search of him to the hotel.

In mercy to Eustace, I consented to wait. What I suffered under the forced necessity for remaining passive at that crisis in my life, no words of mine can tell. It will be better if I go on with my narrative.

Benjamin was the first to ask me what had passed between my husband and myself.

'You may speak freely, my dear,' he said. 'I know what has happened since you have been in Major Fitz-David's house. No one has told me about it; I found it out for myself. If you remember, I was struck by the name "Macallan," when you first mentioned it to me at my cottage. I couldn't guess why, at the time. I know why, now.'

Hearing this, I told them both unreservedly what I had said to Eustace, and how he had received it. To my unspeakable disappointment, they both sided with my husband—treating my view of his position as a mere dream. They said it, as he had said it, 'You have not read the Trial.'

I was really enraged with them. 'The facts are enough for *me*,' I said. 'We know he is innocent. Why is his innocence not proved? It ought to be, it must be, it shall be! If the Trial tells me it can't be done, I refuse to believe the Trial. Where is the book, Major? Let me see for myself, if his lawyers have left nothing for his wife to do. Did they love him as I love him? Give me the book!'

Major Fitz-David looked at Benjamin.

'It will only additionally shock and distress her, if I give her the book,' he said. 'Don't you agree with me?'

I interposed before Benjamin could answer.

'If you refuse my request,' I said, 'you will oblige me, Major, to go to the nearest bookseller, and tell him to buy the Trial for me. I am determined to read it.'

This time, Benjamin sided with me.

'Nothing can make matters worse than they are, sir,' he said. 'If I may be permitted to advise, let her have her own way.'

The Major rose, and took the book out of the Italian cabinet—to which he had consigned it for safe keeping.

'My young friend tells me, that she informed you of her regrettable outbreak of temper a few days since,' he said, as he handed me the volume. 'I was not aware at the time, what book she had in her hand when she so far forgot herself as to destroy the vase. When I left you in the study, I supposed the Report of the Trial to be in its customary place, on the top shelf of the bookcase; and I own I felt some curiosity to know whether you would think of examining that shelf. The broken vase—it is needless to conceal it from you now—was one of a pair presented to me by your husband and his first wife, only a week before the poor woman's terrible death. I felt my first presentiment that you were on the brink of discovery, when I found you looking at the fragments—and I fancy I betrayed to you that something of the kind was disturbing me. You looked as if you noticed it.'

'I did notice it, Major. And I, too, had a vague idea that I was on the way to discovery. Will you look at your watch? Have we waited half-an-hour yet?'

My impatience had misled me. The ordeal of the half-hour was not yet at an end.

Slowly and more slowly, the heavy minutes followed each other—and still there were no signs of my husband's return. We tried to continue our conversation, and failed. Nothing was audible; no sounds but the ordinary sounds of the street disturbed the dreadful silence. Try as I might to repel it, there was one foreboding thought that pressed closer and closer on my mind as the interval of waiting wore its weary way on. I shuddered as I asked myself, if our married life had come to an end—if Eustace had really left me?

The Major saw—what Benjamin's slower perception had not yet discovered—that my fortitude was beginning to sink under the unrelieved oppression of suspense.

'Come!' he said. 'Let us go to the hotel.'

It then wanted nearly five minutes to the half-hour. I *looked* my gratitude to Major Fitz-David for sparing me those last five minutes: I could not speak to him, or to Benjamin. In silence we three got into a cab and drove to the hotel.

The landlady met us in the hall. Nothing had been seen or heard of Eustace. There was a letter waiting for me upstairs, on the table in our sitting-room. It had been left at the hotel by a messenger, only a few minutes since.

Trembling and breathless, I ran up the stairs; the two gentlemen following me. The writing on the address of the letter was in my husband's hand. My heart sank in me as I looked at the lines; there could be but one reason for his writing to me. That closed envelope held his farewell words. I sat with the letter on my lap, stupefied—incapable of opening it.

Kind-hearted Benjamin attempted to comfort and encourage me. The Major, with his larger experience of women, warned the old man to be silent.

'Wait!' I heard him whisper. 'Speaking to her will do no good now. Give her time.'

Acting on a sudden impulse, I held out the letter to him as he spoke. Even moments might be of importance, if Eustace had indeed left me. To give me time, might be to lose the opportunity of recalling him.

'You are his old friend,' I said. 'Open his letter, Major, and read it for me.'

Major Fitz-David opened the letter, and read it through to himself. When he had done, he threw it on the table with a gesture which was almost a gesture of contempt.

'There is but one excuse for him,' he said. 'The man is mad.'

Those words told me all. I knew the worst; and, knowing it, I could read the letter. It ran thus:—

'MY BELOVED VALERIA,—

'When you read these lines, you read my farewell words. I return to my solitary unfriended life—my life before I knew you.

'My darling, you have been cruelly treated. You have been entrapped into marrying a man who has been publicly accused of poisoning his first wife—and who has not been honourably and completely acquitted of the charge. And you know it!

'Can you live on terms of mutual confidence and mutual esteem with me, when I have committed this fraud, and when I stand towards you in this position? It was possible for you to live with me happily, while you were in ignorance of the truth. It is *not* possible, now you know all.

'No! the one atonement I can make is—to leave you. Your one chance of future happiness is to be disassociated, at once and for ever, from my dishonoured life. I love you, Valeria—truly, devotedly, passionately. But the spectre of the poisoned woman rises between us. It makes no difference that I am innocent even of the thought of harming my first wife. My innocence has not been proved. In this world my innocence can never be proved. You are young and loving, and generous and hopeful. Bless others, Valeria, with your rare attractions and your delightful gifts. They are of no avail with *me*. The poisoned woman stands between us. If you live with me now, you will see her as I see her. *That* torture shall never be yours. I love you. I leave you.

'Do you think me hard and cruel? Wait a little, and time will change that way of thinking. As the years go on, you will say to yourself, "Basely as he deceived me, there was some generosity in him. He was man enough to release me of his own free will."

'Yes, Valeria, I fully, freely release you. If it be possible to annul our marriage, let it be done. Recover your liberty by any means that you may be advised to employ; and be assured beforehand of my entire and implicit submission. My lawyers have the necessary instruction on this subject. Your uncle has only to communicate with them, and I think he will be satisfied of my resolution to do you justice. The one interest that I have now left in life, is my interest in your welfare and your happiness in the time to come. Your welfare and your happiness are no longer to be found in your union with Me.

'I can write no more. This letter will wait for you at the hotel. It will be useless to attempt to trace me. I know my own weakness. My heart is all yours; I might yield to you if I let you see me again.

'Show these lines to your uncle, and to any friends whose opinions you may value. I have only to sign my dishonoured name; and every one will understand and applaud my motive for writing as I do. The name justifies—amply justifies—the letter. Forgive me, and forget me. Farewell!

'EUSTACE MACALLAN.'

In those words, he took his leave of me. We had then been married—six days.

CHAPTER XIV

The Woman's Answer

THUS far, I have written of myself with perfect frankness and, I think I may fairly add, with some courage as well. My frankness fails me, and my courage fails me, when I look back to my husband's farewell letter, and try to recall the storm of contending passions that it roused in my mind. No! I cannot tell the truth about myself—I dare not tell the truth about myself—at that terrible time. Men! consult your observation of women, and imagine what I felt. Women! look into your own hearts, and see what I felt, for yourselves.

What I *did*, when my mind was quiet again, is an easier matter to deal with. I answered my husband's letter. My reply to him shall appear in these pages. It will show, in some degree, what effect (of the lasting sort) his desertion of me produced on my mind. It will also reveal the

motives that sustained me, the hopes that animated me, in
the new and strange life which my next chapters must
describe.

I was removed from the hotel, in the care of my fatherly
old friend, Benjamin. A bedroom was prepared for me in
his little villa. There, I passed the first night of my separation from my husband. Towards the morning, my weary
brain got some rest—I slept.

At breakfast-time, Major Fitz-David called to inquire
about me. He had kindly volunteered to go and speak for
me to my husband's lawyers, on the preceding day. They
had admitted that they knew where Eustace had gone; but
they declared at the same time that they were positively
forbidden to communicate his address to any one. In other
respects, their 'Instructions' in relation to the wife of their
client were (as they were pleased to express it) 'generous
to a fault.' I had only to write to them, and they would
furnish me with a copy by return of post.

This was the Major's news. He refrained, with the tact
that distinguished him, from putting any questions to me
beyond questions relating to the state of my health. These
answered, he took his leave of me for that day. He and
Benjamin had a long talk together afterwards, in the garden
of the villa.

I retired to my room, and wrote to my uncle Starkweather; telling him exactly what had happened, and enclosing him a copy of my husband's letter. This done, I
went out for a little while to breathe the fresh air, and to
think. I was soon weary, and went back again to my room
to rest. My kind old Benjamin left me at perfect liberty to
be alone as long as I pleased. Towards the afternoon, I
began to feel a little more like my old self again. I mean by
this, that I could think of Eustace without bursting out
crying, and could speak to Benjamin without distressing
and frightening the dear old man.

That night, I had a little more sleep. The next morning

I was strong enough to confront the first and foremost duty that I now owed to myself—the duty of answering my husband's letter.

I wrote to him in these words:—

'I am still too weak and weary, Eustace, to write to you at any length. But my mind is clear. I have formed my own opinion of you and your letter; and I know what I mean to do now you have left me. Some women, in my situation, might think that you had forfeited all right to their confidence. I don't think that. So I write and tell you what is in my mind, in the plainest and fewest words that I can use.

'You say you love me—and you leave me. I don't understand loving a woman, and leaving her. For my part, in spite of the hard things you have said and written to me, and in spite of the cruel manner in which you have left me, I love you—and I won't give you up. No! As long as I live, I mean to live your wife.

'Does this surprise you? It surprises *me*. If another woman wrote in this manner to a man who had behaved to her as you have behaved, I should be quite at a loss to account for her conduct. I am quite at a loss to account for my own conduct. I ought to hate you—and yet I can't help loving you. I am ashamed of myself; but so it is.

'You need feel no fear of my attempting to find out where you are, and of my trying to persuade you to return to me. I am not quite foolish enough to do that. You are not in a fit state of mind to return to me. You are all wrong, all over, from head to foot. When you get right again, I am vain enough to think that you will return to me of your own accord. And shall I be weak enough to forgive you? Yes, I shall certainly be weak enough to forgive you.

'But how are you to get right again?

'I have puzzled my brains over this question by night and by day—and my opinion is that you will never get right again, unless I help you.

'How am I to help you?

'The question is easily answered. What the Law has failed
to do for you, your Wife must do for you. Do you remember
what I said, when we were together in the back room at
Major Fitz-David's house? I told you that the first thought
that came to me, when I heard what the Scotch Jury had
done, was the thought of setting their vile Verdict right.
Well! Your letter has fixed this idea more firmly in my mind
than ever. The only chance that I can see of winning you
back to me, in the character of a penitent and loving husband, is to change that underhand Scotch Verdict of Not
Proven, into an honest English verdict of Not Guilty.

'Are you surprised at the knowledge of the law which this
way of writing betrays in an ignorant woman? I have been
learning, my dear: the Law and the Lady have begun by
understanding one another. In plain English, I have looked
into Ogilvie's Imperial Dictionary; and Ogilvie tells me: "A
verdict of Not Proven only indicates that, in the opinion of
the Jury, there is a deficiency in the evidence to convict the
prisoner. A verdict of Not Guilty imports the Jury's opinion
that the prisoner is innocent."—Eustace! that shall be the
opinion of the world in general, and of the Scotch Jury in
particular, in your case. To that one object I dedicate my
life to come, if God spares me!

'Who will help me, when I need help, is more than I yet
know. There was a time when I had hoped that we should
go hand in hand together in doing this good work. That
hope is at an end. I no longer expect you, or ask you, to
help me. A man who thinks as you think, can give no help
to anybody—it is his miserable condition to have no hope.
So be it! I will hope for two, and will work for two; and
I shall find some one to help me—never fear—if I deserve
it.

'I will say nothing about my plans—I have not read the
Trial yet. It is quite enough for me that I know you are
innocent. When a man is innocent, there *must* be a way of
proving it: the one thing needful is to find the way. Sooner
or later, with or without assistance, I shall find it. Yes!

before I know any single particular of the Case, I tell you positively—I shall find it!

'You may laugh over this blind confidence on my part, or you may cry over it. I don't pretend to know whether I am an object for ridicule or an object for pity. Of one thing only I am certain. I mean to win you back, a man vindicated before the world, without a stain on his character or his name—thanks to his Wife.

'Write to me sometimes, Eustace; and believe me, through all the bitterness of this bitter business, your faithful and loving

'VALERIA.'

There was my reply! Poor enough as a composition (I could write a much better letter now), it had, if I may presume to say so, one merit. It was the honest expression of what I really meant and felt.

I read it to Benjamin. He held up his hands with his customary gesture when he was thoroughly bewildered and dismayed. 'It seems the rashest letter that ever was written,' said the dear old man. 'I never heard, Valeria, of a woman doing what you propose to do. Lord help us! the new generation is beyond my fathoming. I wish your uncle Starkweather was here: I wonder what he would say? Oh, dear me, what a letter from a wife to a husband! Do you really mean to send it to him?'

I added immeasurably to my old friend's surprise, by not even employing the post-office. I wished to see the 'instructions' which my husband had left behind him. So I took the letter to his lawyers myself.

The firm consisted of two partners. They both received me together. One was a soft lean man, with a sour smile. The other was a hard fat man, with ill-tempered eyebrows. I took a great dislike to both of them. On their side, they appeared to feel a strong distrust of me. We began by disagreeing. They showed me my husband's instructions; providing, among other things, for the payment of one clear

half of his income, as long as he lived, to his wife. I positively refused to touch a farthing of his money.

The lawyers were unaffectedly shocked and astonished at
this decision. Nothing of the sort had ever happened before,
in the whole course of their experience. They argued and
remonstrated with me. The partner with the ill-tempered
eyebrows wanted to know what my reasons were. The partner with the sour smile reminded his colleague satirically
that I was a lady, and had therefore no reasons to give. I
only answered, 'Be so good as to forward my letter,
gentlemen'—and left them.

I have no wish to claim any credit to myself in these pages
which I do not honestly deserve. The truth is that my pride
forbade me to accept help from Eustace, now that he had
left me. My own little fortune (eight hundred a year) had
been settled on myself when I married. It had been more
than I wanted as a single woman, and I was resolved that
it should be enough for me now. Benjamin had insisted on
my considering his cottage as my home. Under these circumstances, the expenses in which my determination to
clear my husband's character might involve me, were the
only expenses for which I had to provide. I could afford to
be independent—and independent I resolved that I would
be.

While I am occupied in confessing my weakness and my
errors, it is only right to add that, dearly as I still loved my
unhappy misguided husband, there was one little fault of
his which I found it not easy to forgive.

Pardoning other things, I could not pardon his concealing
from me that he had been married to a first wife. Why I
should have felt this so bitterly as I did, at certain times
and seasons, I am not able to explain. Jealousy was at the
bottom of it, I suppose. And yet, I was not conscious of
being jealous—especially when I thought of the poor creature's miserable death. Still, at odd times when I was discouraged and out of temper, I used to say to myself,
'Eustace ought not to have kept *that* secret from me.' What

would *he* have said, if I had been a widow, and had never told him of it?

It was getting on towards evening when I returned to the cottage. Benjamin appeared to have been on the look-out for me. Before I could ring at the bell he opened the garden gate.

'Prepare yourself for a surprise, my dear,' he said. 'Your uncle, the Reverend Doctor Starkweather, has arrived from the North, and is waiting to see you. He received your letter this morning, and he took the first train to London as soon as he had read it.'

In another minute my uncle's strong arms were round me. In my forlorn position, I felt the good Vicar's kindness, in travelling all the way to London to see me, very gratefully. It brought the tears into my eyes—tears, without bitterness, that did me good.

'I have come, my dear child, to take you back to your old home,' he said. 'No words can tell how fervently I wish you had never left your aunt and me. Well! well! we won't talk about it. The mischief is done—and the next thing is to mend it as well as we can. If I could only get within arm's length of that husband of yours, Valeria—there! there! God forgive me, I am forgetting that I am a clergyman. What shall I forget next, I wonder? By-the-bye, your aunt sends you her dearest love. She is more superstitious than ever. This miserable business doesn't surprise her a bit. She says it all began with your making that mistake about your name in signing the church register. You remember? Was there ever such stuff? Ah, she's a foolish woman, that wife of mine! But she means well—a good soul at bottom. She would have travelled all the way here along with me, if I would have let her. I said, "No; you stop at home and look after the house and the parish; and I'll bring the child back." You shall have your old bedroom, Valeria, with the white curtains, you know, looped up with blue! We will return to the Vicarage (if you can get up in time) by the nine-forty train to-morrow morning.'

Return to the Vicarage! How could I do that? How could
I hope to gain what was now the one object of my existence,
if I buried myself in a remote north-country village? It was
simply impossible for me to accompany Doctor Starkweather on his return to his own house.

'I thank you, uncle, with all my heart,' I said. 'But I am
afraid I can't leave London for the present.'

'You can't leave London for the present?' he repeated.
'What does the girl mean, Mr Benjamin?'

Benjamin evaded a direct reply.

'She is kindly welcome here, Doctor Starkweather,' he
said, 'as long as she chooses to stay with me.'

'That's no answer,' retorted my uncle, in his rough-and-
ready way. He turned to me. 'What is there to keep you in
London?' he asked. 'You used to hate London. I suppose
there is some reason?'

It was only due to my good guardian and friend that I
should take him into my confidence sooner or later. There
was no help for it but to rouse my courage and tell him
frankly what I had it in my mind to do. The Vicar listened
in breathless dismay. He turned to Benjamin, with distress
as well as surprise in his face, when I had done.

'God help her!' cried the worthy man. 'The poor thing's
troubles have turned her brain!'

'I thought you would disapprove of it, sir,' said Benjamin,
in his mild and moderate way. 'I confess I disapprove of it
myself.'

' "Disapprove of it," isn't the word,' retorted the Vicar.
'Don't put it in that feeble way, if you please. An act of
madness—that's what it is, if she really means what she
says.' He turned my way, and looked as he used to look, at
the afternoon service, when he was catechising an obstinate
child. 'You don't mean it,' he said, 'do you?'

'I am very sorry to forfeit your good opinion, uncle,' I
replied. 'But I must own that I do certainly mean it.'

'In plain English,' retorted the Vicar, 'you are conceited
enough to think that you can succeed where the greatest

lawyers in Scotland have failed. *They* couldn't prove this man's innocence, all working together. And *you* are going to prove it single-handed? Upon my word, you are a wonderful woman,' cried my uncle, suddenly descending from indignation to irony. 'May a plain country parson, who isn't used to lawyers in petticoats, be permitted to ask how you mean to do it?'

'I mean to begin by reading the Trial, uncle.'

'Nice reading for a young woman! You will be wanting a batch of nasty French novels next.* Well, and when you have read the Trial—what then? Have you thought of that?'

'Yes, uncle. I have thought of that. I shall first try to form some conclusion (after reading the Trial) as to the guilty person who really committed the crime. Then, I shall make out a list of the witnesses who spoke in my husband's defence. I shall go to those witnesses, and tell them who I am, and what I want. I shall ask all sorts of questions which grave lawyers might think it beneath their dignity to put. I shall be guided, in what I do next, by the answers I receive. And I shall not be discouraged, no matter what difficulties are thrown in my way. Those are my plans, uncle, so far as I know them now.'

The Vicar and Benjamin looked at each other, as if they doubted the evidence of their own senses. The Vicar spoke.

'Do you mean to tell me,' he said, 'that you are going roaming about the country, to throw yourself on the mercy of strangers, and to risk whatever rough reception you may get in the course of your travels? You! A young woman! Deserted by your husband! With nobody to protect you! Mr Benjamin, do you hear her? And can you believe your ears? I declare to Heaven *I* don't know whether I am awake or dreaming. Look at her—just look at her! There she sits as cool and easy as if she had said nothing at all extraordinary, and was going to do nothing out of the common way! What am I to do with her—that's the serious question— what on earth am I to do with her?'

'Let me try my experiment, uncle, rash as it may look to you,' I said. 'Nothing else will comfort and support me; and God knows I want comfort and support. Don't think me obstinate. I am ready to admit that there are serious difficulties in my way.'

The Vicar resumed his ironical tone.

'Oh!' he said. 'You admit that, do you? Well, there is something gained, at any rate!'

'Many another woman before me,' I went on, 'has faced serious difficulties, and has conquered them—for the sake of the man she loved.'

Doctor Starkweather rose slowly to his feet, with the air of a person whose capacity of toleration had reached its last limits.

'Am I to understand that you are still in love with Mr Eustace Macallan?' he asked.

'Yes,' I answered.

'The hero of the great Poison Trial?' pursued my uncle. 'The man who has deceived and deserted you? You love him?'

'I love him more dearly than ever.'

'Mr Benjamin,' said the Vicar. 'If she recovers her senses between this and nine o'clock to-morrow morning, send her with her luggage to Loxley's Hotel, where I am now staying. Good night, Valeria. I shall consult with your aunt as to what is to be done next. I have no more to say.'

'Give me a kiss, uncle, at parting.'

'Oh, yes. I'll give you a kiss. Anything you like, Valeria. I shall be sixty-five next birthday; and I thought I knew something of women at my time of life. It seems I know nothing. Loxley's Hotel is the address, Mr Benjamin. Good night.'

Benjamin looked very grave when he returned to me, after accompanying Doctor Starkweather to the garden gate.

'Pray be advised, my dear,' he said. 'I don't ask you to consider *my* view of this matter as good for much. But your uncle's opinion is surely worth considering?'

I did not reply. It was useless to say any more. I made up my mind to be misunderstood and discouraged, and to bear it. 'Good night, my dear old friend,' was all I said to Benjamin. Then I turned away—I confess with the tears in my eyes—and took refuge in my bedroom.

The window-blind was up; and the autumn moonlight shone brilliantly into the little room.

As I stood by the window, looking out, the memory came to me of another moonlight night—when Eustace and I were walking together in the Vicarage garden before our marriage. It was the night of which I have written, many pages back, when there were obstacles to our union, and when Eustace had offered to release me from my engagement to him. I saw the dear face again, looking at me in the moonlight; I heard once more his words, and mine. 'Forgive me' (he had said) 'for having loved you—passionately, devotedly loved you. Forgive me, and let me go.'

And I had answered, 'Oh, Eustace, I am only a woman—don't madden me! I can't live without you. I must, and will, be your wife!' And now, after marriage had united us, we were parted! Parted, still loving each other as passionately as ever. And why? Because he had been accused of a crime that he had never committed, and because a Scotch jury had failed to see that he was an innocent man.

I looked at the lovely moonlight, pursuing these remembrances and these thoughts. A new ardour burnt in me. 'No!' I said to myself. 'Neither relations nor friends shall prevail on me to falter and fail in my husband's cause. The assertion of his innocence is the work of my life—I will begin it to-night!'

I drew down the blind, and lit the candles. In the quiet night—alone and unaided—I took my first step on the toilsome and terrible journey that lay before me. From the title-page to the end, without stopping to rest, and without missing a word, I read the Trial of my husband for the murder of his wife.*

CHAPTER XV

The Story of the Trial. The Preliminaries

LET me confess another weakness, on my part, before I begin the story of the Trial. I cannot prevail upon myself to copy, for the second time, the horrible title-page which holds up to public ignominy my husband's name. I have copied it once in my tenth chapter. Let once be enough.

Turning to the second page of the Trial, I found a Note, assuring the reader of the absolute correctness of the Report of the proceedings. The compiler described himself as having enjoyed certain privileges. Thus, the presiding Judge had himself revised his charge to the Jury. And, again, the chief lawyers for the prosecution and the defence, following the Judge's example, had revised their speeches, for, and against, the prisoner. Lastly, particular care had been taken to secure a literally correct report of the evidence given by the various witnesses. It was some relief to me to discover this Note, and to be satisfied at the outset that the Story of the Trial was, in every particular, fully and truly told.

The next page interested me more nearly still. It enumerated the actors in the Judicial Drama—the men who held in their hands my husband's honour, and my husband's life. Here is the List:

THE LORD JUSTICE CLERK,
LORD DRUMFENNICK,   } Judges on the Bench.
LORD NOBLEKIRK,

THE LORD ADVOCATE (Mintlaw),
DONALD DREW, Esquire (Advocate-   } Counsel for
   Depute),   the Crown.

Mr JAMES ARLISS, W.S., Agent for the Crown.

THE DEAN OF FACULTY
  (Farmichael),
ALEXANDER CROCKET, Esquire
  (Advocate),
                  } Counsel for the Panel (otherwise the Prisoner).

Mr THORNIEBANK, W.S.,
Mr PLAYMORE, W.S.,
             } Agents for the Panel.

The Indictment* against the Prisoner then followed. I shall not copy the uncouth language, full of needless repetitions (and, if I know anything of the subject, not guiltless of bad grammar as well), in which my innocent husband was solemnly and falsely accused of poisoning his first wife. The less there is of that false and hateful Indictment on this page, the better and the truer the page will look, to *my* eyes.

To be brief, then, Eustace Macallan was 'indicted and accused, at the instance of David Mintlaw, Esq., Her Majesty's Advocate, for Her Majesty's interest,' of the Murder of his Wife by poison, at his residence called Gleninch, in the county of Mid-Lothian. The poison was alleged to have been wickedly and feloniously given by the prisoner to his wife Sara, on two occasions, in the form of arsenic, administered in tea, medicine, 'or other article or articles of food or drink, to the prosecutor unknown, or in some other manner to the prosecutor unknown.' It was further declared that the prisoner's wife had died of the poison thus administered by her husband, on one or other, or both, of the stated occasions; and that she was thus murdered by her husband. The next paragraph asserted, that the said Eustace Macallan, taken before John Daviot, Esquire, advocate, sheriff-substitute of Mid-Lothian, did in his presence at Edinburgh (on a given date—viz:—the 29th of October), subscribe a Declaration stating his innocence of the alleged crime: this Declaration being reserved in the Indictment—together with certain Documents, papers, and articles, enumerated in an Inventory—to be used in evidence against the prisoner. The Indictment concluded by declaring that, in the event of the offence charged against the prisoner being found proven by the Verdict, he, the said Eustace Macallan, 'ought to be punished with the pains of the law, to deter others from committing the like crimes in all time coming.'

So much for the Indictment! I have done with it—and I am rejoiced to have done with it.

An Inventory of papers, documents, and articles followed at great length, on the three next pages. This, in its turn, was succeeded by the list of the witnesses, and by the names of the jurors (fifteen in number) balloted for, to try the case. And then, at last, the Report of the Trial began. It resolved itself, to my mind, into three great Questions. As it appeared to me at the time, so let me present it here.

CHAPTER XVI

First Question—Did the Woman Die Poisoned?

THE proceedings began at ten o'clock. The prisoner was placed at the Bar, before the High Court of Justiciary,* at Edinburgh. He bowed respectfully to the Bench, and pleaded Not Guilty, in a low voice.

It was observed by every one present, that the prisoner's face betrayed the traces of acute mental suffering. He was deadly pale. His eyes never once wandered to the crowd in the Court. When certain witnesses appeared against him, he looked at them with a momentary attention. At other times, he kept his eyes on the ground. When the evidence touched on his wife's illness and death he was deeply affected, and covered his face with his hands. It was a subject of general remark and general surprise, that the prisoner, in this case (although a man), showed far less self-possession than the last prisoner tried in that Court for murder—a woman, who had been convicted on overwhelming evidence. There were persons present (a small minority only) who considered this want of composure on the part of the prisoner to be a sign in his favour. Self-possession, in his dreadful position, signified to their minds, the stark insensibility of a heartless and shameless criminal, and afforded in itself a presumption—not of innocence—but of guilt.

The first witness called was John Daviot, Esquire, Sheriff-Substitute* of Mid-Lothian. He was examined by the Lord Advocate (as counsel for the prosecution); and said:

'The prisoner was brought before me on the present charge. He made, and subscribed, a Declaration, on the 29th of October. It was freely and voluntarily made; the prisoner having been first duly warned and admonished.'

Having identified the Declaration, the Sheriff-Substitute—being cross-examined by the Dean of Faculty* (as counsel for the defence)—continued his evidence in these words:

'The charge against the prisoner was, Murder. This was communicated to him before he made the Declaration. The questions addressed to the prisoner were put, partly by me, partly by another officer, the Procurator-Fiscal.* The answers were given distinctly, and, so far as I could judge, without reserve. The statements put forward in the Declaration were all made in answer to questions asked by the Procurator-Fiscal or by myself.'

A clerk in the Sheriff-Clerk's office then officially produced the Declaration, and corroborated the evidence of the witness who had preceded him.

The appearance of the next witness created a marked sensation in the Court. This was no less a person than the nurse who had attended Mrs Macallan in her last illness—by name, Christina Ormsay.

After the first formal answers, the nurse (examined by the Lord Advocate*) proceeded to say:

'I was first sent for, to attend the deceased lady, on the

seventh of October. She was then suffering from a severe cold, accompanied by a rheumatic affection of the left knee-joint. Previous to this, I understood that her health had been fairly good. She was not a very difficult person to nurse, when you got used to her, and understood how to manage her. The main difficulty was caused by her temper. She was not a sullen person; she was headstrong and violent—easily excited to fly into a passion, and quite reckless, in her fits of anger, as to what she said or did. At such times, I really hardly think she knew what she was about. My own idea is, that her temper was made still more irritable by unhappiness in her married life. She was far from being a reserved person. Indeed, she was disposed (as I thought) to be a little too communicative about herself and her troubles, with persons, like me, who were beneath her in station. She did not scruple, for instance, to tell me (when we had been long enough together to get used to each other) that she was very unhappy, and fretted a good deal about her husband. One night, when she was wakeful and restless, she said to me——'

The Dean of Faculty here interposed; speaking on the prisoner's behalf. He appealed to the Judges to say whether such loose and unreliable evidence as this, was evidence which could be received by the Court?

The Lord Advocate (speaking on behalf of the Crown) claimed it as his right to produce the evidence. It was of the utmost importance, in this case, to show (on the testimony of an unprejudiced witness) on what terms the husband and wife were living. The witness was a most respectable woman. She had won, and deserved, the confidence of the unhappy lady whom she attended on her deathbed.

After briefly consulting together, the Judges unanimously decided that the evidence could not be admitted. What the witness had herself seen and observed of the relations between the husband and wife, was the only evidence that they could receive.

The Lord Advocate thereupon continued his examination of the witness. Christina Ormsay resumed her evidence as follows:

'My position as nurse led necessarily to my seeing more of Mrs Macallan than any other person in the house. I am able to speak, from experience, of many things not known to others who were only in her room at intervals.

For instance, I had more than one opportunity of personally observing that Mr and Mrs Macallan did not live together very happily. I can give you an example of this, not drawn from what others told me, but from what I noticed for myself.

'Towards the latter part of my attendance on Mrs Macallan, a young widow lady, named Mrs Beauly—a cousin of Mr Macallan's—came to stay at Gleninch. Mrs Macallan was jealous of this lady; and she showed it, in my presence, only the day before her death, when Mr Macallan came into her room to inquire how she had passed the night. "Oh," she said, "never mind how *I* have slept! What do you care whether I sleep well or ill? How has Mrs Beauly passed the night? Is she more beautiful than ever this morning? Go back to her—pray go back to her! Don't waste your time with me." Beginning in that manner, she worked herself into one of her furious rages. I was brushing her hair at the time; and, feeling that my presence was an impropriety under the circumstances, I attempted to leave the room. She forbade me to go. Mr Macallan felt, as I did, that my duty was to withdraw; and he said so in plain words. Mrs Macallan insisted on my staying, in language so insolent to her husband that he said, "If you cannot control yourself, either the nurse leaves the room or I do." She refused to yield even then. "A good excuse," she said, "for getting back to Mrs Beauly. Go!" He took her at her word, and walked out of the room. He had barely closed the door, before she began reviling him to me in the most shocking manner. She declared, among other things she said of him, that the news of all others which he would be glad to hear

would be the news of her death. I ventured, quite respectfully, on remonstrating with her. She took up the hairbrush,
and threw it at me—and, then and there, dismissed me
from my attendance on her. I left her; and waited below
until her fit of passion had worn itself out. Then I returned
to my place at the bedside, and, for a while, things went
on again as usual.

   'It may not be amiss to add a word which may help to
explain Mrs Macallan's jealousy of her husband's cousin.
Mrs Macallan was a very plain woman. She had a cast in
one of her eyes, and (if I may use the expression) one of
the most muddy, blotchy complexions it was ever my misfortune to see in a person's face. Mrs Beauly, on the other
hand, was a most attractive lady. Her eyes were universally
admired; and she had a most beautifully clear and delicate
colour. Poor Mrs Macallan said of her, most untruly, that
she painted.

   'No; the defects in the complexion of the deceased lady
were not in any way attributable to her illness. I should call
them born and bred defects in herself.

   'Her illness, if I am asked to describe it, I should say was
troublesome, nothing more. Until the last day, there were
no symptoms in the least degree serious about the malady
that had taken her. Her rheumatic knee was painful, of
course, acutely painful if you like, when she moved it; and
the confinement to bed was irksome enough, no doubt. But
otherwise there was nothing in the lady's condition, before
the fatal attack came, to alarm her or anybody about her.
She had her books, and her writing-materials, on an invalid
table which worked on a pivot, and could be arranged in
any position most agreeable to her. At times, she read and
wrote a great deal. At other times, she lay quiet, thinking
her own thoughts, or talking with me and with one or two
lady friends in the neighbourhood who came regularly to
see her.

   'Her writing, so far as I knew, was almost entirely of the
poetical sort. She was a great hand at composing poetry.

On one occasion only, she showed me some of her poems. I am no judge of such things. Her poetry was of the dismal kind; despairing about herself, and wondering why she had ever been born, and nonsense like that. Her husband came in more than once for some hard hits at his cruel heart and his ignorance of his wife's merits. In short, she vented her discontent with her pen as well as with her tongue. There were times—and pretty often too—when an angel from heaven would have failed to have satisfied Mrs Macallan.

'Throughout the period of her illness the deceased lady occupied the same room—a large bedroom situated (like all the best bedrooms) on the first floor of the house.

'Yes: the plan of the room now shown to me is quite accurately taken, according to my remembrance of it. One door led into the great passage, or corridor, on which all the doors opened. A second door, at one side (marked B on the plan), led into Mr Macallan's sleeping room. A third door, on the opposite side (marked C on the plan), communicated with a little study or book-room, used, as I was told, by Mr Macallan's mother when she was staying at Gleninch, but seldom or never entered by any one else. Mr Macallan's mother was not at Gleninch while I was there. The door between the bedroom and this study was locked, and the key was taken out. I don't know who had the key, or whether there were more keys than one in existence. The door was never opened, to my knowledge. I only got into the study, to look at it along with the housekeeper, by entering through a second door that opened on to the corridor.

'I beg to say that I can speak, from my own knowledge, positively about Mrs Macallan's illness, and about the sudden change which ended in her death. By the doctor's advice, I made notes, at the time, of dates and hours, and such like. I looked at my notes before coming here.

'From the seventh of October, when I was first called in to nurse her, to the twentieth of the same month, she slowly, but steadily, improved in health. Her knee was still painful, no doubt; but the inflammatory look of it was disappearing. As to the other symptoms, except weakness from lying in bed, and irritability of temper, there was really nothing the matter with her. She slept badly, I ought perhaps to add. But we remedied this, by means of composing-draughts, prescribed for that purpose by the doctor.

'On the morning of the twenty-first, at a few minutes past six, I got my first alarm that something was going wrong with Mrs Macallan.

'I was woke, at the time I have mentioned, by the ringing of the hand-bell which she kept on her bed-table. Let me say for myself that I had only fallen asleep on the sofa in the bedroom, at past two in the morning, from sheer fatigue. Mrs Macallan was then awake. She was in one of her bad humours with me. I had tried to prevail on her to let me remove her dressing-case from her bed-table, after she had used it in making her toilet for the night. It took up a great deal of room; and she could not possibly want it again before the morning. But no—she insisted on my letting it be. There was a glass inside the case; and, plain as she was, she never wearied of looking at herself in that glass! I saw that she was in a bad state of temper, so I gave her her way, and let the dressing-case be. Finding that she was too sullen to speak to me after that, and too obstinate to take her composing-draught from me when I offered it, I laid me down on the sofa at her bed-foot, and fell asleep, as I have said.

'The moment her bell rang, I was up and at the bedside, ready to make myself useful.

'I asked what was the matter with her. She complained of faintness and depression, and said she felt sick. I inquired if she had taken anything in the way of physic or food while I had been asleep. She answered that her husband had come in about an hour since, and, finding her still sleepless, had himself administered the composing-draught. Mr Macallan (sleeping in the next room) joined us while she was speaking. He, too, had been aroused by the bell. He heard what Mrs Macallan said to me about the composing-draught, and made no remark upon it. It seemed to me that he was alarmed at his wife's faintness. I suggested that she should take a little wine, or brandy-and-water. She answered that she could swallow nothing so strong as wine or brandy, having a burning pain in her stomach already. I put my hand on her stomach—quite lightly. She screamed when I touched her.

'This symptom alarmed us. We sent to the village for the medical man who had attended Mrs Macallan during her illness: one Mr Gale.

'The doctor seemed no better able to account for the change for the worse in his patient than we were. Hearing her complaint of thirst, he gave her some milk. Not long after taking it, she was sick. The sickness appeared to relieve her. She soon grew drowsy, and slumbered. Mr Gale left us, with strict injunctions to send for him instantly if she was taken ill again.

'Nothing of the sort happened; no change took place for the next three hours or more. She roused up towards half-past nine, and inquired about her husband. I informed her that he had returned to his own room, and asked if I should send for him. She said, "No." I asked next, if she would like anything to eat or drink. She said, "No," again, in rather a vacant, stupefied way—and then told me to go down stairs and get my breakfast. On my way down I met the housekeeper. She invited me to breakfast with her in her room, instead of in the servants' hall as usual. I remained with the housekeeper but a short time: certainly not more than half an hour.

'Going upstairs again, I met the under-housemaid, sweeping, on one of the landings.

'The girl informed me that Mrs Macallan had taken a cup of tea, during my absence in the housekeeper's room. Mr Macallan's valet had ordered the tea for his mistress, by his master's directions. The under-housemaid made it, and

took it upstairs herself to Mrs Macallan's room. Her master
(she said) opened the door, when she knocked, and took
the teacup from her with his own hand. He opened the door
widely enough for her to see into the bedroom, and to
notice that nobody was with Mrs Macallan but himself.

'After a little talk with the under-housemaid, I returned
to the bedroom. No one was there. Mrs Macallan was lying
perfectly quiet, with her face turned away from me on the
pillow. Approaching the bedside, I kicked against something on the floor. It was a broken teacup. I said to Mrs
Macallan, "How comes the teacup to be broken, ma'am?"
She answered, without turning towards me—in an odd,
muffled kind of voice—"I dropped it." "Before you drank
your tea, ma'am?" I asked. "No," she said; "in handing the
cup back to Mr Macallan after I had done." I had put my
question, wishing to know—in case she had spilt the tea
when she dropped the cup—whether it would be necessary
to get her any more. I am quite sure I remember correctly
my question, and her answer. I inquired next if she had
been long alone. She said, shortly, "Yes; I have been trying
to sleep." I said, "Do you feel pretty comfortable?" She
answered, "Yes," again. All this time she still kept her face
sulkily turned from me towards the wall. Stooping over her
to arrange the bed-clothes, I looked towards her table. The
writing materials which were always kept on it, were disturbed; and there was wet ink on one of the pens. I said,
"Surely, you haven't been writing, ma'am?" "Why not?"
she said; "I couldn't sleep." "Another poem?" I asked. She
laughed to herself—a bitter, short laugh. "Yes," she said;
"another poem." "That's good," I said; "it looks as if you
were getting quite like yourself again. We shan't want the
doctor any more to-day." She made no answer to this,
except an impatient sign with her hand. I didn't understand
the sign. Upon that, she spoke again—and crossly enough,
too! "I want to be alone; leave me."

'I had no choice but to do as I was told. To the best of
my observation there was nothing the matter with her, and

nothing for the nurse to do. I put the bell-rope within reach of her hand, and I went downstairs again.

'Half an hour more, as well as I can guess it, passed. I kept within hearing of the bell; but it never rang. I was not quite at my ease—without exactly knowing why. That odd muffled voice in which she had spoken to me hung on my mind, as it were. I was not quite satisfied about leaving her alone for too long a time together—and then, again, I was unwilling to risk throwing her into one of her fits of passion by going back before she rang for me. It ended in my venturing into the room on the ground floor, called the Morning Room, to consult Mr Macallan. He was usually to be found there in the forenoon of the day.

'On this occasion, however, when I looked into the Morning Room it was empty.

'At the same moment, I heard the master's voice on the terrace outside. I went out, and found him speaking to one Mr Dexter, an old friend of his, and (like Mrs Beauly) a guest staying in the house. Mr Dexter was sitting at the window of his room upstairs (he was a cripple, and could only move himself about in a chair on wheels); and Mr Macallan was speaking to him from the terrace below.

' "Dexter!" I heard Mr Macallan say; "Where is Mrs Beauly? Have you seen anything of her?"

'Mr Dexter answered, in his quick, off-hand way of speaking, "Not I! I know nothing about her."

'Then I advanced, and, begging pardon for intruding, I mentioned to Mr Macallan the difficulty I was in about going back or not to his wife's room, without waiting until she rang for me. Before he could advise me in the matter, the footman made his appearance, and informed me that Mrs Macallan's bell was then ringing—and ringing violently.

'It was close on eleven o'clock. As fast as I could mount the stairs, I hastened back to the bedroom.

'Before I opened the door, I heard Mrs Macallan groaning. She was in dreadful pain; feeling a burning heat in the stomach, and in the throat; together with the same sickness which had troubled her in the early morning. Though no doctor, I could see in her face that this second attack was of a far more serious nature than the first. After ringing the bell for a messenger to send to Mr Macallan, I ran to the door to see if any of the servants happened to be within call.

'The only person I saw in the corridor was Mrs Beauly. She was on her way from her own room, she said, to inquire after Mrs Macallan's health. I said to her, "Mrs Macallan is seriously ill again, ma'am. Would you please tell Mr Macallan, and send for the doctor?" She ran downstairs at once to do as I told her.

'I had not been long back at the bedside when Mr Macallan and Mrs Beauly both came in together. Mrs Macallan cast a strange look on them (a look I cannot at all describe), and made them leave her. Mrs Beauly, looking very much frightened, withdrew immediately. Mr Macallan advanced a step or two nearer to the bed. His wife looked at him again, in the same strange way, and cried out—half as if she was threatening him, half as if she was entreating him— "Leave me with the nurse. Go!" He only waited to say to me in a whisper, "The doctor is sent for"—and then he left the room.

'Before Mr Gale arrived, Mrs Macallan was violently sick. What came from her was muddy and frothy, and faintly streaked with blood. When Mr Gale saw it, he looked very serious; I heard him say to himself, "What does this mean?" He did his best to relieve Mrs Macallan, but with no good result that I could see. After a time, she seemed to suffer less. Then more sickness came on. Then there was another intermission. Whether she was suffering or not, I observed that her hands and feet (whenever I touched them) remained equally cold. Also, the doctor's report of her pulse was always the same—"very small and feeble." I said to Mr Gale, "What is to be done, sir?" And Mr Gale said to me, "I won't take the responsibility on myself any longer; I must have a physician from Edinburgh."

'The fastest horse in the stables at Gleninch was put into a dog-cart; and the coachman drove away full speed to Edinburgh, to fetch the famous Doctor Jerome.

'While we were waiting for the physician, Mr Macallan came into his wife's room, with Mr Gale. Exhausted as she was, she instantly lifted her hand, and signed to him to leave her. He tried by soothing words to persuade her to let him stay. No! She still insisted on sending him out of her room. He seemed to feel it—at such a time, and in the presence of the doctor. Before she was aware of him, he suddenly stepped up to the bedside, and kissed her on the forehead. She shrank from him with a scream. Mr Gale interfered, and led him out of the room.

'In the afternoon, Dr Jerome arrived.

'The great physician came just in time to see her seized with another attack of sickness. He watched her attentively, without speaking a word. In the interval when the sickness stopped, he still studied her, as it were, in perfect silence. I thought he would never have done examining her. When he was at last satisfied, he told me to leave him alone with Mr Gale. "We will ring," he said, "when we want you here again."

'It was a long time before they rang for me. The coachman was sent for, before I was summoned back to the bedroom. He was despatched to Edinburgh, for the second time, with a written message from Doctor Jerome to his head servant, saying that there was no chance of his returning to the city, and to his patients, for some hours to come. Some of us thought this looked badly for Mrs Macallan. Others said it might mean that the doctor had hopes of saving her, but expected to be a long time in doing it.

'At last I was sent for. On my presenting myself in the bedroom, Doctor Jerome went out to speak to Mr Macallan, leaving Mr Gale alone with me. From that time, as long as the poor lady lived, I was never left alone with her. One of the two doctors was always in her room. Refreshments were prepared for them; but still they took it in turns to eat their meal—one relieving the other at the bedside. If they had administered remedies to their patient I should not have been surprised by this proceeding. But they were at the end of their remedies; their only business in the room seemed to be to keep watch. I was puzzled to account for this. Keeping watch was the nurse's business. I thought the conduct of the doctors very strange.

'By the time that the lamp was lit in the sick room, I could see that the end was near. Excepting an occasional feeling of cramp in her legs, she seemed to suffer less. But her eyes looked sunk in her head; her skin was cold and clammy; her lips had turned to a bluish paleness. Nothing roused her now—excepting the last attempt made by her husband to see her. He came in with Dr Jerome, looking like a man terror-struck. She was past speaking; but the moment she saw him, she feebly made signs and sounds which showed that she was just as resolved as ever not to let him come near her. He was so overwhelmed that Mr Gale was obliged to help him out of the room. No other person was allowed to see the patient. Mr Dexter and Mrs Beauly made their inquiries outside the door, and were not invited in. As the evening drew on, the doctors sat on either side of the bed, silently watching her, silently waiting for her death.

'Towards eight o'clock, she seemed to have lost the use of her hands and arms; they lay helpless outside the bedclothes. A little later, she sank into a sort of dull sleep. Little by little, the sound of her heavy breathing grew fainter. At twenty minutes past nine, Doctor Jerome told me to bring the lamp to the bedside. He looked at her, and put his hand on her heart. Then he said to me, "You can go downstairs, nurse: it is all over." He turned to Mr Gale. "Will you inquire if Mr Macallan can see us?" he said. I opened the door for Mr Gale, and followed him out. Doctor Jerome called me back for a moment, and told me to give him the key of the door. I did so, of course—but I thought this also very strange. When I got down to the servants' hall, I found there was a general feeling that something was wrong. We were all uneasy—without knowing why.

'A little later the two doctors left the house. Mr Macallan had been quite incapable of receiving them, and hearing what they had to say. In this difficulty, they had spoken privately with Mr Dexter, as Mr Macallan's old friend, and the only gentleman then staying at Gleninch.

'Before bedtime I went upstairs, to prepare the remains of the deceased lady for the coffin. The room in which she lay was locked; the door leading into Mr Macallan's room being secured as well as the door leading into the corridor. The keys had been taken away by Mr Gale. Two of the men servants were posted outside the bedroom to keep watch. They were to be relieved at four in the morning—that was all they could tell me.

'In the absence of any explanations or directions, I took the liberty of knocking at the door of Mr Dexter's room. From his lips I first heard the startling news. Both the doctors had refused to give the usual certificate of death! There was to be a medical examination of the body the next morning.'

There the examination of the nurse, Christina Ormsay, came to an end.

Ignorant as I was of the law, I could see what impression the evidence (so far) was intended to produce on the minds of the Jury. After first showing that my husband had had two opportunities of administering the poison—once in the medicine and once in the tea—the counsel for the Crown led the Jury to infer that the prisoner had taken those opportunities to rid himself of an ugly and jealous wife whose detestable temper he could no longer endure.

Having directed his examination to the attainment of this object, the Lord Advocate had done with the witness. The Dean of Faculty—acting in the prisoner's interests—then rose to bring out the favourable side of the wife's character by cross-examining the nurse. If he succeeded in this attempt, the Jury might reconsider their conclusion that the wife was a person who had exasperated her husband beyond endurance. In that case, where (so far) was the husband's

motive for poisoning her? and where was the presumption
of the prisoner's guilt?

Pressed by this skilful lawyer, the nurse was obliged to
exhibit my husband's first wife under an entirely new aspect. Here is the substance of what the Dean of Faculty
extracted from Christina Ormsay:

'I persist in declaring that Mrs Macallan had a most
violent temper. But she was certainly in the habit of making amends for the offence that she gave by her violence.
When she was quiet again, she always made her excuses
to me; and she made them with a good grace. Her manners
were engaging at such times as these. She spoke and acted
like a well-bred lady. Then again, as to her personal appearance. Plain as she was in face, she had a good figure;
her hands and feet, I was told, had been modelled by a
sculptor. She had a very pleasant voice; and she was reported when in health to sing beautifully. She was also (if
her maid's account was to be trusted) a pattern, in the
matter of dressing, for the other ladies in the neighbourhood. Then, as to Mrs Beauly, though she was certainly
jealous of the beautiful young widow, she had shown at
the same time that she was capable of controlling that
feeling. It was through Mrs Macallan that Mrs Beauly was
in the house. Mrs Beauly had wished to postpone her visit
on account of the state of Mrs Macallan's health. It was
Mrs Macallan herself—not her husband—who decided
that Mrs Beauly should not be disappointed, and should
pay her visit to Gleninch, then and there. Further, Mrs
Macallan (in spite of her temper) was popular with her
friends, and popular with her servants. There was hardly
a dry eye in the house when it was known she was dying.
And, further still, in those little domestic disagreements at
which the nurse had been present, Mr Macallan had never
lost his temper, and had never used harsh language; he
seemed to be more sorry than angry when the quarrels took
place.'—Moral for the Jury: Was this the sort of woman
who would exasperate a man into poisoning her? And was

this the sort of man who would be capable of poisoning his wife?

Having produced that salutary counter-impression, the Dean of Faculty sat down; and the medical witnesses were called next.

Here, the evidence was simply irresistible.

Doctor Jerome and Mr Gale positively swore that the symptoms of the illness were the symptoms of poisoning by arsenic.* The surgeon who had performed the post-mortem examination followed. He positively swore that the appearance of the internal organs proved Dr Jerome and Mr Gale to be right in declaring that their patient had died poisoned. Lastly, to complete this overwhelming testimony, two analytical chemists actually produced in Court the arsenic which they had found in the body, in a quantity admittedly sufficient to have killed two persons instead of one. In the face of such evidence as this, cross-examination was a mere form. The first Question raised by the Trial—Did the Woman Die Poisoned?—was answered in the affirmative, and answered beyond the possibility of doubt.

The next witnesses called were witnesses concerned with the question that now followed—the obscure and terrible question: Who Poisoned Her?

CHAPTER XVII

Second Question—Who Poisoned her?

THE evidence of the doctors and the chemists closed the proceedings, on the first day of the Trial.

On the second day, the evidence to be produced by the prosecution was anticipated with a general feeling of curiosity and interest. The Court was now to hear what had been seen and done by the persons officially appointed to verify such cases of suspected crime as the case which had occurred at Gleninch. The Procurator-Fiscal—being the person officially appointed to direct the preliminary investigations of the Law—was the first witness called, on the second day of the Trial.

Examined by the Lord Advocate, the Fiscal gave his evidence, as follows:

'On the twenty-sixth of October, I received a communication from Doctor Jerome of Edinburgh, and from Mr Alexander Gale, medical practitioner, residing in the village or hamlet of Dingdovie, near Edinburgh. The communication related to the death, under circumstances of suspicion, of Mrs Eustace Macallan, at her husband's house, hard by Dingdovie, called Gleninch. There was also forwarded to me, enclosed in the document just mentioned, two reports. One described the results of a post-mortem examination of the deceased lady; and the other stated the discoveries made, after a chemical analysis of certain of the interior organs of her body. The result, in both instances, proved to demonstrate that Mrs Eustace Macallan had died of poisoning by arsenic.

'Under these circumstances, I set in motion a search and inquiry in the house at Gleninch, and elsewhere, simply for the purpose of throwing light on the circumstances which had attended the lady's death.

'No criminal charge, in connexion with the death, was made at my office against any person, either in the communication which I received from the medical men, or in any other form. The investigations at Gleninch, and elsewhere, beginning on the twenty-sixth of October, were not completed until the twenty-eighth. Upon this latter date—acting on certain discoveries which were reported to me, and on my own examination of letters and other documents brought to my office—I made a criminal charge against the prisoner; and obtained a warrant for his apprehension. He was examined before the Sheriff, on the twenty-ninth of October, and was committed for Trial before this Court.'

The Fiscal having made his statement, and having been cross-examined (on technical matters only), the persons employed in his office were called next. These men had a story of startling interest to tell. Theirs were the fatal discoveries which had justified the Fiscal in charging my husband with the murder of his wife. The first of the witnesses was a sheriff's officer. He gave his name as Isaiah Schoolcraft.

Examined by Mr Drew—Advocate-Depute, and counsel for the Crown with the Lord Advocate—Isaiah Schoolcraft said:

'I got a warrant on the twenty-sixth of October, to go to the country house near Edinburgh, called Gleninch. I took with me Robert Lorrie, Assistant to the Fiscal. We first examined the room in which Mrs Eustace Macallan had died. On the bed, and on a movable table which was attached to it, we found books and writing materials, and a paper containing some unfinished verses in manuscript; afterwards identified as being in the handwriting of the deceased. We enclosed these articles in paper, and sealed them up.

'We next opened an Indian cabinet in the bedroom. Here we found many more verses, on many more sheets of paper, in the same handwriting. We also discovered, first, some letters—and next a crumpled piece of paper thrown aside in a corner of one of the shelves. On closer examination, a chemist's printed label was discovered on this morsel of paper. We also found in the folds of it a few scattered grains of some white powder. The paper and the letters were carefully enclosed, and sealed up as before.

'Further investigation in the room revealed nothing which could throw any light on the purpose of our inquiry. We examined the clothes, jewellery, and books of the deceased. These we left under lock and key. We also found her dressing case, which we protected by seals, and took away with us to the Fiscal's office, along with all the other articles that we had discovered in the room.

'The next day we continued our examination in the house, having received, in the interval, fresh instructions from the Fiscal. We began our work in the bedroom communicating with the room in which Mrs Macallan had died. It had been kept locked since the death. Finding nothing of any importance here, we went next to another room on the same floor, in which we were informed the prisoner was then lying, ill in bed.

'His illness was described to us as a nervous complaint, caused by the death of his wife, and by the proceedings which had followed it. He was reported to be quite incapable of exerting himself, and quite unfit to see strangers. We insisted nevertheless (in deference to our instructions) on obtaining admission to his room. He made no reply, when we inquired whether he had, or had not, removed anything from the sleeping-room next to his late wife's which he usually occupied, to the sleeping-room in which he now lay. All he did was to close his eyes, as if he was too feeble to speak to us or to notice us. Without further disturbing him, we began to examine the room and the different objects in it.

'While we were so employed, we were interrupted by a strange sound. We likened it to the rumbling of wheels in the corridor outside.

'The door opened, and there came swiftly in a gentleman—a cripple—wheeling himself along in a chair. He wheeled his chair straight up to a little table which stood by the prisoner's bedside, and said something to him in a whisper too low to be overheard. The prisoner opened his eyes, and quickly answered by a sign. We informed the crippled gentleman, quite respectfully, that we could not allow him to be in the room at this time. He appeared to think nothing of what we said. He only answered, "My name is Dexter. I am one of Mr Macallan's old friends. It is you who are intruding here; not I." We again notified to him that he must leave the room; and we pointed out particularly that he had got his chair in such a position against the bedside-table as to prevent us from examining it. He only laughed. "Can't you see for yourselves," he said; "that it is a table, and nothing more?" In reply to this, we warned him that we were acting under a legal warrant, and that he might get into trouble if he obstructed us in the execution of our duty. Finding there was no moving him by fair means, I took his chair and pulled it away, while Robert Lorrie laid hold of the table and carried it to the other end of the room. The crippled gentleman flew into a furious rage with me for presuming to touch his chair. "My chair is Me," he said: "how dare you lay hands on Me?" I first opened the door; and then, by way of accommodating him, gave the chair a good push behind with my stick, instead of my hand—and so sent It, and him, safely and swiftly out of the room.

'Having locked the door, so as to prevent any further intrusion, I joined Robert Lorrie in examining the bedside-table. It had one drawer in it, and that drawer we found secured.

'We asked the prisoner for the key.

'He flatly refused to give it to us, and said we had no right to unlock his drawers. He was so angry that he even declared it was lucky for us he was too weak to rise from his bed. I answered civilly that our duty obliged us to examine the drawer, and that, if he still declined to produce the key, he would only oblige us to take the table away and have the lock opened by a smith.

'While we were still disputing, there was a knock at the door of the room.

'I opened the door cautiously. Instead of the crippled gentleman, whom I had expected to see again, there was another stranger standing outside. The prisoner hailed him as a friend and neighbour, and eagerly called upon him for protection from us. We found this second gentleman pleasant enough to deal with. He informed us readily that he had been sent for by Mr Dexter, and that he was himself a lawyer—and he asked to see our warrant. Having looked at it, he at once informed the prisoner (evidently very much to the prisoner's surprise) that he must submit to have the drawer examined—under protest. And then, without more ado, he got the key, and opened the table drawer for us himself.

'We found inside several letters, and a large book, with a lock to it; having the words "My Diary" inscribed on it in gilt letters. As a matter of course, we took possession of the letters and the Diary, and sealed them up to be given to the Fiscal. At the same time, the gentleman wrote out a protest, on the prisoner's behalf, and handed us his card. The card informed us that he was Mr Playmore—now one of the agents for the prisoner. The card and the protest were deposited, with the other documents, in the care of the Fiscal. No other discoveries of any importance were made at Gleninch.

'Our next inquiries took us to Edinburgh—to the druggist whose label we had found on the crumpled morsel of paper and to other druggists likewise whom we were instructed to question. On the twenty-eighth of October, the Fiscal was in possession of all the information that we could collect, and our duties for the time being came to an end.'

This concluded the evidence of Schoolcraft and Lorrie. It was not shaken on cross-examination; and it was plainly unfavourable to the prisoner.

Matters grew worse still when the next witnesses were called. The druggist whose label had been found on the crumpled bit of paper now appeared on the stand, to make the position of my unhappy husband more critical than ever.

Andrew Kinlay, druggist, of Edinburgh, deposed as follows:

'I keep a special registry-book of the poisons sold by me. I produce the book. On the date therein mentioned, the prisoner at the bar, Mr Eustace Macallan, came into my shop, and said that he wished to purchase some arsenic. I asked him what it was wanted for? He told me it was wanted by his gardener, to be used, in solution, for the killing of insects in the greenhouse. At the same time he mentioned his name—Mr Macallan, of Gleninch. I at once directed my assistant to put up the arsenic (two ounces of it); and I made the necessary entry in my book. Mr Macallan signed the entry; and I signed it afterwards as witness. He paid for the arsenic, and took it away with him wrapped up in two papers—the outer wrapper being labelled with my name and address, and with the word "Poison" in large letters; exactly like the label now produced on the piece of paper found at Gleninch.'

The next witness, Peter Stockdale (also a druggist of Edinburgh), followed, and said:

'The prisoner at the bar called at my shop, on the date indicated on my register—some days later than the date indicated in the register of Mr Kinlay. He wished to purchase sixpenny-worth of arsenic. My assistant, to whom he had addressed himself, called me. It is a rule in my shop that no one sells poisons but myself. I asked the prisoner what he wanted the arsenic for. He answered that he wanted it for killing rats* at his house called Gleninch. I said, "Have I the honour of speaking to Mr Macallan, of Gleninch?" He said that was his name. I sold him the arsenic—about an ounce and a half—and labelled the bottle in which I put it with the word "Poison," in my own handwriting. He signed the Register, and took the arsenic away with him, after paying for it.'

The cross-examination of these two men succeeded in asserting certain technical objections to their evidence. But the terrible fact that my husband himself had actually purchased the arsenic, in both cases, remained unshaken.

The next witnesses—the gardener, and the cook, at Gleninch—wound the chain of hostile evidence round the prisoner more mercilessly still.

On examination, the gardener said, on his oath:

'I never received any arsenic from the prisoner or from any one else, at the date to which you refer, or at any other date. I never used any such thing as a solution of arsenic, or ever allowed the men working under me to use it, in the conservatories, or in the garden, at Gleninch. I disapprove of arsenic as a means of destroying noxious insects infesting flowers and plants.'

The cook, being called next, spoke as positively as the gardener.

'Neither my master, nor any other person, gave me any arsenic to destroy rats, at any time. No such thing was wanted. I declare, on my oath, that I never saw any rats, in, or about, the house—or ever heard of any rats infesting it.'

Other household servants at Gleninch gave similar evidence. Nothing could be extracted from them on cross-examination—except that there might have been rats in the house, though they were not aware of it. The possession of the poison was traced directly to my husband, and to no one else. That he had bought it was actually proved; and that he had kept it, was the one conclusion that the evidence justified.

The witnesses who came next did their best to press the charge against the prisoner home to him. Having the arsenic in his possession, what had he done with it? The evidence led the Jury to infer what he had done with it.

The prisoner's valet deposed that his master had rung for him at twenty minutes to ten, on the morning of the day on which his mistress died, and had ordered a cup of tea for her. The man had received the order at the open door of Mrs Macallan's room, and could positively swear that no other person but his master was there at the time.

The under-housemaid, appearing next, said that she had made the tea, and had herself taken it upstairs, before ten o'clock, to Mrs Macallan's room. Her master had received it from her at the open door. She could look in, and see that he was alone in her mistress's room.

The nurse, Christina Ormsay, being recalled, repeated what Mrs Macallan had said to her, on the day when that lady was first taken ill. She had said (speaking to the nurse at six o'clock in the morning), 'Mr Macallan came in about an hour since; he found me still sleepless, and gave me my composing-draught.' This was at five o'clock in the morning, while Christina Ormsay was asleep on the sofa. The nurse further swore that she had looked at the bottle containing the composing-mixture, and had seen, by the measuring marks on the bottle, that a dose had been poured out since the dose previously given, administered by herself.

On this occasion, special interest was excited by the cross-examination. The closing questions, put to the under-housemaid and the nurse, revealed for the first time what the nature of the defence was to be.

Cross-examining the under-housemaid, the Dean of Faculty said:

'Did you ever notice, when you were setting Mrs Eustace Macallan's room to rights, whether the water left in the basin was of a blackish or bluish colour?' The witness answered, 'I never noticed anything of the sort.'

The Dean of Faculty went on:

'Did you ever find, under the pillow of the bed, or in any other hiding-place in Mrs Macallan's room, any books or pamphlets, telling of remedies used for improving a bad complexion?' The witness answered, 'No.'

The Dean of Faculty persisted:

'Did you ever hear Mrs Macallan speak of arsenic, taken as a wash, or taken as a medicine, as a good thing to improve the complexion?' The witness answered, 'Never.'

Similar questions were next put to the nurse, and were all answered, by this witness also, in the negative.

Here, then—in spite of the negative answers—was the plan of the defence made dimly visible for the first time to the Jury and to the audience. By way of preventing the possibility of a mistake in so serious a matter, the Chief Judge (the Lord Justice Clerk) put this plain question, when the witnesses had retired, to the Counsel for the defence:

'The Court and the Jury,' said his lordship, 'wish distinctly to understand the object of your cross-examination of

the housemaid and the nurse. Is it the theory of the defence,
that Mrs Eustace Macallan used the arsenic which her
husband purchased, for the purpose of improving the defects of her complexion?'

The Dean of Faculty answered:

'That is what we say, my lord, and what we propose to
prove, as the foundation of the defence. We cannot dispute
the medical evidence which declares that Mrs Macallan
died poisoned. But we assert that she died of an overdose
of arsenic, ignorantly taken, in the privacy of her own room,
as a remedy for the defects—the proved and admitted defects—of her complexion.* The Prisoner's declaration before the Sheriff, expressly sets forth that he purchased the
arsenic at the request of his wife.'

The Lord Justice Clerk inquired, upon this, if there was
any objection, on the part of either of the learned counsel,
to have the Declaration read in Court, before the Trial
proceeded further.

To this, the Dean of Faculty replied that he would be
glad to have the Declaration read. If he might use the
expression, it would usefully pave the way, in the minds of
the Jury, for the defence which he had to submit to them.

The Lord Advocate (speaking on the other side) was
happy to be able to accommodate his learned brother in
this matter. So long as the mere assertions which the Declaration contained were not supported by proof, he looked
upon that document as evidence for the prosecution, and
he, too, was quite willing to have it read.

Thereupon, the prisoner's Declaration of his innocence—
on being charged before the Sheriff with the murder of his
wife—was read, in the following terms:

'I bought the two packets of arsenic, on each occasion,
at my wife's own request. On the first occasion, she told
me the poison was wanted by the gardener, for use in the
conservatories. On the second occasion, she said it was
required by the cook for ridding the lower part of the house
of rats.

'I handed both packets of arsenic to my wife immediately on my return home. I had nothing to do with the poison, after buying it. My wife was the person who gave orders to the gardener and the cook—not I. I never held any communication with either of them.

'I asked my wife no questions about the use of the arsenic; feeling no interest in the subject. I never entered the conservatories for months together; I care little about flowers. As for the rats, I left the killing of them to the cook and the other servants—just as I should have left any other part of the domestic business to the cook and the other servants.

'My wife never told me she wanted the arsenic to improve her complexion. Surely, I should be the last person admitted to the knowledge of such a secret of her toilet as that? I implicitly believed what she told me—viz., that the poison was wanted, for the purposes specified, by the gardener and the cook.

'I assert positively, that I lived on friendly terms with my wife; allowing, of course, for the little occasional disagreements and misunderstandings of married life. Any sense of disappointment, in connexion with my marriage, which I might have felt privately, I conceived it to be my duty, as a husband and a gentleman, to conceal from my wife. I was not only shocked and grieved by her untimely death—I was filled with fear that I had not, with all my care, behaved affectionately enough to her in her lifetime.

'Furthermore, I solemnly declare that I know no more of how she took the arsenic found in her body than the babe unborn. I am innocent even of the thought of harming that unhappy woman. I administered the composing-draught, exactly as I found it in the bottle. I afterwards gave her the cup of tea, exactly as I received it from the under-housemaid's hand. I never had access to the arsenic, after I placed the two packages in my wife's possession. I am entirely ignorant of what she did with them, or of where she kept them. I declare, before God, I am innocent of the horrible crime with which I am charged.'

With the reading of those true and touching words the proceedings on the second day of the Trial came to an end.

So far, I must own, the effect on me of reading the Report was to depress my spirits, and to lower my hopes. The whole weight of the evidence, at the close of the second day, was against my husband. Woman, as I was, and partisan, as I was, I could plainly see that.

The merciless Lord Advocate (I confess I hated him!) had proved (1) that Eustace had bought the poison; (2) that the reason which he had given to the druggists for buying the poison was not the true reason; (3) that he had had two opportunities of secretly administering the poison to his wife. On the other side, what had the Dean of Faculty proved? As yet—nothing. The assertions in the prisoner's Declaration of his innocence were still, as the Lord Advocate had remarked, assertions not supported by proof. Not one atom of evidence had been produced to show that it was the wife who had secretly used the arsenic, and used it for her complexion.

My one consolation was, that the reading of the Trial had already revealed to me the helpful figures of two friends, on whose sympathy I might surely rely. The crippled Mr Dexter had especially shown himself to be a thorough good ally of my husband's. My heart warmed to the man who had moved his chair against the bedside-table—the man who had struggled to the last to defend Eustace's papers from the wretches who had seized them! I decided, then and there, that the first person to whom I would confide my aspirations and my hopes should be Mr Dexter. If he felt any difficulty about advising me, I would then apply next to the agent, Mr Playmore—the second good friend, who had formally protested against the seizure of my husband's papers.

Fortified by this resolution, I turned the page, and read the history of the third day of the Trial.

CHAPTER XVIII

Third Question—What was his Motive?

THE first question (Did the Woman die Poisoned?) had been answered, positively. The second question (Who Poisoned Her?) had been answered, apparently. There now remained the third and final question—What Was His Motive? The first evidence called, in answer to that inquiry, was the evidence of relatives and friends of the dead wife.

Lady Brydehaven, widow of Rear Admiral Sir George Brydehaven, examined by Mr Drew (counsel for the Crown with the Lord Advocate), gave evidence as follows:—

'The deceased lady (Mrs Eustace Macallan) was my niece. She was the only child of my sister; and she lived under my roof after the time of her mother's death. I objected to her marriage—on grounds which were considered purely fanciful and sentimental by her other friends. It is extremely painful to me to state the circumstances in public; but I am ready to make the sacrifice, if the ends of justice require it.

'The prisoner at the Bar, at the time of which I am now speaking, was staying as a guest in my house. He met with an accident, while he was out riding, which caused a severe injury to one of his legs. The leg had been previously hurt, while he was serving with the army in India. This circumstance tended greatly to aggravate the injury received in the accident. He was confined to a recumbent position on a sofa for many weeks together; and the ladies in the house took it in turns to sit with him, and while away the weary time by reading to him and talking to him. My niece was foremost among these volunteer nurses. She played admirably on the piano; and the sick man happened—most unfortunately as the event proved—to be fond of music.

'The consequences of the perfectly innocent intercourse thus begun, were deplorable consequences for my niece. She became passionately attached to Mr Eustace Macallan: without awakening any corresponding affection on his side.

'I did my best to interfere, delicately and usefully, while it was still possible to interfere with advantage. Unhappily, my niece refused to place any confidence in me. She persistently denied that she was actuated by any warmer feeling towards Mr Macallan than a feeling of friendly interest. This made it impossible for me to separate them, without openly acknowledging my reason for doing so, and thus producing a scandal which might have affected my niece's reputation. My husband was alive at that time; and the one thing I could do, under the circumstances, was the thing I did. I requested him to speak privately to Mr Macallan, and to appeal to his honour to help us out of the difficulty, without prejudice to my niece.

'Mr Macallan behaved admirably. He was still helpless. But he made an excuse for leaving us which it was impossible to dispute. In two days after my husband had spoken to him, he was removed from the house.

'The remedy was well intended; but it came too late, and it utterly failed. The mischief was done. My niece pined away visibly; neither medical help nor change of air and scene did anything for her. In course of time—after Mr Macallan had recovered from the effects of his accident—I found out that she was carrying on a clandestine correspondence with him, by means of her maid. His letters, I am bound to say, were most considerately and carefully written. Nevertheless, I felt it my duty to stop the correspondence.

'My interference—what else could I do but interfere?—brought matters to a crisis. One day, my niece was missing at breakfast-time. The next day, we discovered that the poor infatuated creature had gone to Mr Macallan's chambers in London, and had been found hidden in his bedroom, by some bachelor friends who came to visit him.

'For this disaster Mr Macallan was in no respect to blame. Hearing footsteps outside, he had only time to take measures for saving her character by concealing her in the nearest room—and the nearest room happened to be his bedchamber. The matter was talked about of course, and motives were misinterpreted in the vilest manner. My husband had another private conversation with Mr Macallan. He again behaved admirably. He publicly declared that my niece had visited him as his betrothed wife. In a fortnight from that time, he silenced scandal in the one way that was possible—he married her.

'I was alone in opposing the marriage. I thought it at the time—what it has proved to be since—a fatal mistake.

'It would have been sad enough, if Mr Macallan had only married her without a particle of love on his side. But, to make the prospect more hopeless still, he was himself, at that very time, the victim of a misplaced attachment to a lady who was engaged to another man. I am well aware that he compassionately denied this—just as he compassionately affected to be in love with my niece when he married her. But his hopeless admiration of the lady whom I have mentioned, was a matter of fact notorious among his friends. It may not be amiss to add, that *her* marriage preceded *his* marriage. He had irretrievably lost the woman he really loved—he was without a hope or an aspiration in life—when he took pity on my niece.

'In conclusion, I can only repeat that no evil which could have happened (if she had remained a single woman) would have been comparable, in my opinion, to the evil of such a marriage as this. Never, I sincerely believe, were two more ill-assorted persons united in the bonds of matrimony, than the prisoner at the bar and his deceased wife.'

The evidence of this witness produced a strong sensation among the audience, and had a marked effect on the minds of the Jury. Cross-examination forced Lady Brydehaven to modify some of her opinions, and to acknowledge that the hopeless attachment of the prisoner to another woman was a matter of rumour only. But the facts in her narrative remained unshaken—and, for that one reason, they invested the crime charged against the prisoner with an appearance of possibility, which it had entirely failed to assume during the earlier part of the Trial.

Two other ladies (intimate friends of Mrs Eustace Macallan) were called next. They differed from Lady Brydehaven in their opinions on the propriety of the marriage; but on all the material points, they supported her testimony, and confirmed the serious impression which the first witness had produced on every person in Court.

The next evidence which the prosecution proposed to put in, was the silent evidence of the letters and the Diary found at Gleninch.

In answer to a question from the Bench, the Lord Advocate stated that the letters were written by friends of the prisoner and of his deceased wife, and that passages in them bore directly on the terms on which the two associated in their married life. The Diary was still more valuable as evidence. It contained the prisoner's daily record of domestic events, and of the thoughts and feelings which they aroused in him at the time.

A most painful scene followed this explanation.

Writing, as I do, long after the events took place, I still cannot prevail upon myself to describe in detail what my unhappy husband said and did, at this distressing period of the Trial. Deeply affected while Lady Brydehaven was giving her evidence, he had with difficulty restrained himself from interrupting her. He now lost all control over his feelings. In piercing tones which rang through the Court, he protested against the contemplated violation of his own most sacred secrets and his wife's most sacred secrets. 'Hang me, innocent as I am!' he cried, 'but spare me *that*!' The effect of this terrible outbreak on the audience is reported to have been indescribable. Some of the women present were in hysterics. The Judges interfered from the Bench—but with no good result. Quiet was at length restored by the Dean of Faculty, who succeeded in soothing the prisoner—and who then addressed the Judges, pleading for indulgence to his unhappy client in most touching and eloquent language. The speech, a masterpiece of impromptu oratory, concluded with a temperate yet strongly-urged protest against the reading of the papers discovered at Gleninch.

The three Judges retired to consider the legal question submitted to them. The sitting was suspended for more than half an hour.

As usual in such cases, the excitement in the Court communicated itself to the crowd outside in the street. The general opinion here—led, as it was supposed, by one of the clerks or other inferior persons connected with the legal proceedings—was decidedly adverse to the prisoner's chance of escaping a sentence of death. 'If the letters and the Diary are read,' said the brutal spokesmen of the mob, 'the letters and the Diary will hang him.'

On the return of the Judges into Court, it was announced that they had decided, by a majority of two to one, on permitting the documents in dispute to be produced in evidence. Each of the Judges, in turn, gave his reasons for the decision at which he had arrived. This done, the Trial proceeded. The reading of the extracts from the letters and the extracts from the Diary began.

The first letters produced were the letters found in the Indian cabinet, in Mrs Eustace Macallan's room. They were addressed to the deceased lady by intimate (female) friends of hers, with whom she was accustomed to correspond. Three separate Extracts, from letters written by three different correspondents, were selected to be read in Court.

FIRST CORRESPONDENT: 'I despair, my dearest Sara, of being able to tell you how your last letter has distressed me. Pray forgive me, if I own to thinking that your very sensitive nature exaggerates or misinterprets, quite unconsciously of course, the neglect that you experience at the hands of your husband. I cannot say anything about *his* peculiarities of character, because I am not well enough acquainted with him to know what they are. But, my dear, I am much older than you, and I have had a much longer experience than yours, of what somebody calls, "the lights and shadows of married life." Speaking from that experience, I must tell you what I have observed. Young married women, like you, who are devotedly attached to their husbands, are apt to make one very serious mistake. As a rule, they all expect too much from their husbands. Men, my poor Sara, are not like *us*. Their love, even when it is quite sincere, is not like our love. It does not last, as it does with us. It is not the one hope and one thought of their lives, as it is with us. We have no alternative—even when we most truly respect and love them—but to make allowance for this difference between the man's nature and the woman's. I do not for one moment excuse your husband's coldness. He is wrong, for example, in never looking at you when he speaks to you, and in never noticing the efforts that you make to please him. He is worse than wrong—he is really cruel if you like—in never returning your kiss when you kiss him. But, my dear, are you quite sure that he is always *designedly* cold and cruel? May not his conduct be sometimes the result of troubles and anxieties which weigh on his mind, and which are troubles and anxieties that you cannot share? If you try to look at his behaviour in this light, you will understand many things which puzzle and pain you now. Be patient with him, my child. Make no complaints; and never approach him with your caresses at times when his mind is preoccupied or his temper ruffled. This may be hard advice to follow, loving him as ardently as you do. But rely on it, the secret of happiness for us women is to be found (alas, only too often!) in such exercise of restraint and resignation as your old friend now recommends. Think, my dear, over what I have written—and let me hear from you again.'

SECOND CORRESPONDENT: 'How can you be so foolish, Sara, as to waste your love on such a cold-blooded brute as your husband seems to be? To be sure, I am not married yet—or perhaps I should not be so surprised at you. But I shall be married one of these days; and if my husband ever treats me as Mr Macallan treats you, I shall insist on a separation. I declare I think I would rather be actually beaten, like the women among the lower orders, than be treated with the polite neglect and contempt which you describe. I burn with indignation when I think of it. It must be quite insufferable. Don't bear it any longer, my poor dear. Leave him, and come and stay with me. My brother is a law-student, as you know. I read to him portions of your letter; and he is of opinion that you might get, what he calls, a judicial separation. Come and consult him.'

THIRD CORRESPONDENT: 'You know, my dear Mrs Macallan, what *my* experience of men has been. Your letter does not surprise me in the least. Your husband's conduct to you points to one conclusion. He is in love with some other woman. There is Somebody in the dark, who gets from him everything that he denies to you. I have been through it all—and I know! Don't give way. Make it the business of your life to find out who the creature is. Perhaps there may be more than one of them. It doesn't matter. One, or many, if you can only discover them, you may make his existence as miserable to him as he makes your existence to you. If you want my experience to help you, say the word, and it is freely at your service. I can come and stay with you, at Gleninch, any time after the fourth of next month.'

With those abominable lines the readings from the letters of the women came to an end. The first and longest of the Extracts produced the most vivid impression in Court. Evidently the writer was, in this case, a worthy and sensible person. It was generally felt, however, that all three of the

letters—no matter how widely they might differ in tone—
justified the same conclusion. The wife's position at Gleninch (if the wife's account of it was to be trusted) was the
position of a neglected and an unhappy woman.

The correspondence of the prisoner, which had been
found, with his Diary, in the locked bed-table drawer, was
produced next. The letters in this case were, with one
exception, all written by men. Though the tone of them
was moderation itself, as compared with the second and
third of the women's letters, the conclusion still pointed the
same way. The life of the husband, at Gleninch, appeared
to be just as intolerable as the life of the wife.

For example, one of the prisoner's male friends wrote,
inviting him to make a yacht voyage round the world.
Another suggested an absence of six months on the Conti-
nent. A third recommended field sports in India. The one
object aimed at by all the writers was plainly to counsel a
separation, more or less plausible and more or less complete, between the married pair.

The last letter read was addressed to the prisoner in a
woman's handwriting, and was signed by a woman's Christian name only.

'Ah, my poor Eustace, what a cruel destiny is ours!' (the
letter began). 'When I think of your life, sacrificed to that
wretched woman, my heart bleeds for you! If *we* had been
man and wife—if it had been *my* unutterable happiness to
love and cherish the best, the dearest of men—what a
paradise of our own we might have lived in, what delicious
hours we might have known! But regret is vain; we are
separated, in this life—separated by ties which we both
mourn, and yet which we must both respect. My Eustace,
there is a world beyond this! There, our souls will fly to
meet each other, and mingle in one long heavenly embrace—in a rapture forbidden to us on earth. The misery
described in your letter—oh! why, why did you marry
her?—has wrung this confession of feeling from me. Let it
comfort you; but let no other eyes see it. Burn my rashly-

written lines, and look (as I look) to the better life which you may yet share with your own HELENA.'

The reading of this outrageous letter provoked a question from the Bench. One of the Judges asked if the writer had attached any date or address to her letter.

In answer to this, the Lord Advocate stated that neither the one nor the other appeared. The envelope showed that the letter had been posted in London. 'We propose,' the learned counsel continued, 'to read certain passages from the prisoner's Diary, in which the name signed at the end of the letters occurs more than once; and we may possibly find other means of identifying the writer, to the satisfaction of your lordships, before the Trial is over.'

The promised passages from my husband's private Diary were now read. The first extract related to a period of nearly a year before the date of Mrs Eustace Macallan's death. It was expressed in these terms:

'News, by this morning's post, which has quite overwhelmed me. Helena's husband died suddenly, two days since, of heart disease. She is free—my beloved Helena is free! And I?

'I am fettered to a woman with whom I have not a single feeling in common. Helena is lost to me, by my own act. Ah! I can understand now, as I never understood before, how irresistible temptation can be, and how easily, sometimes, crime may follow it. I had better shut up these leaves for the night. It maddens me to no purpose to think of my position or to write of it.'

The next passage, dated a few days later, dwelt on the same subject:

'Of all the follies that a man can commit, the greatest is acting on impulse. I acted on impulse when I married the unfortunate creature who is now my wife.

'Helena was then lost to me, as I too hastily supposed. She had married the man to whom she rashly engaged herself, before she met with me. He was younger than I, and, to all appearances, heartier and stronger than I. So far

as I could see, my fate was sealed for life. Helena had
written her farewell letter, taking leave of me in this world,
for good. My prospects were closed; my hopes had ended.
I had not an aspiration left; I had no necessity to stimulate
me to take refuge in work. A chivalrous action, an exertion
of noble self-denial, seemed to be all that was left to me,
all that I was fit for.

'The circumstances of the moment adapted themselves,
with a fatal facility, to this idea. The ill-fated woman who had
become attached to me (Heaven knows without so much as
the shadow of encouragement on my part!), had, just at that
time, rashly placed her reputation at the mercy of the world.
It rested with me to silence the scandalous tongues that re-
viled her. With Helena lost to me, happiness was not to be
expected. All women were equally indifferent to me. A generous action would be the salvation of *this* woman. Why not
perform it? I married her on that impulse—married her, just
as I might have jumped into the water and saved her, if she
had been drowning; just as I might have knocked a man
down, if I had seen him ill-treating her in the street!

'And now, the woman for whom I have made this sacrifice stands between me and my Helena—my Helena, free
to pour out all the treasures of her love on the man who
adores the earth that she touches with her foot!

'Fool! Madman! Why don't I dash out my brains against
the wall that I see opposite to me while I write these lines?

'My gun is there in the corner. I have only to tie a string
to the trigger, and to put the muzzle to my mouth——No!
My mother is alive; my mother's love is sacred. I have no
right to take the life which she gave me. I must suffer and
submit. Oh, Helena! Helena!'

The third Extract—one among many similar passages—
had been written about two months before the death of the
prisoner's wife.

'More reproaches addressed to me! There never was such
a woman for complaining; she lives in a perfect atmosphere
of ill-temper and discontent.

'My new offences are two in number. I never ask her to play to me now; and, when she puts on a new dress, expressly to please me, I never notice it. Notice it! Good Heavens! The effort of my life is *not* to notice her, in anything she does or says. How could I keep my temper, unless I kept as much as possible out of the way of private interviews with her? And I do keep my temper. I am never hard on her; I never use harsh language to her. She has a double claim on my forbearance—she is a woman; and the law has made her my wife. I remember this; but I am human. The less I see of her—except when visitors are present—the more certain I can feel of preserving my self-control.

'I wonder what it is that makes her so utterly distasteful to me. She is a plain woman; but I have seen uglier women than she, whose caresses I could have endured, without the sense of shrinking that comes over me when I am obliged to submit to *her* caresses. I keep the feeling hidden from her. She loves me, poor thing!—and I pity her. I wish I could do more; I wish I could return, in the smallest degree, the feeling with which she regards me. But, no—I can only pity her. If she would be content to live on friendly terms with me, and never to exact demonstrations of tenderness, we might get on pretty well. But she wants love. Unfortunate creature, she wants love!

'Oh, my Helena! I have no love to give her. My heart is yours.

'I dreamt last night, that this unhappy wife of mine was dead. The dream was so vivid that I actually got out of my bed, and opened the door of her room, and listened.

'Her calm regular breathing was distinctly audible in the stillness of the night. She was in a deep sleep. I closed the door again, and lit my candle and read. Helena was in all my thoughts; it was hard work to fix my attention on the book. But anything was better than going to bed again, and dreaming, perhaps, for the second time, that I, too, was free.

'What a life mine is! what a life my wife's is! If the house was to take fire, I wonder whether I should make an effort to save myself, or to save her?'

The last two passages read, referred to later dates still.

'A gleam of brightness has shone over this dismal existence of mine at last.

'Helena is no longer condemned to the seclusion of widowhood. Time enough has passed to permit of her mixing again in society. She is paying visits to friends in our part of Scotland; and, as she and I are cousins, it is universally understood that she cannot leave the North without also spending a few days at my house. She writes me word that the visit, however embarrassing it may be to us privately, is nevertheless a visit that must be made, for the sake of appearances. Blessings on appearances! I shall see this angel in my purgatory—and all because Society in Mid-Lothian would think it strange that my cousin should be visiting in my part of Scotland, and not visit Me!

'But we are to be very careful. Helena says, in so many words, "I come to see you, Eustace, as a sister. You must receive me as a brother, or not receive me at all. I shall write to your wife to propose the day for my visit. I shall not forget—do you not forget—that it is by your wife's permission that I enter your house."

'Only let me see her! I will submit to anything to obtain the unutterable happiness of seeing her!'

The last Extract followed, and consisted of these lines only:

'A new misfortune! My wife has fallen ill. She has taken to her bed, with a bad rheumatic cold, just at the time appointed for Helena's visit to Gleninch. But, on this occasion (I gladly own it!), she has behaved charmingly. She has written to Helena to say that her illness is not serious enough to render a change necessary in the arrangements, and to make it her particular request that my cousin's visit shall take place upon the day originally decided on.

'This is a great sacrifice made to me, on my wife's part.

Jealous of every woman, under forty, who comes near me, she is of course jealous of Helena—and she controls herself, and trusts me!

'I am bound to show my gratitude for this, and I will show it. From this day forth, I vow to live more affectionately with my wife. I tenderly embraced her this very morning—and, I hope, poor soul, she did not discover the effort that it cost me.'

There, the readings from the Diary came to an end.

The most unpleasant pages in the whole Report of the Trial were—to me—the pages which contained the extracts from my husband's Diary. There were expressions, here and there, which not only pained me, but which almost shook Eustace's position in my estimation. I think I would have given everything I possessed to have had the power of annihilating certain lines in that Diary. As for his passionate expressions of love for Mrs Beauly, every one of them went through me like a sting! He had whispered words quite as warm into my ears, in the days of his courtship. I had no reason to doubt that he truly and dearly loved me. But the question was—Had he, just as truly and dearly, loved Mrs Beauly, before me? Had she or I won the first of his heart? He had declared to me, over and over again, that he had only fancied himself to be in love, before the day when we met. I had believed him then. I determined to believe him still. I did believe him. But I hated Mrs Beauly!

As for the painful impression produced in Court by the readings from the letters and the Diary, it seemed to be impossible to increase it. Nevertheless, it *was* perceptibly increased. In other words, it was rendered more unfavourable still towards the prisoner, by the evidence of the next, and last, witness called on the part of the prosecution.

William Enzie, under-gardener at Gleninch, was sworn, and deposed as follows:

'On the twentieth of October, at eleven o'clock in the forenoon, I was at work in the shrubbery, on the side next to the garden called the Dutch Garden. There was a summer-house in the Dutch Garden, having its back set towards the shrubbery. The day was wonderfully fine and warm for the time of year.

'Passing to my work, I passed the back of the summer-house. I heard voices inside—a man's voice and a lady's voice. The lady's voice was strange to me. The man's voice I recognized as the voice of my master. The ground in the shrubbery was soft; and my curiosity was excited. I stepped up to the back of the summer-house, without being heard; and I listened to what was going on inside.

'The first words I could distinguish were spoken in my master's voice. He said, "If I could only have foreseen that you might one day be free, what a happy man I might have been!" The lady's voice answered, "Hush! you must not talk so." My master said, upon that, "I must talk of what is in my mind; it is always in my mind that I have lost you." He stopped a bit there, and then he said on a sudden, "Do me one favour, my angel! Promise me not to marry again." The lady's voice spoke out, thereupon, sharply enough, "What do you mean?" My master said, "I wish no harm to the unhappy creature who is a burden on my life; but suppose——?" "Suppose nothing," the lady said; "come back to the house."

'She led the way into the garden, and turned round, beckoning my master to join her. In that position, I saw her face plainly; and I knew it for the face of the young widow lady who was visiting at the house. She was pointed out to me by the head-gardener, when she first arrived, for the purpose of warning me that I was not to interfere if I found her picking the flowers. The gardens at Gleninch were shown to tourists on certain days; and we made a difference, of course, in the matter of the flowers, between strangers and guests staying in the house. I am quite certain of the identity of the lady who was talking with my master. Mrs Beauly was a comely person—and there was no mistaking her for any other than herself. She and my master withdrew together on the way to the house. I heard nothing more of what passed between them.'

This witness was severely cross-examined as to the correctness of his recollection of the talk in the summer-house, and as to his capacity for identifying both the speakers. On certain minor points he was shaken. But he firmly asserted his accurate remembrance of the last words exchanged between his master and Mrs Beauly; and he personally described the lady, in terms which proved that he had correctly identified her.

With this, the answer to the third Question raised by the Trial—the question of the prisoner's Motive for poisoning his wife—came to an end.

The story for the prosecution was now a story told. The staunchest friends of the prisoner in Court were compelled to acknowledge that the evidence, thus far, pointed clearly and conclusively against him. He seemed to feel this himself. When he withdrew at the close of the third day of the Trial, he was so depressed and exhausted that he was obliged to lean on the arm of the governor of the jail.

CHAPTER XIX

The Evidence for the Defence

THE feeling of interest excited by the Trial was prodigiously increased on the fourth day. The witnesses for the defence were now to be heard; and first and foremost among them was the prisoner's mother. She looked at her son as she lifted her veil to take the oath. He burst into tears. At that moment, the sympathy felt for the mother was generally extended to the unhappy son.

Examined by the Dean of Faculty, Mrs Macallan the elder gave her answers with remarkable dignity and self-control.

Questioned as to certain private conversations which had

passed between her late daughter-in-law and herself, she declared that Mrs Eustace Macallan was morbidly sensitive on the subject of her personal appearance. She was devotedly attached to her husband; the great anxiety of her life was to make herself as attractive to him as possible. The imperfections in her personal appearance—and especially in her complexion—were subjects to her of the bitterest regret. The witness had heard her say, over and over again (referring to her complexion), that there was no risk she would not run, and no pain she would not suffer, to improve it. 'Men' (she had said) 'are all caught by outward appearances: my husband might love me better, if I had a better colour.'

Being asked next if the passages from her son's Diary were to be depended on as evidence—that is to say, if they fairly represented the peculiarities in his character, and his true sentiments towards his wife—Mrs Macallan denied it in the plainest and the strongest terms.

'The extracts from my son's Diary are a libel on his character,' she said. 'And not the less a libel, because they happen to be written by himself. Speaking from a mother's experience of him, I know that he must have written the passages produced, in moments of uncontrollable depression and despair. No just person judges hastily of a man by the rash words which may escape him in his moody and miserable moments. Is my son to be so judged because he happens to have written *his* rash words, instead of speaking them? His pen has been his most deadly enemy, in this case—it has presented him at his very worst. He was not happy in his marriage—I admit that. But I say, at the same time, that he was invariably considerate towards his wife. I was implicitly trusted by both of them; I saw them in their most private moments. I declare—in the face of what she appears to have written to her friends and correspondents— that my son never gave his wife any just cause to assert that he treated her with cruelty and neglect.'

These words, firmly and clearly spoken, produced a

strong impression. The Lord Advocate—evidently perceiving that any attempt to weaken that impression would not be likely to succeed—confined himself, in cross-examination, to two significant questions.

'In speaking to you of the defects in her complexion,' he said, 'did your daughter-in-law refer in any way to the use of arsenic as a remedy?'

The answer to this was, 'No.'

The Lord Advocate proceeded:

'Did you yourself ever recommend arsenic, or mention it casually, in the course of the private conversations which you have described?'

The answer to this was, 'Never.'

The Lord Advocate resumed his seat. Mrs Macallan the elder withdrew.

An interest of a new kind was excited by the appearance of the next witness. This was no less a person than Mrs Beauly herself. The Report describes her as a remarkably attractive person; modest and ladylike in her manner, and, to all appearance, feeling sensitively the public position in which she was placed.

The first portion of her evidence was almost a recapitulation of the evidence given by the prisoner's mother—with this difference, that Mrs Beauly had been actually questioned by the deceased lady on the subject of cosmetic applications to the complexion. Mrs Eustace Macallan had complimented her on the beauty of her complexion, and had asked what artificial means she used to keep it in such good order. Using no artificial means (and knowing nothing whatever of cosmetics), Mrs Beauly had resented the question; and a temporary coolness between the two ladies had been the result.

Interrogated as to her relations with the prisoner, Mrs Beauly indignantly denied that she or Mr Macallan had ever given the deceased lady the slightest cause for jealousy. It was impossible for Mrs Beauly to leave Scotland, after visiting at the houses of her cousin's neighbours, without

also visiting her cousin's house. To take any other course
would have been an act of downright rudeness, and would
have excited remark. She did not deny that Mr Macallan
had admired her in the days when they were both single
people. But there was no further expression of that feeling,
when she had married another man, and when he had
married another woman. From that time, their intercourse
was the innocent intercourse of a brother and sister. Mr
Macallan was a gentleman: he knew what was due to his
wife and to Mrs Beauly—she would not have entered the
house if experience had not satisfied her of that. As for the
evidence of the under-gardener, it was little better than
pure invention. The greater part of the conversation which
he had described himself as overhearing had never taken
place. The little that was really said (as the man reported
it) was said jestingly; and she had checked it immediately—
as the witness had himself confessed. For the rest, Mr
Macallan's behaviour towards his wife was invariably
kind and considerate. He was constantly devising means
to alleviate her sufferings from the rheumatic affection
which confined her to her bed; he had spoken of her, not
once but many times, in terms of the sincerest sympathy.
When she ordered her husband and witness to leave
the room, on the day of her death, Mr Macallan said to
witness afterwards, "We must bear with her jealousy, poor
soul: we know that we don't deserve it." In that patient
manner he submitted to her infirmities of temper, from first
to last.

The main interest in the cross-examination of Mrs Beauly
centred in a question which was put at the end. After
reminding her that she had given her name, on being sworn,
as 'Helena Beauly,' the Lord Advocate said:

'A letter addressed to the prisoner, and signed "Helena,"
has been read in Court. Look at it, if you please. Are you
the writer of that letter?'

Before the witness could reply, the Dean of Faculty protested against the question. The Judges allowed the protest,

and refused to permit the question to be put. Mrs Beauly thereupon withdrew. She had betrayed a very perceptible agitation on hearing the letter referred to, and on having it placed in her hands. This exhibition of feeling was variously interpreted among the audience. Upon the whole, however, Mrs Beauly's evidence was considered to have aided the impression which the mother's evidence had produced in the prisoner's favour.

The next witnesses—both ladies, and both school-friends of Mrs Eustace Macallan—created a new feeling of interest in Court. They supplied the missing link in the evidence for the defence.

The first of the ladies declared that she had mentioned arsenic, as a means of improving the complexion, in conversation with Mrs Eustace Macallan. She had never used it herself, but she had read of the practice of eating arsenic, among the Styrian peasantry, for the purpose of clearing the colour, and of producing a general appearance of plumpness and good health.* She positively swore that she had related this result of her reading to the deceased lady, exactly as she now related it in Court.

The second witness, present at the conversation already mentioned, corroborated the first witness in every particular: and added that she had procured the book relating to the arsenic-eating practices of the Styrian peasantry, and to their results, at Mrs Eustace Macallan's own request. This book she had herself despatched by post to Mrs Eustace Macallan at Gleninch.

There was but one assailable point in this otherwise conclusive evidence. The cross-examination discovered it.

Both the ladies were asked in turn, if Mrs Eustace Macallan had expressed to them, directly or indirectly, any intention of obtaining arsenic, with a view to the improvement of her complexion. In each case the answer to that all-important question was, 'No.' Mrs Eustace Macallan had heard of the remedy, and had received the book. But of her own intentions in the future, she had not said one word. She had begged both the ladies to consider the conversation as strictly private—and there it had ended.

It required no lawyer's eye to discern the fatal defect which was now revealed in the evidence for the defence. Every intelligent person present could see that the prisoner's chance of an honourable acquittal depended on tracing the poison to the possession of his wife—or at least on proving her expressed intention to obtain it. In either of these cases, the prisoner's Declaration of his innocence would claim the support of testimony, which—however indirect it might be—no honest and intelligent men would be likely to resist. Was that testimony forthcoming? Was the counsel for the defence not at the end of his resources yet?

The crowded audience waited, in breathless expectation, for the appearance of the next witness. A whisper went round, among certain well-instructed persons, that the Court was now to see and hear the prisoner's old friend—already often referred to in the course of the Trial, as 'Mr Dexter.'

After a brief interval of delay, there was a sudden commotion among the audience, accompanied by suppressed exclamations of curiosity and surprise. At the same moment the crier summoned the new witness by the extraordinary name of—

'MISERRIMUS DEXTER.'

CHAPTER XX

The End of the Trial

THE calling of the witness produced a burst of laughter from the public seats—due partly, no doubt, to the strange name by which he had been summoned; partly, also, to the instinctive desire of all crowded assemblies, when their interest is painfully excited, to seize on any relief in the shape of the first excuse for merriment which may present itself. A severe rebuke from the Bench restored order among the audience. The Lord Justice Clerk declared that he would 'clear the Court' if the interruption to the proceedings was renewed.

During the silence which followed this announcement, the new witness appeared.

Gliding, self-propelled in his chair on wheels, through the opening made for him among the crowd, a strange and startling creature—literally the half of a man—revealed himself to the general view. A coverlid, which had been thrown over his chair, had fallen off during his progress through the throng. The loss of it exposed to the public curiosity the head, the arms, and the trunk of a living human being: absolutely deprived of the lower limbs. To make this deformity all the more striking and all the more terrible, the victim of it was—as to his face and his body— an unusually handsome, and an unusually well-made man. His long silky hair, of a bright and beautiful chestnut colour, fell over shoulders that were the perfection of strength and grace. His face was bright with vivacity and intelligence. His large, clear blue eyes, and his long, delicate white hands, were like the eyes and hands of a beautiful woman. He would have looked effeminate, but for the manly proportions of his throat and chest: aided in their effect by his flowing beard and long moustache, of a lighter chestnut shade than the colour of his hair. Never had a magnificent head and body been more hopelessly ill-bestowed than in this instance! Never had Nature committed a more careless or a more cruel mistake than in the making of this man!

He was sworn, seated, of course, in his chair. Having given his name, he bowed to the Judges, and requested their permission to preface his evidence with a word of explanation.

'People generally laugh when they first hear my strange Christian name,' he said, in a low, clear, resonant voice, which penetrated to the remotest corners of the Court. 'I may inform the good people here that many names, still common among us, have their significations, and that mine is one of them. "Alexander," for instance, means, in the Greek, "a helper of men." "David" means, in Hebrew, "well-beloved." "Francis" means, in German, "free." My name, "Miserrimus," means, in Latin, "most unhappy."* It was given to me by my father, in allusion to the deformity which you all see—the deformity with which it was my misfortune to be born. You won't laugh at "Miserrimus" again, will you?' He turned to the Dean of Faculty, waiting to examine him for the defence. 'Mr Dean, I am at your service. I apologize for delaying, even for a moment, the proceedings of the Court.'

He delivered his little address with perfect grace and good humour. Examined by the Dean, he gave his evidence clearly, without the slightest appearance of hesitation or reserve.

'I was staying at Gleninch, as a guest in the house, at the time of Mrs Eustace Macallan's death,' he began. 'Doctor Jerome and Mr Gale desired to see me, at a private interview—the prisoner being then in a state of prostration which made it impossible for him to attend to his duties as master of the house. At this interview, the two doctors astonished and horrified me, by declaring that Mrs Eustace Macallan had died poisoned. They left it to me to communicate the dreadful news to her husband; and they warned me that a post-mortem examination must be held on the body.

'If the Fiscal had seen my old friend, when I communicated the doctors' message, I doubt if he would have ventured to charge the prisoner with the murder of his wife. To my mind the charge was nothing less than an outrage. I resisted the seizure of the prisoner's Diary and letters, animated by that feeling. Now that the Diary has been produced, I agree with the prisoner's mother in denying that it is fair evidence to bring against him. A Diary (when it extends beyond a bare record of facts and dates) is, in general, nothing but an expression of the weakest side in the character of the person who keeps it. It is, in nine cases out of ten, the more or less contemptible outpouring of vanity and conceit which the writer dare not exhibit to any mortal but himself. I am the prisoner's oldest friend. I solemnly declare that I never knew he could write down-right nonsense until I heard his Diary read in this Court!

'*He* kill his wife! *He* treat his wife with neglect and cruelty! I venture to say, from twenty years' experience of him, that there is no man in this assembly who is, constitutionally, more incapable of crime, and more incapable of cruelty, than the man who stands at that Bar. While I am about it, I go further still. I even doubt whether a man capable of crime, and capable of cruelty, could have found it in his heart to do evil to the woman whose untimely death is the subject of this inquiry.

'I have heard what the ignorant and prejudiced nurse, Christina Ormsay, has said of the deceased lady. From my own personal observation I contradict every word of it. Mrs Eustace Macallan—granting her personal defects—was nevertheless one of the most charming women I ever met with. She was highly bred, in the best sense of the word. I never saw, in any other person, so sweet a smile as hers, or such grace and beauty of movement as hers. If you liked music, she sang beautifully; and few professed musicians had such a touch on the piano as hers. If you preferred talking, I never yet met with the man (or even the woman, which is saying a great deal more) whom her conversation could not charm. To say that such a wife as this could be first cruelly neglected, and then barbarously murdered, by the man—not by the martyr—who stands there, is to tell me that the sun never shines at noonday, or that the heaven is not above the earth.

'Oh, yes! I know that the letters of her friends show that she wrote to them in bitter complaint of her husband's conduct to her. But remember what one of those friends (the wisest and the best of them) says in reply. "I own to thinking," she writes, "that your sensitive nature exaggerates or misinterprets the neglect that you experience at the hands of your husband." There, in that one sentence, is the whole truth! Mrs Eustace Macallan's nature was the imaginative, self-tormenting nature of a poet. No mortal love could ever have been refined enough for *her*. Trifles, which women of a coarser moral fibre would have passed over without notice, were causes of downright agony to that exquisitely sensitive temperament. There are persons born to be unhappy. That poor lady was one of them. When I have said this, I have said all.

'No! There is one word more still to be added.

'It may be as well to remind the prosecution that Mrs Eustace Macallan's death was, in the pecuniary sense, a serious loss to her husband. He had insisted on having the whole of her fortune settled on herself, and on her relatives after her, when he married. Her income from that fortune helped to keep in splendour the house and grounds at Gleninch. The prisoner's own resources (aided even by his mother's jointure) were quite inadequate fitly to defray the expenses of living at his splendid country seat. Knowing all the circumstances, I can positively assert that the wife's death has deprived the husband of two-thirds of his income. And the prosecution, viewing him as the basest and cruellest of men, declares that he deliberately killed her—with all his pecuniary interests pointing to the preservation of her life!

'It is useless to ask me whether I noticed anything in the conduct of the prisoner and Mrs Beauly, which might justify a wife's jealousy. I never observed Mrs Beauly with any attention; and I never encouraged the prisoner in talking to me about her. He was a general admirer of pretty women—so far as I know, in a perfectly innocent way. That he could prefer Mrs Beauly to his wife, is inconceivable to me—unless he was out of his senses. I never had any reason to believe that he was out of his senses.

'As to the question of the arsenic—I mean the question of tracing the poison to the possession of Mrs Eustace Macallan—I am able to give evidence which may perhaps be worthy of the attention of the Court.

'I was present, in the Fiscal's office, during the examination of the papers, and of the other objects discovered at Gleninch. The dressing-case belonging to the deceased lady was shown to me, after its contents had been officially investigated by the Fiscal himself. I happen to have a very sensitive sense of touch. In handling the lid of the dressing-case, on the inner side, I felt something at a certain place, which induced me to examine the whole structure of the lid very carefully. The result was the discovery of a private repository, concealed in the space between the outer wood and the lining. In that repository I found the bottle which I now produce.'

The further examination of the witness was suspended, while the hidden bottle was compared with the bottles properly belonging to the dressing-case.

These last were of the finest cut glass, and of a very elegant form—entirely unlike the bottle found in the private repository, which was of the commonest manufacture, and of the shape ordinarily in use among chemists. Not a drop of liquid, not the smallest atom of any solid substance, remained in it. No smell exhaled from it—and, more unfortunately still for the interests of the defence, no label was found attached to the bottle when it had been discovered.

The chemist who had sold the second supply of arsenic to the prisoner was recalled, and examined. He declared that the bottle was exactly like the bottle in which he placed the arsenic. It was, however, equally like hundreds of other bottles in his shop. In the absence of the label (on which he had himself written the word 'Poison') it was impossible for him to identify the bottle. The dressing-case, and the deceased lady's bed-room, had been vainly searched for the chemist's missing label—on the chance that it might have become accidentally detached from the mysterious empty bottle. In both instances the search had been without result. Morally, it was a fair conclusion that this might be really the bottle which had contained the poison. Legally, there was not the slightest proof of it.

Thus ended the last effort of the defence to trace the
arsenic purchased by the prisoner to the possession of his
wife. The book relating the practices of the Styrian peasantry (found in the deceased lady's room) had been produced. But could the book prove that she had asked her
husband to buy arsenic for her? The crumpled paper, with
the grains of powder left in it, had been identified by the
chemist, and had been declared to contain grains of arsenic.
But where was the proof that Mrs Eustace Macallan's hand
had placed the packet in the cabinet, and had emptied it of
its contents? No direct evidence anywhere! Nothing but
conjecture!

The renewed examination of Miserrimus Dexter touched
on matters of no general interest. The cross-examination
resolved itself, in substance, into a mental trial of strength
between the witness and the Lord Advocate; the struggle
terminating (according to the general opinion) in favour of
the witness. One question, and one answer only, I will
repeat here. They appeared to me of serious importance to
the object that I had in view in reading the Trial.

'I believe, Mr Dexter,' the Lord Advocate remarked, in
his most ironical manner, 'that you have a theory of your
own, which makes the death of Mrs Eustace Macallan no
mystery to *you?*'

'I may have my own ideas on that subject, as on other
subjects,' the witness replied. 'But let me ask their lordships, the Judges—Am I here to declare theories, or to state
facts?'

I made a note of that answer. Mr Dexter's 'ideas' were
the ideas of a true friend to my husband, and of a man of
far more than average ability. They might be of inestimable
value to me, in the coming time—if I could prevail on him
to communicate them.

I may mention, while I am writing on the subject, that I
added to this first note a second, containing an observation
of my own. In alluding to Mrs Beauly, while he was giving
his evidence, Mr Dexter had spoken of her so slightingly—

so rudely, I might almost say—as to suggest that he had some private reasons for disliking (perhaps for distrusting) this lady. Here, again, it might be of vital importance to me to see Mr Dexter, and to clear up, if I could, what the dignity of the Court had passed over without notice.

The last witness had been now examined. The chair on wheels glided away, with the half-man in it, and was lost in a distant corner of the Court. The Lord Advocate rose to address the Jury for the prosecution.

I do not scruple to say that I never read anything so infamous as this great lawyer's speech. He was not ashamed to declare, at starting, that he firmly believed the prisoner to be guilty. What right had he to say anything of the sort? Was it for *him* to decide? Was he the Judge and Jury both, I should like to know? Having begun by condemning the prisoner, on his own authority, the Lord Advocate proceeded to pervert the most innocent actions of that unhappy man, so as to give them as vile an aspect as possible. Thus: When Eustace kissed his poor wife's forehead, on her death-bed, he did it to create a favourable impression in the minds of the doctor and the nurse! Again, when his grief under his bereavement completely overwhelmed him, he was triumphing in secret, and acting a part! If you looked into his heart, you would see there a diabolical hatred for his wife, and an infatuated passion for Mrs Beauly! In everything he had said, he had lied; in everything he had done, he had acted like a crafty and heartless wretch! So the chief counsel for the prosecution spoke of the prisoner, standing helpless before him at the Bar. In my husband's place, if I could have done nothing more, I would have thrown something at his head. As it was, I tore the pages which contained the speech for the prosecution out of the Report, and trampled them under my feet—and felt all the better, too, for having done it. At the same time, I am a little ashamed of having revenged myself on the harmless printed leaves, now.

The fifth day of the Trial opened with the speech for the defence. Ah, what a contrast to the infamies uttered by the Lord Advocate was the grand burst of eloquence by the Dean of Faculty, speaking on my husband's side!

This illustrious lawyer struck the right note at starting.

'I yield to no one,' he began, 'in the pity I feel for the wife. But I say, the martyr in this case, from first to last, is the husband. Whatever the poor woman may have endured, that unhappy man at the Bar has suffered, and is now suffering, more. If he had not been the kindest of men, the most docile and most devoted of husbands, he would never have occupied his present dreadful situation. A man of a meaner and harder nature would have felt suspicion of his wife's motives, when she asked him to buy poison—would have seen through the wretchedly commonplace excuses she made for wanting it—and would have wisely and cruelly said, "No." The prisoner is not that sort of man. He is too good to his wife, too innocent of any evil thought towards her, or towards any one, to foresee the inconveniences and the dangers to which his fatal compliance may expose him. And what is the result? He stands there, branded as a murderer, because he was too high-minded and too honourable to suspect his wife.'

Speaking thus of the husband, the Dean was just as eloquent and just as unanswerable when he came to speak of the wife.

'The Lord Advocate,' he said, 'has asked, with the bitter irony for which he is celebrated at the Scottish Bar, why we have failed entirely to prove that the prisoner placed the two packets of poison in the possession of his wife? I say, in answer, we have proved, first, that the wife was passionately attached to the husband; secondly, that she felt bitterly the defects in her personal appearance, and especially the defects in her complexion; and, thirdly, that she was informed of arsenic as a supposed remedy for these defects, taken internally. To men who know anything of human nature, there is proof enough! Does my learned friend actually suppose, that women are in the habit of mentioning the secret artifices and applications by which they improve their personal appearance? Is it in his experience of the sex, that a woman who is eagerly bent on making herself attractive to a man, would tell that man, or tell anybody else who might communicate with him, that the charm by which she hoped to win his heart—say the charm of a pretty complexion—had been artificially acquired by the perilous use of a deadly poison? The bare idea of such a thing is absurd. Of course, nobody ever heard Mrs Eustace Macallan speak of arsenic. Of course, nobody ever surprised her in the act of taking arsenic. It is in the evidence, that she would not even confide her intention to try the poison to the friends who had told her of it as a remedy, and who had got her the book. She actually begged them to consider their brief conversation on the subject as strictly private. From first to last, poor creature, she kept her secret; just as she would have kept her secret, if she had worn false hair, or if she had been indebted to the dentist for her teeth. And there you see her husband, in peril of his life, because a woman acted *like* a woman—as your wives, Gentlemen of the Jury, would, in a similar position, act towards You.'

After such glorious oratory as this (I wish I had room to quote more of it!) the next, and last, speech delivered at the Trial—that is to say the Charge of the Judge to the Jury—is dreary reading indeed.

His lordship first told the Jury that they could not expect to have direct evidence of the poisoning. Such evidence hardly ever occurred in cases of poisoning. They must be satisfied with the best circumstantial evidence. All quite true, I dare say. But having told the Jury they might accept circumstantial evidence, he turned back again on his own words, and warned them against being too ready to trust it! 'You must have evidence satisfactory and convincing to your own minds,' he said; 'in which you find no conjectures—but only irresistible and just inferences.' Who is to decide what is a just inference? And what does circumstantial evidence rest on, *but* conjecture?

After this specimen, I need give no further extracts from the summing-up. The Jury, thoroughly bewildered no doubt, took refuge in a compromise. They occupied an hour in considering and debating among themselves, in their own room. (A jury of women would not have taken a minute!) Then they returned into Court, and gave their timid and trimming Scotch Verdict in these words:—

'Not Proven.'

Some slight applause followed, among the audience, which was instantly checked. The prisoner was dismissed from the Bar with the formalities observed on such occasions. He slowly retired, like a man in deep grief; his head sunk on his breast—not looking at any one, and not replying when his friends spoke to him. He knew, poor fellow, the slur that the Verdict left on him. 'We don't say you are innocent of the crime charged against you; we only say, there is not evidence enough to convict you.' In that lame and impotent conclusion the proceedings ended, at the time. And there they would have remained, for all time—but for Me.

CHAPTER XXI

I See my Way

IN the grey light of the new morning, I closed the Report of my husband's Trial for the murder of his first Wife.

No sense of fatigue overpowered me. I had no wish, after my long hours of reading and thinking, to lie down and sleep. It was strange, but it was so. I felt as if I *had* slept, and had now just awakened—a new woman, with a new mind.

I could almost understand Eustace's desertion of me. To a man of his refinement, it would have been a martyrdom to meet his wife, after she had read the things published of him to all the world, in the Report. I felt this, as he would have felt it. At the same time, I thought he might have trusted Me to make amends to him for the martyrdom, and might have come back. Perhaps, it might yet end in his coming back. In the mean while, and in that expectation, I pitied and forgave him with my whole heart.

One little matter only dwelt on my mind disagreeably, in spite of my philosophy. Did Eustace still secretly love Mrs Beauly? or had I extinguished that passion in him? To what order of beauty did this lady belong? Were we, by any chance, the least in the world like one another?

The window of my room looked to the east. I drew up the blind, and saw the sun rising grandly in a clear sky. The temptation to go out and breathe the fresh morning air was irresistible. I put on my hat and shawl, and took the Report of the Trial under my arm. The bolts of the back door were easily drawn. In another minute, I was out in Benjamin's pretty little garden.

Composed and strengthened by the inviting solitude and the delicious air, I found courage enough to face the serious question that now confronted me—the question of the future.

I had read the Trial. I had vowed to devote my life to the sacred object of vindicating my husband's innocence. A solitary, defenceless woman, I stood pledged to myself to carry that desperate resolution through to an end. How was I to begin?

The bold way of beginning was surely the wise way, in such a position as mine. I had good reasons (founded, as I have already mentioned, on the important part played by this witness at the Trial) for believing that the fittest person to advise and assist me, was—Miserrimus Dexter. He might disappoint the expectations that I had fixed on him, or he might refuse to help me, or (like my uncle Starkweather) he might think I had taken leave of my senses. All these events were possible. Nevertheless, I held to my resolution to try the experiment. If he was in the land of the living, I decided that my first step at starting should take me to the deformed man, with the strange name.

Supposing he received me, sympathized with me, understood me? What would he say? The nurse, in her evidence, had reported him as speaking in an off-hand manner. He would say, in all probability, 'What do you mean to do? And how can I help you to do it?'

Had I answers ready, if those two plain questions were put to me? Yes! if I dared own to any human creature what was, at that very moment, secretly fermenting in my mind. Yes! if I could confide to a stranger a suspicion roused in me by the Trial, which I have been thus far afraid to mention even in these pages!

It must, nevertheless, be mentioned now. My suspicion led to results, which are part of my story, and part of my life.

Let me own then, to begin with, that I closed the record of the Trial actually agreeing, in one important particular, with the opinion of my enemy and my husband's enemy— the Lord Advocate! He had characterized the explanation of Mrs Eustace Macallan's death, offered by the defence, as 'a clumsy subterfuge, in which no reasonable being could discern the smallest fragment of probability.' Without going quite so far as this, I, too, could see no reason whatever in the evidence for assuming that the poor woman had taken an over-dose of the poison, by mistake. I believed that she had the arsenic secretly in her possession, and that she had tried, or intended to try, the use of it internally, for the purpose of improving her complexion. But further than this I could not advance. The more I thought of it, the more plainly justified the lawyers for the prosecution seemed to me to be, in declaring that Mrs Eustace Macallan had died by the hand of a poisoner—although they were entirely and certainly mistaken in charging my husband with the crime.

My husband being innocent, somebody else, on my own showing, must be guilty. Who, among the persons inhabiting the house at the time, had poisoned Mrs Eustace Macallan? My suspicion, in answering that question, pointed straight to a woman. And the name of that woman was—Mrs Beauly!

Yes! To that startling conclusion I had arrived. It was, to my mind, the inevitable result of reading the evidence.

Look back for a moment to the letter produced in Court, signed 'Helena,' and addressed to Mr Macallan. No reasonable person can doubt (though the Judges excused her from answering the question) that Mrs Beauly was the writer. Very well. The letter offers, as I think, trustworthy evidence to show the state of the woman's mind when she paid her visit to Gleninch.

Writing to Mr Macallan, at a time when she was married to another man—a man to whom she had engaged herself before she met with Mr Macallan—what does she say! She says, 'When I think of your life sacrificed to that wretched woman, my heart bleeds for you.' And, again, she says, 'If it had been my unutterable happiness to love and cherish the best, the dearest of men, what a paradise of our own we might have lived in, what delicious hours we might have known!'

If this is not the language of a woman shamelessly and furiously in love with a man—not her husband—what is? She is so full of him, that even her idea of another world (see the letter) is the idea of 'embracing' Mr Macallan's 'soul.' In this condition of mind and morals, the lady one day finds herself and her embraces free, through the death of her husband. As soon as she can decently visit, she goes visiting; and, in due course of time, she becomes the guest of the man whom she adores. His wife is ill in her bed. The one other visitor at Gleninch is a cripple, who can only move in his chair on wheels. The lady has the house and the one beloved object in it, all to herself. No obstacle stands between her and 'the unutterable happiness of loving and cherishing the best, the dearest of men'—but a poor sick ugly wife, for whom Mr Macallan never has felt, and never can feel, the smallest particle of love.

Is it perfectly absurd to believe that such a woman as this, impelled by these motives, and surrounded by these circumstances, would be capable of committing a crime—if the safe opportunity offered itself?

What does her own evidence say?

She admits that she had a conversation with Mrs Eustace Macallan, in which that lady 'questioned her on the subject of cosmetic applications to the complexion.' Did nothing else take place at that interview? Did Mrs Beauly make no discoveries (afterwards turned to fatal account) of the dangerous experiment which her hostess was then trying, to improve her ugly complexion? All we know is, that Mrs Beauly said nothing about it.

What does the under-gardener say?

He heard a conversation between Mr Macallan and Mrs Beauly, which shows that the possibility of Mrs Beauly becoming Mrs Eustace Macallan had certainly presented itself to that lady's mind, and was certainly considered by her to be too dangerous a topic of discourse to be pursued. Innocent Mr Macallan would have gone on talking. Mrs Beauly is discreet, and stops him.

And what does the nurse (Christina Ormsay) tell us?

On the day of Mrs Eustace Macallan's death, the nurse is dismissed from attendance, and is sent downstairs. She leaves the sick woman, recovered from her first attack of illness, and able to amuse herself with writing. The nurse remains away for half an hour, and then gets uneasy at not hearing the invalid's bell. She goes to the Morning Room to consult Mr Macallan; and there she hears that Mrs Beauly is missing. Mr Macallan doesn't know where she is, and asks Mr Dexter if he has seen her. Mr Dexter has not set eyes on her. At what time does the disappearance of Mrs Beauly take place? At the very time when Christina Ormsay had left Mrs Eustace Macallan alone in her room!

Meanwhile, the bell rings at last, rings violently. The nurse goes back to the sick room at five minutes to eleven, or thereabouts, and finds that the bad symptoms of the morning have returned in a gravely aggravated form. A second dose of poison—larger than the dose administered in the early morning—has been given, during the absence of the nurse, and (observe) during the disappearance also of Mrs Beauly. The nurse, looking out into the corridor for help, encounters Mrs Beauly herself, innocently on her way from her own room—just up, we are to suppose, at eleven in the morning!—to inquire after the sick woman.

A little later, Mrs Beauly accompanies Mr Macallan to visit the invalid. The dying woman casts a strange look at both of them, and tells them to leave her. Mr Macallan understands this as the fretful outbreak of a person in pain, and waits in the room to tell the nurse that the doctor is sent for. What does Mrs Beauly do? She runs out panic-stricken, the instant Mrs Eustace Macallan looks at her. Even Mrs Beauly, it seems, has a conscience!

Is there nothing to justify suspicion in such circumstances as these—circumstances sworn to, on the oaths of the witnesses?

To me, the conclusion is plain. Mrs Beauly's hand gave that second dose of poison. Admit this; and the inference follows that she also gave the first dose in the early morning. How could she do it? Look again at the evidence. The nurse admits that she was asleep, from past two in the morning to six. She also speaks of a locked door of communication with the sick room, the key of which had been removed, nobody knew by whom. Some person must have stolen that key. Why not Mrs Beauly?

One word more, and all that I had in my mind at that time will be honestly revealed.

Miserrimus Dexter, under cross-examination, had indirectly admitted that he had ideas of his own on the subject of Mrs Eustace Macallan's death. At the same time, he had spoken of Mrs Beauly in a tone which plainly betrayed that he was no friend to that lady. Did *he* suspect her, too? My chief motive in deciding to ask his advice, before I applied to any one else, was to find an opportunity of putting that question to him. If he really thought of her as I did, my course was clear before me. The next step to take would be carefully to conceal my identity—and then to present myself, in the character of a harmless stranger, to Mrs Beauly.

There were difficulties, of course, in my way. The first and greatest difficulty was to obtain an introduction to Miserrimus Dexter.

The composing influence of the fresh air in the garden had, by this time, made me readier to lie down and rest than to occupy my mind in reflecting on my difficulties. Little by little, I grew too drowsy to think—then too lazy to go on walking. My bed looked wonderfully inviting, as I passed by the open window of my room.

In five minutes more I had accepted the invitation of the bed, and had said farewell to my anxieties and my troubles. In five minutes more I was fast asleep.

A discreetly gentle knock at my door was the first sound that roused me. I heard the voice of my good old Benjamin speaking outside.

'My dear! I am afraid you will be starved if I let you sleep any longer. It is half-past one o'clock; and a friend of yours has come to lunch with us.'

A friend of mine? What friends had I? My husband was far away; and my Uncle Starkweather had given me up in despair.

'Who is it?' I cried out from my bed, through the door.

'Major Fitz-David,' Benjamin answered—by the same medium.

I sprang out of bed. The very man I wanted was waiting to see me! Major Fitz-David, as the phrase is, knew everybody. Intimate with my husband, he would certainly know my husband's old friend—Miserrimus Dexter.

Shall I confess that I took particular pains with my toilet, and that I kept the luncheon waiting? The woman doesn't live who would have done otherwise—when she had a particular favour to ask of Major Fitz-David.

CHAPTER XXII

The Major makes Difficulties

As I opened the dining-room door, the Major hastened to meet me. He looked the brightest and the youngest of living elderly gentlemen—with his smart blue frock-coat, his winning smile, his ruby ring, and his ready compliment. It was quite cheering to meet the modern Don Juan once more.

'I don't ask after your health,' said the old gentleman; 'your eyes answer me, my dear lady, before I can put the question. At your age a long sleep is the true beauty-draught. Plenty of bed—there is the simple secret of keeping your good looks and living a long life—plenty of bed!'

'I have not been so long in my bed, Major, as you suppose. To tell the truth, I have been up all night, reading.'

Major Fitz-David lifted his well-painted eyebrows, in polite surprise.

'What is the happy book which has interested you so deeply?' he asked.

'The book,' I answered, 'is the Trial of my husband for the murder of his first wife.'

The Major's smile vanished. He drew back a step, with a look of dismay.

'Don't mention that horrid book!' he exclaimed. 'Don't speak of that dreadful subject! What have beauty and grace to do with Trials, Poisonings, Horrors? Why, my charming friend, profane your lips by talking of such things? Why frighten away the Loves and the Graces that lie hid in your smile? Humour an old fellow who adores the Loves and the Graces and who asks nothing better than to sun himself in your smile. Luncheon is ready. Let us be cheerful. Let us laugh, and lunch.'

He led me to the table and filled my plate and my glass, with the air of a man who considered himself to be engaged in one of the most important occupations of his life. Benjamin kept the conversation going on in the interval.

'Major Fitz-David brings you some news, my dear,' he said. 'Your mother-in-law, Mrs Macallan, is coming here to see you to-day.'

My mother-in-law coming to see me! I turned eagerly to the Major for further information.

'Has Mrs Macallan heard anything of my husband?' I asked. 'Is she coming here to tell me about him?'

'She has heard from him, I believe,' said the Major; 'and she has also heard from your uncle, the Vicar. Our excellent Starkweather has written to her—to what purpose I have not been informed. I only know that on receipt of his letter, she has decided on paying you a visit. I met the old lady last night at a party; and I tried hard to discover whether she was coming to you as your friend or your enemy. My powers of persuasion were completely thrown away on her. The fact is,' said the Major, speaking in the character of a youth of five-and-twenty, making a modest confession, 'I don't get on well with old women. Take the will for the deed, my sweet friend. I have tried to be of some use to you—and I have failed.'

Those words offered me the opportunity for which I was waiting. I determined not to lose it.

'You can be of the greatest use to me,' I said, 'if you will allow me to presume, Major, on your past kindness. I want to ask you a question; and I may have a favour to beg when you have answered me.'

Major Fitz-David set down his wine-glass on its way to his lips, and looked at me with an appearance of breathless interest.

'Command me, my dear lady—I am yours and yours only,' said the gallant old gentleman. 'What do you wish to ask me?'

'I wish to ask you if you know Miserrimus Dexter?'

'Good Heavens!' cried the Major; 'that *is* an unexpected question! Know Miserrimus Dexter? I have known him for more years than I like to reckon up. What *can* be your object——?'

'I can tell you what my object is in two words,' I interposed. 'I want you to give me an introduction to Miserrimus Dexter.'

My impression is that the Major turned pale under his paint. This, at any rate, is certain; his sparkling little grey eyes looked at me in undisguised bewilderment and alarm.

'You want to know Miserrimus Dexter?' he repeated, with the air of a man who doubted the evidence of his own senses. 'Mr Benjamin! have I taken too much of your excellent wine? Am I the victim of a delusion—or did our fair friend really ask me to give her an introduction to Miserrimus Dexter?'

Benjamin looked at me in some bewilderment on his side, and answered quite seriously—

'I think you said so, my dear.'

'I certainly said so,' I rejoined. 'What is there so very surprising in my request?'

'The man is mad!' cried the Major. 'In all England you could not have picked out a person more essentially unfit to be introduced to a lady—to a young lady especially—than Dexter. Have you heard of his horrible deformity?'

'I have heard of it—and it doesn't daunt me.'

'Doesn't daunt you! My dear lady, the man's mind is as deformed as his body. What Voltaire said satirically of the character of his countrymen in general, is literally true of Miserrimus Dexter. He is a mixture of the tiger and the monkey. At one moment, he would frighten you; and at the next, he would set you screaming with laughter. I don't deny that he is clever in some respects—brilliantly clever, I admit. And I don't say that he has ever committed any acts of violence, or ever willingly injured anybody. But, for all that, he is mad, if ever a man was mad yet. Forgive me if the inquiry is impertinent. What can your motive possibly be for wanting an introduction to Miserrimus Dexter?'

'I want to consult him.'

'May I ask on what subject?'

'On the subject of my husband's Trial.'

Major Fitz-David groaned, and sought a momentary consolation in his friend Benjamin's claret.

'That dreadful subject again!' he exclaimed. 'Mr Benjamin, why does she persist in dwelling on that dreadful subject?'

'I must dwell on what is now the one employment and the one hope of my life,' I said. 'I have reason to think that Miserrimus Dexter can help me to clear my husband's character of the stain which the Scotch Verdict has left on it. Tiger and monkey as he may be, I am ready to run the risk of being introduced to him. And I ask you again—rashly and obstinately as I fear you will think—to give me the introduction. It will put you to no inconvenience. I won't trouble you to escort me; a letter to Mr Dexter would do.'

The Major looked piteously at Benjamin, and shook his head. Benjamin looked piteously at the Major, and shook *his* head.

'She appears to insist on it,' said the Major.

'Yes,' said Benjamin. 'She appears to insist on it.'

'I won't take the responsibility, Mr Benjamin, of sending her alone to Miserrimus Dexter.'

'Shall I go with her, sir?'

The Major reflected. Benjamin, in the capacity of protector, did not appear to inspire our military friend with confidence. After a moment's consideration, a new idea seemed to strike him. He turned to me.

'My charming friend,' he said, 'be more charming than ever—consent to a compromise. Let us treat this difficulty about Dexter from a social point of view. What do you say to a little dinner?'

'A little dinner?' I repeated, not in the least understanding him.

'A little dinner,' the Major reiterated. 'At my house. You insist on my introducing you to Dexter; and I refuse to trust you alone with that crack-brained personage. The only alternative under the circumstances is to invite him to meet you, and to let you form your own opinion of him—under the protection of my roof. Who shall we have to meet you, besides?' pursued the Major, brightening with hospitable intentions. 'We want a perfect galaxy of beauty round the table, as a species of compensation, when we have got Miserrimus Dexter for one of the guests. Madame Mirliflore is still in London. You would be sure to like her—she is charming; she possesses your firmness, your extraordinary tenacity of purpose. Yes, we will have Madame Mirliflore. Who else? Shall we say Lady Clarinda? Another charming person, Mr Benjamin! You would be sure to admire her—she is so sympathetic, she resembles is so many respects our fair friend here. Yes, Lady Clarinda shall be one of us; and you shall sit next to her, Mr Benjamin, as a proof of my sincere regard for you. Shall we have my young prima donna to sing to us in the evening? I think so. She is pretty; she will assist in obscuring the deformity of Dexter. Very well; there is our party complete; I will shut myself up this evening, and approach the question of dinner with my cook. Shall we say this day week,' asked the Major, taking out his pocket-book—'at eight o'clock?'

I consented to the proposed compromise—but not very willingly. With a letter of introduction, I might have seen Miserrimus Dexter that afternoon. As it was, the 'little dinner' compelled me to wait in absolute inaction, through a whole week. However, there was no help for it but to submit. Major Fitz-David, in his polite way, could be as obstinate as I was. He had evidently made up his mind; and further opposition on my part would be of no service to me.

'Punctually at eight, Mr Benjamin,' reiterated the Major. 'Put it down in your book.'

Benjamin obeyed—with a side look at me, which I was at no loss to interpret. My good old friend did not relish meeting a man at dinner, who was described as 'half tiger, half monkey;' and the privilege of sitting next to Lady Clarinda rather daunted than delighted him. It was all my doing, and he, too, had no choice but to submit. 'Punctually at eight, sir,' said poor old Benjamin, obediently recording his formal engagement. 'Please to take another glass of wine.'

The Major looked at his watch, and rose—with fluent apologies for abruptly leaving the table.

'It is later than I thought,' he said. 'I have an appointment with a friend—a female friend; a most attractive person. You a little remind me of her, my dear lady—you resemble her in complexion; the same creamy paleness. I adore creamy paleness. As I was saying, I have an appointment with my friend; she does me the honour to ask my opinion on some very remarkable specimens of old lace. I have studied old lace. I study everything that can make me useful or agreeable to your enchanting sex. You won't forget our little dinner? I will send Dexter his invitation the moment I get home.' He took my hand, and looked at it critically, with his head a little on one side. 'A delicious hand,' he said; 'you don't mind my looking at it, you don't mind my kissing it—do you? A delicious hand is one of my weaknesses. Forgive my weaknesses. I promise to repent and amend, one of these days.'

'At your age, Major, do you think you have much time to lose?' asked a strange voice, speaking behind us.

We all three looked round towards the door. There stood my husband's mother, smiling satirically—with Benjamin's shy little maid-servant waiting to announce her.

Major Fitz-David was ready with his answer. The old soldier was not easily taken by surprise.

'Age, my dear Mrs Macallan, is a purely relative expression,' he said. 'There are some people who are never young; and there are other people who are never old. I am one of the other people. *Au revoir!*'

With that answer, the incorrigible Major kissed the tips of his fingers to us, and walked out. Benjamin, bowing with his old-fashioned courtesy, threw open the door of his little library, and, inviting Mrs Macallan and myself to pass in, left us together in the room.

CHAPTER XXIII

My Mother-in-Law Surprises me

I TOOK a chair at a respectful distance from the sofa on which Mrs Macallan seated herself. The old lady smiled, and beckoned to me to take my place by her side. Judging by appearances, she had certainly not come to see me in the character of an enemy. It remained to be discovered whether she was really disposed to be my friend.

'I have received a letter from your uncle, the Vicar,' she began. 'He asks me to visit you; and I am happy—for reasons which you shall presently hear—to comply with his request. Under other circumstances, I doubt very much, my dear child—strange as the confession may appear—whether I should have ventured into your presence. My son has behaved to you so weakly, and (in my opinion) so inexcusably, that I am really, speaking as his mother, almost ashamed to face you.'

Was she in earnest? I listened to her, and looked at her, in amazement.

'Your uncle's letter,' pursued Mrs Macallan, 'tells me how you have behaved under your hard trial, and what you propose to do, now Eustace has left you. Dr Starkweather, poor man, seems inexpressibly shocked by what you said to him when he was in London. He begs me to use my influence to induce you to abandon your present ideas, and to make you return to your old home at the Vicarage. I don't in the least agree with your uncle, my dear! Wild as I believe your plans to be—you have not the slightest chance of succeeding in carrying them out—I admire your courage; your fidelity; your unshaken faith in my unhappy son, after his unpardonable behaviour to you. You are a fine creature, Valeria! And I have come here to tell you so in plain words. Give me a kiss, child. You deserve to be the wife of a hero—and you have married one of the weakest of living mortals. God forgive me for speaking so of my own son! But it's in my mind, and it must come out!'

This way of speaking of Eustace was more than I could suffer—even from his mother. I recovered the use of my tongue, in my husband's defence.

'I am sincerely proud of your good opinion, dear Mrs Macallan,' I said. 'But you distress me—forgive me if I own it plainly—when I hear you speak so disparagingly of Eustace. I cannot agree with you that my husband is the weakest of living mortals.'

'Of course not!' retorted the old lady. 'You are like a good woman—you make a hero of the man you love, whether he deserves it or not. Your husband has hosts of good qualities, child—and perhaps I know them better than you do. But his whole conduct, from the moment when he first entered your uncle's house to the present time, has been (I say again) the conduct of an essentially weak man. What do you think he has done now by way of climax? He has joined a charitable brotherhood; and he is off to the war in Spain with a red cross on his arm,* when he ought to be here on his knees asking his wife to forgive him. I say that is the conduct of a weak man. Some people might call it by a harder name.'

This news startled and distressed me. I might be resigned to his leaving me (for a time); but all my instincts as a woman revolted at his placing himself in a position of danger, during his separation from his wife. He had now deliberately added to my anxieties. I thought it cruel of him—but I would not confess what I thought to his mother. I affected to be as cool as she was; and I disputed her conclusions with all the firmness that I could summon to help me. The terrible old woman only went on abusing him more vehemently than ever.

'What I complain of in my son,' proceeded Mrs Macallan, 'is that he has entirely failed to understand you. If he had married a fool, his conduct would be intelligible enough. He would have done wisely to conceal from a fool that he had been married already, and that he had suffered the horrid public exposure of a Trial for the murder of his wife. Then, again, he would have been quite right, when this same fool had discovered the truth, to take himself off out of her way, before she could suspect him of poisoning her—for the sake of the peace and quiet of both parties. But you are not a fool. I can see that, after only a short experience of you. Why can't he see it, too? Why didn't he trust you with his secret from the first, instead of stealing his way into your affections under an assumed name? Why did he plan (as he confessed to me) to take you away to the Mediterranean, and to keep you abroad, for fear of some officious friends at home betraying him to you as the prisoner of the famous Trial? What is the plain answer to all these questions? What is the one possible explanation of this otherwise unaccountable conduct? There is only one answer, and one explanation. My poor wretched son—he takes after his father; he isn't the least like me!—is weak in his way of judging; weak in his way of acting; and, like all weak people, headstrong and unreasonable to the last degree. There is the truth! Don't get red and angry. I am as fond of him as you are. I can see his merits, too. And one of them is, that he has married a woman of spirit and resolution—so faithful, and so fond of him, that she won't even let his own mother tell her of his faults. Good child! I like you for hating me!'

'Dear madam, don't say that I hate you!' I exclaimed (feeling very much as if I did hate her, though, for all that!). 'I only presume to think that you are confusing a delicate-minded man with a weak-minded man. Our dear unhappy Eustace——'

'Is a delicate-minded man,' said the impenetrable Mrs Macallan, finishing my sentence for me. 'We will leave it there, my dear, and get on to another subject. I wonder whether we shall disagree about that, too?'

'What is the subject, madam?'

'I won't tell you, if you call me madam. Call me, mother. Say, "What is the subject, mother?" '

'What is the subject, mother?'

'Your notion of turning yourself into a Court of Appeal for a new Trial of Eustace, and forcing the world to pronounce a just verdict on him. Do you really mean to try it?'

'I do!'

Mrs Macallan considered for a moment grimly with herself.

'You know how heartily I admire your courage, and your devotion to my unfortunate son,' she said. 'You know, by this time, that *I* don't cant. But I cannot see you attempt to perform impossibilities; I cannot let you uselessly risk your reputation and your happiness, without warning you before it is too late. My child! the thing you have got it in your head to do, is not to be done by you or by anybody. Give it up.'

'I am deeply obliged to you, Mrs Macallan——'

'Mother!'

'I am deeply obliged to you, mother, for the interest that you take in me—but I cannot give it up. Right or wrong, risk or no risk, I must, and I will, try it!'

Mrs Macallan looked at me very attentively, and sighed as she looked.

'Oh, youth, youth!' she said to herself, sadly. 'What a grand thing it is to be young!' She controlled the rising regret, and turned on me suddenly, almost fiercely, with these words: 'What, in God's name, do you mean to do?'

At the instant when she put the question, the idea crossed my mind that Mrs Macallan could introduce me, if she pleased, to Miserrimus Dexter. She must know him, and know him well, as a guest at Gleninch and an old friend of her son.

'I mean to consult Miserrimus Dexter,' I answered, boldly.

Mrs Macallan started back from me, with a loud exclamation of surprise.

'Are you out of your senses?' she asked.

I told her, as I had told Major Fitz-David, that I had reason to think Mr Dexter's advice might be of real assistance to me at starting.

'And I,' rejoined Mrs Macallan, 'have reason to think that your whole project is a mad one, and that in asking Dexter's advice on it you appropriately consult a madman. You needn't start, child! There is no harm in the creature. I don't mean that he will attack you, or be rude to you. I only say that the last person whom a young woman, placed in your painful and delicate position, ought to associate herself with, is Miserrimus Dexter.'

Strange! Here was the Major's warning repeated by Mrs Macallan, almost in the Major's own words. Well! It shared the fate of most warnings. It only made me more and more eager to have my own way.

'You surprise me very much,' I said. 'Mr Dexter's evidence, given at the Trial, seems as clear and reasonable as evidence can be.'

'Of course it is!' answered Mrs Macallan. 'The shorthand writers and reporters put his evidence into presentable language, before they printed it. If you had heard what he really said, as I did, you would have been either very much disgusted with him, or very much amused by him, according to your way of looking at things. He began, fairly enough, with a modest explanation of his absurd Christian name, which at once checked the merriment of the audience. But as he went on, the mad side of him showed itself. He mixed up sense and nonsense in the strangest confusion: he was called to order over and over again; he was even threatened with fine and imprisonment for contempt of Court. In short, he was just like himself—a mixture of the strangest and the most opposite qualities; at one time, perfectly clear and reasonable, as you said just now; at another, breaking out into rhapsodies of the most outrageous kind, like a man in a state of delirium. A more entirely unfit person to advise anybody, I tell you again, never lived. You don't expect Me to introduce you to him, I hope?'

'I did think of such a thing,' I answered. 'But, after what you have said, dear Mrs Macallan, I give up the idea, of course. It is not a great sacrifice—it only obliges me to wait a week for Major Fitz-David's dinner party. He has promised to ask Miserrimus Dexter to meet me.'

'There is the Major all over!' cried the old lady. 'If you pin your faith on that man, I pity you. He is as slippery as an eel. I suppose you asked him to introduce you to Dexter?'

'Yes.'

'Exactly! Dexter despises him, my dear. He knows as well as I do that Dexter won't go to his dinner. And he takes that roundabout way of keeping you apart—instead of saying No to you plainly, like an honest man.'

This was bad news. But I was, as usual, too obstinate to own myself defeated.

'If the worst comes to the worst,' I said, 'I can but write to Mr Dexter, and beg him to grant me an interview.'

'And go to him by yourself if he does grant it?' inquired Mrs Macallan.

'Certainly. By myself.'

'You really mean it?'

'I do, indeed.'

'I won't allow you to go by yourself.'

'May I venture to ask, ma'am, how you propose to prevent me?'

'By going with you, to be sure, you obstinate hussy! Yes, yes—I can be as headstrong as you are, when I like. Mind! I don't want to know what your plans are. I don't want to be mixed up with your plans. My son is resigned to the Scotch Verdict. And I am resigned to the Scotch Verdict. It is you who won't let matters rest as they are. You are a vain and foolhardy young person. But, somehow, I have taken a liking to you; and I won't let you go to Miserrimus Dexter by yourself. Put on your bonnet!'

'Now?' I asked.

'Certainly! My carriage is at the door. And the sooner it's over, the better I shall be pleased. Get ready—and be quick about it!'

I required no second bidding. In ten minutes more, we were on our way to Miserrimus Dexter.

Such was the result of my mother-in-law's visit.

CHAPTER XXIV

Miserrimus Dexter—First View

WE had dawdled over our luncheon, before Mrs Macallan arrived at Benjamin's cottage. The ensuing conversation between the old lady and myself (of which I have only presented a brief abstract) lasted until quite late in the afternoon. The sun was setting in heavy clouds when we got into the carriage, and the dreary twilight began to fall round us while we were still on the road.

The direction in which we drove took us (as well as I could judge) towards the great northern suburb of London. For more than an hour the carriage threaded its way through a dingy brick labyrinth of streets, growing smaller and smaller, and dirtier and dirtier, the further we went. Emerging from the labyrinth, I noticed in the gathering darkness dismal patches of waste ground which seemed to be neither town nor country. Crossing these, we passed some forlorn outlying groups of houses with dim little scattered shops among them, looking like lost country villages wandering on the way to London; disfigured and smoke-dried already by their journey! Darker and darker, and drearier and drearier the prospect grew—until the carriage stopped at last, and Mrs Macallan announced, in her sharply-satirical way, that we had reached the end of our journey. 'Prince Dexter's Palace, my dear,' she said. 'What do you think of it?'

I looked round me—not knowing what to think of it, if the truth must be told.

We had got out of the carriage, and we were standing on a rough half-made gravel path. Right and left of me, in the dim light, I saw the half-completed foundations of new houses in their first stage of existence. Boards and bricks were scattered about us. At places, gaunt scaffolding-poles rose like the branchless trees of the brick-desert. Behind us, on the other side of the high road, stretched another plot of waste ground, as yet not built on. Over the surface of this second desert, the ghastly white figures of vagrant ducks gleamed at intervals in the mystic light. In front of us, at a distance of two hundred yards or so, as well as I could calculate, rose a black mass which gradually resolved itself, as my eyes became accustomed to the twilight, into a long, low, and ancient house, with a hedge of evergreens and a pitch-black paling in front of it. The footman led the way towards the paling, through the boards and the bricks, the oyster-shells and the broken crockery, that strewed the ground. And this was 'Prince Dexter's Palace!'

There was a gate in the pitch-black paling, and a bell-handle—discovered with great difficulty. Pulling at the handle, the footman set in motion, to judge by the sound produced, a bell of prodigious size, fitter for a church than a house.

While we were waiting for admission, Mrs Macallan pointed to the low dark line of the old building.

'There is one of his madnesses!' she said. 'The speculators in this new neighbourhood have offered him, I don't know how many thousand pounds for the ground that house stands on. It was originally the manor-house of the district. Dexter purchased it, many years since, in one of his freaks of fancy. He has no old family associations with the place; the walls are all but tumbling about his ears; and the money offered would really be of use to him. But, no! He refused the proposal of the enterprising speculators, by letter, in these words: "My house is a standing monument of the picturesque and beautiful, amid the mean, dishonest, and grovelling constructions of a mean, dishonest, and grovelling age. I keep my house, gentlemen, as a useful lesson to you. Look at it, while you are building round me—and blush, if you can, for your own work." Was there ever such an absurd letter written yet? Hush! I hear footsteps in the garden. Here comes his cousin. His cousin is a woman. I may as well tell you that, or you might mistake her for a man, in the dark.'

A rough, deep voice, which I should certainly never have supposed to be the voice of a woman, hailed us from the inner side of the paling.

'Who's there?'

'Mrs Macallan,' answered my mother-in-law.

'What do you want?'

'We want to see Dexter.'

'You can't see him.'

'Why not?'

'What did you say your name was?'

'Macallan. Mrs Macallan. Eustace Macallan's mother. *Now* do you understand?'

The voice muttered and grunted behind the paling, and a key turned in the lock of the gate.

Admitted to the garden, in the deep shadow of the shrubs, I could see nothing distinctly of the woman with the rough voice, except that she wore a man's hat. Closing the gate behind us, without a word of welcome or explanation, she led the way to the house. Mrs Macallan followed her easily, knowing the place; and I walked in Mrs Macallan's footsteps as closely as I could. 'This is a nice family,' my mother-in-law whispered to me. 'Dexter's cousin is the only woman in the house, and Dexter's cousin is an idiot.'

We entered a spacious hall, with a low ceiling—dimly lit at its further end by one small oil lamp. I could see that there were pictures on the grim brown walls—but the subjects represented were invisible in the obscure and shadowy light.

Mrs Macallan addressed herself to the speechless cousin with the man's hat.

'Now tell me,' she said. 'Why can't we see Dexter?'

The cousin took a sheet of paper off the hall table, and handed it to Mrs Macallan.

'The Master's writing!' said this strange creature, in a hoarse whisper, as if the bare idea of 'the Master' terrified her. 'Read it. And stay, or go, which you please.'

She opened an invisible side-door in the wall, masked by one of the pictures—disappeared through it like a ghost— and left us together alone in the hall.

Mrs Macallan approached the oil lamp, and looked by its light at the sheet of paper which the woman had given to her. I followed, and peeped over her shoulder, without ceremony. The paper exhibited written characters, traced in a wonderfully large and firm handwriting. Had I caught the infection of madness in the air of the house? Or did I really see before me these words?

'NOTICE.—My immense imagination is at work. Visions of heroes unroll themselves before me. I re-animate in myself the spirits of the departed great. My brains are boiling in my head. Any persons who disturb me, under existing circumstances, will do it at the peril of their lives.— DEXTER.'

Mrs Macallan looked round at me quietly with her sardonic smile.

'Do you still persist in wanting to be introduced to him?' she asked.

The mockery in the tone of the question roused my pride. I determined that I would not be the first to give way.

'Not if I am putting you in peril of your life, ma'am,' I answered, pertly enough, pointing to the paper in her hand.

My mother-in-law returned to the hall-table, and put the paper back on it, without condescending to reply. She then led the way to an arched recess on our right hand, beyond which I dimly discerned a broad flight of oaken stairs.

'Follow me,' said Mrs Macallan, mounting the stairs in the dark. 'I know where to find him.'

We groped our way up the stairs to the first landing. The next flight of steps, turning in the reverse direction, was faintly illuminated, like the hall below, by one oil lamp, placed in some invisible position above us. Ascending the second flight of stairs, and crossing a short corridor, we discovered the lamp, through the open door of a quaintly-shaped circular room, burning on the mantelpiece. Its light illuminated a strip of thick tapestry, hanging loose from the ceiling to the floor, on the wall opposite to the door by which we had entered.

Mrs Macallan drew aside the strip of tapestry, and, signing to me to follow her, passed behind it.

'Listen!' she whispered.

Standing on the inner side of the tapestry, I found myself in a dark recess or passage, at the end of which a ray of light from the lamp showed me a closed door. I listened, and heard, on the other side of the door, a shouting voice, accompanied by an extraordinary rumbling and whistling sound travelling backwards and forwards, as well as I could judge, over a great space. Now the rumbling and the whistling would reach their climax of loudness, and would overcome the resonant notes of the shouting voice. Then, again, those louder sounds gradually retreated into distance, and the shouting voice made itself heard as the more audible sound of the two. The door must have been of prodigious solidity. Listen as intently as I might, I failed to catch the articulate words (if any) which the voice was pronouncing, and I was equally at a loss to penetrate the cause which produced the rumbling and whistling sounds.

'What can possibly be going on,' I whispered to Mrs Macallan, 'on the other side of that door?'

'Step softly,' my mother-in-law answered, 'and come and see.'

She arranged the tapestry behind us, so as completely to shut out the light in the circular room. Then noiselessly turning the handle, she opened the heavy door.

We kept ourselves concealed in the shadow of the recess, and looked through the open doorway.

I saw (or fancied I saw, in the obscurity,) a long room, with a low ceiling. The dying gleam of an ill-kept fire formed the only light by which I could judge of objects and distances. Redly illuminating the central portion of the room, opposite to which we were standing, the firelight left the extremities shadowed in almost total darkness. I had barely time to notice this, before I heard the rumbling and whistling sounds approaching me. A high chair on wheels moved by, through the field of red light, carrying a shadowy figure with floating hair, and arms furiously raised and lowered, working the machinery that propelled the chair at its utmost rate of speed. 'I am Napoleon, at the sunrise of Austerlitz!'* shouted the man in the chair as he swept past me, on his rumbling and whistling wheels, in the red glow of the firelight. 'I give the word; and thrones rock, and kings fall, and nations tremble, and men by tens of thousands fight and bleed and die!' The chair rushed out of sight, and the shouting man in it became another hero. 'I am Nelson!' the ringing voice cried now. 'I am leading the fleet at Trafalgar. I issue my commands, prophetically conscious of victory and death. I see my own apotheosis—my public funeral, my nation's tears, my burial in the glorious church. The ages remember me, and the poets sing my praise in immortal verse!' The strident wheels turned at the far end of the room, and came back. The fantastic and frightful apparition, man and machinery blended in one—the new Centaur,* half man, half chair—flew by me again in the dying light. 'I am Shakspere!' cried the frantic creature, now. 'I am writing "Lear," the tragedy of tragedies. Ancients and moderns, I am the poet who towers over them all. Light! light! the lines flow out like lava from the eruption of my volcanic mind. Light! light! for the poet of all

time to write the words that live for ever!' He ground
and tore his way back towards the middle of the room.
As he approached the fireplace, a last morsel of unburnt
coal (or wood) burst into momentary flame, and showed
the open doorway. In that moment he saw us! The wheel-
chair stopped with a shock that shook the crazy old
floor of the room, altered its course, and flew at us with
the rush of a wild animal. We drew back, just in time to
escape it, against the wall of the recess. The chair passed
on, and burst aside the hanging tapestry. The light of the
lamp in the circular room poured in through the gap. The
creature in the chair checked his furious wheels, and looked
back over his shoulder with an impish curiosity horrible to
see.

'Have I run over them? Have I ground them to powder
for presuming to intrude on me?' he said to himself. As the
expression of this amiable doubt passed his lips, his eyes
lighted on us. His mind instantly veered back again to
Shakspere and 'King Lear.' 'Goneril and Regan!' he cried.
'My two unnatural daughters, my she-devil children, come
to mock at me!'

'Nothing of the sort,' said my mother-in-law, as quietly
as if she was addressing a perfectly reasonable being. 'I am
your old friend, Mrs Macallan; and I have brought Eustace
Macallan's second wife to see you.'

The instant she pronounced those last words, 'Eustace
Macallan's second wife,' the man in the chair sprang out of it
with a shrill cry of horror, as if she had shot him. For one
moment we saw a head and body in the air, absolutely
deprived of the lower limbs. The moment after, the terrible creature touched the floor as lightly as a monkey, on his
hands. The grotesque horror of the scene culminated in his
hopping away, on his hands, at a prodigious speed, until he
reached the fireplace in the long room. There he crouched
over the dying embers, shuddering and shivering, and mut-
tering, 'Oh, pity me, pity me!' dozens and dozens of times
over to himself.

This was the man whose advice I had come to ask—whose assistance I had confidently counted on, in my hour of need!

CHAPTER XXV

Miserrimus Dexter—Second View

THOROUGHLY disheartened and disgusted, and (if I must honestly confess it) thoroughly frightened too, I whispered to Mrs Macallan, 'I was wrong, and you were right. Let us go.'

The ears of Miserrimus Dexter must have been as sensitive as the ears of a dog. He heard me say, 'Let us go.'

'No!' he answered. 'Bring Eustace Macallan's second wife in here. I am a gentleman—I must apologize to her. I am a student of human character—I wish to see her.'

The whole man appeared to have undergone a complete transformation. He spoke in the gentlest of voices—and he sighed hysterically when he had done, like a woman recovering from a burst of tears. Was it reviving courage or reviving curiosity? When Mrs Macallan said to me, 'The fit is over now; do you still wish to go away?' I answered, 'No; I am ready to go in.'

'Have you recovered your belief in him, already?' asked my mother-in-law, in her mercilessly satirical way.

'I have recovered from my terror of him,' I replied.

'I am sorry I terrified you,' said the soft voice at the fireplace. 'Some people think I am a little mad at times. You came, I suppose, at one of the times—if some people are right. I admit that I am a visionary. My imagination runs away with me, and I say and do strange things. On those occasions, anybody who reminds me of that horrible Trial, throws me back into the past, and causes me unutterable nervous suffering. I am a very tender-hearted man.

As the necessary consequence (in such a world as this), I am a miserable wretch. Accept my excuses. Come in, both of you. Come in, and pity me.'

A child would not have been frightened of him now. A child would have gone in, and pitied him.

The room was getting darker and darker. We could just see the crouching figure of Miserrimus Dexter at the expiring fire—and that was all.

'Are we to have no light?' asked Mrs Macallan. 'And is this lady to see you, when the light comes, out of your chair?'

He lifted something bright and metallic, hanging round his neck, and blew on it a series of shrill, trilling, birdlike notes. After an interval, he was answered by a similar series of notes, sounding faintly in some distant region of the house.

'Ariel is coming,' he said. 'Compose yourself, Mama Macallan, Ariel will make me presentable to a lady's eyes.'

He hopped away on his hands into the darkness at the end of the room. 'Wait a little,' said Mrs Macallan; 'and you will have another surprise—you will see the "delicate Ariel." '*

We heard heavy footsteps in the circular room.

'Ariel!' sighed Miserrimus Dexter out of the darkness, in his softest notes.

To my astonishment, the coarse masculine voice of the cousin in the man's hat—the Caliban's, rather than the Ariel's voice—answered, 'Here!'

'My chair, Ariel!'

The person thus strangely misnamed drew aside the tapestry, so as to let in more light—then entered the room, pushing the wheeled chair before her. She stooped, and lifted Miserrimus Dexter from the floor, like a child. Before she could put him into the chair, he sprang out of her arms with a little gleeful cry, and alighted on his seat, like a bird alighting on its perch!

'The lamp,' said Miserrimus Dexter. 'And the looking-glass. Pardon me,' he added, addressing us, 'for turning my back on you. You musn't see me until my hair is set to rights. Ariel! the brush, the comb, and the perfumes.'

Carrying the lamp in one hand, the looking-glass in the other, and the brush (with the comb stuck in it) between her teeth, Ariel the Second, otherwise Dexter's cousin, presented herself plainly before me for the first time. I could now see the girl's round, fleshy, inexpressive face, her rayless and colourless eyes, her coarse nose and heavy chin. A creature half alive; an imperfectly-developed animal in shapeless form, clad in a man's pilot jacket, and treading in a man's heavy laced boots: with nothing but an old red flannel petticoat, and a broken comb in her frowsy flaxen hair, to tell us that she was a woman—such was the inhospitable person who had received us in the darkness, when we first entered the house.

This wonderful valet, collecting her materials for dressing her still more wonderful master's hair, gave him the looking-glass (a hand-mirror), and addressed herself to her work.

She combed, she brushed, she oiled, she perfumed the flowing locks and the long silky beard of Miserrimus Dexter, with the strangest mixture of dulness and dexterity that I ever saw. Done in brute silence, with a lumpish look and a clumsy gait, the work was perfectly well done, nevertheless. The imp in the chair superintended the whole proceeding critically by means of his hand-mirror. He was too deeply interested in this occupation to speak, until some of the concluding touches to his beard brought the misnamed Ariel in front of him, and so turned her full face towards the part of the room in which Mrs Macallan and I were standing. Then he addressed us—taking special care, however, not to turn his head our way while his toilet was still incomplete.

'Mama Macallan,' he said, 'what is the Christian name of your son's second wife?'

'Why do you want to know?' asked my mother-in-law.

'I want to know, because I can't address her as "Mrs Eustace Macallan."'

'Why not?'

'It recalls *the other* Mrs Eustace Macallan. If I am reminded of those horrible days at Gleninch, my fortitude will give way—I shall burst out screaming again.'

Hearing this, I hastened to interpose.

'My name is Valeria,' I said.

'A Roman name,' remarked Miserrimus Dexter. 'I like it. My own name has a Roman ring in it. My bodily build would have been Roman, if I had been born with legs. I shall call you Mrs Valeria. Unless you disapprove of it?'

I hastened to say that I was far from disapproving of it.

'Very good,' said Miserrimus Dexter. 'Mrs Valeria, do you see the face of this creature in front of me?'

He pointed with the hand-mirror to his cousin, as unconcernedly as he might have pointed to a dog. His cousin, on her side, took no more notice than a dog would have taken of the contemptuous phrase by which he had designated her. She went on combing and oiling his beard as composedly as ever.

'It is the face of an idiot, isn't it?' pursued Miserrimus Dexter. 'Look at her! She is a mere vegetable. A cabbage in a garden has as much life and expression in it as that girl exhibits at the present moment. Would you believe there was latent intelligence, affection, pride, fidelity, in such a half-developed being as this?'

I was really ashamed to answer him. Quite needlessly! The impenetrable young woman went on with her master's beard. A machine could not have taken less notice of the life and the talk around it than this incomprehensible creature.

'*I* have got at that latent affection, pride, fidelity, and the rest of it,' resumed Miserrimus Dexter. '*I* hold the key to that dormant Intelligence. Grand thought! Now look at her, when I speak. (I named her, poor wretch, in one of my ironical moments. She has got to like her name, just as a dog gets to like his collar.) Now, Mrs Valeria, look and listen. Ariel!'

The girl's dull face began to brighten. The girl's mechanically-moving hand stopped, and held the comb in suspense.

'Ariel! you have learnt to dress my hair, and anoint my beard—haven't you?'

Her face still brightened. 'Yes! yes! yes!' she answered, eagerly. 'And you say I have learnt to do it well—don't you?'

'I say that. Would you like to let anybody else do it for you?'

Her eyes melted softly into light and life. Her strange unwomanly voice sank to the gentlest tones that I had heard from her yet.

'Nobody else shall do it for me,' she said, at once proudly and tenderly. 'Nobody, as long as I live, shall touch you but me.'

'Not even the lady there?' asked Miserrimus Dexter, pointing backward with his hand-mirror to the place at which I was standing.

Her eyes suddenly flashed, her hand suddenly shook the comb at me, in a burst of jealous rage.

'Let her try!' cried the poor creature, raising her voice again to it hoarsest notes. 'Let her touch you if she dares!'

Dexter laughed at the childish outbreak. 'That will do, my delicate Ariel,' he said. 'I dismiss your Intelligence for the present. Relapse into your former self. Finish my beard.'

She passively resumed her work. The new light in her eyes, the new expression in her face, faded little by little, and died out. In another minute, the face was as vacant and as lumpish as before: the hands did their work again with the lifeless dexterity which had so painfully impressed me when she first took up the brush. Miserrimus Dexter appeared to be perfectly satisfied with these results.

'I thought my little experiment might interest you,' he said. 'You see how it is? The dormant intelligence of my curious cousin is like the dormant sound in a musical instrument. I play upon it—and it answers to my touch. She likes being played upon. But her great delight is to hear me tell a story. I puzzle her to the verge of distraction; and the more I confuse her, the better she likes the story. It is the greatest fun; you really must see it some day.' He indulged himself in a last look at the mirror. 'Ah!' he said, complacently, 'now I shall do. Vanish, Ariel!'

She tramped out of the room in her heavy boots, with the mute obedience of a trained animal. I said 'Good-night' as she passed me. She neither returned the salutation nor looked at me: the words simply produced no effect on her dull senses. The one voice that could reach her was silent. She had relapsed once more into the vacant inanimate creature who had opened the gate to us—until it pleased Miserrimus Dexter to speak to her again.

'Valeria!' said my mother-in-law. 'Our modest host is waiting to see what you think of him.'

While my attention was fixed on his cousin, he had wheeled his chair round, so as to face me—with the light of the lamp falling full on him. In mentioning his appearance as a witness at the Trial, I find I have borrowed (without meaning to do so) from my experience of him at this later time. I saw plainly now the bright intelligent face, and the large clear blue eyes; the lustrous waving hair of a light chestnut colour; the long delicate white hands, and the magnificent throat and chest, which I have elsewhere described. The deformity which degraded and destroyed the manly beauty of his head and breast, was hidden from view by an Oriental robe of many colours, thrown over the chair like a coverlid. He was clothed in a jacket of black velvet, fastened loosely across his chest with large malachite buttons; and he wore lace ruffles at the ends of his sleeves, in the fashion of the last century. It may well have been due to want of perception on my part—but I could see nothing mad in him, nothing in any way repelling, as he now looked at me. The one defect that I could discover in his face was at the outer corners of his eyes, just under the temple. Here, when he laughed, and, in a lesser degree, when he smiled, the skin contracted into quaint little wrinkles and folds, which looked strangely out of harmony with the almost youthful appearance of the rest of his face. As to his other features, the mouth, so far as his beard and moustache permitted me to see it, was small and delicately formed. The nose—perfectly shaped on the straight Grecian model—was perhaps a little too thin, judged by comparison with the full cheeks and the high massive forehead. Looking at him as a whole (and speaking of him, of course, from a woman's, not a physiognomist's, point of view), I can only describe him as being an unusually handsome man. A painter would have revelled in him as a model for St John. And a young girl, ignorant of what the Oriental robe hid from view, would have said to herself the instant she looked at him, 'Here is the hero of my dreams!'

'Well, Mrs Valeria,' he said, quietly, 'do I frighten you now?'

'Certainly not, Mr Dexter.'

His blue eyes—large as the eyes of a woman, clear as the eyes of a child—rested on my face with a strangely varying play of expression, which at once interested and perplexed me.

Now, there was doubt, uneasy painful doubt, in the look: and now again it changed brightly to approval, so open and unrestrained that a vain woman might have fancied she had made a conquest of him at first sight. Suddenly, a new emotion seemed to take possession of him. His eyes sank, his head drooped; he lifted his hands with a gesture of regret. He muttered and murmured to himself; pursuing some secret and melancholy train of thought, which seemed to lead him further and further away from present objects of interest, and to plunge him deeper and deeper in troubled recollections of the past. Here and there, I caught some of the words. Little by little, I found myself trying to fathom what was darkly passing in this strange man's mind.

'A far more charming face,' I heard him say. 'But no—not a more beautiful figure. What figure was ever more beautiful than hers? Something—but not all—of her enchanting grace. Where is the resemblance which has brought her back to me? In the pose of the figure, perhaps? In the movement of the figure, perhaps? Poor martyred angel! What a life! And what a death! what a death!'

Was he comparing me with the victim of the poison—with my husband's first wife? His words seemed to justify the conclusion. If I was right, the dead woman had been evidently a favourite with him. There was no misinterpreting the broken tones of his voice when he spoke of her; he had admired her, living; he mourned her, dead. Supposing that I could prevail upon myself to admit this extraordinary person into my confidence, what would be the result? Should I be the gainer or the loser by the resemblance which he fancied he had discovered? Would the sight of me console him? or pain him? I waited eagerly to hear more on the subject of the first wife. Not a word more escaped his lips. A new change came over him. He lifted his head with a start, and looked about him, as a weary man might look if he was suddenly disturbed in a deep sleep.

'What have I done?' he said. 'Have I been letting my mind drift again?' He shuddered, and sighed. 'Oh, that house of Gleninch!' he murmured sadly to himself. 'Shall I never get away from it in my thoughts? Oh, that house of Gleninch!'

To my infinite disappointment, Mrs Macallan checked the further revelation of what was passing in his mind.

Something in the tone and manner of his allusion to her son's country house seemed to have offended her. She interposed sharply and decisively.

'Gently, my friend, gently!' she said. 'I don't think you quite know what you are talking about.'

His great blue eyes flashed at her fiercely. With one turn of his hand, he brought his chair close at her side. The next instant he caught her by the arm, and forced her to bend

to him, until he could whisper in her ear. He was violently
agitated. His whisper was loud enough to make itself heard
where I was sitting at the time.

'I don't know what I am talking about?' he repeated—
with his eyes fixed attentively, not on my mother-in-law,
but on me. 'You short-sighted old woman! where are your
spectacles? Look at her! Do you see no resemblance—the
figure, not the face!—do you see no resemblance there to
Eustace's first wife?'

'Pure fancy!' rejoined Mrs Macallan. 'I see nothing of the
sort.'

He shook her impatiently.

'Not so loud,' he whispered. 'She will hear you.'

'I have heard you both,' I said. 'You need have no fear,
Mr Dexter, of speaking before me. I know that my husband
had a first wife; and I know how miserably she died. I have
read the Trial.'

'You have read the life and death of a martyr!' cried
Miserrimus Dexter. He suddenly wheeled his chair my way;
he bent over me, almost tenderly; his eyes filled with tears.
'Nobody appreciated her at her true value,' he said, 'but
me. Nobody but me! nobody but me!'

Mrs Macallan walked away impatiently to the end of the
room.

'When you are ready, Valeria, I am,' she said. 'We cannot
keep the servants and the horses waiting much longer in
this bleak place.'

I was too deeply interested in leading Miserrimus Dexter
to pursue the subject on which he had touched, to be
willing to leave him at that moment. I pretended not to
have heard Mrs Macallan. I laid my hand, as if by accident,
on the wheel-chair to keep him near me.

'You showed how highly you esteemed that poor lady in
your evidence at the Trial,' I said. 'I believe, Mr Dexter,
you have ideas of your own about the mystery of her death?'

He had been looking at my hand, resting on the arm of
his chair, until I ventured on my question. At that, he

suddenly raised his eyes, and fixed them with a frowning and furtive suspicion on my face.

'How do you know I have ideas of my own?' he asked, sternly.

'I know it from reading the Trial,' I answered. 'The lawyer who cross-examined you spoke almost in the very words which I have just used. I had no intention of offending you, Mr Dexter.'

His face cleared as rapidly as it had clouded. He smiled, and laid his hand on mine. His touch struck me cold. I felt every nerve in me shivering under it—I drew my hand away quickly.

'I beg your pardon,' he said, 'if I have misunderstood you. I *have* ideas of my own, about that unhappy lady.' He paused, and looked at me in silence, very earnestly. 'Have *you* any ideas?' he asked. 'Ideas about her life? or about her death?'

I was deeply interested; I was burning to hear more. It might encourage him to speak if I was candid with him. I answered, 'Yes.'

'Ideas which you have mentioned to any one?' he went on.

'To no living creature,' I replied—'as yet.'

'This is very strange!' he said, still earnestly reading my face. 'What interest can *you* have in a dead woman whom you never knew? Why did you ask me that question, just now? Have you any motive in coming here to see me?'

I boldly acknowledged the truth. I said, 'I have a motive.'

'Is it connected with Eustace Macallan's first wife?'

'It is.'

'With anything that happened in her lifetime?'

'No.'

'With her death?'

'Yes.'

He suddenly clasped his hands, with a wild gesture of despair—and then pressed them both on his head, as if he was struck by some sudden pain.

'I can't hear it to-night!' he said; 'I would give worlds to hear it—but I daren't; I should lose all hold over myself in the state I am in now. I am not equal to raking up the horror and the mystery of the past; I have not courage enough to open the grave of the martyred dead. Did you hear me, when you came here? I have an immense imagination. It runs riot at times. It makes an actor of me. I play the parts of all the heroes that ever lived. I feel their characters. I merge myself in their individualities. For the time, I *am* the man I fancy myself to be. I can't help it. I am obliged to do it. If I restrained my imagination, when the fit is on me, I should go mad. I let myself loose. It lasts for hours. It leaves me, with my energies worn out, with my sensibilities frightfully acute. Rouse any melancholy or terrible associations in me, at such times; and I am capable of hysterics, I am capable of screaming. You heard me scream. You shall *not* see me in hysterics. No, Mrs Valeria—no, you innocent reflection of the dead and gone—I would not frighten you for the world. Will you come here to-morrow in the day-time? I have got a chaise and a pony. Ariel, my delicate Ariel, can drive. She shall call at Mama Macallan's and fetch you. We will talk to-morrow, when I am fit for it. I am dying to hear you. I will be fit for you in the morning. I will be civil, intelligent, communicative in the morning. No more of it now! Away with the subject! The too-exciting, the too-interesting subject! I must compose myself, or my brains will explode in my head. Music is the true narcotic for excitable brains. My harp! my harp!'

He rushed away in his chair to the far end of the room—passing Mrs Macallan as she returned to me, bent on hastening our departure.

'Come!' said the old lady, irritably. 'You have seen him, and he has made a good show of himself. More of him might be tiresome. Come away.'

The chair returned to us more slowly. Miserrimus Dexter was working it with one hand only. In the other, he held a harp, of a pattern which I had hitherto only seen in pictures.

The strings were few in number; and the instrument was so small that I could have held it easily on my lap. It was the ancient harp of the pictured Muses and the legendary Welsh Bards.

'Good night, Dexter,' said Mrs Macallan.

He held up one hand imperatively.

'Wait!' he said. 'Let her hear me sing.' He turned to me. 'I decline to be indebted to other people for my poetry and my music,' he went on. 'I compose my own poetry, and my own music. I improvise. Give me a moment to think. I will improvise for You.'

He closed his eyes, and rested his head on the frame of the harp. His fingers gently touched the strings while he was thinking. In a few minutes he lifted his head, looked at me, and struck the first notes—the prelude to the song.

Was it good music? or bad? I cannot decide whether it was music at all. It was a wild barbaric succession of sounds; utterly unlike any modern composition. Sometimes, it suggested a slow and undulating Oriental dance. Sometimes it modulated into tones which reminded me of the severer harmonies of the old Gregorian chants. The words, when they followed the prelude, were as wild, as recklessly free from all restraint of critical rules, as the music. They were assuredly inspired by the occasion; I was the theme of the strange song. And thus—in one of the finest tenor voices I ever heard—my poet sang of me:

> Why does she come?
> She reminds me of the lost;
> She reminds me of the dead:
> In her form like the other,
> In her walk like the other:
> Why does she come?

> Does Destiny bring her?
> Shall we range together
> The mazes of the past?

Shall we search together
The secrets of the past?
Shall we interchange thoughts, surmises, suspicions?
Does Destiny bring her?

The Future will show.
Let the night pass;
Let the day come.
I shall see into Her mind:
She will look into Mine.
The Future will show.

His voice sank, his fingers touched the strings more and
more feebly as he approached the last lines. The over-
wrought brain needed, and took, its re-animating repose.
At the final words, his eyes slowly closed. His head lay back
on the chair. He slept with his arms round his harp, as a
child sleeps, hugging its last new toy.

We stole out of the room on tiptoe, and left Miserrimus
Dexter—poet, composer, and madman—in his peaceful
sleep.

CHAPTER XXVI

More of my Obstinacy

ARIEL was downstairs in the shadowy hall, half asleep, half
awake, waiting to see the visitors clear of the house. Without speaking to us, without looking at us, she led the way
down the dark garden walk, and locked the gate behind us.
'Good night, Ariel,' I called out to her over the paling.
Nothing answered me but the tramp of her heavy footsteps
returning to the house, and the dull thump, a moment
afterwards, of the closing door.

The footman had thoughtfully lit the carriage lamps. Carrying one of them to serve as a lantern, he lighted us over

the wilds of the brick-desert, and landed us safely on the path by the high road.

'Well!' said my mother-in-law, when we were comfortably seated in the carriage again. 'You have seen Miserrimus Dexter; and I hope you are satisfied. I will do him the justice to declare that I never, in all my experience, saw him more completely crazy than he was to-night. What do *you* say?'

'I don't presume to dispute your opinion,' I answered. 'But, speaking for myself, I am not quite sure that he is mad.'

'Not mad!' cried Mrs Macallan, 'after those frantic performances in his chair? Not mad, after the exhibition he made of his unfortunate cousin? Not mad, after the song that he sang in your honour, and the falling asleep by way of conclusion? Oh, Valeria! Valeria! Well said the wisdom of our ancestors—there are none so blind as those who won't see!'

'Pardon me, dear Mrs Macallan—I saw everything that you mention; and I never felt more surprised, or more confounded, in my life. But now I have recovered from my amazement, and can think over it quietly, I must still venture to doubt whether this strange man is really mad, in the true meaning of the word. It seems to me that he openly expresses—I admit in a very reckless and boisterous way— thoughts and feelings which most of us are ashamed of as weaknesses, and which we keep to ourselves accordingly. I confess I have often fancied myself transformed into some other person, and have felt a certain pleasure in seeing myself in my new character. One of our first amusements as children (if we have any imagination at all) is to get out of our own characters, and to try the characters of other personages as a change—to be fairies, to be queens, to be anything, in short, but what we really are. Mr Dexter lets out the secret, just as the children do—and, if that is madness, he is certainly mad. But I noticed that when his imagination cooled down, he became Miserrimus Dexter again—he no more believed himself, than we believed him, to be Napoleon or Shakspere. Besides, some allowance is surely to be made for the solitary, sedentary life that he leads. I am not learned enough to trace the influence of that life in making him what he is. But I think I can see the result in an over-excited imagination; and I fancy I can trace his exhibiting his power over the poor cousin, and his singing of that wonderful song, to no more formidable cause than inordinate self-conceit. I hope the confession will not lower me seriously in your good opinion—but I must say I have enjoyed my visit; and, worse still, Miserrimus Dexter really interests me!'

'Does this learned discourse on Dexter mean that you are going to see him again?' asked Mrs Macallan.

'I don't know how I may feel about it to-morrow morning,' I said. 'But my impulse at this moment is decidedly to see him again. I had a little talk with him, while you were away at the other end of the room; and I believe he really can be of use to me——'

'Of use to you, in what?' interposed my mother-in-law.

'In the one object which I have in view—the object, dear Mrs Macallan, which, I regret to say, you do not approve.'

'And you are going to take him into your confidence? to open your whole mind to such a man as the man we have just left?'

'Yes—if I think of it to-morrow as I think of it to-night. I dare say it is a risk; but I must run risks. I know I am not prudent; but prudence won't help a woman in my position, with my end to gain.'

Mrs Macallan made no further remonstrance, in words. She opened a capacious pocket in front of the carriage, and took from it a box of matches and a railway reading-lamp.

'You provoke me,' said the old lady, 'into showing you what your husband thinks of this new whim of yours. I have got his letter with me—his last letter from Spain. You shall judge for yourself, you poor deluded young creature, whether my son is worthy of the sacrifice, the useless and hopeless sacrifice, which you are bent on making of yourself, for his sake. Strike a light!'

I willingly obeyed her. Ever since she had informed me of Eustace's departure to Spain, I had been eager for more news of him—for something to sustain my spirits, after so much that had disappointed and depressed me. Thus far, I did not even know whether my husband thought of me sometimes in his self-imposed exile. As to his regretting already the rash act which had separated us, it was still too soon to begin hoping for that.

The lamp having been lit, and fixed in its place between the two front windows of the carriage, Mrs Macallan produced her son's letter. There is no folly like the folly of love. It cost me a hard struggle to restrain myself from kissing the paper on which the dear hand had rested.

'There!' said my mother-in-law. 'Begin on the second page; the page devoted to you. Read straight down to the last line at the bottom—and, in God's name, come back to your senses, child, before it is too late!'

I followed my instructions, and read these words:

'Can I trust myself to write of Valeria? I *must* write of her! Tell me how she is, how she looks, what she is doing. I am always thinking of her. Not a day passes but I mourn the loss of her. Oh, if she had only been contented to let matters rest as they were! Oh, if she had never discovered the miserable truth!

'She spoke of reading the Trial, when I saw her last. Has she persisted in doing so? I believe—I say this seriously, mother—I believe the shame and the horror of it would have been the death of me, if I had met her face to face, when she first knew of the ignominy that I have suffered, of the infamous suspicion of which I have been publicly made the subject. Think of those pure eyes looking at a man who has been accused (and never wholly absolved) of the foulest and the vilest of all murders—and then think of what that man must feel, if he has any heart and any sense of shame left in him. I sicken as I write of it.

'Does she still meditate that hopeless project—the off-spring, poor angel, of her artless, unthinking generosity? Does she still fancy that it is in *her* power to assert my innocence before the world? Oh, mother (if she does), use your utmost influence to make her give up the idea! Spare her the humiliation, the disappointment, the insult perhaps, to which she may innocently expose herself. For her sake, for my sake, leave no means untried to attain this righteous, this merciful end.

'I send her no message—I dare not do it. Say nothing when you see her, which can recall me to her memory. On the contrary, help her to forget me as soon as possible. The kindest thing I can do—the one atonement I can make to her—is to drop out of her life.'

With those wretched words it ended. I handed his letter back to his mother in silence. She said but little, on her side.

'If *this* doesn't discourage you,' she remarked, slowly folding up the letter, 'nothing will. Let us leave it there, and say no more.'

I made no answer—I was crying behind my veil. My domestic prospect looked so dreary; my unfortunate husband was so hopelessly misguided, so pitiably wrong! The one chance for both of us (and the one consolation for poor Me) was to hold by my desperate resolution more firmly than ever. If I had wanted anything to confirm me in this view, and to arm me against the remonstrances of every one of my friends, Eustace's letter would have proved more than sufficient to answer the purpose. At least, he had not forgotten me; he thought of me, and he mourned the loss of me, every day of his life. That was encouragement enough—for the present. 'If Ariel calls for me in the pony-chaise to-morrow,' I thought to myself, 'with Ariel I go.'

Mrs Macallan set me down at Benjamin's door.

I mentioned to her, at parting—I stood sufficiently in awe of her to put it off till the last moment—that Miserrimus Dexter had arranged to send his cousin and his pony-chaise to her residence, on the next day; and I inquired thereupon whether my mother-in-law would permit me to call at her house to wait for the appearance of the cousin, or whether she would prefer sending the chaise on to Benjamin's cottage. I fully expected an explosion of anger to follow this bold avowal of my plans for the next day. The old lady agreeably surprised me. She proved that she had really taken a liking to me: she kept her temper.

'If you persist in going back to Dexter, you certainly shall not go to him from my door,' she said. 'But I hope you will *not* persist. I hope you will wake a wiser woman to-morrow morning.'

The morning came. A little before noon the arrival of the pony-chaise was announced at the door, and a letter was brought in to me from Mrs Macallan.

'I have no right to control your movements,' my mother-in-law wrote. 'I send the chaise to Mr Benjamin's house; and I sincerely trust that you will not take your place in it. I wish I could persuade you, Valeria, how truly I am your friend. I have been thinking about you anxiously in the wakeful hours of the night. *How* anxiously, you will understand, when I tell you that I now reproach myself for not having done more than I did to prevent your unhappy marriage. And yet, what I could have done I don't really know. My son admitted to me that he was courting you under an assumed name—but he never told me what the name was, or who you were, or where your friends lived. Perhaps, I ought to have taken measures to find this out. Perhaps, if I had succeeded, I ought to have interfered and enlightened you, even at the sad sacrifice of making an enemy of my own son. I honestly thought I did my duty in expressing my disapproval, and in refusing to be present at the marriage. Was I too easily satisfied? It is too late to ask. Why do I trouble you with an old woman's vain misgivings and regrets? My child, if you come to any harm, I shall feel (indirectly) responsible for it. It is this uneasy state of mind which sets me writing, with nothing to say that can interest

you. Don't go to Dexter! The fear has been pursuing me
all night that your going to Dexter will end badly. Write
him an excuse. Valeria! I firmly believe you will repent it if
you return to that house.'

Was ever a woman more plainly warned, more carefully
advised, than I? And yet, warning and advice were both
thrown away on me!

Let me say for myself that I was really touched by the
kindness of my mother-in-law's letter—though I was not
shaken by it in the smallest degree. As long as I lived,
moved, and thought, my one purpose now was to make
Miserrimus Dexter confide to me his ideas on the subject
of Mrs Eustace Macallan's death. To those ideas I looked
as my guiding stars along the dark way on which I was
going. I wrote back to Mrs Macallan, as I really felt, gratefully and penitently. And then I went out to the chaise.

CHAPTER XXVII

Mr Dexter at Home

I FOUND all the idle boys in the neighbourhood collected
round the pony-chaise, expressing, in the occult language of
slang, their high enjoyment and appreciation of the appearance of 'Ariel' in her man's jacket and hat. The pony was
fidgety—*he* felt the influence of the popular uproar. His
driver sat, whip in hand, magnificently impenetrable to the
jibes and jests that were flying round her. I said, 'Good
morning,' on getting into the chaise. Ariel only said, 'Gee
up!' and started the pony.

I made up my mind to perform the journey to the distant
northern suburb in silence. It was evidently useless for me
to attempt to speak; and experience informed me that I
need not expect to hear a word fall from the lips of my
companion. Experience, however, is not always infallible.

After driving for half an hour in stolid silence, Ariel astounded me by suddenly bursting into speech.

'Do you know what we are coming to?' she asked, keeping her eyes straight between the pony's ears.

'No,' I answered. 'I don't know the road. What are we coming to?'

'We are coming to a canal.'

'Well?'

'Well! I have half a mind to upset you in the canal.'

This formidable announcement appeared to me to require some explanation. I took the liberty of asking for it.

'Why should you upset me?' I inquired.

'Because I hate you,' was the cool and candid reply.

'What have I done to offend you?' I asked next.

'What do you want with The Master?' Ariel asked, in her turn.

'Do you mean Mr Dexter?'

'Yes.'

'I want to have some talk with Mr Dexter.'

'You don't! You want to take my place. You want to brush his hair and oil his beard, instead of me. You wretch!'

I now began to understand. The idea which Miserrimus Dexter had jestingly put into her head, in exhibiting her to us on the previous night, had been ripening slowly in that dull brain, and had found its way outwards into words, about fifteen hours afterwards, under the irritating influence of my presence!

'I don't want to touch his hair or his beard,' I said. 'I leave that entirely to you.'

She looked round at me; her fat face flushing, her dull eyes dilating, with the unaccustomed effort to express herself in speech, and to understand what was said to her in return.

'Say that again,' she burst out. 'And say it slower this time.'

I said it again, and I said it slower.

'Swear it!' she cried, getting more and more excited.

I preserved my gravity (the canal was just visible in the distance), and swore it.

'Are you satisfied now?' I asked.

There was no answer. Her last resources of speech were exhausted. The strange creature looked back again straight between the pony's ears, emitted hoarsely a grunt of relief; and never more looked at me, never more spoke to me, for the rest of the journey. We drove past the banks of the canal; and I escaped immersion. We rattled, in our jingling little vehicle, through the streets and across the waste patches of ground, which I dimly remembered in the darkness, and which looked more squalid and more hideous than ever in the broad daylight. The chaise turned down a lane, too narrow for the passage of any larger vehicle, and stopped at a wall and a gate that were new objects to me. Opening the gate with her key, and leading the pony, Ariel introduced me to the back garden and yard of Miserrimus Dexter's rotten and rambling old house. The pony walked off independently to his stable, with the chaise behind him. My silent companion led me through a bleak and barren kitchen, and along a stone passage. Opening a door at the end, she admitted me to the back of the hall, into which Mrs Macallan and I had penetrated by the front entrance to the house. Here, Ariel lifted a whistle which hung round her neck, and blew the shrill trilling notes, with the sound of which I was already familiar as the means of communication between Miserrimus Dexter and his slave. The whistling over, the slave's unwilling lips struggled into speech, for the last time.

'Wait till you hear The Master's whistle,' she said. 'Then go upstairs.'

So! I was to be whistled for like a dog. And worse still, there was no help for it but to submit like a dog. Had Ariel any excuses to make? Nothing of the sort! She turned her shapeless back on me, and vanished into the kitchen region of the house.

After waiting for a minute or two, and hearing no signal from the floor above, I advanced into the broader and brighter part of the hall, to look by daylight at the pictures which I had only imperfectly discovered in the darkness of the night. A painted inscription in many colours, just under the cornice of the ceiling, informed me that the works on the walls were the production of the all-accomplished Dexter himself. Not satisfied with being poet and composer, he was painter as well. On one wall the subjects were described as 'Illustrations of the Passions'; on the other, as 'Episodes in the Life of the Wandering Jew.'* Chance spectators like myself were gravely warned, by means of the inscription, to view the pictures as efforts of pure imagination. 'Persons who look for mere Nature in works of Art' (the inscription announced) 'are persons to whom Mr Dexter does not address himself with the brush. He relies entirely on his imagination. Nature puts him out.'

Taking due care to dismiss all ideas of Nature from my mind, to begin with, I looked at the pictures which represented the Passions, first.

Little as I knew critically of Art, I could see that Miserrimus Dexter knew still less of the rules of drawing, colour, and composition. His pictures were, in the strictest meaning of that expressive word—Daubs. The diseased and riotous delight of the painter in representing Horrors, was (with certain exceptions to be hereafter mentioned) the one remarkable quality that I could discover in the series of his works.

The first of the Passion-pictures illustrated Revenge. A corpse, in fancy costume, lay on the bank of a foaming river, under the shade of a giant tree. An infuriated man, also in fancy costume, stood astride over the dead body, with his sword lifted to the lowering sky, and watched, with a horrid expression of delight, the blood of the man whom he had just killed, dripping slowly in a procession of big red drops down the broad blade of his weapon. The next picture illustrated Cruelty, in many compartments. In one, I saw a disembowelled horse savagely spurred on by his rider at a bull-fight. In another, an aged philosopher was dissecting

a live cat, and gloating over his work. In a third, two Pagans
politely congratulated each other on the torture of two
saints: one saint was roasting on a gridiron; the other, hung
up to a tree by his heels, had just been skinned, and was
not quite dead yet. Feeling no great desire, after these
specimens, to look at any more of the illustrated Passions,
I turned to the opposite wall to be instructed in the career
of the Wandering Jew. Here, a second inscription informed
me that the painter considered the Flying Dutchman* to be
no other than the Wandering Jew, pursuing his interminable
journey by sea. The marine adventures of this mysterious
personage were the adventures chosen for representation
by Dexter's brush. The first picture showed me a harbour
on a rocky coast. A vessel was at anchor, with the helmsman
singing on the deck. The sea in the offing was black and
rolling; thunder-clouds lay low on the horizon, split by
broad flashes of lightning. In the glare of the lightning,
heaving and pitching, appeared the misty form of the Phantom Ship approaching the shore. In this work, badly as it
was painted, there were really signs of a powerful imagination, and even of a poetical feeling for the supernatural.
The next picture showed the Phantom Ship, moored (to
the horror and astonishment of the helmsman) behind the
earthly vessel in the harbour. The Jew had stepped on
shore. His boat was on the beach. His crew—little men with
stony white faces, dressed in funereal black—sat in silent
rows on the seats of the boat, with their oars in their lean
long hands. The Jew, also in black, stood with his eyes and
hands raised imploringly to the thunderous heaven. The
wild creatures of land and sea—the tiger, the rhinoceros,
the crocodile; the sea-serpent, the shark, and the devil-
fish—surrounded the accursed Wanderer in a mystic circle,
daunted and fascinated at the sight of him. The lightning
was gone. The sky and sea had darkened to a great black
blank. A faint and lurid light lit the scene, falling downward
from a torch, brandished by an avenging Spirit that hovered
over the Jew on outspread vulture-wings. Wild as the pic-

ture might be in its conception, there was a suggestive power in it which I confess strongly impressed me. The mysterious silence in the house, and my strange position at the moment, no doubt had their effect on my mind. While I was still looking at the ghastly composition before me, the shrill trilling sound of the whistle upstairs burst on the stillness. For the moment, my nerves were so completely upset, that I started with a cry of alarm. I felt a momentary impulse to open the door, and run out. The idea of trusting myself alone with the man who had painted those frightful pictures, actually terrified me; I was obliged to sit down on one of the hall chairs. Some minutes passed before my mind recovered its balance, and I began to feel like my ordinary self again. The whistle sounded impatiently for the second time. I rose, and ascended the broad flight of stairs which led to the ante-room. To draw back at the point which I had now reached would have utterly degraded me in my own estimation. Still, my heart did certainly beat faster than usual when I found myself on the top of the stairs; and I honestly acknowledge that I saw my own imprudence, just then, in a singularly vivid light.

There was a glass over the mantelpiece in the ante-room. I lingered for a moment (nervous as I was) to see how I looked in the glass.

The hanging tapestry over the inner door had been left partially drawn aside. Softly as I moved, the dog's ears of Miserrimus Dexter caught the sound of my dress on the floor. The fine tenor voice, which I had last heard singing, called to me gently.

'Is that Mrs Valeria? Please don't wait there. Come in!'

I entered the inner room.

The wheeled chair advanced to meet me, so slowly and so softly that I hardly knew it again. Miserrimus Dexter languidly held out his hand. His head inclined pensively to one side; his large blue eyes looked at me piteously. Not a vestige seemed to be left of the raging, shouting creature of my first visit, who was Napoleon at one moment and Shakspere at another. Mr Dexter of the morning was a mild, thoughtful, melancholy man, who only recalled Mr Dexter of the night by the inveterate oddity of his dress. His jacket, on this occasion, was of pink quilted silk. The coverlid which hid his deformity matched the jacket in pale sea-green satin; and, to complete these strange vagaries of costume, his wrists were actually adorned with massive bracelets of gold, formed on the severely-simple models which have descended to us from ancient times!

'How good of you to cheer and charm me by coming here!' he said, in his most mournful and most musical tones. 'I have dressed, expressly to receive you, in the prettiest clothes I have. Don't be surprised. Except in this ignoble and material nineteenth century, men have always worn precious stuffs and beautiful colours as well as women. A hundred years ago, a gentleman in pink silk was a gentleman properly dressed. Fifteen hundred years ago, the patricians of the classic times wore bracelets exactly like mine. I despise the brutish contempt for beauty and the mean dread of expense which degrade a gentleman's costume to black cloth, and limit a gentleman's ornaments to a finger ring, in the age I live in. I like to be bright and beautiful, especially when brightness and beauty come to see me. You don't know how precious your society is to me. This is one of my melancholy days. Tears rise unbidden to my eyes. I sigh and sorrow over myself; I languish for pity. Just think of what I am! A poor solitary creature, cursed with a frightful deformity. How pitiable! how dreadful! My affectionate heart—wasted. My extraordinary talents—useless or misapplied. Sad! sad! sad! Please pity me.'

His eyes were positively filled with tears—tears of compassion for himself. He looked at me and spoke to me with the wailing querulous entreaty of a sick child wanting to be nursed. I was quite at a loss what to do. It was perfectly ridiculous—but I was never more embarrassed in my life.

'Please pity me!' he repeated. 'Don't be cruel. I only ask a little thing. Pretty Mrs Valeria, say you pity me!'

I said I pitied him—and I felt that I blushed as I did it.

'Thank you,' said Miserrimus Dexter, humbly. 'It does me good. Go a little further. Pat my hand.'

I tried to restrain myself; but my sense of the absurdity of this last petition (quite gravely addressed to me, remember!) was too strong to be controlled. I burst out laughing.

Miserrimus Dexter looked at me with a blank astonishment which only increased my merriment. Had I offended him? Apparently not. Recovering from his astonishment, he laid his head luxuriously on the back of his chair, with the expression of a man who was listening critically to a performance of some sort. When I had quite exhausted myself, he raised his head, and clapped his shapely white hands, and honoured me with an 'encore.'

'Do it again,' he said, still in the same childish way. 'Merry Mrs Valeria, *you* have a musical laugh—*I* have a musical ear. Do it again.'

I was serious enough by this time. 'I am ashamed of myself, Mr Dexter,' I said. 'Pray forgive me.'

He made no answer to this; I doubt if he heard me. His variable temper appeared to be in course of undergoing some new change. He sat looking at my dress (as I supposed) with a steady and anxious attention, gravely forming his own conclusions, steadfastly pursuing his own train of thought.

'Mrs Valeria,' he burst out suddenly, 'you are not comfortable in that chair.'

'Pardon me,' I replied; 'I am quite comfortable.'

'Pardon *me*,' he rejoined. 'There is a chair of Indian basket-work at the end of the room, which is much better suited to you. Will you accept my apologies if I am rude enough to allow you to fetch it for yourself? I have a reason.'

He had a reason! What new piece of eccentricity was he about to exhibit? I rose and fetched the chair: it was light enough to be quite easily carried. As I returned to him, I noticed that his eyes were still strangely employed in what seemed to me to be the closest scrutiny of my dress. And stranger still, the result of this appeared to be, partly to interest and partly to distress him.

I placed the chair near him, and was about to take my seat in it, when he sent me back again, on another errand, to the end of the room.

'Oblige me indescribably,' he said. 'There is a hand-screen hanging on the wall, which matches the chair. We are rather near the fire here. You may find the screen useful. Once more forgive me for letting you fetch it for yourself. Once more let me assure you that I have a reason.'

Here was his 'reason,' reiterated, emphatically reiterated, for the second time! Curiosity made me as completely the obedient servant of his caprices as Ariel herself. I fetched the hand-screen. Returning with it, I met his eyes still fixed with the same incomprehensible attention on my perfectly plain and unpretending dress, and still expressing the same curious mixture of interest and regret.

'Thank you a thousand times,' he said. 'You have (quite innocently) wrung my heart. But you have not the less done me an inestimable kindness. Will you promise not to be offended with me, if I confess the truth?'

He was approaching his explanation! I never gave a promise more readily in my life.

'I have rudely allowed you to fetch your chair and your screen for yourself,' he went on. 'My motive will seem a very strange one, I am afraid. Did you observe that I noticed you very attentively—too attentively, perhaps?'

'Yes,' I said. 'I thought you were noticing my dress.'

He shook his head, and sighed bitterly.

'Not your dress,' he said. 'And not your face. Your dress is not pretty. Your face is still strange to me. Dear Mrs Valeria, I wanted to see you walk.'

To see me walk! What did he mean? Where was that erratic mind of his wandering to now?

'You have a rare accomplishment for an Englishwoman,' he resumed; 'you walk well. *She* walked well. I couldn't resist the temptation of seeing her again, in seeing you. It was *her* movement, *her* sweet simple unsought grace (not yours) when you walked to the end of the room and returned to me. You raised her from the dead, when you fetched the chair and the screen. Pardon me for making use of you; the idea was innocent, the motive was sacred. You have distressed, and delighted me. My heart bleeds—and thanks you.'

He paused for a moment: he let his head droop on his breast—then suddenly raised it again.

'Surely we were talking about her last night,' he said. 'What did I say? What did you say? My memory is confused; I half remember, half forget. Please remind me. You're not offended with me—are you?'

I might have been offended with another man. Not with him. I was far too anxious to find my way into his confidence—now that he had touched of his own accord on the subject of Eustace's first wife—to be offended with Miserrimus Dexter.

'We were speaking,' I answered, 'of Mrs Eustace Macallan's death; and we were saying to one another——'

He interrupted me, leaning forward eagerly in his chair. 'Yes! yes!' he exclaimed. 'And I was wondering what interest *you* could have in penetrating the mystery of her death. Tell me! Confide in me! I am dying to know!'

'Not even you have a stronger interest in that subject than the interest that I feel,' I said. 'The happiness of my whole life to come depends on my clearing up the mystery of her death.'

'Good God!—why?' he cried. 'Stop! I am exciting myself. I mustn't do that. I must have all my wits about me; I mustn't wander. The thing is too serious. Wait a minute!'

An elegant little basket was hooked on to one of the arms of his chair. He opened it, and drew out a strip of embroidery partially finished, with the necessary materials for working, all complete. We looked at each other across the embroidery. He noticed my surprise.

'Women,' he said, 'wisely compose their minds, and help themselves to think quietly, by doing needlework. Why are men such fools as to deny themselves the same admirable resource—the simple and soothing occupation which keeps the nerves steady and leaves the mind calm and free? As a man, I follow the women's wise example. Mrs Valeria, permit me to compose myself.'

Gravely arranging his embroidery, this extraordinary being began to work with the patient and nimble dexterity of an accomplished needlewoman.

'Now,' said Miserrimus Dexter, 'if you are ready, I am. You talk—I work. Please begin.'

I obeyed him, and began.

CHAPTER XXVIII

In the Dark

WITH such a man as Miserrimus Dexter, and with such a purpose I had in view, no half-confidences were possible. I must either risk the most unreserved acknowledgment of the interests that I really had at stake, or I must make the best excuse that occurred to me for abandoning my contemplated experiment at the last moment. In my present critical situation, no such refuge as a middle course lay before me—even if I had been inclined to take it. As things were, I ran all risks, and plunged headlong into my own affairs at starting.

'Thus far, you know little or nothing about me, Mr Dexter,' I said. 'You are, as I believe, quite unaware that my husband and I are not living together at the present time?'

'Is it necessary to mention your husband?' he asked, coldly, without looking up from his embroidery, and without pausing in his work.

'It is absolutely necessary,' I answered. 'I can explain myself to you in no other way.'

He bent his head, and sighed resignedly.

'You and your husband are not living together, at the present time?' he resumed. 'Does that mean that Eustace has left you?'

'He has left me, and has gone abroad.'

'Without any necessity for it?'

'Without the least necessity.'

'Has he appointed no time for his return to you?'

'If he perseveres in his present resolution, Mr Dexter, Eustace will never return to me.'

For the first time, he raised his head from his embroidery—with a sudden appearance of interest.

'Is the quarrel so serious as that?' he asked. 'Are you free of each other, pretty Mrs Valeria, by common consent of both parties?'

The tone in which he put the question was not at all to my liking. The look he fixed on me was a look which unpleasantly suggested that I had trusted myself alone with him, and that he might end in taking advantage of it. I reminded him quietly, by my manner more than by my words, of the respect which he owed to me.

'You are entirely mistaken,' I said. 'There is no anger—there is not even a misunderstanding between us. Our parting has caused bitter sorrow, Mr Dexter, to him and to me.'

He submitted to be set right with ironical resignation. 'I am all attention,' he said, threading his needle. 'Pray go on; I won't interrupt you again.' Acting on this invitation, I told him the truth about my husband and myself quite unreservedly, taking care, however, at the same time, to put Eustace's motives in the best light that they would bear. Miserrimus Dexter laid aside his embroidery on the chair, and laughed softly to himself, with an impish enjoyment of my poor little narrative, which set every nerve in me on edge as I looked at him.

'I see nothing to laugh at,' I said, sharply.

His beautiful blue eyes rested on me with a look of innocent surprise.

'Nothing to laugh at,' he repeated, 'in such an exhibition of human folly as you have described!' His expression suddenly changed; his face darkened and hardened very strangely. 'Stop!' he cried, before I could answer him. 'There can be only one reason for your taking it as seriously as you do. Mrs Valeria, you are fond of your husband.'

'Fond of him isn't strong enough to express it,' I retorted. 'I love him with my whole heart.'

Miserrimus Dexter stroked his magnificent beard, and contemplatively repeated my words. 'You love him with your whole heart? Do you know why?'

'Because I can't help it,' I answered, doggedly.

He smiled satirically, and went on with his embroidery. 'Curious!' he said to himself; 'Eustace's first wife loved him, too. There are some men whom the women all like; and there are other men whom the women never care for. Without the least reason for it in either case. The one man is just as good as the other; just as handsome, as agreeable, as honourable, and as high in rank as the other. And yet, for Number One, they will go through fire and water; and for Number Two, they won't so much as turn their heads to look at him. Why? They don't know themselves—as Mrs Valeria has just said! Is there a physical reason for it? Is there some potent magnetic emanation from Number One, which Number Two doesn't possess? I must investigate this when I have the time, and when I find myself in the humour.' Having so far settled the question to his own entire satisfaction, he looked up at me again. 'I am still in the dark about you and your motives,' he said. 'I am still as far as ever from understanding what your interest is in investigating that hideous tragedy at Gleninch. Clever Mrs Valeria, please take me by the hand, and lead me into the light. You're not offended with me—are you? Make it up; and I will give you this pretty piece of embroidery when I have done it. I am only a poor, solitary, deformed wretch, with a quaint turn of mind; I mean no harm. Forgive me! indulge me! enlighten me!'

He resumed his childish ways; he recovered his innocent smile, with the odd little puckers and wrinkles accompanying it at the corners of his eyes. I began to doubt whether I might not have been unreasonably hard on him. I penitently resolved to be more considerate towards his infirmities of mind and body, during the remainder of my visit.

'Let me go back for a moment, Mr Dexter, to past times at Gleninch,' I said. 'You agree with me in believing Eustace to be absolutely innocent of the crime for which he was tried. Your evidence at the Trial tells me that.'

He paused over his work, and looked at me with a grave and stern attention which presented his face in quite a new light.

'That is *our* opinion,' I resumed. 'But it was not the opinion of the Jury. Their verdict, you remember, was Not Proven. In plain English, the Jury who tried my husband declined to express their opinion, positively and publicly, that he was innocent. Am I right?'

Instead of answering, he suddenly put his embroidery back in the basket, and moved the machinery of his chair, so as to bring it close by mine.

'Who told you this?' he asked.

'I found it for myself, in a book.'

Thus far, his face had expressed steady attention—and no more. Now, for the first time, I thought I saw something darkly passing over him which betrayed itself to my mind as rising distrust.

'Ladies are not generally in the habit of troubling their heads about dry questions of law,' he said. 'Mrs Eustace Macallan the Second, you must have some very powerful motive for turning your studies that way.'

'I have a very powerful motive, Mr Dexter. My husband is resigned to the Scotch Verdict. His mother is resigned to it. His friends (so far as I know) are resigned to it——'

'Well?'

'Well! I don't agree with my husband, or his mother, or his friends. I refuse to submit to the Scotch Verdict.'

The instant I said those words, the madness in him, which I had hitherto denied, seemed to break out. He suddenly stretched himself over his chair: he pounced on me, with a hand on each of my shoulders; his wild eyes questioned me fiercely, frantically, within a few inches of my face.

'What do you mean?' he shouted, at the utmost pitch of his ringing and resonant voice.

A deadly fear of him shook me. I did my best to hide the outward betrayal of it. By look and word, I showed him, as firmly as I could, that I resented the liberty he had taken with me.

'Remove your hands, sir,' I said. 'And retire to your proper place.'

He obeyed me mechanically. He apologised to me mechanically. His whole mind was evidently still filled with the words that I had spoken to him, and still bent on discovering what those words meant.

'I beg your pardon,' he said; 'I humbly beg your pardon. The subject excites me, frightens me, maddens me. You don't know what a difficulty I have in controlling myself. Never mind. Don't take me seriously. Don't be frightened at me. I am so ashamed of myself—I feel so small and so miserable at having offended you. Make me suffer for it. Take a stick and beat me. Tie me down in my chair. Call up Ariel, who is as strong as a horse, and tell her to hold me. Dear Mrs Valeria! Injured Mrs Valeria! I'll endure anything in the way of punishment, if you will only tell me what you mean by not submitting to the Scotch Verdict?' He backed his chair penitently, as he made that entreaty. 'Am I far enough away yet?' he asked, with a rueful look. 'Do I still frighten you? I'll drop out of sight, if you prefer it, in the bottom of the chair.'

He lifted the sea-green coverlid. In another moment he

would have disappeared, like a puppet in a show, if I had not stopped him.

'Say nothing more, and do nothing more; I accept your apologies,' I said. 'When I tell you that I refuse to submit to the opinion of the Scotch Jury, I mean exactly what my words express. That Verdict has left a stain on my husband's character. He feels the stain bitterly. How bitterly no one knows so well as I do. His sense of his degradation is the sense that has parted him from me. It is not enough for *him* that I am persuaded of his innocence. Nothing will bring him back to me—nothing will persuade Eustace that I think him worthy to be the guide and companion of my life—but the proof of his innocence, set before the Jury which doubts it, and the public which doubts it, to this day. He, and his friends, and his lawyers all despair of ever finding that proof, now. But I am his wife; and none of you love him as I love him. I alone refuse to despair; I alone refuse to listen to reason. If God spares me, Mr Dexter, I dedicate my life to the vindication of my husband's innocence. You are his old friend—I am here to ask you to help me.'

It appeared to be now my turn to frighten *him*. The colour left his face. He passed his hand restlessly over his forehead, as if he was trying to brush some delusion out of his brain.

'Is this one of my dreams?' he asked, faintly. 'Are you a vision of the night?'

'I am only a friendless woman,' I said, 'who has lost all that she loved and prized, and who is trying to win it back again.'

He began to move in his chair nearer to me once more. I lifted my hand. He stopped the chair directly. There was a moment of silence. We sat watching one another. I saw his hands tremble as he laid them on the coverlid; I saw his face grow paler and paler, and his under lip drop. What dead and buried remembrances had I brought to life in him, in all their olden horror?

He was the first to speak again.

'So this is your interest,' he said, 'in clearing up the mystery of Mrs Eustace Macallan's death?'

'Yes.'

'And you believe that I can help you?'

'I do.'

He slowly lifted one of his hands, and pointed at me with his long forefinger.

'You suspect somebody,' he said.

The tone in which he spoke was low and threatening: it warned me to be careful. At the same time, if I now shut him out of my confidence, I should lose the reward that might yet be to come, for all that I had suffered and risked at that perilous interview.

'You suspect somebody,' he repeated.

'Perhaps!' was all I said in return.

'Is the person within your reach?'

'Not yet.'

'Do you know where the person is?'

'No.'

He laid his head languidly on the back of his chair, with a trembling long-drawn sigh. Was he disappointed? Or was he relieved? or was he simply exhausted in mind and body alike? Who could fathom him? Who could say?

'Will you give me five minutes?' he asked, feebly and wearily, without raising his head. 'You know already how any reference to events at Gleninch excites and shakes me. I shall be fit for it again, if you will kindly give me a few minutes to myself. There are books in the next room. Please excuse me.'

I at once retired to the circular ante-chamber. He followed me in his chair, and closed the door between us.

CHAPTER XXIX

In the Light

A LITTLE interval of solitude was a relief to me, as well as to Miserrimus Dexter.

Startling doubts beset me as I walked restlessly backwards and forwards, now in the ante-room, and now in the corridor outside. It was plain that I had (quite innocently) disturbed the repose of some formidable secrets in Miserrimus Dexter's mind. I confused and wearied my poor brains in trying to guess what the secrets might be. All my ingenuity—as after events showed me—was wasted on speculations not one of which even approached the truth. I was on surer ground, when I arrived at the conclusion that Dexter had really kept every mortal creature out of his confidence. He could never have betrayed such serious signs of disturbance as I had noticed in him, if he had publicly acknowledged at the Trial, or if he had privately communicated to any chosen friend, all that he knew of the tragic and terrible drama acted in the bed-chamber at Glen-inch. What powerful influence had induced him to close his lips? Had he been silent in mercy to others? or in dread of consequences to himself? Impossible to tell! Could I hope that he would confide to Me what he had kept secret from Justice and Friendship alike? When he knew what I really wanted of him, would he arm me, out of his own stores of knowledge, with the weapon that would win me victory in the struggle to come? The chances were all against it—there was no denying that. Still, the end was worth trying for. The caprice of the moment might yet stand my friend, with such a wayward being as Miserrimus Dexter. My plans and projects were sufficiently strange, sufficiently wide of the ordinary limits of a woman's thoughts and actions, to attract his sympathies. 'Who knows' (I thought to myself) 'if I may not take his confidence by surprise, by simply telling him the truth!'

The interval expired; the door was thrown open; the voice of my host summoned me again to the inner room.

'Welcome back!' said Miserrimus Dexter. 'Dear Mrs Valeria, I am quite myself again. How are you?'

He looked and spoke with the easy cordiality of an old friend. During the period of my absence, short as it was, another change had passed over this most multiform of living beings. His eyes sparkled with good humour; his cheeks were flushing under a new excitement of some sort. Even his dress had undergone alteration since I had seen it last. He now wore an extemporised cap of white paper; his ruffles were tucked up; a clean apron was thrown over the seagreen coverlid. He backed his chair before me, bowing and smiling; and waved me to a seat with the grace of a dancing-master, chastened by the dignity of a lord in waiting.

'I am going to cook,' he announced, with the most engaging simplicity. 'We both stand in need of refreshment, before we return to the serious business of our interview. You see me in my cook's dress—forgive it. There is a form in these things; I am a great stickler for forms. I have been taking some wine. Please sanction that proceeding by taking some wine too.'

He filled a goblet of ancient Venetian glass with a purple red liquor, beautiful to see.

'Burgundy!' he said. 'The King of Wines. And this is the King of Burgundies—Clos Vougeot. I drink to your health and happiness!'

He filled a second goblet for himself, and honoured the toast by draining it to the bottom. I now understood the sparkle in his eyes and the flush in his cheeks! It was my interest not to offend him. I drank a little of his wine—and I quite agreed with him; I thought it delicious.

'What shall we eat?' he asked. 'It must be something

worthy of our Clos Vougeot. Ariel is good at roasting and boiling joints, poor wretch! But I don't insult your taste by offering you Ariel's cookery. Plain joints!' he exclaimed, with an expression of refined disgust. 'Bah! A man who eats a plain joint is only one remove from a cannibal—or a butcher. Will you leave it to me to discover something more worthy of us? Let us go to the kitchen.'

He wheeled his chair round; and invited me to accompany him with a courteous wave of his hand.

I followed the chair to some closed curtains at one end of the room, which I had not hitherto noticed. Drawing aside the curtains, he revealed to view an alcove, in which stood a neat little gas stove for cooking. Drawers and cupboards, plates, dishes, and saucepans were ranged round the alcove—all on a miniature scale, all scrupulously bright and clean. 'Welcome to the kitchen!' said Miserrimus Dexter. He drew out of a recess in the wall a marble slab which served as a table, and reflected profoundly with his hand to his head. 'I have it!' he cried—and opening one of the cupboards next, took from it a black bottle of a form that was new to me. Sounding this bottle with a spike, he pierced and produced to view some little irregularly formed black objects, which might have been familiar enough to a woman accustomed to the luxurious tables of the rich; but which were a new revelation to a person like myself, who had led a simple country life in the house of a clergyman with small means. When I saw my host carefully lay out these occult substances, of uninviting appearance, on a clean napkin, and then plunge once more into profound reflection at the sight of them, my curiosity could be no longer restrained. I ventured to say, 'What are those things, Mr Dexter? and are we really going to eat them?'

He started at the rash question, and looked at me, with hands outspread in irrepressible astonishment.

'Where is our boasted progress?' he cried. 'What is education but a name? Here is a cultivated person who doesn't know Truffles when she sees them!'

'I have heard of truffles,' I answered humbly. 'But I never saw them before. We had no such foreign luxuries as those, Mr Dexter, at home in the North.'

Miserrimus Dexter lifted one of the truffles tenderly on his spike, and held it up to me in a favourable light.

'Make the most of one of the few first sensations in this life, which has no ingredient of disappointment lurking under the surface,' he said. 'Look at it; meditate over it. You shall eat it, Mrs Valeria, stewed in Burgundy!'

He lit the gas for cooking, with the air of a man who was about to offer me an inestimable proof of his good will.

'Forgive me if I observe the most absolute silence,' he said, 'dating from the moment when I take this in my hand.' He produced a bright little stew-pan from his collection of culinary utensils as he spoke. 'Properly pursued, the Art of Cookery allows of no divided attention,' he continued gravely. 'In that observation you will find the reason why no woman ever has reached, or ever will reach, the highest distinction as a cook. As a rule, women are incapable of absolutely concentrating their attention on any one occupation, for any given time. Their minds will run on something else—say typically, for the sake of illustration, their sweetheart, or their new bonnet. The one obstacle, Mrs Valeria, to your rising equal to the men in the various industrial processes of life is not raised, as the women vainly suppose, by the defective institutions of the age they live in. No! the obstacle is in themselves. No institutions that can be devised to encourage them will ever be strong enough to contend successfully with the sweetheart and the new bonnet. A little while ago, for instance, I was instrumental in getting women employed in our local post-office here. The other day I took the trouble—a serious business to me—of getting downstairs, and wheeling myself away to the office to see how they were getting on. I took a letter with me to register. It had an unusually long address. The registering-women began copying the address on the receipt-form, in a business-like manner cheering and delightful to see. Half-way through, a little child, sister of one of the other women employed, trotted into the office, and popped under the counter to go and speak to her relative. The registering-woman's mind instantly gave way. Her pencil stopped; her eyes wandered off to the child, with a charming expression of interest. "Well, Lucy!" she said, "how-d'ye-do?" Then she remembered business again, and returned to her receipt. When I took it across the counter, an important line in the address of my letter was left out in the copy. Thanks to Lucy. Now a man in the same position would not have seen Lucy—he would have been too closely occupied with what he was about at the moment. There is the whole difference between the mental constitution of the sexes, which no legislation will ever alter as long as the world lasts! What does it matter? Women are infinitely superior to men in the moral qualities which are the true adornments of humanity. Be content—oh, my mistaken sisters, be content with that!'

He twisted his chair round towards the stove. It was useless to dispute the question with him, even if I had felt inclined to do so. He absorbed himself in his stew-pan.

I looked about me in the room.

The same insatiable relish for horrors exhibited downstairs by the pictures in the hall, was displayed again here. The photographs hanging on the wall, represented the various forms of madness taken from the life. The plaster casts ranged on the shelf opposite, were casts (after death) of the heads of famous murderers. A frightful little skeleton of a woman hung in a cupboard, behind a glazed door, with this cynical inscription placed above the skull—'Behold the scaffolding on which beauty is built!' In a corresponding cupboard, with the door wide open, there hung in loose folds a shirt (as I took it to be) of chamois leather. Touching it (and finding it to be far softer than any chamois leather that my fingers had ever felt before), I disarranged the folds, and disclosed a ticket pinned among them, describing the thing in these horrid lines:—'Skin of a French Marquis, tanned in the Revolution of Ninety Three.* Who says the nobility are not good for something? They make good leather.'

After this last specimen of my host's taste in curiosities, I pursued my investigation no farther. I returned to my chair, and waited for the Truffles.

After a brief interval, the voice of the poet-painter-composer-and-cook summoned me back to the alcove.

The gas was out. The stew-pan and its accompaniments had vanished. On the marble slab were two plates, two napkins, two rolls of bread—and a dish, with another napkin in it, on which reposed two quaint little black balls. Miserrimus Dexter, regarding me with a smile of benevolent interest, put one of the balls on my plate, and took the other himself. 'Compose yourself, Mrs Valeria,' he said. 'This is an epoch in your life. Your first Truffle! Don't touch it with the knife. Use the fork alone. And—pardon me; this is most important—eat slowly.'

I followed my instructions, and assumed an enthusiasm which I honestly confess I did not feel. I privately thought the new vegetable a great deal too rich, and, in other respects, quite unworthy of the fuss that had been made about it. Miserrimus Dexter lingered and languished over his truffles, and sipped his wonderful Burgundy, and sang his own praises as a cook—until I was really almost mad with impatience to return to the real object of my visit. In the reckless state of mind which this feeling produced, I abruptly reminded my host that he was wasting our time, by the most dangerous question that I could possibly put to him.

'Mr Dexter,' I said, 'have you heard anything lately of Mrs Beauly?'

The easy sense of enjoyment expressed in his face left it at those rash words, and went out like a suddenly-extinguished light. That furtive distrust of me which I had already noticed, instantly made itself felt again in his manner and in his voice.

'Do you know Mrs Beauly?' he asked.

'I only know her,' I answered, 'by what I have read of her in the Trial.'

He was not satisfied with that reply.

'You must have an interest of some sort in Mrs Beauly,' he said, 'or you would not have asked me about her. Is it the interest of a friend? or the interest of an enemy?'

Rash as I might be, I was not quite reckless enough yet, to meet that plain question by an equally plain reply. I saw enough in his face to warn me to be careful with him before it was too late.

'I can only answer you in one way,' I rejoined. 'I must return to a subject which is very painful to you—the subject of the Trial.'

'Go on!' he said with one of his grim outbursts of humour. 'Here I am at your mercy—a martyr at the stake. Poke the fire! poke the fire!'

'I am only an ignorant woman,' I resumed; 'and I daresay I am quite wrong. But there is one part of my husband's trial which doesn't at all satisfy me. The defence set up for him seems to me to have been a complete mistake.'

'A complete mistake?' he repeated. 'Strange language, Mrs Valeria, to say the least of it!' He tried to speak lightly; he took up his goblet of wine. But I could see that I had produced an effect on him. His hand trembled as it carried the wine to his lips.

'I don't doubt that Eustace's first wife really asked him to buy the arsenic,' I continued. 'I don't doubt that she used it secretly to improve her complexion. But what I do *not* believe is—that she died of an overdose of the poison, taken by mistake.'

He put back the goblet of wine on the table near him, so unsteadily that he spilt the greater part of it. For a moment his eyes met mine; then looked down again.

'How do you believe she died?' he inquired, in tones so low that I could hardly hear them.

'By the hand of a poisoner,' I answered.

He made a movement as if he was about to start up in the chair, and sank back again, seized apparently with a sudden faintness.

'Not my husband!' I hastened to add. 'You know that I am satisfied of *his* innocence.'

I saw him shudder. I saw his hands fasten their hold convulsively on the arms of his chair.

'Who poisoned her?' he asked—still lying helplessly back in the chair.

At the critical moment, my courage failed me. I was afraid to tell him in what direction my suspicions pointed. 'Can't you guess?' I said.

There was a pause. I supposed him to be secretly following his own train of thought. It was not for long. On a sudden, he started up in his chair. The prostration which had possessed him appeared to vanish in an instant. His eyes recovered their wild light; his hands were steady again; his colour was brighter than ever. Had he been pondering over the secret of my interest in Mrs Beauly, and had he guessed? He had!

'Answer me on your word of honour!' he cried. 'Don't attempt to deceive me. Is it a woman?'

'It is.'

'What is the first letter of her name? Is it one of the first three letters of the alphabet?'

'Yes.'

'B?'

'Yes.'

'Beauly?'

'Beauly.'

He threw his hands up above his head, and burst into a frantic fit of laughter.

'I have lived long enough!' he broke out wildly. 'At last I have discovered one other person in the world who sees it as plainly as I do. Cruel Mrs Valeria! why did you torture me? Why didn't you own it before?'

'What!' I exclaimed, catching the infection of his excitement. 'Are *your* ideas, *my* ideas? Is it possible that *you* suspect Mrs Beauly, too?'

He made this remarkable reply:

'Suspect?' he repeated, contemptuously. 'There isn't the shadow of a doubt about it. Mrs Beauly poisoned her.'*

CHAPTER XXX

The Indictment of Mrs Beauly

I STARTED to my feet, and looked at Miserrimus Dexter. I was too much agitated to be able to speak to him.

My utmost expectations had not prepared me for the tone of absolute conviction in which he had spoken. At the best, I had anticipated that he might, by the barest chance, agree with me in suspecting Mrs Beauly. And now, his own lips had said it, without hesitation or reserve! 'There isn't the shadow of a doubt; Mrs Beauly poisoned her.'

'Sit down,' he said, quietly. 'There's nothing to be afraid of. Nobody can hear us in this room.'

I sat down again, and recovered myself a little.

'Have you never told any one else what you have told me?' was the first question I put to him.

'Never. No one else suspected her.'

'Not even the lawyers?'

'Not even the lawyers. There is no legal evidence against Mrs Beauly. There is nothing but moral certainty.'

'Surely you might have found the evidence, if you had tried?'

He laughed at the idea.

'Look at me!' he said. 'How is a man to hunt up evidence who is tied to this chair? Besides, there were other difficulties in my way. I am not generally in the habit of needlessly betraying myself—I am a cautious man, though you may not have noticed it. But my immeasurable hatred of Mrs

Beauly was not to be concealed. If eyes can tell secrets, she must have discovered, in my eyes, that I hungered and thirsted to see her in the hangman's hands. From first to last, I tell you, Mrs Borgia-Beauly* was on her guard against me. Can I describe her cunning? All my resources of language are not equal to the task. Take the degrees of comparison to give you a faint idea of it. I am positively cunning; the devil is comparatively cunning; Mrs Beauly is superlatively cunning. No! no! If she is ever discovered, at this distance of time, it will not be done by a man—it will be done by a woman, a woman whom she doesn't suspect; a woman who can watch her with the patience of a tigress in a state of starvation——'

'Say a woman like Me!' I broke out. 'I am ready to try.'

His eyes glittered; his teeth showed themselves viciously under his moustache; he drummed fiercely with both hands on the arms of his chair.

'Do you really mean it?' he asked.

'Put me in your position,' I answered. 'Enlighten me with your moral certainty (as you call it)—and you shall see.'

'I'll do it!' he said. 'Tell me one thing first. How did an outside stranger, like you, come to suspect her?'

I set before him, to the best of my ability, the various elements of suspicion which I had collected from the evidence at the Trial; and I laid especial stress on the fact (sworn to by the nurse) that Mrs Beauly was missing, exactly at the time when Christina Ormsay had left Mrs Eustace Macallan alone in her room.

'You have hit it!' cried Miserrimus Dexter. 'You are a wonderful woman! What was she doing on the morning of the day when Mrs Eustace Macallan died poisoned? And where was she, during the dark hours of the night? I can tell you where she was *not:*—she was not in her own room.'

'Not in her own room?' I repeated. 'Are you really sure of that?'

'I am sure of everything that I say, when I am speaking of Mrs Beauly. Mind that; and now listen! This is a drama;

and I excel in dramatic narrative. You shall judge for yourself. Date, the twentieth of October. Scene, The Corridor, called The Guests' Corridor, at Gleninch. On one side, a row of windows looking out into the garden. On the other, a row of four bedrooms, with dressing-rooms attached. First bedroom (beginning from the staircase), occupied by Mrs Beauly. Second bedroom, empty. Third bedroom, occupied by Miserrimus Dexter. Fourth bedroom, empty. So much for the Scene! The time comes next—the time is eleven at night. Dexter discovered in his bedroom, reading. Enter to him Eustace Macallan. Eustace speaks:—"My dear fellow, be particularly careful not to make any noise; don't bowl your chair up and down the corridor to-night." Dexter inquires, "Why?" Eustace answers, "Mrs Beauly has been dining with some friends in Edinburgh, and has come back terribly fatigued; she has gone up to her room to rest." Dexter makes another inquiry (satirical inquiry, this time):—"How does she look when she is terribly fatigued? As beautiful as ever?" Answer:—"I don't know; I have not seen her; she slipped upstairs, without speaking to anybody." Third inquiry by Dexter (logical inquiry, on this occasion):—"If she spoke to nobody, how do you know she is fatigued?" Eustace hands me a morsel of paper, and answers, "Don't be a fool! I found this on the hall table. Remember what I have told you about keeping quiet; good night!" Eustace retires. Dexter looks at the paper, and reads these lines in pencil:—"Just returned. Please forgive me for going to bed without saying good night. I have over-exerted myself; I am dreadfully fatigued. (Signed) HELENA." Dexter is by nature suspicious; Dexter suspects Mrs Beauly. Never mind his reasons; there is no time to enter into his reasons now. He puts the case to himself thus:—"A weary woman would never have given herself the trouble to write this. She would have found it much less fatiguing to knock at the drawing-room door as she passed, and to make her apologies by word of mouth. I see something here out of the ordinary way: I shall make a night of it in my chair."

Very good. Dexter proceeds to make a night of it. He opens
his door; wheels himself softly into the corridor; locks the
doors of the two empty bedrooms, and returns (with the
keys in his pocket) to his own room. "Now," says D. to
himself, "if I hear a door softly opened in this part of the
house, I shall know for certain it is Mrs Beauly's door!"
Upon that, he closes his own door, leaving the tiniest little
chink to look through; puts out his light; and waits and
watches at his tiny little chink, like a cat at a mousehole.
The corridor is the only place he wants to see; and a lamp
burns there all night. Twelve o'clock strikes; he hears the
doors below bolted and locked, and nothing happens. Half-
past twelve—and nothing still. The house is as silent as the
grave. One o'clock; two o'clock—same silence. Half-past
two—and something happens at last. Dexter hears a sound
close by, in the corridor. It is the sound of a handle turning
very softly in a door—in the only door that can be opened,
the door of Mrs Beauly's room. Dexter drops noiselessly
from his chair, on to his hands; lies flat on the floor at his
chink; and listens. He hears the handle closed again; he sees
a dark object flit by him; he pops his head out of his door,
down on the floor where nobody would think of looking for
him. And, what does he see? Mrs Beauly! There she goes,
with the long brown cloak over her shoulders which she
wears when she is driving, floating behind her. In a moment
more, she disappears, past the fourth bedroom, and turns
at a right angle, into a second corridor, called the South
Corridor. What rooms are in the South Corridor? There
are three rooms. First room, the little study, mentioned in
the nurse's evidence. Second room, Mrs Eustace Macallan's bedchamber. Third room, her husband's bedchamber.
What does Mrs Beauly (supposed to be worn out by
fatigue) want in that part of the house, at half-past two in
the morning? Dexter decides on running his risk of being
seen—and sets forth on a voyage of discovery. Do you know
how he gets from place to place, without his chair? Have
you seen the poor deformed creature hop on his hands?

Shall he show you how he does it, before he goes on with his story?'

I hastened to stop the proposed exhibition.

'I saw you hop last night,' I said. 'Go on! pray go on with your story!'

'Do you like my dramatic style of narrative?' he asked. 'Am I interesting?'

'Indescribably interesting, Mr Dexter. I am eager to hear more.'

He smiled in high approval of his own abilities.

'I am equally good at the autobiographical style,' he said. 'Shall we try that next, by way of variety?'

'Anything you like,' I cried, losing all patience with him, 'if you will only go on!'

'Part Two: Autobiographical Style,' he announced, with a wave of his hand. 'I hopped along the Guests' Corridor, and turned into the South Corridor. I stopped at the little study. Door open; nobody there. I crossed the study to the second door, communicating with Mrs Macallan's bedchamber. Locked! I looked through the keyhole. Was there something hanging over it, on the other side? I can't say—I only know there was nothing to be seen, but blank darkness. I listened. Nothing to be heard. Same blank darkness, same absolute silence, inside the locked second door of Mrs Eustace's room, opening on the corridor. I went on to her husband's bedchamber. I had the worst possible opinion of Mrs Beauly—I should not have been in the least surprised if I had caught her in Eustace's room. I looked through the keyhole. In this case, the key was out of it—or was turned the right way for me—I don't know which. Eustace's bed was opposite the door. No discovery. I could see him, by his nightlight, innocently asleep. I reflected a little. The back staircase was at the end of the corridor, beyond me. I slid down the stairs, and looked about me on the lower floor, by the light of the night-lamp. Doors all fast locked, and keys outside, so that I could try them myself. House door barred and bolted. Door leading into the servants'

offices barred and bolted. I got back to my own room, and
thought it out quietly. Where could she be? Certainly *in* the
house, somewhere. Where? I had made sure of the other
rooms; the field of search was exhausted. She could only
be in Mrs Macallan's room—the *one* room which had baf-
fled my investigations; the *only* room which had not lent
itself to examination. Add to this, that the key of the door
in the study, communicating with Mrs Macallan's room,
was stated in the nurse's evidence to be missing; and don't
forget that the dearest object of Mrs Beauly's life (on the
showing of her own letter, read at the Trial) was to be
Eustace Macallan's happy wife. Put these things together
in your own mind, and you will know what my thoughts
were, as I sat waiting for events in my chair, without my
telling you. Towards four o'clock, strong as I am, fatigue
got the better of me. I fell asleep. Not for long. I woke with
a start and looked at my watch. Twenty-five minutes past
four. Had she got back to her room while I was asleep? I
hopped to her door, and listened. Not a sound. I softly
opened the door. The room was empty. I went back again
to my own room to wait and watch. It was hard work to
keep my eyes open. I drew up the window to let the cool
air refresh me; I fought hard with exhausted nature; and
exhausted nature won. I fell asleep again. This time it was
eight in the morning when I woke. I have goodish ears, as
you may have noticed. I heard women's voices talking
under my open window. I peeped out. Mrs Beauly and her
maid, in close confabulation! Mrs Beauly and her maid,
looking guiltily about them to make sure that they were
neither seen nor heard! "Take care, ma'am," I heard the
maid say; "that horrid deformed monster is as sly as a fox.
Mind he doesn't discover you." Mrs Beauly answered,
"You go first, and look out in front; I will follow you; and
make sure there is nobody behind us." With that, they
disappeared round the corner of the house. In five minutes
more I heard the door of Mrs Beauly's room softly opened
and closed again. Three hours later, the nurse met her in

the corridor, innocently on her way to make inquiries at Mrs Eustace Macallan's door. What do you think of these circumstances? What do you think of Mrs Beauly and her maid having something to say to each other, which they didn't dare say in the house—for fear of my being behind some door listening to them? What do you think of these discoveries of mine being made, on the very morning when Mrs Eustace was taken ill—on the very day when she died by a poisoner's hand? Do you see your way to the guilty person? And has mad Miserrimus Dexter been of some assistance to you, so far?'

I was too violently excited to answer him. The way to the vindication of my husband's innocence was opened to me at last!

'Where is she?' I cried. 'And where is that servant who is in her confidence?'

'I can't tell you,' he said. 'I don't know.'

'Where can I inquire? Can you tell me that?'

He considered a little.

'There is one man who must know where she is—or who could find it out for you,' he said.

'Who is he? What is his name?'

'He is a friend of Eustace's. Major Fitz-David.'

'I know him! I am going to dine with him next week. He has asked you to dine too.'

Miserrimus Dexter laughed contemptuously.

'Major Fitz-David may do very well for the ladies,' he said. 'The ladies can treat him as a species of elderly human lap-dog. I don't dine with lap-dogs; I have said, No. You go. He, or some of his ladies, may be of use to you. Who are the guests? Did he tell you?'

'There was a French lady whose name I forget,' I said, 'and Lady Clarinda——'

'That will do! She is a friend of Mrs Beauly's. She is sure to know where Mrs Beauly is. Come to me, the moment you have got your information. Find out if the maid is with her: she is the easiest to deal with of the two. Only make the maid open her lips; and we have got Mrs Beauly. We crush her,' he cried, bringing his hand down like lightning on the last languid fly of the season, crawling over the arm of his chair, 'we crush her as I crush this fly. Stop! A question; a most important question in dealing with the maid. Have you got any money?'

'Plenty of money.'

He snapped his fingers joyously.

'The maid is ours!' he cried. 'It's a matter of pounds, shillings, and pence, with the maid. Wait! Another question. About your name? If you approach Mrs Beauly in your own character as Eustace's wife, you approach her as the woman who has taken her place—you make a mortal enemy of her at starting. Beware of that!'

My jealousy of Mrs Beauly, smouldering in me all through the interview, burst into flame at those words. I could resist it no longer—I was obliged to ask him if my husband had ever loved her.

'Tell me the truth,' I said. 'Did Eustace really——?'

He burst out laughing maliciously; he penetrated my jealousy, and guessed my question almost before it had passed my lips.

'Yes,' he said, 'Eustace did really love her—and no mistake about it. She had every reason to believe (before the Trial) that the wife's death would put her in the wife's place. But the Trial made another man of Eustace. Mrs Beauly had been a witness of the public degradation of him. That was enough to prevent his marrying Mrs Beauly. He broke off with her at once and for ever—for the same reason precisely which has led him to separate himself from you. Existence with a woman who knew that he had been tried for his life as a murderer, was an existence that he was not hero enough to face. You wanted the truth. There it is! You have need to be cautious of Mrs Beauly—you have no need to be jealous of her. Take the safe course. Arrange with the Major, when you meet Lady Clarinda at his dinner, that you meet her under an assumed name.'

'I can go to the dinner,' I said, 'under the name in which Eustace married me. I can go as "Mrs Woodville."'

'The very thing!' he exclaimed. 'What would I not give to be present when Lady Clarinda introduces you to Mrs Beauly! Think of the situation. A woman with a hideous secret, hidden in her inmost soul: and another woman who knows of it—another woman who is bent, by fair means or foul, on dragging that secret into the light of day. What a struggle! What a plot for a novel! I am in a fever when I think of it. I am beside myself when I look into the future, and see Mrs Borgia-Beauly brought to her knees at last. Don't be alarmed!' he cried, with the wild light flashing once more in his eyes. 'My brains are beginning to boil again in my head. I must take refuge in physical exercise. I must blow off the steam, or I shall explode in my pink jacket on the spot!'

The old madness seized on him again. I made for the door, to secure my retreat in case of necessity—and then ventured to look round at him.

He was off on his furious wheels—half man, half chair—flying like a whirlwind to the other end of the room. Even this exercise was not violent enough for him, in his present mood. In an instant he was down on the floor; poised on his hands, and looking in the distance like a monstrous frog. Hopping down the room, he overthrew, one after another, all the smaller and lighter chairs as he passed them. Arrived at the end, he turned, surveyed the prostrate chairs, encouraged himself with a scream of triumph, and leapt rapidly over chair after chair, on his hands—his limbless body, now thrown back from the shoulders, and now thrown forward to keep the balance, in a manner at once wonderful and horrible to behold. 'Dexter's Leapfrog!' he cried, cheerfully, perching himself, with his bird-like lightness, on the last of the prostrate chairs, when he had reached the further end of the room. 'I'm pretty active, Mrs Valeria, considering I'm a cripple. Let us drink to the hanging of Mrs Beauly, in another bottle of Burgundy!'

I seized desperately on the first excuse that occurred to me for getting away from him.

'You forget,' I said—'I must go at once to the Major. If I don't warn him in time, he may speak of me to Lady Clarinda by the wrong name.'

Ideas of hurry and movement were just the ideas to take his fancy, in his present state. He blew furiously on the whistle that summoned Ariel from the kitchen regions, and danced up and down on his hands in the full frenzy of his delight.

'Ariel shall get you a cab!' he cried. 'Drive at a gallop to the Major's. Set the trap for her without losing a moment. Oh, what a day of days this has been! Oh, what a relief to get rid of my dreadful secret, and share it with You! I am suffocating with happiness—I am like the Spirit of the Earth in Shelley's poem.' He broke out with the magnificent lines in 'Prometheus Unbound,'* in which the Earth feels the Spirit of Love, and bursts into speech. ' "The joy, the triumph, the delight, the madness! The boundless, over-flowing, bursting gladness, The vaporous exultation not to be confined! Ha! ha! the animation of delight, Which wraps me like an atmosphere of light, And bears me as a cloud is borne by its own wind." That's how I feel, Valeria! that's how I feel!'

I crossed the threshold while he was still speaking. The last I saw of him, he was pouring out that glorious flood of words—his deformed body, poised on the overthrown chair, his face lifted in rapture to some fantastic Heaven of his own making. I slipped out softly into the antechamber. Even as I crossed the room, he changed once more. I heard his ringing cry; I heard the soft thump-thump of his hands on the floor. He was going down the room again, in 'Dexter's Leapfrog,' flying over the prostrate chairs!

In the hall, Ariel was on the watch for me.

As I approached her, I happened to be putting on my gloves. She stopped me; and taking my right arm, lifted my hand towards her face. Was she going to kiss it? or to bite it? Neither. She smelt it like a dog—and dropped it again with a hoarse chuckling laugh.

'You don't smell of his perfumes,' she said. 'You *haven't* touched his beard. *Now* I believe you. Want a cab?'

'Thank you. I'll walk till I meet a cab.'

She was bent on being polite to me—now I had *not* touched his beard.

'I say!' she burst out, in her deepest notes.

'Yes?'

'I'm glad I didn't upset you in the canal. There now!'

She gave me a friendly smack on the shoulder which nearly knocked me down—relapsed, the instant after, into her leaden stolidity of look and manner—and led the way out by the front door. I heard her hoarse chuckling laugh as she locked the gate behind me. My star was at last in the ascendant! In one and the same day, I had found my way into the confidence of Ariel, and Ariel's Master!

CHAPTER XXXI

The Defence of Mrs Beauly

THE days that elapsed before Major Fitz-David's dinner-party were precious days to me.

My long interview with Miserrimus Dexter had disturbed me far more seriously than I suspected at the time. It was not until some hours after I had left him, that I really began to feel how my nerves had been tried by all that I had seen and heard, during my visit at his house. I started at the slightest noises; I dreamed of dreadful things; I was ready to cry without reason, at one moment, and to fly into a passion without reason, at another. Absolute rest was what I wanted, and (thanks to my good Benjamin) was what I got.

The dear old man controlled his anxieties on my account, and spared me the questions which his fatherly interest in my welfare made him eager to ask. It was tacitly understood between us that all conversation on the subject of my visit to Miserrimus Dexter (of which, it is needless to say, he strongly disapproved), should be deferred until repose had restored my energies of body and mind. I saw no visitors. Mrs Macallan came to the cottage, and Major Fitz-David came to the cottage—one of them to hear what had passed between Miserrimus Dexter and myself: the other to amuse me with the latest gossip about the guests at the forthcoming dinner. Benjamin took it on himself to make my apologies, and to spare me the exertion of receiving my visitors. We hired a little open carriage, and took long drives in the pretty country lanes, still left flourishing within a few miles of the northern suburb of London. At home, we sat and talked quietly of old times, or played at backgammon and dominoes—and so, for a few happy days, led the peaceful, unadventurous life which was good for me. When the day of the dinner arrived, I felt restored to my customary health. I was ready again, and eager again, for the introduction to Lady Clarinda, and the discovery of Mrs Beauly.

Benjamin looked a little sadly at my flushed face, as we drove to Major Fitz-David's house.

'Ah, my dear,' he said, in his simple way, 'I see you are well again! You have had enough of our quiet life already.'

My recollection of events and persons, in general, at the dinner-party, is singularly indistinct. I remember that we were very merry, and as easy and familiar with one another as if we had been old friends. I remember that Madame Mirliflore was unapproachably superior to the other women present, in the perfect beauty of her dress, and in the ample justice which she did to the luxurious dinner set before us. I remember the Major's young prima-donna, more round-eyed, more over-dressed, more shrill and strident as the coming 'Queen of Song,' than ever. I remember the Major himself, always kissing our hands, always luring us to indulge in dainty dishes and drinks, always making love, always detecting resemblances between us, always 'under the charm,' and never once out of his character as elderly Don Juan, from the beginning of the evening to the end. I remember dear old Benjamin completely bewildered, shrinking into corners, blushing when he was personally drawn into the conversation, frightened at Madame Mirliflore, bashful with Lady Clarinda, submissive to the Major, suffering under the music; and, from the bottom of his honest old heart, wishing himself home again. And there, as to the members of that cheerful little gathering, my memory finds its limits—with one exception. The appearance of Lady Clarinda is as present to me as if I had met her yesterday; and of the memorable conversation which we two held together privately, towards the close of the evening, it is no exaggeration to say that I can still call to mind almost every word.

I see her dress, I hear her voice again, while I write.

She was attired, I remember, with that extreme assumption of simplicity which always defeats its own end, by irresistibly suggesting art. She wore plain white muslin, over white silk, without trimming or ornament of any kind. Her rich brown hair, dressed in defiance of the prevailing fashion, was thrown back from her forehead, and gathered into a simple knot behind, without adornment of any sort. A little white ribbon encircled her neck, fastened by the only article of jewellery that she wore—a tiny diamond brooch. She was unquestionably handsome; but her beauty was of the somewhat hard and angular type which is so often seen in English women of her race: the nose and chin too prominent and too firmly shaped; the well-opened grey eyes full of spirit and dignity, but wanting in tenderness and mobility of expression. Her manner had all the charm which fine breeding can confer—exquisitely polite, easily cordial; showing that perfect yet unobtrusive confidence in herself, which (in England) seems to be the natural outgrowth of pre-eminent social rank. If you had accepted her for what she was, on the surface, you would have said, Here is the model of a noble woman who is perfectly free from pride. And if you had taken a liberty with her, on the strength of that conviction, she would have made you remember it to the end of your life.

We got on together admirably. I was introduced as 'Mrs Woodville,' by previous arrangement with the Major, effected through Benjamin. Before the dinner was over, we had promised to exchange visits. Nothing but the opportunity was wanting to lead Lady Clarinda into talking, as I wanted her to talk, of Mrs Beauly.

Late in the evening, the opportunity came.

I had taken refuge from the terrible bravura singing of the Major's strident prima-donna, in the back drawing-room. As I had hoped and anticipated, after a while, Lady Clarinda (missing me from the group round the piano) came in search of me. She seated herself by my side, out of sight and out of hearing of our friends in the front room; and, to my infinite relief and delight, touched on the subject of Miserrimus Dexter, of her own accord. Something I had said of him, when his name had been accidentally mentioned at dinner, remained in her memory, and led us, by perfectly natural gradations, into speaking of Mrs Beauly. 'At last,' I thought to myself, 'the Major's little dinner will bring me my reward!'

And what a reward it was, when it came! My heart sinks in me again—as it sank on that never-to-be-forgotten evening—while I sit at my desk, thinking of it.

'So Dexter really spoke to you of Mrs Beauly!' exclaimed Lady Clarinda. 'You have no idea how you surprise me.'

'May I ask why?'

'He hates her! The last time I saw him, he wouldn't allow me to mention her name. It is one of his innumerable oddities. If any such feeling as sympathy is a possible feeling in such a nature as his, he ought to like Helena Beauly. She is the most completely unconventional person I know. When she does break out, poor dear, she says things and does things, which are almost reckless enough to be worthy of Dexter himself. I wonder whether you would like her?'

'You have kindly asked me to visit you, Lady Clarinda. Perhaps I may meet her at your house?'

Lady Clarinda laughed as if the idea amused her.

'I hope you will not wait until *that* is likely to happen,' she said. 'Helena's last whim is to fancy that she has got— the gout, of all the maladies in the world! She is away at some wonderful baths in Hungary, or Bohemia (I don't remember which)—and where she will go, or what she will do, next, it is perfectly impossible to say. Dear Mrs Wood-ville! is the heat of the fire too much for you? You are looking quite pale.'

I *felt* that I was looking pale. The discovery of Mrs Beauly's absence from England was a shock for which I was quite unprepared. For the moment, it unnerved me.

'Shall we go into the other room?' asked Lady Clarinda.

To go into the other room would be to drop the conversation. I was determined not to let that catastrophe happen. It was just possible that Mrs Beauly's maid might have quitted her service, or might have been left behind in England. My information would not be complete, until I knew what had become of the maid. I pushed my chair back a little from the fire-place, and took a hand-screen from a table near me. It might be made useful in hiding my face, if any more disappointments were in store for me.

'Thank you, Lady Clarinda: I was only a little too near the fire. I shall do admirably here. You surprise me about Mrs Beauly. From what Mr Dexter said to me, I had im-agined——'

'Oh, you must not believe anything Dexter tells you!' interposed Lady Clarinda. 'He delights in mystifying people; and he purposely misled you, I have no doubt. If all that I hear is true, *he* ought to know more of Helena Beauly's strange freaks and fancies than most people. He all but discovered her, in one of her adventures (down in Scotland), which reminds me of the story in Auber's charm-

ing opera—what is it called? I shall forget my own name
next! I mean the opera in which the two nuns slip out of
the convent, and go to the ball. Listen! how very odd! That
vulgar girl is singing the castanet song in the second act, at
this moment. Major! what opera is the young lady singing
from?'

The Major was scandalised at the interruption. He bustled into the back room—whispered 'Hush! hush! my dear
lady. The *Domino Noir*'*—and bustled back again to the
piano.

'Of course!' said Lady Clarinda. 'How stupid of me! The
Domino Noir. And how strange that you should forget it
too!'

I had remembered it perfectly; but I could not trust
myself to speak. If, as I believed, the 'adventure' mentioned
by Lady Clarinda was connected, in some way, with Mrs
Beauly's mysterious proceedings on the morning of the
twenty-first of October, I was on the brink of the very
discovery which it was the one interest of my life to make!
I held the screen so as to hide my face; and I said, in the
steadiest voice that I could command at the moment,—

'Pray go on! Pray tell me what the adventure was!'

Lady Clarinda was quite flattered by my eager desire to
bear the coming narrative.

'I hope my story will be worthy of the interest which you
are so good as to feel in it,' she said. 'If you only knew
Helena—it is *so* like her! I have it, you must know, from
her maid. She has taken a woman who speaks foreign languages with her to Hungary, and she has left the maid with
me. A perfect treasure! I should only be too glad if I could
keep her in my service: she has but one defect, a name I
hate—Phœbe. Well! Phœbe and her mistress were staying
at a place near Edinburgh, called (I think) Gleninch. The
house belonged to that Mr Macallan, who was afterwards
tried—you remember it, of course?—for poisoning his wife.
A dreadful case; but don't be alarmed—my story has nothing to do with it; my story has to do with Helena Beauly.

One evening (while she was staying at Gleninch) she was engaged to dine with some English friends visiting Edinburgh. The same night—also in Edinburgh—there was a masked ball, given by somebody whose name I forget. The ball (almost an unparalleled event in Scotland!) was reported to be not at all a reputable affair. All sorts of amusing people were to be there. Ladies of doubtful virtue, you know; and gentlemen on the outlying limits of society, and so on. Helena's friends had contrived to get cards, and were going, in spite of the objections—in the strictest incognito, of course; trusting to their masks. And Helena herself was bent on going with them, if she could only manage it without being discovered at Gleninch. Mr Macallan was one of the strait-laced people who disapproved of the ball. No lady, he said, could show herself at such an entertainment without compromising her reputation. What stuff! Well, Helena, in one of her wildest moments, hit on a way of going to the ball without discovery, which was really as ingenious as a plot in a French play. She went to the dinner in the carriage from Gleninch, having sent Phœbe to Edinburgh before her. It was not a grand dinner—a little friendly gathering; no evening dress. When the time came for going back to Gleninch, what do you think Helena did? She sent her maid back in the carriage, instead of herself! Phœbe was dressed in her mistress's cloak and bonnet and veil. She was instructed to run upstairs the moment she got to the house; leaving on the hall-table a little note of apology (written by Helena of course!) pleading fatigue as an excuse for not saying good night to her host. The mistress and the maid were about the same height; and the servants naturally never discovered the trick. Phœbe got up to her mistress's room, safely enough. There, her instructions were to wait until the house was quiet for the night, and then to steal up to her own room. While she was waiting, the girl fell asleep. She only woke at two in the morning, or later. It didn't much matter, as she thought. She stole out on tip-toe, and closed the door behind her. Before she was at the end of the corridor, she fancied she heard something. She waited till she was safe on the upper storey, and then she looked over the banisters. There was Dexter—so like him!—hopping about on his hands (did you ever see it? the most grotesquely-horrible exhibition you can imagine!)—there was Dexter, hopping about, and looking through key-holes—evidently in search of the person who had left her room at two in the morning; and no doubt taking Phœbe for her mistress, seeing that she had forgotten to take her mistress's cloak off her shoulders. The next morning early, Helena came back in a hired carriage from Edinburgh, with a hat and mantle borrowed from her English friends. She left the carriage in the road; and got into the house by way of the garden—without being discovered, this time, by Dexter, or by anybody. Clever and daring, wasn't it? And, as I said just now, quite a new version of the *Domino Noir*. You will wonder, as I did, how it was that Dexter didn't make mischief in the morning? He would have done it no doubt. But even *he* was silenced (as Phœbe told me) by the dread-ful event that happened in the house on the same day.——My dear Mrs Woodville! the heat of this room is certainly too much for you. Take my smelling-bottle. Let me open the window.'

I was just able to answer, 'Pray say nothing! Let me slip out into the air!'

I made my way unobserved to the landing, and sat down on the stairs to compose myself, where nobody could see me. In a moment more, I felt a hand laid gently on my shoulder, and discovered good Benjamin looking at me in dismay. Lady Clarinda had considerately spoken to him, and had assisted him in quietly making his retreat from the room, while his host's attention was still absorbed by the music.

'My dear child!' he whispered, 'what is the matter?'

'Take me home, and I will tell you,' was all that I could say.

CHAPTER XXXII

A Specimen of my Wisdom

THE scene must follow my erratic movements—the scene must close on London for a while, and open in Edinburgh.

Two days had passed since Major Fitz-David's dinner-party. I was able to breathe again freely, after the utter destruction of all my plans for the future, and of all the hopes that I had founded on them. I could now see that I had been trebly in the wrong—wrong in hastily and cruelly suspecting an innocent woman; wrong in communicating my suspicions (without an attempt to verify them previously) to another person; wrong in accepting the flighty inferences and conclusions of Miserrimus Dexter as if they had been solid truths. I was so ashamed of my folly, when I thought of the past; so completely discouraged, so rudely shaken in my confidence in myself, when I thought of the future, that, for once in a way, I accepted sensible advice when it was offered to me. 'My dear,' said good old Benjamin, after we had thoroughly talked over my discomfiture on our return from the dinner-party, 'judging by what you tell me of him, I don't fancy Mr Dexter. Promise me that you will not go back to him, until you have first consulted some person who is fitter to guide you through this dangerous business than I am.'

I gave him my promise, on one condition. 'If I fail to find the person,' I said, 'will you undertake to help me?'

Benjamin pledged himself to help me, cheerfully.

The next morning, when I was brushing my hair, and thinking over my affairs, I called to mind a forgotten resolution of mine, at the time when I first read the Report of my husband's Trial. I mean the resolution—if Miserrimus Dexter failed me—to apply to one of the two agents (or solicitors, as we should term them) who had prepared Eustace's defence, namely, Mr Playmore. This gentleman, it may be remembered, had especially recommended himself to my confidence by his friendly interference, when the sheriff's officers were in search of my husband's papers. Referring back to the evidence of 'Isaiah Schoolcraft,' I found that Mr Playmore had been called in to assist and advise Eustace, by Miserrimus Dexter. He was therefore not only a friend on whom I might rely, but a friend who was personally acquainted with Dexter as well. Could there be a fitter man to apply to for enlightenment in the darkness that had now gathered round me? Benjamin, when I put the question to him, acknowledged that I had made a sensible choice on this occasion, and at once exerted himself to help me. He discovered (through his own lawyer) the address of Mr Playmore's London agents; and from these gentlemen he obtained for me a letter of introduction to Mr Playmore himself. I had nothing to conceal from my new adviser; and I was properly described in the letter as Eustace Macallan's second wife.

The same evening, we two set forth (Benjamin refused to let me travel alone) by the night mail for Edinburgh.

I had previously written to Miserrimus Dexter (by my old friend's advice), merely saying that I had been unexpectedly called away from London for a few days, and that I would report to him the result of my interview with Lady Clarinda on my return. A characteristic answer was brought back to the cottage by Ariel. 'Mrs Valeria, I happen to be a man of quick perceptions; and I can read the *unwritten* part of your letter. Lady Clarinda has shaken your confidence in me. Very good. I pledge myself to shake your confidence in Lady Clarinda. In the mean time, I am not offended. In serene composure I wait the honour and the happiness of your visit. Send me word by telegraph, whether you would like Truffles again, or whether you would prefer something simpler and lighter—say that incomparable French dish, Pig's Eyelids and Tamarinds. Believe me always your ally and admirer, your poet and cook—DEXTER.'

Arrived in Edinburgh, Benjamin and I had a little discussion. The question in dispute between us was, whether I should go with him, or go alone, to Mr Playmore. I was all for going alone.

'My experience of the world is not a very large one,' I said. 'But I have observed that, in nine cases out of ten, a man will make concessions to a woman, if she approaches him by herself, which he would hesitate even to consider, if another man was within hearing. I don't know how it is—I only know that it is so. If I find that I get on badly with Mr Playmore, I will ask him for a second appointment, and, in that case, you shall accompany me. Don't think me self-willed. Let me try my luck alone, and let us see what comes of it.'

Benjamin yielded, with his customary consideration for me. I sent my letter of introduction to Mr Playmore's office—his private house being in the neighbourhood of Gleninch. My messenger brought back a polite answer, inviting me to visit him at an early hour in the afternoon. At the appointed time to the moment, I rang the bell at the office door.

CHAPTER XXXIII

A Specimen of my Folly

THE incomprehensible submission of Scotchmen to the ecclesiastical tyranny of their Established Church, has produced—not unnaturally as I think—a very mistaken impression of the national character in the popular mind.

Public opinion looks at the institution of 'The Sabbath' in Scotland; finds it unparalleled in Christendom for its senseless and savage austerity; sees a nation content to be deprived by its priesthood of every social privilege on one day in every week—forbidden to travel; forbidden to telegraph; forbidden to eat a hot dinner; forbidden to read a newspaper; in short, allowed the use of two liberties only, the liberty of exhibiting oneself at the Church, and the liberty of secluding oneself over the bottle—public opinion sees this, and arrives at the not unreasonable conclusion that the people who submit to such social laws as these are the most stolid, stern, and joyless people on the face of the earth. Such are Scotchmen supposed to be, when viewed at a distance. But how do Scotchmen appear when they are seen under a closer light, and judged by the test of personal experience? There are no people more cheerful, more companionable, more hospitable, more liberal in their ideas, to be found on the face of the civilized globe than the very people who submit to the Scotch Sunday! On the six days of the week, there is an atmosphere of quiet humour, a radiation of genial common sense, about Scotchmen in general, which is simply delightful to feel. But on the seventh day, these same men will hear one of their ministers seriously tell them that he views taking a walk on the Sabbath in the light of an act of profanity, and will be the only people in existence who can let a man talk downright nonsense without laughing at him.

I am not clever enough to be able to account for this anomaly in the national character; I can only notice it by way of necessary preparation for the appearance in my little narrative of a personage not frequently seen, in writing—a cheerful Scotchman.

In all other respects I found Mr Playmore only negatively remarkable. He was neither old nor young, neither handsome nor ugly; he was personally not in the least like the popular idea of a lawyer; and he spoke perfectly good English, touched with only the slightest possible flavour of a Scotch accent.

'I have the honour to be an old friend of Mr Macallan,' he said, cordially shaking hands with me; 'and I am honestly happy to become acquainted with Mr Macallan's wife. Where will you sit? Near the light? You are young enough not to be afraid of the daylight, just yet. Is this your first visit to Edinburgh? Pray let me make it as pleasant to you as I can. I shall be delighted to present Mrs Playmore to you. We are staying in Edinburgh for a little while. The Italian opera is here; and we have a box for to-night. Will you kindly waive all ceremony, and dine with us and go to the music afterwards?'

'You are very kind,' I answered. 'But I have some anxieties just now which will make me a very poor companion for Mrs Playmore at the opera. My letter to you mentions, I think, that I have to ask your advice on matters which are of very serious importance to me.'

'Does it?' he rejoined. 'To tell you the truth, I have not read the letter through. I observed your name in it, and I gathered from your message that you wished to see me here. I sent my note to your hotel—and then went on with something else. Pray pardon me. Is this a professional consultation? For your own sake, I sincerely hope not.'

'It is hardly a professional consultation, Mr Playmore. I find myself in a very painful position; and I come to you to advise me, under very unusual circumstances. I shall greatly surprise you when you hear what I have to say; and I am afraid I shall occupy more than my fair share of your time.'

'I, and my time, are entirely at your disposal,' he said. 'Tell me what I can do for you—and tell it in your own way.'

The kindness of his language was more than matched by the kindness of his manner. I spoke to him freely and fully—I told him my strange story, exaggerating nothing, and suppressing nothing.

He showed the varying impressions that I produced on his mind, without the slightest concealment. My separation from Eustace distressed him. My resolution to dispute the Scotch Verdict, and my unjust suspicions of Mrs Beauly, first amused, then surprised him. It was not, however, until I had described my extraordinary interview with Miserrimus Dexter, and my hardly less remarkable conversation with Lady Clarinda, that I produced the greatest effect on the lawyer's mind. I saw him change colour for the first time. He started, and muttered to himself, as if he had completely forgotten me. 'Good God!' I heard him say— 'Can it be possible? Does the truth lie *that* way, after all?'

I took the liberty of interrupting him. I had no idea of allowing him to keep his thoughts to himself.

'I seem to have surprised you?' I said.

He started at the sound of my voice.

'I beg ten thousand pardons!' he exclaimed. 'You have not only surprised me—you have opened an entirely new view to my mind. I see a possibility, a really startling possibility, in connexion with the poisoning at Gleninch, which never occurred to me until the present moment. This is a nice state of things,' he added, falling back again into his ordinary humour. 'Here is the client leading the lawyer. My dear Mrs Eustace, which is it—do you want my advice? or do I want yours?'

'May I hear the new idea?' I asked.

'Not just yet, if you will excuse me,' he answered. 'Make allowances for my professional caution. I don't want to be professional with You—my great anxiety is to avoid it. But the lawyer gets the better of the man, and refuses to be suppressed. I really hesitate to realize what is passing in my own mind, without some further inquiry. Do me a great favour. Let us go over a part of the ground again, and let me ask you some questions as we proceed. Do you feel any objection to obliging me in this matter?'

'Certainly not, Mr Playmore. How far shall we go back?'

'To your visit to Dexter, with your mother-in-law. When you first asked him if he had any ideas of his own, on the subject of Mrs Macallan's death, did I understand you to say that he looked at you suspiciously?'

'Very suspiciously.'

'And his face cleared up again, when you told him that your question was only suggested by what you had read in the Report of the Trial?'

'Yes.'

He drew a slip of paper out of the drawer in his desk, dipped his pen in the ink, considered a little, and placed a chair for me close at his side.

'The lawyer disappears,' he said, 'and the man resumes his proper place. There shall be no professional mysteries between you and me. As your husband's old friend, Mrs Eustace, I feel no common interest in you. I see a serious necessity for warning you before it is too late; and I can only do so to any good purpose, by running a risk on which few men in my place would venture. Personally and professionally, I am going to trust you—though I *am* a Scotchman and a lawyer! Sit here and look over my shoulder while I make my notes. You will see what is passing in my mind, if you see what I write.'

I sat down by him and looked over his shoulder, without the smallest pretence of hesitation.

He began to write as follows:—

'The poisoning at Gleninch. Queries: In what position does Miserrimus Dexter stand towards the poisoning? And what does he (presumably) know about that matter?

'He has ideas which are secrets. He suspects that he has betrayed them, or that they have been discovered in some way, inconceivable to himself. He is palpably relieved when he finds that this is not the case.'

The pen stopped; and the question went on.

'Let us advance to your second visit,' said Mr Playmore, 'when you saw Dexter alone. Tell me again what he did, and how he looked, when you informed him that you were not satisfied with the Scotch Verdict.'

I repeated what I have already written. The pen went back to the paper again, and added these lines:—

'He hears nothing more remarkable than that a person visiting him, who is interested in the case, refuses to accept the verdict at the Macallan Trial, as a final verdict, and proposes to re-open the inquiry. What does he do upon that?

'He exhibits all the symptoms of a panic of terror; he sees himself in some incomprehensible danger; he is frantic at one moment, and servile at the next; he must and will know what this disturbing person really means. And when he is informed on that point, he first turns pale and doubts the evidence of his own senses; and next, with nothing said to justify it, gratuitously accuses his visitor of suspecting somebody. Query here: When a small sum of money is missing in a household, and the servants in general are called together to be informed of the circumstance, what do we think of the one servant, in particular, who speaks first, and who says, "Do you suspect *me?*"'

He laid down the pen again.

'Is that right?' he asked.

I began to see the end to which the notes were drifting. Instead of answering his question, I entreated him to enter into the explanations that were still wanting to convince my own mind. He held up a warning forefinger and stopped me.

'Not yet,' he said. 'Once again, am I right—so far?'

'Quite right.'

'Very well. Now tell me what Dexter did next. Don't mind repeating yourself. Give me all the details, one after another to the end.'

I gave him all the details, exactly as I remembered them. Mr Playmore returned to his writing for the third and last time. Thus the notes ended:—

'He is indirectly assured that *he* at least is not the person suspected. He sinks back in his chair; he draws a long breath; he asks to be left awhile by himself, under the pretence that the subject excites him. When the visitor returns, Dexter has been drinking in the interval. The visitor resumes the subject—not Dexter. The visitor is convinced that Mrs Eustace Macallan died by the hand of a poisoner, and openly says so. Dexter sinks back in his chair like a man fainting. What is the horror that has got possession of him? It is easy to understand, if we call it guilty horror. It is beyond all understanding, if we call it anything else. And how does it leave him? He flies from one extreme to another; he is indescribably delighted when he discovers that the visitor's suspicions are all fixed on an absent person. And then, and then only, he takes refuge in the declaration that he has been of one mind with his guest, in the matter of suspicion, from the first! These are facts. To what plain conclusion do they point?'

He shut up his notes, and, steadily watching my face waited for me to speak first.

'I understand you, Mr Playmore,' I began, impetuously. 'You believe that Mr Dexter——'

His warning forefinger stopped me there.

'Tell me,' he interposed, 'what Dexter said to you when he was so good as to confirm your opinion of poor Mrs Beauly?'

'He said, "There isn't a doubt about it. Mrs Beauly poisoned her." '

'I can't do better than follow so good an example—with one trifling difference. I say too, There isn't a doubt about it! Dexter poisoned her.'

'Are you joking, Mr Playmore?'

'I never was more in earnest in my life. Your rash visit to Dexter, and your extraordinary imprudence in taking him into your confidence, have led to astonishing results. The light which the whole machinery of the Law was unable to throw on the poisoning case at Gleninch, has been accidentally let in on it, by a Lady who refuses to listen to reason and who insists on having her own way. Quite incredible, and nevertheless quite true!'

'Impossible!' I exclaimed.

'What is impossible!' he asked, coolly.

'That Dexter poisoned my husband's first wife.'

'And why is that impossible, if you please?'

I began to be almost enraged with Mr Playmore.

'Can you ask the question?' I replied, indignantly, 'I have told you that I heard him speak of her, in terms of respect and affection of which any woman might be proud. He lives in the memory of her. I owe his friendly reception of me to some resemblance which he fancies he sees between my figure and hers. I have seen tears in his eyes, I have heard his voice falter and fail him, when he spoke of her. He may be the falsest of men in all besides; but he is true to *her*—he has not misled me in that one thing. There are signs that never deceive a woman, when a man is talking to her of what is really near his heart. I saw those signs. It is as true that I poisoned her, as that he did. I am ashamed to set my opinion against yours, Mr Playmore; but I really cannot help it. I declare I am almost angry with you!'

He seemed to be pleased, instead of offended, by the bold manner in which I expressed myself.

'My dear Mrs Eustace, you have no reason to be angry with me! In one respect, I entirely share your view—with this difference, that I go a little further than you do.'

'I don't understand you.'

'You will understand me directly. You describe Dexter's feeling for the late Mrs Eustace, as a happy mixture of respect and affection. I can tell you, it was a much warmer feeling towards her than that. I have my information from the poor lady herself—who honoured me with her confidence and friendship for the best part of her life. Before she married Mr Macallan—she kept it a secret from him, and you had better keep it a secret too—Miserrimus Dexter was in love with her. Miserrimus Dexter asked her—deformed as he was, seriously asked her—to be his wife.'

'And in the face of that,' I cried, 'you say that he poisoned her!'

'I do. I see no other conclusion possible, after what happened during your visit to him. You all but frightened him into a fainting-fit. What was he afraid of?'

I tried hard to find an answer to that. I even embarked on an answer, without quite knowing where my own words might lead me.

'Mr Dexter is an old and true friend of my husband's,' I

began. 'When he heard me say I was not satisfied with the Verdict, he might have felt alarmed——'

'He might have felt alarmed at the possible consequences to your husband of re-opening the inquiry,' said Mr Playmore, ironically finishing the sentence for me. 'Rather far-fetched, Mrs Eustace! and not very consistent with your faith in your husband's innocence! Clear your mind of one mistake,' he continued, seriously, 'which may fatally mislead you, if you persist in pursuing your present course. Miserrimus Dexter, you may take my word for it, ceased to be your husband's friend on the day when your husband married his first wife. Dexter has kept up appearances, I grant you—both in public and in private. His evidence in his friend's favour at the Trial, was given with the deep feeling which everybody expected from him. Nevertheless I firmly believe, looking under the surface, that Mr Macallan has no bitterer enemy living than Miserrimus Dexter.'

He turned me cold. I felt that here, at least, he was right. My husband had wooed and won the woman who had refused Dexter's offer of marriage. Was Dexter the man to forgive that? My own experience answered me—and said, No.

'Bear in mind what I have told you,' Mr Playmore proceeded. 'And now let us get on to your own position in this matter, and to the interests that you have at stake. Try to adopt my point of view for the moment; and let us inquire what chance we have of making any further advance towards a discovery of the truth. It is one thing to be morally convinced (as I am) that Miserrimus Dexter is the man who ought to have been tried for the murder at Gleninch; and it is another thing, at this distance of time, to lay our hands on the plain evidence which can alone justify anything like a public assertion of his guilt. There, as I see it, is the insuperable difficulty in the case. Unless I am completely mistaken, the question is now narrowed to this plain issue: The public assertion of your husband's innocence depends entirely on the public assertion of Dexter's guilt. How are you to arrive at that result? There is not a particle of evidence against him. You can only convict Dexter on Dexter's own confession. Are you listening to me?'

I was listening, most unwillingly. If he was right, things had indeed come to that terrible pass. But I could not—with all my respect for his superior knowledge and experience—I could not persuade myself that he *was* right. And I owned it, with the humility which I really felt.

He smiled good-humouredly.

'At any rate,' he said, 'you will admit that Dexter has not freely opened his mind to you, thus far? He is still keeping something from your knowledge, which you are interested in discovering?'

'Yes. I admit that.'

'Very good. What applies to your view of the case, applies to mine. I say, he is keeping from you the confession of his guilt. You say, he is keeping from you information which may fasten the guilt on some other person. Let us start from that point. Confession, or information, how are you to get at what he is now withholding from you? What influence can you bring to bear on him, when you see him again?'

'Surely, I might persuade him?'

'Certainly. And if persuasion fails—what then? Do you think you can entrap him into speaking out? or terrify him into speaking out?'

'If you will look at your notes, Mr Playmore, you will see that I have already succeeded in terrifying him—though I am only a woman, and though I didn't mean to do it.'

'Very well answered! You mark the trick. What you have done once, you think you can do again. Well! as you are determined to try the experiment, it can do you no harm to know a little more of Dexter than you know now. Before you go back to London, suppose we apply for information to somebody who can help us?'

I started, and looked round the room. He made me do it: he spoke as if the person who was to help us was close at our elbows.

'Don't be alarmed,' he said. 'The oracle is silent; and the oracle is here.'

He unlocked one of the drawers of his desk; produced a bundle of letters; and picked out one.

'When we were arranging your husband's defence,' he said, 'we felt some difficulty about including Miserrimus Dexter among our witnesses. We had not the slightest suspicion of him—I need hardly tell you. But we were all afraid of his eccentricity; and some among us even feared that the excitement of appearing at the Trial might drive him completely out of his mind. In this emergency we applied to a doctor to help us. Under some pretext, which I forget now, we introduced him to Dexter. And in due course of time we received his report. Here it is.'

He opened the letter; and, marking a certain passage in it with a pencil, handed it to me.

'Read the lines which I have marked,' he said; 'they will be quite sufficient for our purpose.'

I read these words:—

'Summing up the results of my observation, I may give it as my opinion that there is undoubtedly latent insanity in this case; but that no active symptoms of madness have presented themselves as yet. You may, I think, produce him at the Trial, without fear of consequences. He may say and do all sorts of odd things; but he has his mind under the control of his will,* and you may trust his self-esteem to exhibit him in the character of a substantially intelligent witness.

'As to the future, I am, of course, not able to speak positively. I can only state my views.

'That he will end in madness (if he lives), I entertain little or no doubt. The question of *when* the madness will show itself, depends entirely on the state of his health. His nervous system is highly sensitive; and there are signs that his way of life has already damaged it. If he conquers the bad habits to which I have alluded in an earlier part of my report, and if he passes many hours of every day quietly in the open air, he may last as a sane man for years to come.

If he persists in his present way of life—or, in other words, if further mischief occurs to that sensitive nervous system—his lapse into insanity must infallibly take place when the mischief has reached its culminating point. Without warning to himself or to others, the whole mental structure will give way; and, at a moment's notice, while he is acting as quietly or speaking as intelligently as at his best time, the man will drop (if I may use the expression) into madness or idiocy. In either case, when the catastrophe has happened, it is only due to his friends to add, that they can (as I believe) entertain no hope of his cure. The balance once lost, will be lost for life.'

There it ended. Mr Playmore put the letter back in his drawer.

'You have just read the opinion of one of our highest living authorities,' he said. 'Does Dexter strike you as a likely man to give his nervous system a chance of recovery? Do you see no obstacles and no perils in your way?'

My silence answered him.

'Suppose you go back to Dexter,' he proceeded. 'And suppose that the doctor's opinion exaggerates the peril, in his case. What are you to do? The last time you saw him, you had the immense advantage of taking him by surprise. Those sensitive nerves of his gave way; and he betrayed the fear that you roused in him. Can you take him by surprise again? Not you! He is prepared for you now; and he will be on his guard. If you encounter nothing worse, you will have his cunning to deal with, next. Are you his match at that? But for Lady Clarinda he would have hopelessly misled you on the subject of Mrs Beauly.'

There was no answering this, either. I was foolish enough to try to answer it, for all that.

'He told me the truth, so far as he knew it,' I rejoined. 'He really saw, what he said he saw, in the corridor at Gleninch.'

'He told you the truth,' returned Mr Playmore, 'because he was cunning enough to see that the truth would help him in irritating your suspicions. You don't really believe that he shared your suspicions?'

'Why not?' I said. 'He was as ignorant of what Mrs Beauly was really doing on that night, as I was—until I met Lady Clarinda. It remains to be seen whether he will not be as much astonished as I was, when I tell him what Lady Clarinda told me.'

This smart reply produced an effect which I had not anticipated.

To my surprise, Mr Playmore abruptly dropped all further discussion on his side. He appeared to despair of convincing me, and he owned it indirectly in his next words.

'Will nothing that I can say to you,' he asked, 'induce you to think as I think in this matter?'

'I have not your ability, or your experience,' I answered. 'I am sorry to say, I can't think as you think.'

'And are you really determined to see Miserrimus Dexter again?'

'I have engaged myself to see him again.'

He waited a little, and thought over it.

'You have honoured me by asking for my advice,' he said. 'I earnestly advise you, Mrs Eustace, to break your engagement. I go even further than that. I *entreat* you not to see Dexter again.'

Just what my mother-in-law had said! just what Benjamin and Major Fitz-David had said! They were all against me. And still I held out. I wonder, when I look back at it, at my own obstinacy. I am almost ashamed to relate that I made Mr Playmore no reply. He waited, still looking at me. I felt irritated by that fixed look. I rose, and stood before him with my eyes on the floor.

He rose in his turn. He understood that the conference was over.

'Well! well!' he said, with a kind of sad good-humour, 'I suppose it is unreasonable of me to expect that a young woman like you should share any opinion with an old lawyer like me. Let me only remind you that our conversation must remain strictly confidential, for the present—and then let us change the subject. Is there anything that I can do for you? Are you alone in Edinburgh?'

'No. I am travelling with an old friend of mine, who has known me from childhood.'

'And do you stay here to-morrow?'

'I think so.'

'Will you do me one favour? Will you think over what has passed between us, and will you come back to me in the morning?'

'Willingly, Mr Playmore, if it is only to thank you again for your kindness.'

On that understanding we parted. He sighed—the cheerful man sighed—as he opened the door for me. Women are contradictory creatures. That sigh affected me more than all his arguments. I felt myself blush for my own headstrong resistance to him, as I took my leave and turned away into the street.

CHAPTER XXXIV

Gleninch

I FOUND Benjamin at the hotel, poring over a cheap periodical; absorbed in guessing one of the weekly 'Enigmas'* which the Editor presented to his readers. My old friend was a great admirer of these verbal 'puzzles,' and had won all sorts of cheap prizes by his ingenuity in arriving at the right solution of the problems submitted to him. On ordinary occasions, it was useless to attempt to attract his attention, while he was occupied with his favourite amusement. But his interest in hearing the result of my interview with the lawyer proved to be even keener than his interest in solving the problem before him. He shut up his journal the moment I entered the room, and asked, eagerly, 'What news, Valeria? What news?'

In telling him what had happened, I of course respected Mr Playmore's confidence in me. Not a word relating to the lawyer's horrible suspicion of Miserrimus Dexter passed my lips.*

'Aha!' said Benjamin, complacently. 'So the lawyer thinks as I do. You will listen to Mr Playmore (won't you?), though you wouldn't listen to me?'

'You must forgive me, my old friend,' I replied. 'I am afraid it has come to this—try as I may, I can listen to nobody who advises me. On our way here, I honestly meant to be guided by Mr Playmore—we should never have taken this long journey, if I had *not* honestly meant it. I have tried, tried hard, to be a teachable, reasonable woman. But there is something in me that won't be taught. I am afraid I shall go back to Dexter.'

Even Benjamin lost all patience with me, this time.

'What is bred in the bone,' he said, quoting the old proverb, 'will never come out of the flesh. In years gone by, you were the most obstinate child that ever made a mess in a nursery. Oh, dear me, we might as well have stayed in London!'

'No,' I replied, 'now we have travelled to Edinburgh, we will see something (interesting to *me* at any rate), which we should never have seen if we had not left London. My husband's country house is within a few miles of us, here. To-morrow we will go to Gleninch.'

'Where the poor lady was poisoned?' asked Benjamin, with a look of dismay. 'You mean that place?'

'Yes. I want to see the room in which she died; I want to go all over the house.'

Benjamin crossed his hands resignedly on his lap. 'I try to understand the new generation,' said the old man, sadly. 'But I can't manage it. The new generation beats me.'

I sat down to write to Mr Playmore about the visit to Gleninch. The house in which the tragedy had occurred

that had blighted my husband's life, was, to my mind, the
most interesting house on the habitable globe. The prospect
of visiting Gleninch had, indeed (to tell the truth), strongly
influenced my resolution to consult the Edinburgh lawyer.
I sent my note to Mr Playmore by a messenger, and received the kindest reply in return. If I would wait until the
afternoon, he would get the day's business done, and would
take us to Gleninch in his own carriage.

Benjamin's obstinacy—in its own quiet way, and on certain occasions only—was quite a match for mine. He had
privately determined, as one of the old generation, to have
nothing to do with Gleninch. Not a word on the subject
escaped him, until Mr Playmore's carriage was at the hotel
door. At that appropriate moment, Benjamin remembered
an old friend of his in Edinburgh. 'Will you please to excuse
me, Valeria? My friend's name is Saunders—and he will
take it unkindly of me if I don't dine with him to-day.'

Apart from the associations that I connected with it, there
was nothing to interest a traveller at Gleninch.

The country round was pretty and well cultivated, and
nothing more. The park was, to an English eye, wild and
badly kept. The house had been built within the last seventy
or eighty years. Outside, it was as bare of all ornament as
a factory, and as gloomily heavy in effect as a prison. Inside,
the deadly dreariness, the close oppressive solitude, of a
deserted dwelling wearied the eye and weighed on the
mind, from the roof to the basement. The house had been
shut up since the time of the Trial. A lonely old couple,
man and wife, had the keys, and the charge of it. The man
shook his head in silent and sorrowful disapproval of our
intrusion, when Mr Playmore ordered him to open the
doors and shutters, and let the light in on the dark, deserted
place. Fires were burning in the library and the picture
gallery, to preserve the treasures which they contained from
the damp. It was not easy, at first, to look at the cheerful
blaze, without fancying that the inhabitants of the house
must surely come in and warm themselves! Ascending to

the upper floor, I saw the rooms made familiar to me by the Report of the Trial. I entered the little study, with the old books on the shelves, and the key still missing from the locked door of communication with the bedchamber. I looked into the room in which the unhappy mistress of Gleninch had suffered and died. The bed was left in its place; the sofa on which the nurse had snatched her intervals of repose was at its foot; the Indian cabinet, in which the crumpled paper with the grains of arsenic had been found, still held its little collection of curiosities. I moved on its pivot the invalid table on which she had taken her meals, and written her poems, poor soul. The place was dreary and dreadful; the heavy air felt as if it was still burdened with its horrid load of misery and distrust. I was glad to get out (after a passing glance at the room which Eustace had occupied, in those days) into the Guests' Corridor. There was the bedroom, at the door of which Miserrimus Dexter had waited and watched! There was the oaken floor along which he had hopped, in his horrible way, following the footsteps of the servant disguised in her mistress's clothes! Go where I might, the ghosts of the dead and the absent went with me, step by step. Go where I might, the lonely horror of the house had its still and awful voice for Me:—'I keep the secret of the Poison! *I* hide the mystery of the death!'

The oppression of the place became unendurable. I longed for the pure sky, and the free air. My companion noticed and understood me.

'Come!' he said. 'We have had enough of the house. Let us look at the grounds.'

In the grey quiet of the evening, we roamed about the lonely gardens, and threaded our way through the rank, neglected shrubberies. Wandering here and wandering there, we drifted into the kitchen garden—with one little patch still sparely cultivated by the old man and his wife, and all the rest a wilderness of weeds. Beyond the far end of the garden, divided from it by a low paling of wood, there stretched a piece of waste ground, sheltered on three sides by trees. In one lost corner of the ground, an object, common enough elsewhere, attracted my attention here. The object was a dust-heap. The great size of it, and the curious situation in which it was placed, roused a moment's languid curiosity in me. I stopped, and looked at the dust and ashes, at the broken crockery and the old iron. Here, there was a torn hat; and there, some fragments of rotten old boots; and, scattered round, a small attendant litter of waste paper and frowsy rags.

'What are you looking at?' asked Mr Playmore.

'At nothing more remarkable than the dust-heap,' I answered.

'In tidy England, I suppose you would have all that carted away, out of sight,' said the lawyer. 'We don't mind in Scotland, as long as the dust-heap is far enough away not to be smelt at the house. Besides, some of it, sifted, comes in usefully as manure for the garden. Here, the place is deserted, and the rubbish in consequence has not been disturbed. Everything at Gleninch, Mrs Eustace (the big dust-heap included), is waiting for the new mistress to set it to rights. One of these days, you may be queen here—who knows!'

'I have done with Gleninch, Mr Playmore, when I leave it to-day!'

'Don't be too sure of that,' returned my companion. 'Time has its surprises in store for all of us.'*

We turned away, and walked back in silence to the park gate, at which the carriage was waiting.

On the return to Edinburgh, Mr Playmore directed the conversation to topics entirely unconnected with my visit to Gleninch. He saw that my mind stood in need of relief; and he most goodnaturedly, and successfully, exerted himself to amuse me. It was not until we were close to the city that he touched on the subject of my return to London.

'Have you decided yet on the day when you leave Edinburgh?' he asked.

'We leave Edinburgh,' I replied, 'by the train of to-morrow morning.'

'Do you still see no reason to alter the opinions which you expressed yesterday? Does your speedy departure mean that?'

'I am afraid it does, Mr Playmore. When I am an older woman, I may be a wiser woman. In the mean time, I can only trust to your indulgence if I still blindly blunder on, in my own way.'

He smiled pleasantly, and patted my hand—then changed on a sudden, and looked at me gravely and attentively, before he opened his lips again.

'This is my last opportunity of speaking to you before you go,' he said. 'May I speak freely?'

'As freely as you please, Mr Playmore! Whatever you may say to me, will only add to my grateful sense of your kindness.'

'I have very little to say, Mrs Eustace—and that little begins with a word of caution. You told me yesterday that, when you paid your last visit to Miserrimus Dexter, you went to him alone. Don't do that again. Take somebody with you.'

'Do you think I am in any danger, then?'

'Not in the ordinary sense of the word. I only think that a friend may be useful in keeping Dexter's audacity (he is one of the most impudent men living) within proper limits. Then, again, in case anything worth remembering and acting on *should* fall from him in his talk, a friend may be valuable as witness. In your place, I should have a witness with me who could take notes—but then I am a lawyer, and my business is to make a fuss about trifles. Let me only say—go with a companion, when you next visit Dexter; and be on your guard against yourself, when the talk turns on Mrs Beauly.'

'On my guard against myself? What do you mean?'

'Practice, my dear Mrs Eustace, has given me an eye for the little weaknesses of human nature. You are (quite naturally) disposed to be jealous of Mrs Beauly; and you are, in consequence, not in full possession of your excellent common sense, when Dexter uses that lady as a means of blindfolding you. Am I speaking too freely?'

'Certainly not! It is very degrading to me to be jealous of Mrs Beauly. My vanity suffers dreadfully when I think of it. But my common sense yields to conviction. I dare say you are right.'

'I am delighted to find that we agree on one point,' he rejoined, drily. 'I don't despair yet of convincing you, in that far more serious matter which is still in dispute between us. And, what is more, if you will throw no obstacles in the way, I look to Dexter himself to help me.'

This roused my curiosity. How Miserrimus Dexter could help him, in that or in any other way, was a riddle beyond my reading.

'You propose to repeat to Dexter all that Lady Clarinda told you about Mrs Beauly,' he went on. 'And you think it is likely that Dexter will be overwhelmed, as you were overwhelmed, when he hears the story. I am going to venture on a prophecy. I say that Dexter will disappoint you. Far from showing any astonishment, he will boldly tell you that you have been duped by a deliberately false statement of facts, invented and set afloat, in her own guilty interests, by Mrs Beauly. Now tell me—if he really tries, in that way, to renew your unfounded suspicion of an innocent woman, will *that* shake your confidence in your own opinion?'

'It will entirely destroy my confidence in my own opinion, Mr Playmore.'

'Very good. I shall expect you to write to me, in any case; and I believe we shall be of one mind, before the week is out. Keep strictly secret all that I said to you yesterday about Dexter. Don't even mention my name, when you see him. Thinking of him as I think now, I would as soon touch the hand of the hangman as the hand of that monster! God bless you! Good bye.'

So he said his farewell words at the door of the hotel. Kind, genial, clever—but oh, how easily prejudiced, how shockingly obstinate in holding to his own opinion! And *what* an opinion! I shuddered as I thought of it.

CHAPTER XXXV

Mr Playmore's Prophecy

WE reached London between eight and nine in the evening. Strictly methodical in all his habits, Benjamin had telegraphed to his housekeeper, from Edinburgh, to have supper ready for us by ten o'clock, and to send the cabman whom he always employed to meet us at the station.

Arriving at the villa, we were obliged to wait for a moment to let a pony-chaise get by us before we could draw up at Benjamin's door. The chaise passed very slowly, driven by a rough-looking man, with a pipe in his mouth. But for the man, I might have doubted whether the pony was quite a stranger to me. As things were, I thought no more of the matter.

Benjamin's respectable old housekeeper opened the garden gate, and startled me by bursting into a devout ejaculation of gratitude at the sight of her master. 'The Lord be praised, Sir!' she cried. 'I thought you would never come back!'

'Anything wrong?' asked Benjamin, in his own impenetrably quiet way.

The housekeeper trembled at the question, and answered in these enigmatical words:—

'My mind's upset, Sir; and whether things are wrong or whether things are right, is more than I can say. Hours ago, a strange man came in and asked'—she stopped as if she was completely bewildered—looked for a moment vacantly at her master—and suddenly addressed herself to me. 'And asked,' she proceeded, 'when *you* was expected back, ma'am. I told him what my master had telegraphed, and the man says upon that, "Wait a bit" (he says); "I'm coming back." He came back in a minute or less; and he carried a Thing in his arms which curdled my blood—it did!—and set me shaking from the crown of my head to the sole of my foot. I know I ought to have stopped it; but I couldn't stand upon my legs—much less put the man out of the house. In he went, without *with* your leave, or *by* your leave, Mr Benjamin, Sir—in he went with the Thing in his arms, straight through to your library. And there It has been all these hours. And there It is now. I've spoken to the Police; but they wouldn't interfere—and what to do next, is more than my poor head can tell. Don't you go in by yourself, ma'am! You'll be frightened out of your wits—you will!'

I persisted in entering the house, for all that. Aided by the pony, I easily solved the mystery of the housekeeper's otherwise unintelligible narrative. Passing through the dining-room (where the supper table was already laid for us), I looked through the half-opened library door.

Yes; there was Miserrimus Dexter, arrayed in his pink jacket, fast asleep in Benjamin's favourite arm-chair! No coverlid hid his horrible deformity. Nothing was sacrificed to conventional ideas of propriety, in his extraordinary dress. I could hardly wonder that the poor old housekeeper trembled from head to foot when she spoke of him!

'Valeria!' said Benjamin, pointing to the Portent in the chair. 'Which is it—an Indian idol? or a man?'

I have already described Miserrimus Dexter as possessing the sensitive ear of a dog. He now showed that he also slept the light sleep of a dog. Quietly as Benjamin had spoken, the strange voice roused him on the instant. He rubbed his eyes, and smiled as innocently as a waking child.

'How do you do, Mrs Valeria?' he said. 'I have had a nice little sleep. You don't know how happy I am to see you again. Who is this?'

He rubbed his eyes once more, and looked at Benjamin. Not knowing what else to do in this extraordinary emergency, I presented my visitor to the master of the house.

'Excuse my getting up, Sir,' said Miserrimus Dexter. 'I can't get up—I have got no legs. You look as if you thought I was occupying your chair? If I am committing an intrusion, be so good as to put your umbrella under me, and give me a jerk. I shall fall on my hands, and I shan't be offended with you. I will submit to a tumble and a scolding—but please don't break my heart by sending me away. That beautiful woman, there, can be very cruel sometimes, Sir, when the fit takes her. She went away when I stood in the sorest need of a little talk with her—she went away, and left me to my loneliness and my suspense. I am a poor deformed wretch, with a warm heart, and (perhaps) an insatiable curiosity as well. Insatiable curiosity (have you ever felt it?) is a curse. I bore it till my brains began to boil in my head; and then I sent for my gardener, and made him drive me here. I like being here. The air of your library soothes me; the sight of Mrs Valeria is balm to my wounded heart. She has something to tell me—something that I am dying to hear. If she is not too tired after her journey, and if you will let her tell it, I promise to have myself taken away when she has done. Dear Mr Benjamin, you look like the refuge of the afflicted. I am afflicted. Shake hands like a good Christian, and take me in.'

He held out his hand. His soft blue eyes melted into an expression of piteous entreaty. Completely stupefied by the amazing harangue of which he had been made the object, Benjamin took the offered hand, with the air of a man in a dream. 'I hope I see you well, Sir,' he said, mechanically—and then looked round at me to know what he was to do next.

'I understand Mr Dexter,' I whispered. 'Leave him to me.'

Benjamin stole a last bewildered look at the Object in the chair; bowed to it, with the instinct of politeness which never failed him; and (still with the air of a man in a dream) withdrew into the next room.

Left together, we looked at each other, for the first moment, in silence.

Whether I unconsciously drew on that inexhaustible store
of indulgence which a woman always keeps in reserve for a
man who owns that he has need of her—or whether, resent-
ing as I did Mr Playmore's horrible suspicion of him, my
heart was especially accessible to feelings of compassion, in
his unhappy case—I cannot tell. I only know that I pitied
Miserrimus Dexter, at that moment, as I had never pitied
him yet; and that I spared him the reproof which I should
certainly have administered to any other man, who had
taken the liberty of establishing himself, uninvited, in Benjamin's house.

He was the first to speak.

'Lady Clarinda has destroyed your confidence in me!' he
began, wildly.

'Lady Clarinda has done nothing of the sort,' I replied.
'She has not attempted to influence my opinion. I was really
obliged to leave London, as I told you.'

He sighed, and closed his eyes contentedly, as if I had
relieved him of a heavy weight of anxiety.

'Be merciful to me,' he said; 'and tell me something
more. I have been so miserable in your absence.' He suddenly opened his eyes again, and looked at me with an
appearance of the greatest interest. 'Are you very much
fatigued with travelling?' he proceeded. 'I am hungry for
news of what happened at the Major's dinner-party. Is it
cruel of me to tell you so, when you have not rested after
your journey? Only one question to-night! and I will leave
the rest till to-morrow. What did Lady Clarinda say about
Mrs Beauly? All that you wanted to hear?'

'All, and more,' I answered.

'What? what? what?' he cried, wild with impatience in a
moment.

Mr Playmore's last prophetic words were vividly present
to my mind. He had declared, in the most positive manner,
that Dexter would persist in misleading me, and would
show no signs of astonishment when I repeated what Lady
Clarinda had told me of Mrs Beauly. I resolved to put the

lawyer's prophecy—so far as the question of astonishment was concerned—to the sharpest attainable test. I said not a word to Miserrimus Dexter, in the way of preface or preparation; I burst on him with my news as abruptly as possible.

'The person you saw in the corridor was *not* Mrs Beauly,' I said. 'It was the maid, dressed in her mistress's cloak and hat. Mrs Beauly herself was not in the house at all. Mrs Beauly herself was dancing at a masked ball in Edinburgh. There is what the maid told Lady Clarinda; and there is what Lady Clarinda told *me*.'

In the absorbing interest of the moment, I poured out those words one after another as fast as they could pass my lips. Miserrimus Dexter completely falsified the lawyer's prediction. He shuddered under the shock. His eyes opened wide with amazement. 'Say it again!' he cried. 'I can't take it all in at once. You stun me.'

I was more than contented with this result—I triumphed in my victory. For once, I had really some reason to feel satisfied with myself. I had taken the Christian and merciful side in my discussion with Mr Playmore; and I had won my reward. I could sit in the same room with Miserrimus Dexter, and feel the blessed conviction that I was not breathing the same air with a poisoner. Was it not worth the visit to Edinburgh to have made sure of that?

In repeating, at his own desire, what I had already said to him, I took care to add the details which made Lady Clarinda's narrative coherent and credible. He listened throughout with breathless attention—here and there repeating the words after me to impress them the more surely and the more deeply on his mind.

'What is to be said? what is to be done?' he asked, with a look of blank despair. 'I can't disbelieve it. From first to last, strange as it is, it sounds true.'

(How would Mr Playmore have felt, if he had heard those words? I did him the justice to believe that he would have felt heartily ashamed of himself!)

'There is nothing to be said,' I rejoined; 'except that Mrs Beauly is innocent, and that you and I have done her a grievous wrong. Don't you agree with me?'

'I entirely agree with you,' he answered, without an instant's hesitation. 'Mrs Beauly is an innocent woman. The defence at the Trial was the right defence after all.'

He folded his arms complacently; he looked perfectly satisfied to leave the matter there.

I was not of his mind. To my own amazement, I now found myself the least reasonable person of the two!

Miserrimus Dexter (to use the popular phrase) had given me more than I had bargained for. He had not only done all that I had anticipated, in the way of falsifying Mr Playmore's prediction—he had actually advanced beyond my limits. I could go the length of recognising Mrs Beauly's innocence; but at that point I stopped. If the Defence at the Trial was the right defence—farewell to all hope of asserting my husband's innocence! I held to that hope, as I held to my love and my life.

'Speak for yourself,' I said. 'My opinion of the Defence remains unchanged.'

He started and knit his brows, as if I had disappointed and displeased him.

'Does that mean that you are determined to go on?'

'It does.'

He was downright angry with me. He cast his customary politeness to the winds.

'Absurd! Impossible!' he cried, contemptuously. 'You have yourself declared that we wronged an innocent woman, when we suspected Mrs Beauly. Is there any one else whom we can suspect? It is ridiculous to ask the question! There is no alternative left but to accept the facts as they are, and to stir no further in the matter of the poisoning at Gleninch. It is childish to dispute plain conclusions. You *must* give up.'

'You may be angry with me, if you will, Mr Dexter. Neither your anger nor your arguments will make me give up.'

He controlled himself by an effort—he was quiet and polite again, when he next spoke to me.

'Very well. Pardon me for a moment, if I absorb myself in my own thoughts. I want to do something which I have not done yet.'

'What may that be, Mr Dexter?'

'I am going to put myself into Mrs Beauly's skin, and to think with Mrs Beauly's mind. Give me a minute. Thank you.'

What did he mean? What new transformation of him was passing before my eyes? Was there ever such a puzzle of a man as this? Who that saw him now, intently pursuing his new train of thought, would have recognised him as the childish creature who had woke up so innocently, and who had amazed Benjamin by the infantine nonsense which he talked? It is said, and said truly, that there are many sides to every human character. Dexter's many sides were developing themselves at such a rapid rate of progress, that they were already beyond my counting!

He lifted his head, and fixed a look of keen inquiry on me.

'I have come out of Mrs Beauly's skin,' he announced. 'And I have arrived at this result:—We are two impetuous people; and we have been a little hasty in rushing at a conclusion.'

He stopped. I said nothing. Was the shadow of a doubt of him beginning to rise in my mind? I waited, and listened.

'I am as fully satisfied as ever of the truth of what Lady Clarinda told you,' he proceeded. 'But I see, on consideration, what I failed to see at the time. The story admits of two interpretations. One on the surface, and another under the surface. I look under the surface, in your interests; and I say, it is just possible that Mrs Beauly may have been cunning enough to forestall suspicion, and to set up an Alibi.'*

I am ashamed to own that I did not understand what he meant by the last word—Alibi. He saw that I was not following him, and he spoke out more plainly.

'Was the maid something more than her mistress's passive accomplice?' he said. 'Was she the Hand that her mistress used? Was she on her way to give the first dose of poison, when she passed me in the corridor? Did Mrs Beauly spend the night in Edinburgh—so as to have her defence ready, if suspicion fell upon her?'

My shadowy doubt of him became substantial doubt, when I heard that. Had I absolved him a little too readily? Was he really trying to renew my suspicions of Mrs Beauly, as Mr Playmore had foretold? This time I was obliged to answer him. In doing so, I unconsciously employed one of the phrases which the lawyer had used to me, during my first interview with him.

'That sounds rather far-fetched, Mr Dexter,' I said.

To my relief, he made no attempt to defend the new view that he had advanced.

'It *is* far-fetched,' he admitted. 'When I said it was just possible—though I didn't claim much for my idea—I said more for it perhaps than it deserved. Dismiss my view as ridiculous; what are you to do next? If Mrs Beauly is not the poisoner (either by herself or by her maid), who is? She is innocent, and Eustace is innocent. Where is the other person whom you can suspect? Have *I* poisoned her?' he cried, with eyes flashing, and his voice rising to its highest notes. 'Do you, does anybody, suspect Me? I loved her; I adored her; I have never been the same man since her death. Hush! I will trust you with a secret. (Don't tell your husband; it might be the destruction of our friendship.) I would have married her, before she met with Eustace, if she would have taken me. When the doctors told me she had died poisoned—ask Doctor Jerome what I suffered! *he* can tell you! All through that horrible night, I was awake: watching my opportunity until I found my way to her! I got into the room, and took my last leave of the cold remains of the angel whom I loved. I cried over her. I kissed her, for the first and last time. I stole one little lock of her hair. I have worn it ever since; I have kissed it night and day.

Oh, God! the room comes back to me! the dead face comes back to me! Look! look!'

He tore from its place of concealment in his bosom a little locket, fastened by a ribbon round his neck. He threw it to me where I sat; and burst into a passion of tears.

A man in my place might have known what to do. Being only a woman, I yielded to the compassionate impulse of the moment.

I got up and crossed the room to him. I gave him back his locket, and put my hand, without knowing what I was about, on the poor wretch's shoulder. 'I am incapable of suspecting you, Mr Dexter,' I said, gently. 'No such idea ever entered my head. I pity you from the bottom of my heart.'

He caught my hand in his, and devoured it with kisses. His lips burnt me like fire. He twisted himself suddenly in the chair, and wound his arm round my waist. In the terror and indignation of the moment, vainly struggling with him, I cried out for help.*

The door opened, and Benjamin appeared on the threshold. Dexter let go his hold of me.

I ran to Benjamin and prevented him from advancing into the room. In all my long experience of my fatherly old friend, I had never seen him really angry yet. I saw him more than angry now. He was pale—the patient, gentle old man was pale with rage! I held him at the door with all my strength.

'You can't lay your hand on a cripple,' I said. 'Send for his servant outside to take him away.'

I drew Benjamin out of the room, and closed and locked the library door. The housekeeper was in the dining-room. I sent her out to call the driver of the pony-chaise into the house.

The man came in—the rough man whom I had noticed when we were approaching the garden gate. Benjamin opened the library door in stern silence. It was perhaps unworthy of me—but I could *not* resist the temptation to look in.

Miserrimus Dexter had sunk down in the chair. The rough man lifted his master with a gentleness that surprised me. 'Hide my face,' I heard Dexter say to him, in broken tones. He opened his coarse pilot jacket, and hid his master's head under it, and so went silently out—with the deformed creature held to his bosom, like a woman sheltering her child.

CHAPTER XXXVI

Ariel

I PASSED a sleepless night.

The outrage that had been offered to me was bad enough in itself. But consequences were associated with it which might affect me more seriously still. In so far as the attainment of the one object of my life might yet depend on my personal association with Miserrimus Dexter, an insurmountable obstacle appeared to be now placed in my way. Even in my husband's interests, ought I to permit a man who had grossly insulted me, to approach me again? Although I was no prude, I recoiled from the thought of it.

I rose late, and sat down at my desk, trying to summon energy enough to write to Mr Playmore—and trying in vain.

Towards noon (while Benjamin happened to be out for a little while), the housekeeper announced the arrival of another strange visitor at the gate of the villa.

'It's a woman this time, ma'am—or something like one,' said this worthy person, confidentially. 'A great, stout, awkward, stupid creature, with a man's hat on, and a man's stick in her hand. She says she has got a note for you, and she won't give it to anybody *but* you. I'd better not let her in—had I?'

Recognising the original of the picture, I astonished the housekeeper by consenting to receive the messenger immediately.

Ariel entered the room—in stolid silence, as usual. But I noticed a change in her which puzzled me. Her dull eyes were red and bloodshot. Traces of tears (as I fancied) were visible on her fat, shapeless cheeks. She crossed the room, on her way to my chair, with a less determined tread than was customary with her. Could Ariel (I asked myself) be woman enough to cry? Was it within the limits of possibility that Ariel should approach me in sorrow and in fear?

'I hear you have brought something for me?' I said. 'Won't you sit down?'

She handed me a letter—without answering, and without taking a chair. I opened the envelope. The letter inside was written by Miserrimus Dexter. It contained these lines:—

'Try to pity me, if you have any pity left for a miserable man; I have bitterly expiated the madness of a moment. If you could see me—even you would own that my punishment has been heavy enough. For God's sake, don't abandon me! I was beside myself when I let the feeling that you have awakened in me get the better of my control. It shall never show itself again; it shall be a secret that dies with me. Can I expect you to believe this? No. I won't ask you to believe me; I won't ask you to trust me in the future. If you ever consent to see me again, let it be in the presence of any third person whom you may appoint to protect you. I deserve that—I will submit to it; I will wait till time has composed your angry feeling against me. All I ask now, is leave to hope. Say to Ariel, "I forgive him; and one day I will let him see me again." She will remember it, for love of me. If you send her back without a message, you send me to the madhouse. Ask her, if you don't believe me.— MISERRIMUS DEXTER.'

I finished the strange letter, and looked at Ariel.

She stood with her eyes on the floor, and held out to me the thick walking-stick which she carried in her hand.

'Take the stick'—were the first words she said to me.

'Why am I to take it?' I asked.

She struggled a little with her sluggishly-working mind, and slowly put her thoughts into words.

'You're angry with the Master,' she said. 'Take it out on Me. Here's the stick. Beat me.'

'Beat you!' I exclaimed.

'My back's broad,' said the poor creature. 'I won't make a row. I'll bear it. Drat you, take the stick! Don't vex *him*. Whack it out on my back. Beat *me*.'

She roughly forced the stick into my hand; she turned her poor shapeless shoulders to me, waiting for the blow. It was at once dreadful and touching to see her. The tears rose in my eyes. I tried, gently and patiently, to reason with her. Quite useless! The idea of taking the Master's punishment on herself was the one idea in her mind. 'Don't vex *him*,' she repeated. 'Beat *me*.'

'What do you mean by "vexing him"?' I asked.

She tried to explain, and failed to find the words. She showed me by imitation, as a savage might have shown me, what she meant. Striding to the fireplace, she crouched on the rug, and looked into the fire with a horrible vacant stare. Then she clasped her hands over her forehead, and rocked slowly to and fro, still staring into the fire. 'There's how he sits!' she said, with a sudden burst of speech. 'Hours on hours, there's how he sits! Notices nobody. Cries about *you*.'

The picture she presented recalled to my memory the Report of Dexter's health, and the doctor's plain warning of peril waiting for him in the future. Even if I could have resisted Ariel, I must have yielded to the vague dread of consequences which now shook me in secret.

'Don't do that!' I cried. She was still rocking herself in imitation of the 'Master,' and still staring into the fire with her hands to her head. 'Get up, pray! I am not angry with him now. I forgive him.'

She rose on her hands and knees, and waited, looking up intently into my face. In that attitude—more like a dog than a human being—she repeated her customary petition, when she wanted to fix words that interested her in her mind.

'Say it again!'

I did as she bade me. She was not satisfied.

'Say it as it is in the letter,' she went on. 'Say it as the Master said it to Me.'

I looked back at the letter, and repeated the form of message contained in the latter part of it, word for word: 'I forgive him; and one day I will let him see me again.'

She sprang to her feet at a bound. For the first time since she had entered the room, her dull face began to break slowly into light and life.

'That's it!' she cried. 'Hear if I can say it, too! Hear if I've got it by heart.'

Teaching her, exactly as I should have taught a child, I slowly fastened the message, word by word, on her mind.

'Now rest yourself,' I said; 'and let me give you something to eat and drink, after your long walk.'

I might as well have spoken to one of the chairs! She snatched up her stick from the floor, and burst out with a hoarse shout of joy. 'I've got it by heart!' she cried. 'This will cool the Master's head! Hooray!' She dashed out into the passage, like a wild animal escaping from its cage. I was just in time to see her tear open the garden gate, and set forth on her walk back, at a pace which made it hopeless to attempt to follow and stop her.

I returned to the sitting-room, pondering on a question which has perplexed wiser heads than mine. Could a man who was hopelessly and entirely wicked, have inspired such devoted attachment to him as Dexter had inspired in the faithful woman who had just left me—in the rough gardener, who had carried him out so gently on the previous night? Who can decide? The greatest scoundrel living always has a friend—in a woman, or a dog.

I sat down again at the desk, and made another attempt to write to Mr Playmore.

Recalling, for the purpose of my letter, all that Miserrimus Dexter had said to me, my memory dwelt, with special interest, on the strange outbreak of feeling which had led him to betray the secret of his infatuation for Eustace's first wife. I saw again the ghastly scene in the death-chamber—the deformed creature crying over the corpse, in the stillness of the first dark hours of the new day. The horrible picture took a strange hold on my mind. I rose, and walked up and down, and tried to turn my thoughts some other way. It was not to be done: the scene was too familiar to be easily dismissed. I had myself walked in the corridor which Dexter had crossed, on his way to take his last leave of her.

The corridor? I stopped. My thoughts suddenly took a new direction, uninfluenced by any effort of my will.

What other association, besides the associations with Dexter, did I connect with the corridor? Was it something I had seen, during my visit to Gleninch? No. Was it something I had read? I snatched up the Report of the Trial to see. It opened at a page which contained the nurse's evidence. I read the evidence through again, without recovering the lost remembrance, until I came to these lines close at the end:—

'Before bedtime I went upstairs to prepare the remains of the deceased lady for the coffin. The room in which she lay was locked; the door leading into Mr Macallan's room being secured, as well as the door leading into the corridor. The keys had been taken away by Mr Gale. Two of the men-servants were posted outside the bedroom to keep watch. They were to be relieved at four in the morning—that was all they could tell me.'

There was my lost association with the corridor! There was what I ought to have remembered when Miserrimus Dexter was telling me of his visit to the dead!

How had he got into the bedroom—the doors being locked, and the keys being taken away by Mr Gale? There was but one of the locked doors, of which Mr Gale had not got the key: the door of communication between the study and the bedroom. The key was missing from this. Had it been stolen? And was Dexter the thief? He might have passed by the men on the watch, while they were asleep; or he might have crossed the corridor, in an unguarded interval while the men were being relieved. But how could he have got into the bedchamber, except by way of the locked study door? He *must* have had the key! And he *must* have secreted it, weeks before Mrs Eustace Macallan's death! When the nurse first arrived at Gleninch, on the seventh of the month, her evidence declared the key of the door of communication to be then missing.

To what conclusion did these considerations and discoveries point? Had Miserrimus Dexter, in a moment of ungovernable agitation, unconsciously placed the clue in my hands? Was the pivot on which turned the whole mystery of the poisoning at Gleninch, the missing key?

I went back for the third time to my desk. The one person who might be trusted to find the answer to those questions was Mr Playmore. I wrote him a full and careful account of all that had happened; I begged him to forgive and forget my ungracious reception of the advice which he had so kindly offered to me; and I promised beforehand to do nothing, without first consulting his opinion, in the new emergency which now confronted me.

The day was fine, for the time of year; and by way of getting a little wholesome exercise, after the surprises and occupations of the morning, I took my letter to Mr Playmore to the post.

Returning to the villa, I was informed that another visitor was waiting to see me; a civilized visitor this time, who had given her name. My mother-in-law—Mrs Macallan.

CHAPTER XXXVII

At the Bedside

BEFORE she had uttered a word, I saw in my mother-in-law's face that she brought bad news.

'Eustace?' I said.

She answered me by a look.

'Let me hear it at once!' I cried. 'I can bear anything but suspense.'

Mrs Macallan lifted her hand, and showed me a telegraphic despatch which she had hitherto kept concealed in the folds of her dress.

'I can trust your courage,' she said. 'There is no need, my child, to prevaricate with you. Read that.'

I read the telegram. It was sent by the chief surgeon of a field-hospital; and it was dated from a village in the north of Spain.

'Mr Eustace severely wounded in a skirmish, by a stray shot. Not in danger, so far. Every care taken of him. Wait for another telegram.'

I turned away my face, and bore as best I might the pang that wrung me when I read those words. I thought I knew how dearly I loved him. I had never known it till that moment.

My mother-in-law put her arm round me, and held me to her tenderly. She knew me well enough not to speak to me at that moment.

I rallied my courage, and pointed to the last sentence in the telegram.

'Do you mean to wait?' I asked.

'Not a day!' she answered. 'I am going to the Foreign Office about my passport—I have some interest there: they can give me letters; they can advise and assist me. I leave to-night by the mail train to Calais!'

'*You* leave?' I said. 'Do you suppose I will let you go without me? Get my passport when you get yours. At seven this evening, I will be at your house.'

She attempted to remonstrate; she spoke of the perils of the journey. At the first words, I stopped her. 'Don't you know yet, mother, how obstinate I am? They may keep you waiting at the Foreign Office. Why do you waste the precious hours here?'

She yielded with a gentleness that was not in her everyday character. 'Will my poor Eustace ever know what a wife he has got!' That was all she said. She kissed me, and went away in her carriage.

My remembrances of our journey are strangely vague and imperfect.

As I try to recall them, the memory of those more recent and more interesting events which occurred after my return to England, gets between me and my adventures in Spain, and seems to force these last into a shadowy background, until they look like adventures that happened many years since. I confusedly recollect delays and alarms that tried our patience and our courage. I remember our finding friends (thanks to our letters of recommendation) in a Secretary to the Embassy, and in a Queen's Messenger,* who assisted and protected us at a critical point in the journey. I recall to mind a long succession of men, in our employment as travellers, all equally remarkable for their dirty cloaks and their clean linen, for their highly-civilised courtesy to women, and their utterly-barbarous cruelty to horses. Last, and most important of all, I see again, more clearly than I can see anything else, the one wretched bedroom of a squalid village inn, in which we found our poor darling, prostrate between life and death, insensible to everything that passed in the narrow little world that lay round his bedside.

There was nothing romantic or interesting in the accident which had put my husband's life in peril.

He had ventured too near the scene of the conflict (a miserable affair) to rescue a poor lad who lay wounded on the field—mortally wounded as the event proved. A rifle-bullet had struck him in the body. His brethren of the field-hospital had carried him back to their quarters, at the risk of their lives. He was a great favourite with all of them; patient, and gentle, and brave; only wanting a little more judgment to be the most valuable recruit who had joined the brotherhood.

In telling me this, the surgeon kindly and delicately added a word of warning as well.

The fever caused by the wound had brought with it delirium as usual. My poor husband's mind, in so far as his wandering words might interpret it, was filled by the one image of his wife. The medical attendant had heard enough, in the course of his ministrations at the bedside, to satisfy him that any sudden recognition of me by Eustace (if he recovered) might be attended by the most lamentable results. As things were at that sad time, I might take my turn at nursing him, without the slightest chance of his discovering me, perhaps for weeks and weeks to come. But on the day when he was declared out of danger—if that happy day ever arrived—I must resign my place at his bedside, and must wait to show myself until the surgeon gave me leave.

My mother-in-law and I relieved each other regularly, day and night, in the sick room.

In the hours of his delirium—hours that recurred with a pitiless regularity—my name was always on my poor darling's fevered lips. The ruling idea in him was the one dreadful idea which I had vainly combated at our last interview. In the face of the verdict pronounced at the Trial, it was impossible even for his wife to be really and truly persuaded that he was an innocent man. All the wild pictures which his distempered imagination drew, were equally inspired by that one obstinate conviction. He fancied himself to be still living with me, under those dreaded conditions. Do what he might, I was always recalling to him the terrible ordeal through which he had passed. He acted his part, and he acted mine. He gave me a cup of tea; and I said to him, 'We quarrelled yesterday, Eustace. Is it poisoned?' He kissed me, in token of our reconciliation; and I laughed and said, 'It's morning now, my dear. Shall I die by nine o'clock to-night?' I was ill in bed, and he gave me my medicine. I looked at him with a doubting eye. I said to him, 'You are in love with another woman. Is there anything in the medicine that the doctor doesn't know of?' Such was the horrible drama which now perpetually acted itself in his mind. Hundreds and hundreds of times I heard him repeat it, almost always in the same words. On other occasions, his thoughts wandered away to my desperate project of proving him to be an innocent man. Sometimes, he laughed at it. Sometimes, he mourned over it. Sometimes, he devised cunning schemes for placing unsuspected obstacles in my way. He was especially hard on me when he was inventing his preventive stratagems—he cheerfully instructed the visionary people who assisted him, not to hesitate at offending or distressing me. 'Never mind if you make her angry; never mind if you make her cry. It's all for her good; it's all to save the poor fool from dangers she doesn't dream of. You mustn't pity her when she says she does it for my sake. See! she is going to be insulted; she is going to be deceived; she is going to disgrace herself without knowing it. Stop her! stop her!' It was weak of me I know; I ought to have kept the plain fact that he was out of his senses always present to my mind. Still, it is true that my hours passed at my husband's pillow were, many of them, hours of mortification and misery of which he, poor dear, was the innocent and only cause.

The weeks passed; and he still hovered between life and death.

I kept no record of the time, and I cannot now recall the exact date on which the first favourable change took place. I only remember that it was towards sunrise on a fine winter morning, when we were relieved at last of our heavy burden of suspense. The surgeon happened to be by the bedside, when his patient woke. The first thing he did, after looking at Eustace, was to caution me by a sign to be silent, and to keep out of sight. My mother-in-law and I both knew what this meant. With full hearts we thanked God together for giving us back the husband and the son.

The same evening, being alone, we ventured to speak of the future—for the first time since we had left home.

'The surgeon tells me,' said Mrs Macallan, 'that Eustace is too weak to be capable of bearing anything in the nature of a surprise, for some days to come. We have time to consider whether he is, or is not, to be told that he owes his life as much to your care as to mine. Can you find it in your heart to leave him, Valeria, now that God's mercy has restored him to you and to me?'

'If I only consulted my own heart,' I answered, 'I should never leave him again.'

Mrs Macallan looked at me in grave surprise.

'What else have you to consult?' she asked.

'If we both live,' I replied, 'I have to think of the happiness of his life, and the happiness of mine, in the years that are to come. I can bear a great deal mother, but I cannot endure the misery of his leaving me for the second time.'

'You wrong him, Valeria—I firmly believe you wrong him—in thinking it possible that he can leave you again!'

'Dear Mrs Macallan, have you forgotten what we have both heard him say of me, while we have been sitting by his bedside?'

'We have heard the ravings of a man in delirium. It is surely hard to hold Eustace responsible for what he said when he was out of his senses?'

'It is harder still,' I said, 'to resist his mother when she is pleading for him. Dearest and best of friends! I don't hold Eustace responsible for what he said in the fever—but I *do* take warning by it. The wildest words that fell from him were, one and all, the faithful echo of what he said to me

in the best days of his health and his strength. What hope
have I that he will recover with an altered mind towards
me? Absence has not changed it; suffering has not changed
it. In the delirium of fever, and in the full possession of his
reason, he has the same dreadful doubt of me. I see but
one way of winning him back. I must destroy at its root his
motive for leaving me. It is hopeless to persuade him that
I believe in his innocence: I must show him that belief is
no longer necessary; I must prove to him that his position
towards me has become the position of an innocent man.'

'Valeria! Valeria! you are wasting time and words. You
have tried the experiment; and you know as well as I do,
the thing is not to be done.'

I had no answer to that. I could say no more than I had
said already.

'Suppose you go back to Dexter, out of sheer compassion
for a mad and miserable wretch who has already insulted
you,' proceeded my mother-in-law. 'You can only go back,
accompanied by me, or by some other trustworthy person.
You can only stay long enough to humour the creature's
wayward fancy, and to keep his crazy brain quiet for a time.
That done, all is done—you leave him. Even supposing
Dexter to be still capable of helping you, how can you make
use of him but by admitting him to terms of confidence and
familiarity—by treating him, in short, on the footing of an
intimate friend? Answer me honestly: can you bring yourself to do that, after what happened at Mr Benjamin's
house?'

I had told her of my last interview with Miserrimus Dexter, in the natural confidence that she inspired in me as
relative and fellow-traveller; and this was the use to which
she turned her information! I suppose I had no right to
blame her; I suppose the motive sanctioned everything. At
any rate, I had no choice but to give offence, or to give an
answer. I gave it. I acknowledged that I could never again
permit Miserrimus Dexter to treat me on terms of familiarity, as a trusted and intimate friend.

Mrs Macallan pitilessly pressed the advantage that she had won.

'Very well,' she said, 'that resource being no longer open to you, what hope is left? Which way are you to turn next?'

There was no meeting those questions, in my present situation, by any adequate reply. I felt strangely unlike myself—I submitted in silence. Mrs Macallan struck the last blow that completed her victory.

'My poor Eustace is weak and wayward,' she said; 'but he is not an ungrateful man. My child! you have returned him good for evil—you have proved how faithfully and how devotedly you love him, by suffering hardships and by risking dangers for his sake. Trust me, and trust him! He cannot resist you. Let him see the dear face that he has been dreaming of, looking at him again with all the old love in it; and he is yours once more, my daughter—yours for life.' She rose and touched my forehead with her lips; her voice sank to tones of tenderness which I had never heard from her yet. 'Say yes, Valeria,' she whispered; 'and be dearer to me and dearer to him than ever!'

My heart sided with her. My energies were worn out. No letter had arrived from Mr Playmore, to guide and to encourage me. I had resisted so long and so vainly; I had tried and suffered so much; I had met with such cruel disasters and such reiterated disappointments—and *he* was in the room beneath me, feebly finding his way back to consciousness and to life—how could I resist? It was all over! In saying Yes (if Eustace confirmed his mother's confidence in him), I was saying adieu to the one cherished ambition, the one dear and noble hope of my life. I knew it—and I said Yes.

And so good-bye to the grand struggle! And so welcome to the new resignation which owned that I had failed!

My mother-in-law and I slept together under the only shelter that the inn could offer to us—a sort of loft at the top of the house. The night that followed our conversation was bitterly cold. We felt the chilly temperature, in spite of the protection of our dressing gowns and our travelling wrappers. My mother-in-law slept; but no rest came to me. I was too anxious and too wretched, thinking over my changed position, and doubting how my husband would receive me, to be able to sleep.

Some hours, as I suppose, must have passed, and I was still absorbed in my own melancholy thoughts—when I suddenly became conscious of a new and strange sensation which astonished and alarmed me. I started up in the bed, breathless and bewildered. The movement awakened Mrs Macallan. 'Are you ill?' she asked. 'What is the matter with you?' I tried to tell her, as well as I could. She seemed to understand me before I had done; she took me tenderly in her arms, and pressed me to her bosom. 'My poor innocent child,' she said, 'is it possible you don't know? Must I really tell you?' She whispered her next words. Shall I ever forget the tumult of feelings which the whisper aroused in me—the strange medley of joy and fear, and wonder and relief, and pride and humility, which filled my whole being, and made a new woman of me from that moment? Now, for the first time, I knew it! If God spared me for a few months more, the most enduring and the most sacred of all human joys might be mine—the joy of being a mother.

I don't know how the rest of the night passed. I only found my memory again, when the morning came, and when I went out by myself to breathe the crisp wintry air on the open moor behind the inn.

I have said that I felt like a new woman. The morning found me with a new resolution and a new courage. When I thought of the future, I had not only my husband to consider now. His good name was no longer his own and mine—it might soon become the most precious inheritance that he could leave to his child. What had I done, while I was in ignorance of this? I had resigned the hope of cleansing his name from the stain that had rested on it—a stain still, no matter how little it might look in the eye of the Law. Our child might live to hear malicious tongues say, 'Your father was tried for the vilest of all murders, and was never absolutely acquitted of the charge.' Could I face the glorious perils of childbirth, with that possibility present to my mind? No! not until I had made one more effort to lay the conscience of Miserrimus Dexter bare to my view! not until I had once again renewed the struggle, and brought the truth that vindicated the husband and the father to the light of day!

I went back to the house, with my new courage to sustain me. I opened my heart to my friend and mother, and told her frankly of the change that had come over me, since we had last spoken of Eustace.

She was more than disappointed, she was almost offended with me. The one thing needful had happened, she said. The happiness that was coming to us would form a new tie between my husband and me. Every other consideration but this, she treated as purely fanciful. If I left Eustace now, I did a heartless thing and a foolish thing. I should regret, to the end of my days, having thrown away the one golden opportunity of my married life.

It cost me a hard struggle, it oppressed me with many a painful doubt; but I held firm, this time. The honour of the father, the inheritance of the child—I kept those thoughts as constantly as possible before my mind. Sometimes they failed me, and left me nothing better than a poor fool who had some fitful bursts of crying, and was ashamed of herself afterwards. But my native obstinacy (as Mrs Macallan said) carried me through. Now and then, I had a peep at Eustace, while he was asleep, and that helped me too. Though they made my heart ache and shook me sadly at the time, those furtive visits to my husband fortified me afterwards. I cannot explain how this happened (it seems so contradictory); I can only repeat it as one of my experiences at that troubled time.

I made one concession to Mrs Macallan—I consented to wait for two days, before I took any steps for returning to

England, on the chance that my mind might change in the interval.

It was well for me that I yielded so far. On the second day, the director of the field-hospital sent to the post-office, at our nearest town, for letters addressed to him or to his care. The messenger brought back a letter for me. I thought I recognized the handwriting, and I was right. Mr Playmore's answer had reached me at last!

If I had been in any danger of changing my mind, the good lawyer would have saved me in the nick of time. The extract that follows contains the pith of his letter; and shows how he encouraged me, when I stood in sore need of a few cheering and friendly words.

'Let me now tell you' (he wrote) 'what I have done towards verifying the conclusion to which your letter points.

'I have traced one of the servants who was appointed to keep watch in the corridor, on the night when the first Mrs Eustace died at Gleninch. The man perfectly remembers that Miserrimus Dexter appeared before him and his fellow-servant (in his chair), after the house was quiet for the night. Dexter said to them, "I suppose there is no harm in my going into the study to read? I can't sleep after what has happened; I must relieve my mind somehow." The men had no orders to keep any one out of the study. They knew that the door of communication with the bedchamber was locked, and that the keys of the two other doors of communication were in the possession of Mr Gale. They accordingly permitted Dexter to go into the study. He closed the door (the door that opened on the corridor), and remained absent for some time—in the study as the men supposed; in the bedchamber as *we* know, from what he let out at his interview with you. Now, he could enter that room, as you rightly imagine, in but one way—by being in possession of the missing key. How long he remained there, I cannot discover. The point is of little consequence. The servant remembers that he came out of the study again "as pale as death," and that he passed on without a word, on his way back to his own room.

'These are facts. The conclusion to which they lead is serious in the last degree. It justifies everything that I confided to you in my office at Edinburgh. You remember what passed between us. I say no more.

'As to yourself next. You have innocently aroused in Miserrimus Dexter a feeling towards you, which I need not attempt to characterize. There is a certain something—I saw it myself—in your figure, and in some of your movements, which does recall the late Mrs Eustace to those who knew her well, and which has evidently had its effect on Dexter's morbid mind. Without dwelling further on this subject, let me only remind you that he has shown himself (as a consequence of your influence over him) to be incapable, in his moments of agitation, of thinking before he speaks, while he is in your presence. It is not merely possible, it is highly probable, that he may betray himself far more seriously than he has betrayed himself yet, if you give him the opportunity. I owe it to you (knowing what your interests are) to express myself plainly on this point. I have no sort of doubt that you have advanced one step nearer to the end which you have in view, in the brief interval since you left Edinburgh. I see in your letter (and in my discoveries) irresistible evidence that Dexter must have been in secret communication with the deceased lady (innocent communication, I am certain, so far as *she* was concerned), not only at the time of her death, but probably for weeks before it. I cannot disguise from myself, or from you, my own strong persuasion that, if you succeed in discovering the nature of this communication, in all human likelihood you prove your husband's innocence by the discovery of the truth. As an honest man, I am bound not to conceal this. And, as an honest man also, I am equally bound to add that, not even with your reward in view, can I find it in my conscience to advise you to risk what you must risk, if you see Miserrimus Dexter again. In this difficult and delicate matter, I cannot, and will not, take the responsibility. The final decision must rest with yourself. One favour only I entreat you to grant—let me hear what you resolve to do as soon as you know it yourself.'

The difficulties which my worthy correspondent felt were no difficulties to me. I did not possess Mr Playmore's judicial mind. My resolution (come what might of it) to see Miserrimus Dexter again, was settled before I had read his letter to the end.

The mail to France crossed the frontier the next day. There was a place for me under the protection of the conductor, if I chose to take it. Without consulting a living creature—rash as usual, headlong as usual—I took it.

CHAPTER XXXVIII

On the Journey Back

IF I had been travelling homeward in my own carriage, the remaining chapters of this narrative would never have been written. Before we had been an hour on the road, I should have called to the driver, and should have told him to turn back.

Who can be always resolute?

In asking that question, I speak of the women, not of the men. I had been resolute in turning a deaf ear to Mr Playmore's doubts and cautions; resolute in holding out against my mother-in-law; resolute in taking my place by the French mail. Until ten minutes after we had driven away from the inn my courage held out—and then it failed me; then I said to myself, 'You wretch, you have deserted your husband!' For hours afterwards, if I could have stopped the mail, I would have done it. I hated the conductor, the kindest of men. I hated the Spanish ponies that drew us, the cheeriest animals that ever jingled a string of

bells. I hated the bright day that *would* make things pleasant, and the bracing air that forced me to feel the luxury
of breathing, whether I liked it or not. Never was a journey
more miserable than my safe and easy journey to the frontier! But one little comfort helped me to bear my heart-ache
resignedly—a stolen morsel of Eustace's hair. We had
started at an hour of the morning when he was still sound
asleep. I could creep into his room, and kiss him, and cry
over him softly, and cut off a stray lock of his hair, without
danger of discovery. How I summoned resolution enough
to leave him is, to this hour, not clear to my mind. I think
my mother-in-law must have helped me, without meaning
to do it. She came into the room with an erect head, and
a cold eye: she said, with an unmerciful emphasis on the
word, 'If you *mean* to go, Valeria, the carriage is here.' Any
woman with a spark of spirit in her would have 'meant' it
under those circumstances. I meant it—and did it.

And then I was sorry for it. Poor humanity!

Time has got all the credit of being the great consoler of
afflicted mortals. In my opinion, Time has been over-rated
in this matter. Distance does the same beneficent work, far
more speedily, and (when assisted by Change) far more
effectually as well. On the railroad to Paris, I became capable of taking a sensible view of my position. I could now
remind myself that my husband's reception of me—after
the first surprise and the first happiness had passed away—
might not have justified his mother's confidence in him.
Admitting that I ran a risk in going back to Miserrimus
Dexter, should I not have been equally rash, in another way,
if I had returned, uninvited, to a husband who had declared
that our conjugal happiness was impossible, and that our
married life was at an end? Besides, who could say that the
events of the future might not yet justify me—not only to
myself, but to him? I might yet hear him say, 'She was
inquisitive when she had no business to inquire; she was
obstinate when she ought to have listened to reason; she
left my bedside when other women would have remained:

but in the end she atoned for it all—she turned out to be right!'

I rested a day at Paris, and wrote three letters.

One to Benjamin, telling him to expect me the next evening. One to Mr Playmore, warning him in good time, that I meant to make a last effort to penetrate the mystery at Gleninch. One to Eustace (of a few lines only), owning that I had helped to nurse him through the dangerous part of his illness; confessing the one reason which had prevailed with me to leave him; and entreating him to suspend his opinion of me, until time had proved that I loved him more dearly than ever. This last letter I enclosed to my mother-in-law; leaving it to her discretion to choose the right time for giving it to her son. I positively forbade Mrs Macallan, however, to tell Eustace of the new tie between us. Although he *had* separated himself from me, I was determined that he should not hear of it from other lips than mine. Never mind why! There are certain little matters which I must keep to myself; and this is one of them.

My letters being written, my duty was done. I was free to play my last card in the game—the darkly-doubtful game which was neither quite for me, nor quite against me, as the chances now stood.

CHAPTER XXXIX

On the Way to Dexter

'I DECLARE to Heaven, Valeria, I believe that monster's madness is infectious—and you have caught it!'

This was Benjamin's opinion of me (on my arrival at the villa); after I had announced my intention of returning Miserrimus Dexter's visit, in his company.

Being determined to carry my point, I could afford to try the influence of mild persuasion. I begged my good friend

to have a little patience with me. 'And do remember what
I have already told you,' I added. 'It is of serious importance to me to see Dexter again.'

I only heaped fuel on the fire. 'See him again?' Benjamin
repeated, indignantly. 'See him, after he grossly insulted
you, under my roof, in this very room? I can't be awake; I
must be asleep and dreaming.'

It was wrong of me, I know. But Benjamin's virtuous
indignation was so very virtuous that it let the spirit of
mischief loose in me. I really could not resist the temptation
to outrage his sense of propriety, by taking an audaciously
liberal view of the whole matter.

'Gently, my good friend, gently!' I said. 'We must make
allowances for a man who suffers under Dexter's infirmities, and lives Dexter's life. And really we must not let
our modesty lead us beyond reasonable limits. I begin to
think that I took rather a prudish view of the thing myself,
at the time. A woman who respects herself, and whose
whole heart is with her husband, is not so very seriously
injured when a wretched crippled creature is rude enough
to put his arm round her waist. Virtuous indignation (if I
may venture to say so) is sometimes very cheap indignation.
Besides, I have forgiven him—and you must forgive him,
too. There is no fear of his forgetting himself again, while
you are with me. His house is quite a curiosity; it is sure to
interest you; the pictures alone are worth the journey. I will
write to him to-day, and we will go and see him together
to-morrow. We owe it to ourselves (if we don't owe it to
Mr Dexter) to pay this visit. If you will look about you,
Benjamin, you will see that benevolence towards everybody
is the great virtue of the time we live in. Poor Mr Dexter
must have the benefit of the prevailing fashion. Come,
come, march with the age! Open your mind to the new
ideas!'

Instead of accepting this polite invitation, worthy old
Benjamin flew at the age we lived in, like a bull at a red
cloth.

'Oh, the new ideas! the new ideas! By all manner of means, Valeria, let us have the new ideas! The old morality's all wrong, the old ways are all worn out. Let's march with the age we live in. Nothing comes amiss to the age we live in. The wife in England and the husband in Spain, married or not married, living together or not living together—it's all one to the new ideas. I'll go with you, Valeria; I'll be worthy of the generation I live in. When we have done with Dexter, don't let's do things by halves. Let's go and get crammed with ready-made science at a lecture—let's hear the last new professor, the man who has been behind the scenes at Creation, and knows to a T how the world was made, and how long it took to make it. There's the other fellow, too: mind we don't forget the modern Solomon who has left his proverbs behind him—the bran-new philosopher who considers the consolations of religion in the light of harmless playthings, and who is kind enough to say that he might have been all the happier if he could only have been childish enough to play with them himself. Oh, the new ideas, the new ideas, what consoling, elevating, beautiful discoveries have been made by the new ideas! We were all monkeys before we were men, and molecules before we were monkeys!* And what does it matter? And what does anything matter to anybody? I'm with you, Valeria—I'm ready! The sooner the better. Come to Dexter! Come to Dexter!'

'I am so glad you agree with me,' I said. 'But let us do nothing in a hurry. Three o'clock to-morrow will be time enough for Mr Dexter. I will write at once and tell him to expect us. Where are you going?'

'I am going to clear my mind of cant,' said Benjamin, sternly. 'I am going into the library.'

'What are you going to read?'

'I am going to read——"Puss in Boots," and "Jack and the Bean-Stalk," and anything else I can find that doesn't march with the age we live in.'

With that parting shot at the new ideas, my old friend left me for a time.

Having despatched my note, I found myself beginning to revert, with a certain feeling of anxiety, to the subject of Miserrimus Dexter's health. How had he passed through the interval of my absence from England? Could anybody, within my reach, tell me news of him? To inquire of Benjamin would only be to provoke a new outbreak. While I was still considering, the housekeeper entered the room on some domestic errand. I asked, at a venture, if she had heard anything more, while I had been away, of the extraordinary person who had so seriously alarmed her on a former occasion.

The housekeeper shook her head, and looked as if she thought it in bad taste to mention the subject at all.

'About a week after you had gone away, ma'am,' she said, with extreme severity of manner, and with excessive carefulness in her choice of words, 'the Person you mention had the impudence to send a letter to you. The messenger was informed, by my master's orders, that you had gone abroad, and he and his letter were both sent about their business together. Not long afterwards, ma'am, I happened, while drinking tea with Mrs Macallan's housekeeper, to hear of the Person again. He himself called in his chaise, at Mrs Macallan's, to inquire about you there. How he can contrive to sit, without legs to balance him, is beyond my understanding—but that is neither here nor there. Legs or no legs, the housekeeper saw him, and she says, as I say, she will never forget him to her dying day. She told him (as soon as she recovered herself) of Mr Eustace's illness, and of you and Mrs Macallan being in foreign parts nursing him. He went away, so the housekeeper told me, with tears in his eyes, and oaths and curses on his lips—a sight shocking to see. That's all I know about the Person, ma'am, and I hope to be excused if I venture to say that the subject is (for good reasons) extremely disagreeable to me.'

She made a formal curtsey, and quitted the room.

Left by myself, I felt more anxious and more uncertain than ever, when I thought of the experiment that was to be tried on the next day. Making due allowance for exaggeration, the description of Miserrimus Dexter, on his departure from Mrs Macallan's house, suggested that he had not endured my long absence very patiently, and that he was still as far as ever from giving his shattered nervous system its fair chance of repose.

The next morning brought me Mr Playmore's reply to the letter which I had addressed to him from Paris.

He wrote very briefly, neither approving nor blaming my decision, but strongly reiterating his opinion that I should do well to choose a competent witness as my companion at my coming interview with Dexter. The most interesting part of the letter was at the end. 'You must be prepared,' Mr Playmore wrote, 'to see a change for the worse in Dexter. A friend of mine was with him on a matter of business a few days since, and was struck by the alteration in him. Your presence is sure to have its effect one way or another. I can give you no instructions for managing him—you must be guided by the circumstances. Your own tact will tell you whether it is wise, or not, to encourage him to speak of the late Mrs Eustace. The chances of his betraying himself all revolve (as I think) round that one topic: keep him to it if you can.' To this was added, in a postscript: 'Ask Mr Benjamin if he was near enough to the library door to hear Dexter tell you of his entering the bedchamber, on the night of Mrs Eustace Macallan's death.'

I put the question to Benjamin when we met at the luncheon-table, before setting forth for the distant suburb in which Miserrimus Dexter lived. My old friend disapproved of the contemplated expedition as strongly as ever. He was unusually grave and unusually sparing of words, when he answered me.

'I am no listener,' he said. 'But some people have voices which insist on being heard. Mr Dexter is one of them.'

'Does that mean that you heard him?' I asked.

'The door couldn't muffle him, and the wall couldn't muffle him,' Benjamin rejoined. 'I heard him—and I thought it infamous. There!'

'I may want you to do more than hear him, this time,' I ventured to say. 'I may want you to make notes of our conversation, while Mr Dexter is speaking to me. You used to write down what my father said, when he was dictating his letters to you. Have you got one of your little note-books to spare?'

Benjamin looked up from his plate with an aspect of stern surprise.

'It is one thing,' he said, 'to write under the dictation of a great merchant, conducting a vast correspondence by which thousands of pounds change hands in due course of post. And it's another thing to take down the gibberish of a maundering mad monster who ought to be kept in a cage. Your good father, Valeria, would never have asked me to do that.'

'Forgive me, Benjamin: I must really ask you to do it. It is Mr Playmore's idea, mind!—not mine. Come! give way this once, dear, for my sake.'

Benjamin looked down again at his plate, with a rueful resignation which told me that I had carried my point.

'I have been tied to her apron-string all my life,' I heard him grumble to himself. 'And it's too late in the day to get loose from her now.' He looked up again at me. 'I thought I had retired from business,' he said. 'But it seems I must turn clerk again. Well? What is the new stroke of work that's expected from me, this time?'

The cab was announced to be waiting for us at the gate, as he asked the question. I rose and took his arm, and gave him a grateful kiss on his rosy old cheek.

'Only two things,' I said. 'Sit down behind Mr Dexter's chair, so that he can't see you. But take care to place yourself, at the same time, so that you can see me.'

'The less I see of Mr Dexter, the better I shall be pleased,' growled Benjamin. 'What am I to do, after I have taken my place behind him?'

'You are to wait until I make you a sign; and when you see it you are to begin writing down in your note-book what

Mr Dexter is saying—and you are to go on, until I make another sign which means, Leave off!'

'Well?' said Benjamin, 'What's the sign for, Begin? and what's the sign for, Leave off?'

I was not quite prepared with an answer to this. I asked him to help me with a hint. No! Benjamin would take no active part in the matter. He was resigned to be employed in the capacity of passive instrument—and there all concession ended, so far as he was concerned.

Left to my own resources, I found it no easy matter to invent a telegraphic system which should sufficiently inform Benjamin, without awakening Dexter's quick suspicion. I looked into the glass to see if I could find the necessary suggestion in anything that I wore. My earrings supplied me with the idea of which I was in search.

'I shall take care to sit in an arm-chair,' I said. 'When you see me rest my elbow on the chair, and lift my hand to my earring, as if I was playing with it—write down what he says; and go on until—well, suppose we say, until you hear me move my chair. At that sound, stop. You understand me?'

'I understand you.'

We started for Dexter's house.

CHAPTER XL

Nemesis at Last!

THE gardener opened the gate to us on this occasion. He had evidently received his orders, in anticipation of my arrival.

'Mrs Valeria?' he asked.

'Yes.'

'And friend?'

'And friend.'

'Please to step upstairs. You know the house.'

Crossing the hall, I stopped for a moment, and looked at a favourite walking-cane which Benjamin still kept in his hand.

'Your cane will only be in your way,' I said. 'Had you not better leave it here?'

'My cane may be useful upstairs,' retorted Benjamin gruffly. '*I* haven't forgotten what happened in the library.'

It was no time to contend with him. I led the way up the stairs.

Arriving at the upper flight of steps, I was startled by hearing a sudden cry from the room above. It was like the cry of a person in pain; and it was twice repeated, before we entered the circular ante-chamber. I was the first to approach the inner room, and to see the many-sided Miserrimus Dexter in another new aspect of his character.

The unfortunate Ariel was standing before a table, with a dish of little cakes placed in front of her. Round each of her wrists was tied a string, the free end of which (at a distance of a few yards) was held in Miserrimus Dexter's hands. 'Try again, my beauty!' I heard him say, as I stopped on the threshold of the door. 'Take a cake.' At the word of command, Ariel submissively stretched out one arm towards the dish. Just as she touched a cake with the tips of her fingers, her hand was jerked away by a pull at the string, so savagely cruel in the nimble and devilish violence of it, that I felt inclined to snatch Benjamin's cane out of his hand, and break it over Miserrimus Dexter's back. Ariel suffered the pain this time in Spartan silence. The position in which she stood enabled her to be the first to see me at the door. She had discovered me. Her teeth were set; her face was flushed under the struggle to restrain herself. Not even a sigh escaped her in my presence.

'Drop the strings!' I called out, indignantly. 'Release her, Mr Dexter, or I shall leave the house.'

At the sound of my voice he burst out with a shrill cry of welcome. His eyes fastened on me with a fierce, devouring delight.

'Come in! come in!' he cried. 'See what I am reduced to, in the maddening suspense of waiting for you. See how I kill the time when the time parts us. Come in! come in! I am in one of my malicious humours this morning, caused entirely, Mrs Valeria, by my anxiety to see you. When I am in my malicious humours I must tease something. I am teasing Ariel. Look at her! She has had nothing to eat all day, and she hasn't been quick enough to snatch a morsel of cake yet. You needn't pity her. Ariel has no nerves—I don't hurt her.'

'Ariel has no nerves,' echoed the poor creature, frowning at me for interfering between her master and herself. 'He doesn't hurt me.'

I heard Benjamin beginning to swing his cane behind me.

'Drop the strings!' I reiterated, more vehemently than ever. 'Drop them—or I shall instantly leave you.'

Miserrimus Dexter's delicate nerves shuddered at my violence. 'What a glorious voice!' he exclaimed—and dropped the strings. 'Take the cakes,' he added, addressing Ariel in his most imperial manner.

She passed me, with the strings hanging from her swollen wrists, and the dish of cakes in her hand. She nodded her head at me defiantly.

'Ariel has got no nerves,' she repeated, proudly. 'He doesn't hurt me.'

'You see,' said Miserrimus Dexter, 'there is no harm done—and I dropped the strings when you told me. Don't *begin* by being hard on me, Mrs Valeria, after your long, long absence.' He paused. Benjamin, standing silent in the doorway, attracted his attention for the first time. 'Who is this?' he asked; and wheeled his chair suspiciously nearer to the door. 'I know!' he cried, before I could answer. 'This is the benevolent gentleman who looked like the refuge of the afflicted, when I saw him last. You have altered for the worse since then, Sir. You have stepped into quite a new character—you personify Retributive Justice, now. Your new protector, Mrs Valeria—I understand!' He bowed low to Benjamin, with ferocious irony. 'Your humble servant, Mr Retributive Justice! I have deserved you—and I submit to you. Walk in, Sir! I will take care that your new office shall be a sinecure. This lady is the Light of my Life. Catch me failing in respect towards her, if you can!' He backed his chair before Benjamin (who listened to him in contemptuous silence) until he reached the part of the room in which I was standing. 'Your hand, Light of my Life!' he murmured, in his gentlest tones. 'Your hand—only to show you have forgiven me!' I gave him my hand. 'One?' he whispered, entreatingly. 'Only one?' He kissed my hand once, respectfully—and dropped it with a heavy sigh. 'Ah, poor Dexter!' he said, pitying himself with the whole sincerity of his egotism. 'A warm heart, wasted in solitude, mocked by deformity. Sad! sad! Ah, poor Dexter!' He looked round again at Benjamin, with another flash of his ferocious irony. 'A beautiful day, Sir,' he said, with mock-conventional courtesy. 'Seasonable weather indeed after the late long-continued rains. Can I offer you any refreshment? Won't you sit down? Retributive Justice, when it is no taller than you are, looks best in a chair.'

'And a monkey looks best in a cage,' rejoined Benjamin, enraged at the satirical reference to his shortness of stature. 'I was waiting, Sir, to see you get into your swing.'

The retort produced no effect on Miserrimus Dexter: it appeared to have passed by him unheard. He had changed again; he was thoughtful, he was subdued; his eyes were fixed on me with a sad and rapt attention. I took the nearest arm-chair; first casting a glance at Benjamin, which he immediately understood. He placed himself behind Dexter, at an angle which commanded a view of my chair. Ariel, silently devouring her cakes, crouched on a stool at 'the Master's' feet, and looked up at him like a faithful dog. There was an interval of quiet and repose. I was able to observe Miserrimus Dexter uninterruptedly, for the first time since I had entered the room.

I was not surprised—I was nothing less than alarmed by

the change for the worse in him, since we had last met. Mr Playmore's letter had not prepared me for the serious deterioration in him which I could now discern.

His features were pinched and worn; the whole face seemed to have wasted strangely in substance and size, since I had last seen it. The softness in his eyes was gone. Blood-red veins were intertwined all over them now; they were set in a piteous and vacant stare. His once firm hands looked withered; they trembled as they lay on the coverlid. The paleness of his face (exaggerated, perhaps, by the black velvet jacket that he wore) had a sodden and sickly look—the fine outline was gone. The multitudinous little wrinkles at the corners of his eyes had deepened. His head sank into his shoulders when he leaned forward in his chair. Years appeared to have passed over him, instead of months, while I had been absent from England. Remembering the medical report which Mr Playmore had given me to read—recalling the doctor's positively-declared opinion that the preservation of Dexter's sanity depended on the healthy condition of his nerves—I could not but feel that I had done wisely (if I might still hope for success) in hastening my return from Spain. Knowing what I knew, fearing what I feared, I believed that his time was near. I felt, when our eyes met by accident, that I was looking at a doomed man.

I pitied him.

Yes! yes! I know that compassion for him was utterly inconsistent with the motive which had taken me to his house—utterly inconsistent with the doubt, still present to my mind whether Mr Playmore had really wronged him in believing that his was the guilt which had compassed the first Mrs Eustace's death. I felt this: I knew him to be cruel; I believed him to be false. And yet, I pitied him! Is there a common fund of wickedness in us all? Is the suppression or the development of that wickedness a mere question of training and temptation? And is there something in our deeper sympathies which mutely acknowledges this, when we feel for the wicked; when we crowd to a criminal trial; when we shake hands at parting (if we happen to be present officially) with the vilest monster that ever swung on a gallows? It is not for me to decide. I can only say that I pitied Miserrimus Dexter—and that he found it out.

'Thank you,' he said, suddenly. 'You see I am ill, and you feel for me. Dear and good Valeria!'

'This lady's name, Sir, is Mrs Eustace Macallan,' interposed Benjamin, speaking sternly behind him. 'The next time you address her, remember, if you please, that you have no business with her Christian name.'

Benjamin's rebuke passed, like Benjamin's retort, unheeded and unheard. To all appearance, Miserrimus Dexter had completely forgotten that there was such a person in the room.

'You have delighted me with the sight of you,' he went on. 'Add to the pleasure by letting me hear your voice. Talk to me of yourself. Tell me what you have been doing since you left England.'

It was necessary to my object to set the conversation afloat; and this was as good a way of doing it as any other. I told him plainly how I had been employed during my absence.

'So you are still fond of Eustace?' he said, bitterly.

'I love him more dearly than ever.'

He lifted his hands, and hid his face. After waiting awhile, he went on; speaking in an odd, muffled manner, still under cover of his hands.

'And you leave Eustace in Spain?' he said; 'and you return to England by yourself! What made you do that?'

'What made me first come here, and ask you to help me, Mr Dexter?'

He dropped his hands, and looked at me. I saw in his eyes, not amazement only, but alarm.

'Is it possible,' he exclaimed, 'that you won't let that miserable matter rest even yet? Are you still determined to meddle with the mystery at Gleninch!'

'I am still determined, Mr Dexter; and I still hope that you may be able to help me.'

The old distrust that I remembered so well, darkened again over his face the moment I said those words.

'How can I help you?' he asked. 'Can I alter facts?' He stopped. His face brightened again, as if some sudden sense of relief had come to him. 'I *did* try to help you,' he went on. 'I told you that Mrs Beauly's absence was a device to screen herself from suspicion; I told you that the poison might have been given by Mrs Beauly's maid. Has reflection convinced you? Do you see something in the idea?'

This return to Mrs Beauly gave me my first chance of leading the talk to the right topic.

'I see nothing in the idea,' I answered. 'I see no motive. Had the maid any reason to be an enemy to the late Mrs Eustace?'

'Nobody had any reason to be an enemy to the late Mrs Eustace!' he broke out, loudly and vehemently. 'She was all goodness, all kindness; she never injured any human creature in thought or deed. She was a saint upon earth. Respect her memory! Let the martyr rest in her grave!' He covered his face again with his hands, and shook and shuddered under the paroxysm of emotion that I had roused in him.

Ariel suddenly and softly left her stool and approached me.

'Do you see my ten claws?' she whispered, holding out her hands. 'Vex the Master again—and you will feel my ten claws on your throat!'

Benjamin rose from his seat: he had seen the action, without hearing the words. I signed to him to keep his place. Ariel returned to her stool, and looked up again at the Master.

'Don't cry,' she said. 'Come on. Here are the strings. Tease me again. Make me screech with the smart of it.'

He never answered and never moved.

Ariel bent her slow mind to meet the difficulty of attract-
ing his attention. I saw it in her frowning brows, in her
colourless eyes looking at me vacantly. On a sudden, she
joyfully struck the open palm of one of her hands with the
fist of the other. She had triumphed. She had got an idea.
'Master!' she cried. 'Master! You haven't told me a story
for ever so long. Puzzle my thick head. Make my flesh
creep. Come on. A good long story. All blood and crimes.'

Had she accidentally hit on the right suggestion to strike
his wayward fancy? I knew his high opinion of his own skill
in 'dramatic narrative.' I knew that one of his favourite
amusements was to puzzle Ariel by telling her stories that
she could not understand. Would he wander away into the
region of wild romance? Or would he remember that my
obstinacy still threatened him with re-opening the inquiry
into the tragedy at Gleninch? and would he set his cunning
at work to mislead me by some new stratagem? This latter
course was the course which my past experience of him
suggested that he would take. But, to my surprise and
alarm, I found my past experience at fault. Ariel succeeded
in diverting his mind from the subject which had been in
full possession of it the moment before she spoke! He
showed his face again. It was overspread by a broad smile
of gratified self-esteem. He was weak enough now to
let even Ariel find her way to his vanity! I saw it, with a
sense of misgiving, with a doubt whether I had not delayed
my visit until too late, which turned me cold, from head to
foot.

Miserrimus Dexter spoke—to Ariel, not to me.

'Poor devil!' he said, patting her head complacently. 'You
don't understand a word of my stories, do you? And yet I
can make the flesh creep on your great clumsy body—and
yet I can stir your stagnant mind, and make you like it! Poor
devil!' He leaned back serenely in his chair, and looked my
way again. Would the sight of me remind him of the words
that had passed between us, not a minute since? No! There
was the pleasantly-tickled self-conceit smiling at me exactly

as it had smiled at Ariel. 'I excel in dramatic narrative, Mrs Valeria,' he said. 'And this creature here on the stool, is a remarkable proof of it. She is quite a psychological study, when I tell her one of my stories. It is really amusing to see the half-witted wretch's desperate efforts to understand me. You shall have a specimen. I have been out of spirits, while you were away—I haven't told her a story for weeks past; I will tell her one now. Don't suppose it's any effort to me! My invention is inexhaustible. You are sure to be amused— you are naturally serious—but you are sure to be amused. I am naturally serious, too: and I always laugh at her.'

Ariel clapped her great shapeless hands. 'He always laughs at me!' she said, with a proud look of superiority, directed straight at Me.

I was at a loss, seriously at a loss, what to do. The outbreak which I had provoked in leading him to speak of the late Mrs Eustace warned me to be careful, and to wait for my opportunity, before I reverted to *that* subject. How else could I turn the conversation, so as to lead him, little by little, towards the betrayal of the secrets which he was keeping from me? In this uncertainty, one thing only seemed to be plain. To let him tell his story, would be simply to let him waste the precious minutes. With a vivid remembrance of Ariel's 'ten claws,' I decided nevertheless on discouraging Dexter's new whim, at every opportunity and by every means in my power.

'Now, Mrs Valeria!' he began, loudly and loftily. 'Listen. Now, Ariel! Bring your brains to a focus. I improvise poetry; I improvise fiction. We will begin with the good old formula of the fairy stories. Once upon a time——'

I was waiting for my opportunity to interrupt him, when he interrupted himself. He stopped, with a bewildered look. He put his hand to his head, and passed it backwards and forwards over his forehead. He laughed feebly.

'I seem to want rousing,' he said.

Was his mind gone? There had been no signs of it, until I had unhappily stirred his memory of the dead mistress of

Gleninch. Was the weakness which I had already noticed, was the bewilderment which I now saw, attributable to the influence of a passing disturbance only? In other words, had I witnessed nothing more serious than a first warning to him, and to us? Would he soon recover himself, if we were patient, and gave him time? Even Benjamin was interested at last; I saw him trying to look at Dexter round the corner of the chair. Even Ariel was surprised and uneasy. She had no dark glances to cast at me now.

We all waited to see what he would do, to hear what he would say, next.

'My harp!' he cried. 'Music will rouse me.'

Ariel brought him his harp.

'Master!' she said, wonderingly. 'What's come to you?' He waved his hand, commanding her to be silent.

'Ode to Invention,' he announced loftily, addressing himself to me. 'Poetry and music improvised by Dexter. Silence! Attention!'

His fingers wandered feebly over the harp-strings; awakening no melody, suggesting no words. In a little while, his hand dropped; his head sank forward gently, and rested on the frame of the harp. I started to my feet and approached him. Was it a sleep? or was it a swoon?

I touched his arm, and called to him by his name.

Ariel instantly stepped between us, with a threatening look at me. At the same moment, Miserrimus Dexter raised his head. My voice had reached him. He looked at me with a curious contemplative quietness in his eyes, which I had never seen in them before.

'Take away the harp,' he said to Ariel, speaking in languid tones, like a man who was very weary.

The mischievous half-witted creature—in sheer stupidity, or in downright malice towards me, I am not sure which—irritated him once more.

'Why, Master?' she asked, staring at him with the harp hugged in her arms. 'What has come to you? Where is the story?'

'We don't want the story,' I interposed. 'I have many things to say to Mr Dexter which I have not said yet.'

Ariel lifted her heavy hand. 'You *will* have it!' she said, and advanced towards me. At the same moment the Master's voice stopped her.

'Put away the harp, you fool!' he repeated sternly. 'And wait for the story until I choose to tell it.'

She took the harp submissively back to its place at the end of the room. Miserrimus Dexter moved his chair a little closer to mine. 'I know what will rouse me,' he said, confidentially. 'Exercise will do it. I have had no exercise lately. Wait a little, and you will see.'

He put his hands on the machinery of the chair, and started on his customary course down the room. Here again, the ominous change in him showed itself under a new form. The pace at which he travelled was not the furious pace that I remembered; the chair no longer rushed under him on rumbling and whistling wheels. It went, but it went slowly. Up the room, and down the room, he painfully urged it—and then he stopped, for want of breath.

We followed him. Ariel was first, and Benjamin was by my side. He motioned impatiently to both of them to stand back, and to let me approach him alone.

'I'm out of practice,' he said, faintly. 'I hadn't the heart to make the wheels roar, and the floor tremble, while you were away.'

Who would not have pitied him? Who would have remembered his misdeeds at that moment? Even Ariel felt it. I heard her beginning to whine and whimper behind me. The magician who alone could rouse the dormant sensibilities in her nature had awakened them now by his neglect. Her fatal cry was heard again, in mournful, moaning tones.

'What's come to you, Master? Have you forgot me? Where's the story?'

'Never mind her,' I whispered to him. 'You want the fresh air. Send for the gardener. Let us take a drive in your pony-chaise.'

It was useless. Ariel would be noticed. The mournful cry came once more.

'Where's the story? Where's the story?'

The sinking spirit leapt up in Dexter again.

'You wretch! you fiend!' he cried, whirling his chair round, and facing her. 'The story is coming. I *can* tell it! I *will* tell it! Wine! You whimpering idiot, get me the wine. Why didn't I think of it before? The kingly Burgundy! that's what I want, Valeria, to set my invention alight and flaming in my head. Glasses for everybody! Honour to the King of the Vintages—the Royal Clos Vougeot!'

Ariel opened the cupboard in the alcove, and produced the wine and the high Venetian glasses. Dexter drained his goblet full of Burgundy at a draught; he forced us to drink (or at least pretend to drink) with him. Even Ariel had her share, this time, and emptied her glass in rivalry with her master. The powerful wine mounted almost instantly to her weak head. She began to sing hoarsely a song of her own devising, in imitation of Dexter. It was nothing but the repetition, the endless mechanical repetition, of her demand for the story. 'Tell us the story. Master! master! tell us the story!' Absorbed over his wine, the Master silently filled his goblet for the second time. Benjamin whispered to me, while his eye was off us, 'Take my advice, Valeria, for once; let us go.'

'One last effort,' I whispered back. 'Only one!'

Ariel went drowsily on with her song.

'Tell us the story. Master! master! tell us the story.'

Miserrimus Dexter looked up from his glass. The generous stimulant was beginning to do its work. I saw the colour rising in his face. I saw the bright intelligence flashing again in his eyes. The Burgundy *had* roused him! The good wine offered me a last chance!

'Now for the story!' he cried.

'No story!' I said. 'I want to talk to you, Mr Dexter. I am not in the humour for a story.'

'Not in the humour!' he repeated, with a gleam of the old

impish irony showing itself again in his face. 'That's an excuse. I see what it is! You think my invention is gone—and you are not frank enough to confess it. I'll show you you're wrong. I'll show you that Dexter is himself again. Silence, you Ariel, or you shall leave the room! I have got it, Mrs Valeria, all laid out here, with scenes and characters complete.' He touched his forehead, and looked at me with a furtive and smiling cunning, before he added his next words. 'It's the very thing to interest *you*, my fair friend. It's the Story of a Mistress and a Maid. Come back to the fire and hear it.'

The Story of a Mistress and a Maid? If that meant anything, it meant the story of Mrs Beauly and her maid, told in disguise!

The title, and the look which had escaped him when he announced it, revived the hope that was well-nigh dead in me. He had rallied at last. He was again in possession of his natural foresight and his natural cunning. Under pretence of telling Ariel her story, he was evidently about to make the attempt to mislead me, for the second time. The conclusion was irresistible. To use his own words—Dexter was himself again.

I took Benjamin's arm as we followed him back to the fireplace in the middle of the room. 'There is a chance for me yet,' I whispered. 'Don't forget the signals.'

We returned to the places which we had already occupied. Ariel cast another threatening look at me. She had just sense enough left, after emptying her goblet of wine, to be on the watch for a new interruption on my part. I took care, of course, that nothing of the sort should happen. I was now as eager as Ariel to hear the story. The subject was full of snares for the narrator. At any moment, in the excitement of speaking, Dexter's memory of the true events might show itself reflected in the circumstances of the fiction. At any moment, he might betray himself.

He looked round him, and began.

'My public, are you seated? My public, are you ready?'

he asked, gaily. 'Your face a little more this way,' he added, in his softest and tenderest tones, motioning to me to turn my full face towards him. 'Surely I am not asking too much? You look at the meanest creature that crawls—look at Me. Let me find my inspiration in your eyes. Let me feed my hungry admiration on your form. Come! have one little pitying smile left for the man whose happiness you have wrecked. Thank you. Light of my Life, thank you!' He kissed his hand to me, and threw himself back luxuriously in his chair. 'The story,' he resumed. 'The story at last! In what form shall I cast it? In the dramatic form—the oldest way, the truest way, the shortest way of telling a story! Title, first. A short title, a taking title: "Mistress and Maid." Scene, the land of romance—Italy. Time, the age of romance—the fifteenth century. Ha! look at Ariel. She knows no more about the fifteenth century than the cat in the kitchen, and yet she is interested already. Happy Ariel!'

Ariel looked at me again, in the double intoxication of the wine and the triumph.

'I know no more than the cat in the kitchen,' she repeated, with a broad grin of gratified vanity. 'I am "happy Ariel!" What are You?'

Miserrimus Dexter laughed uproariously.

'Didn't I tell you?' he said. 'Isn't she fun? Persons of the Drama,' he resumed:—'Three in number. Women only. Angelica, a noble lady; noble alike in spirit and in birth. Cunegonda, a beautiful devil, in woman's form. Damoride, her unfortunate maid. First scene. A dark vaulted chamber in a castle. Time, evening. The owls are hooting in the wood; the frogs are croaking in the marsh. Look at Ariel! Her flesh creeps; she shudders audibly. Admirable Ariel!'

My rival in the Master's favour eyed me defiantly. 'Admirable Ariel!' she repeated, in drowsy accents. Miserrimus Dexter paused to take up his goblet of Burgundy—placed close at hand on a little sliding table attached to his chair. I watched him narrowly, as he sipped the wine. The flush was still mounting in his face; the light was still brightening in his eyes. He set down his glass again, with a jovial smack of his lips—and went on.

'Persons present in the vaulted chamber:—Cunegonda and Damoride. Cunegonda speaks. "Damoride!" "Madam?" "Who lies ill in the chamber above us?" "Madam, the noble lady, Angelica." (A pause. Cunegonda speaks again.) "Damoride!" "Madam?" "How does Angelica like you?" "Madam, the noble lady, sweet and good to all who approach her, is sweet and good to me." "Have you attended on her, Damoride?" "Sometimes, madam, when the nurse was weary." "Has she taken her healing medicine from your hand?" "Once or twice, madam, when I happened to be by." "Damoride, take this key, and open the casket on the table there." (Damoride obeys.) "Do you see a green vial in the casket?" "I see it, madam." "Take it out." (Damoride obeys.) "Do you see a liquid in the green vial? can you guess what it is?" "No, madam." "Shall I tell you?" (Damoride bows respectfully.) "Poison is in the vial." (Damoride starts; she shrinks from the poison; she would fain put it aside. Her mistress signs to her to keep it in her hand; her mistress speaks.) "Damoride, I have told you one of my secrets; shall I tell you another?" (Damoride waits, fearing what is to come. Her mistress speaks.) "I hate the Lady Angelica. Her life stands between me and the joy of my heart. You hold her life in your hand." (Damoride drops on her knees; she is a devout person; she crosses herself, and then she speaks.) "Mistress, you terrify me. Mistress, what do I hear?" (Cunegonda advances, stands over her, looks down on her with terrible eyes, whispers the next words.) "Damoride, the Lady Angelica must die—and I must not be suspected. The Lady Angelica must die—and by your hand." '

He paused again. To sip the wine once more? No; to drink a deep draught of it, this time.

Was the stimulant beginning to fail him already?

I looked at him attentively, as he laid himself back again in his chair, to consider for a moment before he went on.

The flush on his face was as deep as ever; but the brightness in his eyes was beginning to fade already. I had noticed that he spoke more and more slowly as he advanced to the later dialogue of the scene. Was he feeling the effort of invention already? Had the time come when the wine had done all that the wine could do for him?

We waited. Ariel sat watching him, with vacantly-staring eyes and vacantly-open mouth. Benjamin, impenetrably expecting the signal, kept his open note-book on his knee, covered by his hand.

Miserrimus Dexter went on.

'Damoride hears those terrible words; Damoride clasps her hands in entreaty. "Oh, madam! madam! how can I kill the dear and noble lady? What motive have I for harming her?" Cunegonda answers, "You have the motive of obeying Me." Damoride falls with her face on the floor, at her mistress's feet. "Madam, I cannot do it! Madam, I dare not do it!" Cunegonda answers, "You run no risk: I have my plan for diverting discovery from myself, and my plan for diverting discovery from you." Damoride repeats, "I cannot do it! I dare not do it!" Cunegonda's eyes flash lightnings of rage. She takes from its place of concealment in her bosom——'

He stopped in the middle of the sentence, and put his hand to his head. Not like a man in pain, but like a man who had lost his idea.

Would it be well if I tried to help him to recover his idea? or would it be wiser (if I could only do it) to keep silence?

I could see the drift of his story plainly enough. His object, under the thin disguise of the Italian romance, was to meet my unanswerable objection to suspecting Mrs Beauly's maid—the objection that the woman had no motive for committing herself to an act of murder. If he could practically contradict this, by discovering a perfectly reasonable and perfectly probable motive, his end would be gained. Those enquiries which I had pledged myself to pursue—those inquiries which might, at any moment, take a turn that directly concerned him—would, in that case, be successfully diverted from the right to the wrong person. The innocent maid would set my strictest scrutiny at defiance; and Dexter would be safely shielded behind her.

I determined to give him time. Not a word passed my lips.

The minutes followed each other. I waited in the deepest anxiety. It was a trying and a critical moment. If he succeeded in inventing a probable motive, and in shaping it neatly to suit the purpose of his story, he would prove, by that act alone, that there were reserves of mental power still left in him, which the practised eye of the Scotch doctor had failed to see. But the question was—would he do it?

He did it! Not in a new way; not in a convincing way; not without a painfully-evident effort. Still, well done, or ill done, he found a motive for the maid.

'Cunegonda,' he resumed, 'takes from its place of concealment in her bosom a written paper, and unfolds it. "Look at this," she says. Damoride looks at the paper, and sinks again at her mistress's feet in a paroxysm of horror and despair. Cunegonda is in possession of a shameful secret in the maid's past life. Cunegonda can say to her, "Choose your alternative. Either submit to an exposure which disgraces you, and disgraces your parents, for ever— or make up your mind to obey Me." Damoride might submit to the disgrace if it only affected herself. But her parents are honest people; she cannot disgrace her parents. She is driven to her last refuge—there is no hope of melting the hard heart of Cunegonda. Her only resource is to raise difficulties; she tries to show that there are obstacles between her and the crime. "Madam! madam!" she cries, "how can I do it, when the nurse is there to see me?" Cunegonda answers, "Sometimes the nurse sleeps; sometimes the nurse is away." Damoride still persists. "Madam! madam! the door is kept locked, and the nurse has got the key." '

The key! I instantly thought of the missing key at Gleninch. Had *he* thought of it too? He certainly checked himself

as the word escaped him. I resolved to make the signal! I
rested my elbow on the arm of my chair, and played with
my earring. Benjamin took out his pencil, and arranged his
note-book, so that Ariel could not see what he was about,
if she happened to look his way.

We waited, until it pleased Miserrimus Dexter to proceed. The interval was a long one. His hand went up again
to his forehead. A duller and duller look was palpable
stealing over his eyes. When he did speak, it was not to go
on with the narrative, but to put a question.

'Where did I leave off?' he asked.

My hopes sank again as rapidly as they had risen. I
managed to answer him, however, without showing any
change in my manner.

'You left off,' I said, 'where Damoride was speaking to
Cunegonda——'

'Yes! yes!' he interposed. 'And what did she say?'

'She said, "The door is kept locked, and the nurse has
got the key." '

He instantly leaned forward in his chair.

'No!' he answered, vehemently. 'You're wrong. "Key?"
Nonsense! I never said "Key." '

'I thought you did, Mr. Dexter.'

'I never did! I said something else; and you have forgotten
it.'

I refrained from disputing with him, in fear of what might
follow. We waited again. Benjamin, sullenly submitting to
my caprices, had taken down the questions and answers
that had passed between Dexter and myself. He still mechanically kept his page open, and still held his pencil in
readiness to go on. Ariel, quietly submitting to the drowsy
influence of the wine while Dexter's voice was in her ears,
felt uneasily the change to silence. She glanced round her
restlessly; she lifted her eyes to 'the Master.'

There he sat, silent, with his hand to his head, still
struggling to marshal his wandering thoughts; still trying to
see light through the darkness that was closing round him.

'Master!' cried Ariel, piteously, 'what's become of the story?'

He started as if she had awakened him out of a sleep: he shook his head impatiently, as though he wanted to throw off some oppression that weighed upon it.

'Patience! patience!' he said. 'The story is going on again.'

He dashed at it desperately: he picked up the first lost thread that fell in his way, reckless whether it was the right thread or the wrong one.

'Damoride fell on her knees. She burst into tears. She said——'

He stopped, and looked about him with vacant eyes.

'What name did I give the other woman?' he asked; not putting the question to me, or to either of my companions: asking it of himself, or asking it of the empty air.

'You called the other woman, Cunegonda,' I said.

At the sound of my voice, his eyes turned slowly—turned on me, and yet failed to look at me. Dull and absent, still and changeless, they were eyes that seemed to be fixed on something far away. Even his voice was altered when he spoke next. It had dropped to a quiet, vacant, monotonous tone. I had heard something like it while I was watching by my husband's bedside, at the time of his delirium—when Eustace's mind appeared to be too weary to follow his speech. Was the end so near as this?

'I called her Cunegonda,' he repeated. 'And I called the other——'

He stopped once more.

'And you called the other Damoride,' I said.

Ariel looked up at him with a broad stare of bewilderment. She pulled impatiently at the sleeve of his jacket, to attract his notice.

'Is this the story, Master?' she asked.

He answered without looking at her; his changeless eyes still fixed, as it seemed, on something far away.

'This is the story,' he said, absently. 'But why Cunegonda?

why Damoride? Why not Mistress and Maid? It's easier to remember Mistress and Maid——'

He hesitated; he shivered as he tried to raise himself in his chair. Then he seemed to rally. 'What did the Maid say to the Mistress?' he muttered. 'What? what? what?' He hesitated again. Then, something seemed to dawn upon him, unexpectedly. Was it some new thought that had struck him? Or some lost thought that he had recovered? Impossible to say! He went on, suddenly and rapidly went on, in these strange words.

' "The letter." The Maid said, "The letter." Oh, my heart! Every word a dagger. A dagger in my heart. Oh, you letter. Horrible, horrible, horrible letter.'

What, in God's name, was he talking about? What did those words mean?

Was he unconsciously pursuing his faint and fragmentary recollections of a past time at Gleninch, under the delusion that he was going on with the story? In the wreck of the other faculties, was memory the last to sink? Was the truth, the dreadful truth, glimmering on me dimly, through the awful shadow cast before it by the advancing eclipse of the brain? My breath failed me; a nameless horror crept through my whole being.

Benjamin, with his pencil in his hand, cast one warning look at me. Ariel was quiet and satisfied. 'Go on, Master,' was all she said. 'I like it! I like it! Go on with the story.'

He went on—like a man sleeping with his eyes open, and talking in his sleep.

'The Maid said to the Mistress. No: the Mistress said to the Maid. The Mistress said, "Show him the letter. Must, must, must do it." The Maid said, "No. Mustn't do it, Shan't show it. Stuff. Nonsense. Let him suffer. We can get him off. Show it? No. Let the worst come to the worst. Show it then." The Mistress said——' He paused, and waved his hand rapidly to and fro before his eyes, as if he was brushing away some visionary confusion or entanglement. 'Which was it last?' he said, 'Mistress or Maid?

Mistress? No. Maid speaks, of course. Loud. Positive. "You scoundrels. Keep away from that table. The Diary's there. Number Nine, Caldershaws. Ask for Dandie. You shan't have the Diary. A secret in your ear. The Diary will hang him. I won't have him hanged. How dare you touch my chair? My chair is Me? How dare you touch Me?'

The last words burst on me like a gleam of light! I had read them in the Report of the Trial—in the evidence of the sheriff's officer. Miserrimus Dexter had spoken in those very terms, when he had tried vainly to prevent the men from seizing my husband's papers, and when the men had pushed his chair out of the room. There was no doubt now of what his memory was busy with. The mystery at Gleninch! His last backward flight of thought circled, feebly and more feebly, nearer and nearer to the mystery at Gleninch!

Ariel roused him again. She had no mercy on him; she insisted on hearing the whole story.

'Why do you stop, Master? Get along with it! get along with it! Tell us quick—what did the Missus say to the Maid?'

He laughed feebly, and tried to imitate her.

'What did the Missus say to the Maid?' he repeated. His laugh died away. He went on speaking, more and more vacantly, more and more rapidly. 'The Mistress said to the Maid, "We've got him off. What about the letter? Burn it now. No fire in the grate. No matches in the box. House topsy-turvy. Servants all gone. Tear it up. Shake it up in the basket. Along with the rest. Shake it up. Waste paper. Throw it away. Gone for ever. Oh, Sara, Sara, Sara. Gone for ever." '

Ariel clapped her hands, and mimicked him, in her turn. ' "Oh, Sara, Sara, Sara," ' she repeated. ' "Gone for ever." That's prime, Master! Tell us—who was Sara?'

His lips moved. But his voice sank so low that I could barely hear him. He began again, with the old melancholy refrain.

'The Maid said to the Mistress. No: the Mistress said to the Maid——' He stopped abruptly, and raised himself erect in the chair; he threw up both his hands above his head; and burst into a frightful screaming laugh. 'Aha-ha-ha-ha! How funny! Why don't you laugh? Funny, funny, funny, funny. Aha-ha-ha-ha-ha——'

He fell back in the chair. The shrill and dreadful laugh died away into a low sob. Then there was one long, deep, wearily-drawn breath. Then, nothing but a mute vacant face turned up to the ceiling, with eyes that looked blindly, with lips parted in a senseless, changeless grin. Nemesis at last! The foretold doom had fallen on him. The night had come.

But one feeling animated me, when the first shock was over. Even the horror of that fearful sight seemed only to increase the pity that I felt for the stricken wretch. I started impulsively to my feet. Seeing nothing, thinking of nothing, but the helpless figure in the chair, I sprang forward to raise him; to revive him; to recall him (if such a thing might be possible) to himself. At the first step that I took, I felt hands on me—I was violently drawn back. 'Are you blind?' cried Benjamin, dragging me nearer and nearer to the door.

Look there!'

He pointed; and I looked.

Ariel had been beforehand with me. She had raised her master in the chair; she had got one arm round him. In her free hand she brandished an Indian club, torn from a 'trophy' of Oriental weapons that ornamented the wall over the fireplace. The creature was transfigured! Her dull eyes glared like the eyes of a wild animal. She gnashed her teeth in the frenzy that possessed her. 'You have done this!' she shouted to me, waving the club furiously round and round over her head. 'Come near him; and I'll dash your brains out! I'll mash you till there's not a whole bone left in your skin!' Benjamin, still holding me with one hand, opened the door with the other. I let him do with me as he would; Ariel fascinated me; I could look at nothing but Ariel. Her frenzy vanished as she saw us retreating. She dropped the club: she threw both arms round him, and nestled her head on his bosom, and sobbed and wept over him. 'Master! Master! They shan't vex you any more. Look up again. Laugh at me as you used to do. Say, "Ariel; you're a fool." Be like yourself again!' I was forced into the next room. I heard a long, low, wailing cry of misery from a poor creature who loved him with a dog's fidelity and a woman's devotion. The heavy door was closed between us. I was in the quiet antechamber; crying over that piteous sight; clinging to my kind old friend, as helpless and as useless as a child.

Benjamin turned the key in the lock.

'There's no use in crying about it,' he said quietly. 'It would be more to the purpose, Valeria, if you thanked God that you have got out of that room, safe and sound. Come with me.'

He took the key out of the lock, and led me downstairs into the hall. After a little consideration, he opened the front door of the house. The gardener was still quietly at work in the grounds.

'Your master is taken ill,' Benjamin said; 'and the woman who attends upon him has lost her head—if she ever had a head to lose. Where does the nearest doctor live?'

The man's devotion to Dexter showed itself as the woman's devotion had shown itself—in the man's rough way. He threw down the spade, with an oath.

'The Master taken bad?' he said. 'I'll fetch the doctor. I shall find him sooner than you will.'

'Tell the doctor to bring a man with him,' Benjamin added. 'He may want help.'

The gardener turned round sternly.

'*I'm* the man,' he said. 'Nobody shall help but me.'

He left us. I sat down on one of the chairs in the hall, and did my best to compose myself. Benjamin walked to and fro, deep in thought. 'Both of them fond of him,' I heard my old friend say to himself. 'Half monkey, half man—and both of them fond of him. *That* beats me.'

The gardener returned with the doctor—a quiet, dark, resolute man. Benjamin advanced to meet them. 'I have got the key,' he said. 'Shall I go upstairs with you?'

Without answering, the doctor drew Benjamin aside into a corner of the hall. The two talked together in low voices. At the end of it, the doctor said, 'Give me the key. You can be of no use; you will only irritate her.'

With those words, he beckoned to the gardener. He was about to lead the way up the stairs, when I ventured to stop him.

'May I stay in the hall, Sir?' I said. 'I am very anxious to hear how it ends.'

He looked at me for a moment before he replied.

'You had better go home, Madam,' he said. 'Is the gardener acquainted with your address?'

'Yes, Sir.'

'Very well. I will let you know how it ends, by means of the gardener. Take my advice. Go home.'

Benjamin placed my arm in his. I looked back, and saw the doctor and the gardener ascending the stairs together, on their way to the locked-up room.

'Never mind the doctor!' I whispered. 'Let's wait in the garden.'

Benjamin would not hear of deceiving the doctor. 'I mean to take you home,' he said. I looked at him in amazement. My old friend, who was all meekness and submission, so long as there was no emergency to try him, now showed the dormant reserve of manly spirit and decision in his nature, as he had never (in my experience) shown it yet. He led me into the garden. We had kept our cab: it was waiting for us at the gate.

On our way home, Benjamin produced his note-book.

'What's to be done, my dear, with the gibberish that I have written here?' he said.

'Have you written it all down?' I asked, in surprise.

'When I undertake a duty I do it,' he answered. 'You never gave me the signal to leave off—you never moved your chair. I have written every word of it. What shall I do? Throw it out of the cab-window?'

'Give it to me!'

'What are you going to do with it?'

'I don't know yet. I will ask Mr Playmore.'

CHAPTER XLI

Mr Playmore in a New Character

BY that night's post—although I was far from being fit to make the exertion—I wrote to Mr Playmore, to tell him what had taken place, and to beg for his earliest assistance and advice.

The notes in Benjamin's book were partly written in shorthand, and were, on that account, of no use to me in their existing condition. At my request, he made two fair copies. One of the copies I enclosed in my letter to Mr Playmore. The other I laid by me, on my bedside table when I went to rest.

Over and over again, through the long hours of the wakeful night, I read and re-read the last words which had dropped from Miserrimus Dexter's lips. Was it possible to interpret them to any useful purpose? At the very outset, they seemed to set interpretation at defiance. After trying vainly to solve the hopeless problem, I did at last what I might as well have done at first—I threw down the paper in despair. Where were my bright visions of discovery and success now? Scattered to the winds! Was there the faintest chance of the stricken man's return to reason? I remembered too well what I had seen to hope for it. The closing lines of the medical report which I had read in Mr Playmore's office recurred to my memory, in the stillness of the night. 'When the catastrophe has happened, his friends can entertain no hope of his cure: the balance once lost, will be lost for life.'

The confirmation of that terrible sentence was not long in reaching me. The next morning the gardener brought a note, containing the information which the doctor had promised to give me on the previous day.

Miserrimus Dexter and Ariel were still where Benjamin and I had left them together—in the long room. They were watched by skilled attendants; waiting the decision of Dexter's nearest relative (a younger brother), who lived in the country, and who had been communicated with by telegraph. It had been found impossible to part the faithful Ariel from her Master, without using the bodily restraints adopted in cases of raging insanity. The doctor and the gardener (both unusually strong men) had failed to hold the poor creature, when they first attempted to remove her on entering the room. Directly they permitted her to return to her Master, the frenzy vanished: she was perfectly quiet and contented, so long as they let her sit at his feet and look at him.

Sad as this was, the report of Miserrimus Dexter's condition was more melancholy still.

'My patient is in a state of absolute imbecility'—those were the words in the doctor's letter; and the gardener's simple narrative confirmed them as the truest words that could have been used. Dexter was unconscious of poor Ariel's devotion to him—he did not even appear to know that she was present in the room. For hours together, he remained in a state of utter lethargy in his chair. He showed an animal interest in his meals, and a greedy animal enjoyment of eating and drinking as much as he could get—and that was all. 'This morning,' the honest gardener said to me, at parting, 'we thought he seemed to wake up a bit. Looked about him, you know, and made queer signs with his hands. I couldn't make out what he meant; no more could the doctor. She knew, poor thing— she did. Went and got him his harp, and put his hand up to it. Lord bless you, no use! He couldn't play, no more than I can. Twanged at it anyhow, and grinned and gabbled to himself. No: he'll never come right again. Any person can see that, without the doctor to help 'em. Enjoys his meals, as I told you; and that's all. It would be the best thing that could happen, if it would please God to take him. There's no more to be said. I wish you good morning, Ma'am.'

He went away with the tears in his eyes; and left me, I own it, with the tears in mine.

An hour later, there came some news which revived me. I received a telegram from Mr Playmore, expressed in these welcome words: 'Obliged to go to London by tonight's mail train. Expect me to breakfast to-morrow morning.'

The appearance of the lawyer at our breakfast-table duly followed the appearance of his telegram. His first words cheered me. To my infinite surprise and relief, he was far from sharing the despondent view which I took of my position.

'I don't deny,' he said, 'that there are some serious obstacles in your way. But I should never have called here before I attend to my professional business in London, if Mr Benjamin's notes had not produced a very strong impression on my mind. For the first time, as *I* think—you really have a prospect of success. For the first time, I feel justified in offering (under certain restrictions) to help you. That miserable wretch, in the collapse of his intelligence, has done what he would never have done in the possession of his sense and cunning—he has let us see the first precious glimmerings of the light of truth.'

'Are you sure it *is* the truth?' I asked.

'In two important particulars,' he answered, 'I know it to be the truth. Your idea about him is the right one. His memory (as you suppose) was the least injured of his faculties, and was the last to give way, under the strain of trying to tell that story. I believe his memory to have been speaking to you (unconsciously to himself) in all that he said— from the moment when the first reference to "the letter" escaped him, to the end.'

'But what does the reference to the letter mean?' I asked. 'For my part, I am entirely in the dark about it.'

'So am I,' he answered, frankly. 'The chief one among the obstacles which I mentioned just now, is the obstacle presented by that same "letter." The late Mrs Eustace must have been connected with it in some way—or Dexter would never have spoken of it as "a dagger in his heart"; Dexter would never have coupled her name with the words which describe the tearing up of the letter, and the throwing of it away. I can arrive with some certainty at this result, and I can get no further. I have no more idea than you have of who wrote the letter, or of what was written in it. If we are ever to make that discovery—probably the most important discovery of all—we must despatch our first inquiries a distance of three thousand miles. In plain English, my dear lady, we must send to America.'

This naturally enough, took me completely by surprise. I waited eagerly to hear why we were to send to America.

'It rests with you,' he proceeded, 'when you hear what I have to tell you, to say whether you will go to the expense of sending a man to New York, or not. I can find the right man for the purpose; and I estimate the expense (including a telegram)——'

'Never mind the expense!' I interposed, losing all patience with the eminently Scotch view of the case which put my purse in the first place of importance. 'I don't care for the expense; I want to know what you have discovered.'

He smiled. 'She doesn't care for the expense,' he said to himself, pleasantly. 'How like a woman!'

I might have retorted, 'He thinks of the expense, before he thinks of anything else. How like a Scotchman!' As it was, I was too anxious to be witty. I only drummed impatiently with my fingers on the table; and said, 'Tell me! tell me!

He took out the fair copy from Benjamin's note-book, which I had sent to him, and showed me these among Dexter's closing words:—'What about the letter? Burn it now. No fire in the grate. No matches in the box. House topsy-turvy. Servants all gone.'

'Do you really understand what those words mean?' I asked.

'I look back into my own experience,' he answered; 'and I understand perfectly what the words mean.'

'And can you make me understand them too?'

'Easily. In those incomprehensible sentences, Dexter's memory has correctly recalled certain facts. I have only to tell you the facts; and you will be as wise as I am. At the time of the Trial, your husband surprised and distressed me by insisting on the instant dismissal of all the household servants at Gleninch. I was instructed to pay them a quarter's wages in advance; to give them the excellent written characters which their good conduct thoroughly deserved, and to see the house clear of them at an hour's notice. Eustace's motive for this summary proceeding was much the same motive which animated his conduct towards you. "If I am ever to return to Gleninch," he said, "I cannot face my honest servants, after the infamy of having stood my trial for murder." There was his reason! Nothing that I could say to him, poor fellow, shook his resolution. I dismissed the servants accordingly. At an hour's notice, they quitted the house, leaving their work for the day all undone. The only persons placed in charge of Gleninch were persons who lived on the outskirts of the park—that is to say, the lodge-keeper and his wife and daughter. On the last day of the Trial, I instructed the daughter to do her best to make the rooms tidy. She was a good girl enough; but she had no experience as a housemaid: it would never enter her head to lay the bedroom fires ready for lighting, or to replenish the empty match-boxes. Those chance words that dropped from Dexter would, no doubt, exactly describe the state of his room, when he returned to Gleninch, with the prisoner and his mother, from Edinburgh. That he tore up the mysterious letter in his bedroom, and (finding no means immediately at hand for burning it) that he threw the fragments into the empty grate, or into the waste-paper basket, seems to be the most reasonable conclusion that we can draw from what we know. In any case, he would not have much time to think about it. Everything was done in a hurry on that day. Eustace and his mother, accompanied by Dexter, left for England the same evening by the night-train. I myself locked up the house, and gave the keys to the lodge-keeper. It was understood that he was to look after the preservation of the reception-rooms on the ground floor; and that his wife and daughter were to perform the same service, between them, in the rooms upstairs. On receiving your letter, I drove at once to Gleninch, to question the old woman on the subject of the bedrooms, and of Dexter's room especially. She remembered the time when the house was shut up, by associating it with the time when she was confined to her bed by an attack of sciatica. She had not crossed the lodge-door, she was sure, for at least a week (if not longer) after Gleninch had been left in charge of her husband and herself. Whatever was done in the way of keeping the bedrooms aired and tidy, during her illness, was done by her daughter. She, and she only, must have disposed of any litter which might have been lying about in Dexter's room. Not a vestige of torn paper, as I can myself certify, is to be discovered in any part of the room, now. Where did the girl find the fragments of the letter? and what did she do with them? Those are the questions (if you approve of it) which we must send three thousand miles away to ask— for this sufficient reason, that the lodge-keeper's daughter was married more than a year since, and that she is settled with her husband in business at New York. It rests with you to decide what is to be done. Don't let me mislead you with false hopes! Don't let me tempt you to throw away your money! Even if this woman does remember what she did with the torn paper, the chances, at this distance of time, are enormously against our ever recovering a single morsel of it. Be in no haste to decide. I have my work to do in the City—I can give you the whole day to think it over.'

'Send the man to New York by the next steamer,' I said. 'There is my decision, Mr Playmore, without keeping you waiting for it!'

He shook his head, in grave disapproval of my impetuosity. In my former interview with him, we had never once touched on the question of money. I was now, for the first time, to make acquaintance with Mr Playmore on the purely Scotch side of his character!

'Why, you don't even know what it will cost you!' he exclaimed, taking out his pocket-book with the air of a man who was equally startled and scandalised. 'Wait till I tot it up,' he said, 'in English and American money.'

'I can't wait! I want to make more discoveries!'

He took no notice of my interruption: he went on impenetrably with his calculations.

'The man will go second-class and will take a return-ticket. Very well. His ticket includes his food; and (being, thank God, a teetotaller) he won't waste your money in buying liquor on board. Arrived at New York, he will go to a cheap German house, where he will, as I am credibly informed, be boarded and lodged at the rate——'

By this time (my patience being completely worn out) I had taken my cheque-book from the table-drawer; had signed my name; and had handed the blank cheque across the table to my legal adviser.

'Fill it in with whatever the man wants,' I said. 'And for Heaven's sake let us get back to Dexter!'

Mr Playmore fell back in his chair, and lifted his hands and eyes to the ceiling. I was not in the least impressed by that solemn appeal to the unseen powers of arithmetic and money. I insisted positively on being fed with more information.

'Listen to this,' I went on; reading from Benjamin's notes. 'What did Dexter mean, when he said, "Number Nine, Caldershaws. Ask for Dandie. You shan't have the Diary. A secret in your ear. The Diary will hang him?" How came Dexter to know what was in my husband's Diary?

And what does he mean by "Number Nine, Caldershaws," and the rest of it? Facts again?'

'Facts again!' Mr Playmore answered, 'muddled up together, as you may say—but positive facts for all that. Caldershaws, you must know, is one of the most disreputable districts in Edinburgh. One of my clerks (whom I am in the habit of employing confidentially) volunteered to inquire for "Dandie," at "Number nine." It was a ticklish business, in every way; and my man wisely took a person with him who was known in the neighbourhood. "Number nine" turned out to be (ostensibly) a shop for the sale of rags and old iron; and "Dandie" was suspected of trading now and then, additionally, as a receiver of stolen goods. Thanks to the influence of his companion, backed by a bank-note (which can be repaid, by the way, out of the fund for the American expenses), my clerk succeeded in making the fellow speak. Not to trouble you with needless details, the result in substance was this. A fortnight or more before the date of Mrs Eustace's death, "Dandie" made two keys from wax models supplied to him by a new customer. The mystery observed in the matter by the agent who managed it, excited Dandie's distrust. He had the man privately watched before he delivered the keys; and he ended in discovering that his customer was—Miserrimus Dexter. Wait a little! I have not done yet. Add to this information Dexter's incomprehensible knowledge of the contents of your husband's Diary; and the product is—that the wax models sent to the old iron shop in Caldershaws, were models taken by the theft from the key of the Diary and the key of the table-drawer in which it was kept. I have my own idea of the revelations that are still to come, if this matter is properly followed up. Never mind going into that, at present. Dexter (I tell you again) is answerable for the late Mrs Eustace's death. *How* he is answerable, I believe you are in a fair way of finding out. And, more than that, I say now, what I could not venture to say before—it is a duty towards Justice, as well as a duty towards your husband, to bring the truth to light. As for the difficulties to be encountered, I don't think they need daunt you. The greatest difficulties give way in the end, when they are attacked by the united alliance of patience, resolution,—*and* economy.'

With a strong emphasis on the last words, my worthy adviser, mindful of the flight of time and the claims of business, rose to take his leave.

'One word more,' I said, as he held out his hand. 'Can you manage to see Miserrimus Dexter before you go back to Edinburgh? From what the gardener told me, his brother must be with him by this time. It would be a relief to me to hear the latest news of him, and to hear it from you.'

'It is part of my business in London to see him,' said Mr Playmore. 'But, mind! I have no hope of his recovery: I only wish to satisfy myself that his brother is able and willing to take care of him. So far as *we* are concerned, Mrs Eustace, that unhappy man has said his last words.'

He opened the door—stopped—considered—and came back to me.

'With regard to that matter of sending the agent to America,' he resumed. 'I propose to have the honour of submitting to you a brief abstract——'

'Oh, Mr Playmore!'

'A brief abstract in writing, Mrs Eustace, of the estimated expenses of the whole proceeding. You will be good enough maturely to consider the same; making any remarks on it, tending to economy, which may suggest themselves to your mind at the time. And you will further oblige me, if you approve of the abstract, by yourself filling in the blank space on your cheque with the needful amount in words and figures. No, Madam! I really cannot justify it to my conscience to carry about my person any such loose and reckless document as a blank cheque. There's a total disregard of the first claims of prudence and economy implied in this small slip of paper, which is nothing less than a flat contradiction of the principles that have governed my whole life. I can't submit to flat contradiction. Good morning, Mrs Eustace—good morning.'

He laid my cheque on the table with a low bow, and left me. Among the curious developments of human stupidity which occasionally present themselves to view, surely the least excusable is the stupidity which, to this day, persists in wondering why the Scotch succeed so well in life!

CHAPTER XLII

More Surprises

THE same evening I received my 'abstract' by the hands of a clerk.

It was an intensely characteristic document. My expenses were remorselessly calculated down to shillings and even to pence; and our unfortunate messenger's instructions, in respect of his expenditure, were reduced to a nicety which must have made his life in America nothing less than a burden to him. In mercy to the man, I took the liberty, when I wrote back to Mr Playmore, of slightly increasing the indicated amount of the figures which were to appear on the cheque. I ought to have better known the corre- spondent whom I had to deal with. Mr Playmore's reply (informing me that our emissary had started on his voyage) returned a receipt in due form—and the whole of the sur- plus money, to the last farthing!

A few hurried lines accompanied the 'abstract,' and stated the result of the lawyer's visit to Miserrimus Dexter.

There was no change for the better—there was no change at all. Mr Dexter (the brother) had arrived at the house, accompanied by a medical man accustomed to the charge of the insane. The new doctor declined to give any definite opinion on the case until he had studied it carefully with plenty of time at his disposal. It had been accordingly arranged that he should remove Miserrimus Dexter to the asylum of which he was the proprietor, as soon as the preparations for receiving the patient could be completed. The one difficulty that still remained to be met, related to the disposal of the faithful creature who had never left her master, night or day, since the catastrophe had happened. Ariel had no friends, and no money. The proprietor of the asylum could not be expected to receive her without the customary payment; and Mr Dexter's brother 'regretted to say that he was not rich enough to find the money.' A forcible separation from the one human being whom she loved, and a removal in the character of a pauper to a public asylum—such was the prospect which awaited the unfortunate creature, unless some one interfered in her favour before the end of the week.

Under these sad circumstances, good Mr Playmore—passing over the claims of economy in favour of the claims of humanity—suggested that we should privately start a Subscription, and offered to head the list liberally himself.

I must have written all these pages to very little purpose, if it is necessary for me to add that I instantly sent a letter to Mr Dexter (the brother) undertaking to be answerable for whatever money was required, while the subscriptions were being collected, and only stipulating that when Miserrimus Dexter was removed to the asylum, Ariel should accompany him. This was readily conceded. But serious objections were raised, when I further requested that she might be permitted to attend on her master in the asylum, as she had attended on him in the house. The rules of the establishment forbade it, and the universal practice in such cases forbade it, and so on, and so on. However, by dint of perseverance and persuasion, I so far carried my point as to gain a reasonable concession. During certain hours in the day, and under certain wise restrictions, Ariel was to be allowed the privilege of waiting on the Master in his room, as well as of accompanying him when he was brought out in his chair to take the air in the garden. For the honour of humanity, let me add, that the liability which I had undertaken made no very serious demands on my resources.

Placed in Benjamin's charge, our subscription list prospered. Friends, and even strangers sometimes, opened their hearts and their purses when they heard Ariel's melancholy story.

The day which followed the day of Mr Playmore's visit brought me news from Spain, in a letter from my mother-in-law. To describe what I felt, when I broke the seal, and read the first lines, is simply impossible. Let Mrs Macallan be heard on this occasion in my place.

Thus she wrote:—

'Prepare yourself, my dearest Valeria, for a delightful surprise. Eustace has justified my confidence in him. When he returns to England, he returns—if you will let him—to his wife.

'This resolution, let me hasten to assure you, has not been brought about by any persuasions of mine. It is the natural outgrowth of your husband's gratitude and your husband's love. The first words he said to me, when he was able to speak, were these: "If I live to return to England, and if I go to Valeria, do you think she will forgive me?" We can only leave it to you, my dear, to give the answer. If you love us, answer us by return of post.

'Having now told you what he said, when I first informed him that you had been his nurse—and remember, if it seems very little, that he is still too weak to speak, except with difficulty—I shall purposely keep my letter back for a few days. My object is to give him time to think, and to frankly tell you of it, if the interval produces any change in his resolution.

'Three days have passed; and there is no change. He has but one feeling now—he longs for the day which is to unite him again to his wife.

'But there is something else connected with Eustace, that you ought to know, and that I ought to tell you.

'Greatly as time and suffering have altered him, in many respects, there is no change, Valeria, in the aversion—the horror I may even say—with which he views your design of inquiring anew into the circumstances which attended the lamentable death of his first wife. I dare not give him your letter: if I touch on the subject, I irritate and distress him. "Has she given up that idea? Can you positively say she has given up that idea?" Over and over again, he has put those questions to me. I have answered—what else could I do, in the miserably feeble state in which he still lies?—I have answered in such a manner as to soothe and satisfy him. I have said, "Relieve your mind of all anxiety on that subject: Valeria has no choice but to give up the idea; the obstacles in her way have proved to be insurmountable—the obstacles have conquered her." This, if you remember, was what I really believed would happen when you and I spoke of that painful topic; and I have heard nothing from you since which has tended to shake my opinion in the smallest degree. If I am right (as I pray God I may be) in the view that I take, you have only to confirm me in your reply, and all will be well. In the other event—that is to say, if you are still determined to persevere in your hopeless project—then make up your mind to face the result. Set Eustace's prejudices at defiance in this particular; and you lose your hold on his gratitude, his penitence, and his love—you will in my belief, never see him again.

'I express myself strongly, in your own interests, my dear, and for your own sake. When you reply, write a few lines to Eustace, enclosed in your letter to me.

'As for the date of our departure, it is still impossible for me to give you any definite information. Eustace recovers very slowly: the doctor has not yet allowed him to leave his bed. And when we do travel, we must journey by easy stages. It will be at least six weeks, at the earliest, before we can hope to be back again in dear Old England.

'Affectionately yours,

CATHERINE MACALLAN.'

I laid down the letter, and did my best (vainly enough for some time) to compose my spirits. To understand the position in which I now found myself, it is only necessary to remember one circumstance. The messenger to whom we had committed our inquiries was, at that moment, crossing the Atlantic on his way to New York.

What was to be done?

I hesitated. Shocking as it may seem to some people, I hesitated. There was really no need to hurry my decision. I had the whole day before me.

I went out, and took a wretched lonely walk, and turned the matter over in my mind. I came home again, and turned the matter over once more, by the fireside. To offend and repel my darling when he was returning to me, penitently returning of his own free will, was what no woman in my position, and feeling as I did, could under any earthly circumstances have brought herself to do. And yet, on the other hand, how, in Heaven's name, could I give up my grand enterprise, at the very time when even wise and prudent Mr Playmore saw such a prospect of succeeding in it that he had actually volunteered to help me! Placed between those two cruel alternatives, which could I choose? Think of your own frailties; and have some mercy on mine.

I turned my back on both the alternatives. Those two agreeable fiends, Prevarication and Deceit, took me as it were softly by the hand: 'Don't commit yourself either way, my dear,' they said, in their most persuasive manner. 'Write just enough to compose your mother-in-law, and to satisfy your husband. You have got time before you. Wait and see if Time doesn't stand your friend, and get you out of the difficulty.'

Infamous advice! And yet, I took it—I, who had been well brought up, and who ought to have known better. You who read this shameful confession, would have known better, I am sure. *You* are not included, in the Prayer Book category, among the 'miserable sinners.'

Well! well! let me have virtue enough to tell the truth. In writing to my mother-in-law, I informed her that it had been found necessary to remove Miserrimus Dexter to an asylum—and I left her to draw her own conclusions from that fact, unenlightened by so much as one word of additional information. In the same way, I told my husband a part of the truth, and no more. I said I forgave him with all my heart—and I did! I said he had only to come to me, and I would receive him with open arms—and so I would! As for the rest, let me say with Hamlet: 'The rest is silence.'

Having despatched my unworthy letters, I found myself growing restless, and feeling the want of a change. It would be necessary to wait at least eight or nine days before we could hope to hear by telegraph from New York. I bade farewell for a time to my dear and admirable Benjamin, and betook myself to my old home in the North, at the vicarage of my Uncle Starkweather. My journey to Spain to nurse Eustace had made my peace with my worthy relatives; we had exchanged friendly letters; and I had promised to be their guest as soon as it was possible for me to leave London.

I passed a quiet, and (all things considered) a happy time, among the old scenes. I visited once more the bank by the river side, where Eustace and I had first met. I walked again on the lawn, and loitered through the shrubbery—those favourite haunts in which we had so often talked over our troubles, and so often forgotten them in a kiss. How sadly and strangely had our lives been parted since that time! How uncertain still was the fortune which the future had in store for us!

The associations amid which I was now living, had their softening effect on my heart, their elevating influence over my mind. I reproached myself, bitterly reproached myself, for not having written more fully and frankly to Eustace. Why had I hesitated to sacrifice to him my hopes and my interests in the coming investigation? *He* had not hesitated, poor fellow—*his* first thought was the thought of his wife!

I had passed a fortnight with my uncle and aunt, before I heard again from Mr Playmore. When a letter from him arrived at last, it disappointed me indescribably. A telegram from our messenger informed us that the lodge-keeper's

daughter and her husband had left New York, and that he
was still in search of a trace of them.

There was nothing to be done but to wait as patiently as
we could, on the chance of hearing better news. I remained
in the North, by Mr Playmore's advice, so as to be within
an easy journey to Edinburgh—in case it might be necessary
for me to consult him personally. Three more weeks of
weary expectation passed, before a second letter reached
me. This time it was impossible to say whether the news
was good or bad. It might have been either—it was simply
bewildering. Even Mr Playmore himself was taken by surprise. These were the last wonderful words—limited of
course by considerations of economy—which reached us
(by telegram) from our agent in America:—

'Open the dust-heap at Gleninch.'

CHAPTER XLIII

At Last!

MY letter from Mr Playmore, enclosing the agent's extraordinary telegram, was not inspired by the sanguine view
of our prospects which he had expressed to me when we
met at Benjamin's house.

'If the telegram means anything,' he wrote, 'it means that
the fragments of the torn letter have been cast into the
housemaid's bucket (along with the dust, the ashes, and the
rest of the litter in the room), and have been emptied on
the dust-heap at Gleninch. Since this was done, the accumulated refuse collected from the periodical cleansings of
the house, during a term of nearly three years—including,
of course, the ashes from the fires kept burning, for the
greater part of the year, in the library and picture gallery—
have been poured upon the heap, and have buried the
precious morsels of paper deeper and deeper, day by day.

Even if we have a fair chance of finding these fragments, what hope can we feel, at this distance of time, of recovering them with the writing in a state of preservation? I shall be glad to hear, by return of post, if possible, how the matter strikes you. If you could make it convenient to consult with me personally in Edinburgh, we should save time, when time may be of serious importance to us. While you are at Doctor Starkweather's, you are within easy reach of this place. Please think of it.'

I thought of it seriously enough. The foremost question which I had to consider was the question of my husband.

The departure of the mother and son from Spain had been so long delayed, by the surgeon's orders, that the travellers had only advanced on their homeward journey as far as Bordeaux, when I had last heard from Mrs Macallan three or four days since. Allowing for an interval of repose at Bordeaux, and for the slow rate at which they would be compelled to move afterwards, I might still expect them to arrive in England some time before a letter from the agent in America could reach Mr Playmore. How, in this position of affairs, I could contrive to join the lawyer in Edinburgh, after meeting my husband in London, it was not easy to see. The wise way and the right way, as I thought, was to tell Mr Playmore frankly that I was not mistress of my own movements, and that he had better address his next letter to me at Benjamin's house.

Writing to my legal adviser in this sense, I had a word of my own to add, about the dust-heap and the torn letter.

In the last years of my father's life I had travelled with him in Italy; and I had seen in the Museum at Naples the wonderful relics of a bygone time discovered among the ruins of Pompeii. By way of encouraging Mr Playmore, I now reminded him that the eruption which had over-whelmed the town* had preserved, for more than sixteen hundred years, such perishable things as the straw in which pottery had been packed; the paintings on house walls; the dresses worn by the inhabitants; and (most noticeable of all, in our case) a piece of ancient paper, still attached to the volcanic ashes which had fallen over it. If these discoveries had been made after a lapse of sixteen centuries, under a layer of dust and ashes on a large scale, surely we might hope to meet with similar cases of preservation, after a lapse of three or four years only, under a layer of dust and ashes on a small scale? Taking for granted (what was perhaps doubtful enough) that the fragments of the letter could be recovered, my own conviction was that the writing on them, though it might be faded, would certainly still be legible. The very accumulations which Mr Playmore deplored would be the means of preserving them from the rain and the damp. With these modest hints I closed my letter; and thus for once, thanks to my Continental experience, I was able to instruct my lawyer!

Another day passed; and I heard nothing of the travellers.

I began to feel anxious. I made my preparations for the journey southward, over night; and I resolved to start for London the next day—unless I heard of some change in Mrs Macallan's travelling arrangements in the interval.

The post of the next morning decided my course of action. It brought me a letter from my mother-in-law, which added one more to the memorable dates in my domestic calendar.

Eustace and his mother had advanced as far as Paris on their homeward journey, when a cruel disaster had befallen them. The fatigues of travelling, and the excitement of his anticipated meeting with me, had proved together to be too much for my husband. He had held out as far as Paris with the greatest difficulty; and he was now confined to his bed again, struck down by a relapse. The doctors, this time, had no fear for his life; provided that his patience would support him through a lengthened period of the most absolute repose.

'It now rests with you, Valeria,' Mrs Macallan wrote, 'to fortify and comfort Eustace under this new calamity. Do not suppose that he has ever blamed, or thought of blaming, you, for leaving him in Spain, when the surgeon had pronounced him to be out of danger. "It was *I* who left *her*," he said to me, when we first talked about it; "and it is my wife's right to expect that I should go back to her." Those were his words, my dear; and he has done all he can to abide by them. Helpless in his bed, he now asks you to take the will for the deed, and to join him in Paris. I think I know you well enough, my child, to be sure that you will do this; and I need only add one word of caution, before I close my letter. Avoid all reference, not only to the Trial (you will do that of your own accord), but even to our house at Gleninch. You will understand how he feels, in his present state of nervous depression, when I tell you that I should never have ventured on asking you to join him here, if your letter had not informed me that your visits to Dexter were at an end. Would you believe it?—his horror of anything which recalls our past troubles is still so vivid, that he has actually asked me to give my consent to selling Gleninch!'

So Eustace's mother wrote of him. But she had not trusted entirely to her own powers of persuasion. A slip of paper was enclosed in her letter, containing these two lines, traced in pencil—oh, so feebly and so wearily!—by my poor darling himself:—'I am too weak to travel any farther, Valeria. Will you come to me and forgive me?' A few pencil-marks followed; but they were illegible. The writing of those two short sentences had exhausted him.

It is not saying much for myself I know—but, having confessed it when I was wrong, let me at least record it when I did what was right—I decided instantly on giving up all further connexion with the recovery of the torn letter. If Eustace asked me the question, I was resolved to be able to answer truly:—'I have made the sacrifice that assures your tranquillity. When resignation was hardest, I have given way for my husband's sake.'

The motive which had determined me on returning to England, when I first knew that I was mother as well as wife, was still present to my mind when I arrived at this resolution. The one change in me was, that I now treated my husband's tranquillity as the first and foremost consideration. In making this concession, I was not without hope to sustain me. Eustace might yet see the duty of asserting his innocence, in a new light—he might see it as a duty which the father owed to the child.

That morning, I wrote again to Mr Playmore; telling him what my position was, and withdrawing, definitely, from all share in investigating the mystery which lay hidden under the dust-heap at Gleninch.

CHAPTER XLIV

Our New Honeymoon

IT is not to be disguised or denied that my spirits were depressed, on my journey to London.

To resign the one cherished purpose of my life, when I had suffered so much in pursuing it, and when I had (to all appearance) so nearly reached the realisation of my hopes, was putting to a hard trial a woman's fortitude, and a woman's sense of duty. Still, even if the opportunity had been offered to me, I would not have recalled my letter to Mr Playmore. 'It is done, and well done,' I said to myself; 'and I have only to wait a day to be reconciled to it—when I give my husband my first kiss.'

I had planned and hoped to reach London, in time to start for Paris by the night-mail. But the train was twice delayed on the long journey from the North; and there was no help for it but to sleep at Benjamin's villa, and to defer my departure until the morning.

It was, of course, impossible for me to warn my old friend of the change in my plans. My arrival took him by surprise. I found him alone in his library, with a wonderful illumination of lamps and candles; absorbed over some morsels of torn paper scattered on the table before him.

'What in the world are you about?' I asked.

Benjamin blushed—I was going to say, like a young girl. But young girls have given up blushing in these latter days of the age we live in.

'Oh, nothing, nothing!' he said, confusedly. Don't notice it.'

He stretched out his hand to brush the morsels of paper off the table. Those morsels raised a sudden suspicion in my mind. I stopped him.

'You have heard from Mr Playmore!' I said. 'Tell me the truth, Benjamin. Yes, or No?'

Benjamin blushed a shade deeper, and answered 'Yes.'

'Where is the letter?'

'I mustn't show it to you, Valeria.'

This (need I say it?) made me determined to see the letter. My best way of persuading Benjamin to show it to me was to tell him of the sacrifice that I had made to my husband's wishes. 'I have no further voice in the matter,' I added, when I had done. 'It now rests entirely with Mr Playmore to go on or to give up; and this is my last opportunity of discovering what he really thinks about it. Don't I deserve some little indulgence? Have I no claim to look at the letter?'

Benjamin was too much surprised, and too much pleased with me, when he heard what had happened, to be able to resist my entreaties. He gave me the letter.

Mr Playmore wrote, to appeal confidentially to Benjamin as a commercial man. In the long course of his occupation in business, it was just possible that he might have heard of cases in which documents had been put together again, after having been torn up, by design or by accident. Even if his experience failed in this particular, he might be able to refer to some authority in London who would be capable of giving an opinion on the subject. By way of explaining his strange request, Mr Playmore reverted to the notes which Benjamin had taken at Miserrimus Dexter's house, and informed him of the serious importance of 'the gibberish' which he had reported under protest. The letter closed by recommending that any correspondence which ensued should be kept a secret from me—on the ground that it might excite false hopes in my mind if I was informed of it.

I now understood the tone which my worthy adviser had adopted in writing to me. His interest in the recovery of the letter was evidently so overpowering that common prudence compelled him to conceal it from me, in case of ultimate failure. This did not look as if Mr Playmore was likely to give up the investigation, on my withdrawal from it. I glanced again at the fragments of paper on Benjamin's table, with an interest in them which I had not felt yet.

'Has anything been found in Gleninch?' I asked.

'No,' said Benjamin. 'I have only been trying experiments with a little note of my own, before I wrote to Mr Playmore.'

'Oh, you have torn up your little note yourself, then?'

'Yes. And, to make it all the more difficult to put them together again, I shook up the pieces in a basket. It's a childish thing to do, my dear, at my age——'

He stopped, looking very much ashamed of himself.

'Well,' I went on; 'and have you succeeded in putting the pieces together again?'

'It's not very easy, Valeria. But I have made a beginning. It's the same principle as the principle in the "Puzzles" which we used to put together when I was a boy. Only get one central bit of it right, and the rest of the Puzzle falls into its place in a longer or a shorter time. Please don't tell anybody, my dear. People might say I was in my dotage.'

People might have said that, who did not know Benjamin as I knew him. I remembered my old friend's delight in guessing riddles in the columns of the cheap periodicals— and I perfectly understood the strong hold that the new 'Puzzle' had taken on his fancy. 'It's almost as interesting as solving Enigmas—isn't it?' I said slyly.

'Enigmas!' Benjamin repeated, contemptuously. 'It's better than any Enigma I ever guessed yet. To think of that gibberish in my note-book having a meaning in it, after all! I only got Mr Playmore's letter this morning; and—I am really almost ashamed to mention it—I have been trying experiments, off and on, ever since. You won't tell upon me, will you?'

I answered the dear old man by a hearty embrace. Now that he had lost his steady moral balance, and had caught the infection of my enthusiasm, I loved him better than ever!

But I was not quite happy, though I tried to appear so. Struggle against it as I might, I felt a little mortified, when I remembered that I had resigned all further connexion with the search for the letter at such a time as this. My one comfort was to think of Eustace. My one encouragement was to keep my mind fixed as constantly as possible on the bright change for the better that now appeared in the domestic prospect. Here, at least, there was no disaster to fear; here I could honestly feel that I had triumphed. My husband had come back to me of his own free will; he had not given way, under the hard weight of evidence—he had yielded to the nobler influences of his gratitude and his love. And I had taken him to my heart again—not because I had made discoveries which left him no other alternative than to live with me, but because I believed in the better mind that had come to him, and loved and trusted him without reserve. Was it not worth some sacrifice to have arrived at this result! True—most true! And yet I was a little out of spirits. Ah, well! well! the remedy was within a day's journey. The sooner I was with Eustace the better.

Early the next morning, I left London for Paris, by the tidal-train. Benjamin accompanied me to the Terminus.

'I shall write to Edinburgh by to-day's post,' he said, in the interval before the train moved out of the station. 'I think I can find the man Mr Playmore wants to help him, if he decides to go on. Have you any message to send, Valeria?'

'No. I have done with it, Benjamin; I have nothing more to say.'

'Shall I write and tell you how it ends, if Mr Playmore does really try the experiment at Gleninch?'

I answered, as I felt, a little bitterly.

Yes,' I said. 'Write and tell me, if the experiment fails.'

My old friend smiled. He knew me better than I knew myself.

'All right!' he said, resignedly. 'I have got the address of your banker's correspondent in Paris. You will have to go there for money, my dear; and you *may* find a letter waiting for you in the office, when you least expect it. Let me hear how your husband goes on. Good-bye—and God bless you!'

That evening, I was restored to Eustace.

He was too weak, poor fellow, even to raise his head from the pillow. I knelt down at the bedside and kissed him. His languid weary eyes kindled with a new life, as my lips touched his. 'I must try to live now,' he whispered, 'for your sake.'

My mother-in-law had delicately left us together. When he said those words, the temptation to tell him of the new hope that had come to brighten our lives was more than I could resist.

'You must try to live now, Eustace,' I said, 'for some one else, besides me.'

His eyes looked wonderingly into mine.

'Do you mean my mother?' he asked.

I laid my head on his bosom, and whispered back,

'I mean your child.'

I had all my reward for all that I had given up! I forgot Mr Playmore; I forgot Gleninch. Our new honeymoon dates, in my remembrance, from that day.

The quiet time passed, in the bye street in which we lived. The outer stir and tumult of Parisian life ran its daily course around us, unnoticed and unheard. Steadily, though slowly, Eustace gained strength. The doctors, with a word or two of caution, left him almost entirely to me. 'You are his physician,' they said; 'the happier you make him, the sooner he will recover.' The quiet monotonous round of my new life was far from wearying me. I, too, wanted repose—I had no interests, no pleasures, out of my husband's room.

Once, and only once, the placid surface of our lives was just gently ruffled by an allusion to the past. Something that I accidentally said, reminded Eustace of our last interview at Major Fitz-David's house. He referred, very delicately, to what I had then said of the Verdict pronounced on him at the Trial; and he left me to infer that a word from my lips, confirming what his mother had already told him, would quiet his mind at once and for ever.

My answer involved no embarrassments or difficulties: I could, and did, honestly tell him that I had made his wishes my law. But it was hardly in womanhood, I am afraid, to be satisfied with merely replying, and to leave it there. I thought it due to me that Eustace too should concede something, in the way of an assurance which might quiet *my* mind. As usual with me, the words followed the impulse to speak them. 'Eustace,' I asked, 'are you quite cured of those cruel doubts which once made you leave me?'

His answer (as he afterwards said) made me blush with pleasure. 'Ah, Valeria, I should never have gone away, if I had known you then as well as I know you now!'

So the last shadows of distrust melted away out of our lives.

The very remembrance of the turmoil and the trouble of my past days in London seemed now to fade from my memory. We were lovers again; we were absorbed again in each other; we could almost fancy that our marriage dated back once more to only a day or two since. But one last victory over myself was wanting to make my happiness complete. I still felt secret longings, in those dangerous moments when I was left to myself, to know whether the search for the torn letter had, or had not, taken place. What wayward creatures we are! With everything that a woman could want to make her happy, I was ready to put that happiness in peril, rather than remain ignorant of what was going on at Gleninch! I actually hailed the day when my empty purse gave me an excuse for going to my banker's correspondent on business, and so receiving any letters waiting for me which might be placed in my hands.

I applied for my money without knowing what I was about; wondering all the time whether Benjamin had written to me or not. My eyes wandered over the desks and tables in the office, looking for letters furtively. Nothing of the sort was visible. But a man appeared from an inner office: an ugly man, who was yet beautiful to my eyes, for this sufficient reason—he had a letter in his hand, and he said, 'Is this for you, ma'am?'

A glance at the address showed me Benjamin's handwriting.

Had they tried the experiment of recovering the letter? and had they failed?

Somebody put my money in my bag, and politely led me out to the little hired carriage which was waiting for me at the door. I remember nothing distinctly, until I looked at my news from Benjamin on my way home. His first words told me that the dust-heap had been examined, and that the fragments of the torn letter had been found!

CHAPTER XLV

The Dust-Heap Disturbed

MY head turned giddy. I was obliged to wait and let my overpowering agitation subside, before I could read any more.

Looking at the letter again, after an interval, my eyes fell accidentally on a sentence near the end, which surprised and startled me.

I stopped the driver of the carriage, at the entrance to the street in which our lodgings were situated, and told him to take me to the beautiful Park of Paris—the famous Bois de Boulogne. My object was to gain time enough, in this way, to read the letter carefully through by myself, and to ascertain whether I ought, or ought not, to keep the receipt of it a secret, before I confronted my husband and his mother at home.

This precaution taken, I read the narrative which my good Benjamin had so wisely and so thoughtfully written for me. Treating the various incidents methodically, he began with the Report which had arrived, in due course of mail, from our agent in America.

Our man had successfully traced the lodge-keeper's daughter and her husband to a small town in one of the Western States. Mr Playmore's letter of introduction at once secured him a cordial reception from the married pair, and a patient hearing when he stated the object of his voyage across the Atlantic.

His first questions led to no very encouraging results. The woman was confused and surprised, and was apparently quite unable to exert her memory to any useful purpose. Fortunately, her husband proved to be a very intelligent man. He took the agent privately aside, and said to him, 'I understand my wife, and you don't. Tell me exactly what it is you want to know, and leave it to me to discover how much she remembers, and how much she forgets.'

This sensible suggestion was readily accepted. The agent waited for events, a day and a night.

Early the next morning, the husband said to him,—'Talk to my wife now, and you will find she has something to tell you. Only mind this! Don't laugh at her when she speaks of trifles. She is half ashamed to speak of trifles, even to me. Thinks men are above such matters, you know. Listen quietly, and let her talk—and you will get at it all in that way.'

The agent followed his instructions, and 'got at it' as follows:—

The woman remembered, perfectly well, being sent to clean the bedrooms and put them tidy, after the gentlefolks had all left Gleninch. Her mother had a bad hip at the time, and could not go with her and help her. She did not much fancy being alone in the great house, after what had happened in it. On her way to her work, she passed two of the cottagers' children in the neighbourhood, at play in the park. Mr Macallan was always kind to his poor tenants, and never objected to the young ones round about having a run on the grass. The two children idly followed her to the house. She took them inside, along with her; not liking the place, as already mentioned, and feeling that they would be company in the solitary rooms.

She began her work in the Guests' Corridor—leaving the room in the other Corridor, in which the death had happened, to the last.

There was very little to do in the two first rooms. There was not litter enough, when she had swept the floors and cleaned the grates, to even half fill the housemaid's bucket which she carried with her. The children followed her about; and, all things considered, were 'very good company,' in the lonely place.

The third room (that is to say, the bedchamber which had been occupied by Miserrimus Dexter) was in a much worse state than the other two, and wanted a great deal of tidying. She did not much notice the children here, being occupied with her work. The litter was swept up from the carpet, and the cinders and ashes were taken out of the grate, and the whole of it was in the bucket, when her attention was recalled to the children by hearing one of them cry.

She looked about the room without at first discovering them.

A fresh outburst of crying led her in the right direction, and showed her the children under a table in a corner of the room. The youngest of the two had got into a waste-paper basket. The eldest had found an old bottle of gum, with a brush fixed in the cork, and was gravely painting the face of the smaller child with what little remained of the contents of the bottle. Some natural struggles, on the part of the little creature, had ended in the overthrow of the basket and the usual outburst of crying had followed as a matter of course.

In this state of things the remedy was soon applied. The woman took the bottle away from the eldest child, and gave it a 'box on the ear.' The younger one she set on its legs again, and she put the two 'in the corner' to keep them quiet. This done, she swept up such fragments of the torn paper in the basket as had fallen on the floor; threw them back again into the basket, along with the gum-bottle; fetched the bucket, and emptied the basket into it; and then proceeded to the fourth and last room in the corridor, where she finished her work for that day.

Leaving the house, with the children after her, she took the filled bucket to the dust-heap, and emptied it in a hollow place among the rubbish, about half-way up the mound. Then she took the children home; and there was an end of it, for the day.

Such was the result of the appeal made to the woman's memory of domestic events at Gleninch.

The conclusion at which Mr Playmore arrived, from the facts submitted to him, was, that we might now hope to recover the letter. Thrown on the refuse ashes in the house-maid's bucket, and afterwards covered by litter from the fourth room, the torn morsels would be protected above as well as below, when they were emptied on the dust-heap.

Succeeding weeks and months would add to that protection, by adding to the accumulated refuse. In the neglected condition of the grounds, the dust-heap had not been disturbed in search of manure. There it stood, untouched, from the time when the family left Gleninch to the present day. And there, hidden deep somewhere in the mound, the fragments of the letter must be!*

Such were the lawyer's conclusions. He had written im-

mediately to communicate them to Benjamin. And, thereupon, what had Benjamin done?

After having tried his powers of reconstruction on his
own correspondence, the prospect of experimenting on the
mysterious letter itself had proved to be a temptation too
powerful for the old man to resist. 'I almost fancy, my dear,
this business of yours has bewitched me,' he wrote. 'You
see I have the misfortune to be an idle man. I have time to
spare and money to spare. And the end of it is, that I am
here at Gleninch, engaged on my own responsibility (with
good Mr Playmore's permission), in searching the dust-
heap!'

Benjamin's description of his first view of the field of
action at Gleninch followed these characteristic lines of
apology.

I passed over the description, without ceremony. My
remembrance of the scene was too vivid to require any
prompting of that sort. I saw again, in the dim evening
light, the unsightly mound which had so strangely attracted
my attention at Gleninch. I heard again the words in which
Mr Playmore had explained to me the custom of the dust-
heap in Scotch country-houses. What had Benjamin and
Mr Playmore done? What had Benjamin and Mr Playmore
found? For me, the true interest in the narrative was there—
and to that portion of it I eagerly turned next.

They had proceeded methodically, of course, with one
eye on the pounds, shillings, and pence, and the other on
the object in view. In Benjamin, the lawyer had found what
he had not met with in me—a sympathetic mind, alive to
the value of 'an abstract of the expenses,' and conscious of
that most remunerative of human virtues, the virtue of
economy.

At so much a week, they had engaged men to dig into
the mound and to sift the ashes. At so much a week, they
had hired a tent to shelter the open dust-heap from wind
and weather. At so much a week, they had engaged the
services of a young man (personally known to Benjamin),

who was employed in a laboratory under a professor of chemistry, and who had distinguished himself by his skilful manipulation of paper in a recent case of forgery on a well-known London firm. Armed with these preparations, they had begun the work; Benjamin and the young chemist living at Gleninch, and taking it in turns to superintend the proceedings.

Three days of labour with the spade and the sieve produced no results of the slightest importance. However, the matter was in the hands of two quietly-determined men. They declined to be discouraged. They went on.

On the fourth day, the first morsels of paper were found.

Upon examination, they proved to be the fragments of a tradesman's prospectus. Nothing dismayed, Benjamin and the young chemist still persevered. At the end of the day's work, more pieces of paper were turned up. These proved to be covered with written characters. Mr Playmore (arriving at Gleninch, as usual, every evening on the conclusion of his labours in the law) was consulted as to the handwriting. After careful examination, he declared that the mutilated portions of sentences submitted to him had been written, beyond all doubt, by Eustace Macallan's first wife!

This discovery roused the enthusiasm of the searchers to fever height.

Spades and sieves were from that moment forbidden utensils. However unpleasant the task might be, hands alone were used in the farther examination of the mound. The first and foremost necessity was to place the morsels of paper (in flat cardboard boxes prepared for the purpose), in their order as they were found. Night came; the labourers were dismissed; Benjamin and his two colleagues worked on by lamplight. The morsels of paper were turned up by dozens, instead of by ones and twos. For awhile the search prospered in this way; and then the morsels appeared no more. Had they all been recovered? or would renewed hand digging yield more yet? The next light layers of rubbish were carefully removed—and the grand discovery of the day

followed. There (upside down) was the gum-bottle, which
the lodge-keeper's daughter had spoken of! And, more
precious still, under it, were more fragments of written
paper, all stuck together in a little lump, by the last drip-
pings from the gum-bottle dropping upon them as they lay
in the dust-heap!

The scene now shifted to the interior of the house. When
the searchers next assembled, they met at the great table in
the library at Gleninch.

Benjamin's experience with the 'Puzzles' which he had
put together in the days of his boyhood proved to be of
some use to his companions. The fragments accidentally
stuck together, would, in all probability, be found to fit each
other, and would certainly (in any case) be the easiest
fragments to reconstruct, as a centre to start from.

The delicate business of separating these pieces of paper,
and of preserving them in the order in which they had
adhered to each other, was assigned to the practised fingers
of the chemist. But the difficulties of his task did not end
here. The writing was (as usual in letters) traced on both
sides of the paper, and it could only be preserved for the
purpose of reconstruction by splitting each morsel into
two—so as artificially to make a blank side, on which could
be spread the fine cement used for reuniting the fragments
in their original form.

To Mr Playmore and Benjamin, the prospect of successfully putting the letter together, under these disadvantages,
seemed to be almost hopeless. Their skilled colleague soon
satisfied them that they were wrong.

He drew their attention to the thickness of the paper—
note-paper of the strongest and best quality—on which the
writing was traced. It was of more than twice the substance
of the last paper on which he had operated, when he was
engaged in the forgery case; and it was, on that account,
comparatively easy for him (aided by the mechanical ap-
pliances which he had brought from London) to split the
morsels of the torn paper, within a given space of time

which might permit them to begin the reconstruction of the letter that night.

With these explanations, he quietly devoted himself to his work. While Benjamin and the lawyer were still poring over the scattered morsels of the letter which had been first discovered, and trying to piece them together again, the chemist had divided the greater part of the fragments specially confided to him into two halves each; and had correctly put together some five or six sentences of the letter, on the smooth sheet of cardboard prepared for that purpose.

They looked eagerly at the reconstructed writing, so far. It was correctly done: the sense was perfect. The first result gained by examination was remarkable enough to reward them for all their exertions. The language used, plainly identified the person to whom the late Mrs Eustace had addressed her letter.

That person was—my husband.

And the letter thus addressed—if the plainest circumstantial evidence could be trusted—was identical with the letter which Miserrimus Dexter had suppressed until the Trial was over, and had then destroyed by tearing it up.

These were the discoveries that had been made, at the time when Benjamin wrote to me. He had been on the point of posting his letter, when Mr Playmore had suggested that he should keep it by him for a few days longer, on the chance of having more still to tell me.

'We are indebted to her for these results,' the lawyer had said. 'But for her resolution, and her influence over Miserrimus Dexter, we should never have discovered what the dust-heap was hiding from us—we should never have seen so much as a glimmering of the truth. She has the first claim to the fullest information. Let her have it.'

The letter had been accordingly kept back for three days. That interval being at an end, it was hurriedly resumed, and concluded in terms which indescribably alarmed me.

'The chemist is advancing rapidly with his part of the work' (Benjamin wrote); 'and I have succeeded in putting together a separate portion of the torn writing which makes sense. Comparison of what he has accomplished with what I have accomplished has led to startling conclusions. Unless Mr Playmore and I are entirely wrong (and God grant we may be so!) there is a serious necessity for your keeping the reconstruction of the letter strictly secret from everybody about you. The disclosures suggested by what has come to light are so heart-rending and so dreadful, that I cannot bring myself to write about them, until I am absolutely obliged to do so. Please forgive me for disturbing you with this news. We are bound, sooner or later, to consult with you in the matter; and we think it right to prepare your mind for what may be to come.'

To this there was added a postscript in Mr Playmore's handwriting.

'Pray observe strictly the caution which Mr Benjamin impresses on you. And bear this in mind, as a warning from *me*. If we succeed in reconstructing the entire letter, the last person living who ought (in my opinion) to be allowed to see it, is—your husband.'*

I read those startling words; and I asked myself what I was to do next.

As matters now stood, my husband's tranquillity was, so to speak, committed to my charge. It was surely due to *himself*, that I should not receive Benjamin's letter and Mr Playmore's postscript in silence. At the same time, it was due to myself that I should honestly tell Eustace I was in correspondence with Gleninch—only waiting to speak until I knew more than I knew now.

Thus I reasoned with myself. And, to this day, I am not quite sure whether I was right or wrong.

CHAPTER XLVI

The Crisis Deferred

'TAKE care, Valeria!' said Mrs Macallan. 'I ask you no questions; I only caution you, for your own sake. Eustace has noticed, what I have noticed—Eustace has seen a change in you. Take care!'

So my mother-in-law spoke to me, later in the day, when we happened to be alone. I had done my best to conceal all traces of the effect produced on me by the strange and terrible news from Gleninch. But who could read what I had read—who could feel what I now felt—and still maintain an undisturbed serenity of look and manner? If I had been the vilest hypocrite living, I doubt, even then, if my face could have kept my secret, while my mind was full of Benjamin's letter.

Having spoken her word of caution, Mrs Macallan made no further advance to me. I dare say she was right. Still, it seemed hard to be left, without a word of advice or of sympathy, to decide for myself what it was my duty to my husband to do next.

To show him Benjamin's narrative, in his state of health, and in the face of the warning addressed to me, was simply out of the question. At the same time, it was equally impossible, after I had already betrayed myself, to keep him entirely in the dark. I thought over it anxiously in the night. When the morning came, I decided to appeal to my husband's confidence in me.

I went straight to the point, in these terms:

'Eustace, your mother said yesterday that you noticed a change in me, when I came back from my drive. Is she right?'

'Quite right, Valeria,' he answered—speaking in lower tones than usual, and not looking at me.

'We have no concealments from each other, now,' I answered. 'I ought to tell you, and I do tell you, that I found a letter from England waiting at the banker's, which has caused me some agitation and alarm. Will you leave it to me to choose my own time for speaking more plainly? And will you believe, love, that I am really doing my duty towards you, as a good wife, in making this request?'

I paused. He made no answer: I could see that he was secretly struggling with himself. Had I ventured too far? Had I over-estimated the strength of my influence? My heart beat fast, my voice faltered—but I summoned courage enough to take his hand, and to make a last appeal to him. 'Eustace!' I said. 'Don't you know me, yet, well enough to trust me?'

He turned towards me for the first time. I saw a last vanishing trace of doubt in his eyes as they looked into mine.

'You promise, sooner or later, to tell me the whole truth?' he said.

'I promise with all my heart!'

'I trust you, Valeria!'

His brightening eyes told me that he really meant what he said. We sealed our compact with a kiss. Pardon me for mentioning these trifles—I am still writing (if you will kindly remember it) of our new honeymoon.

By that day's post I answered Benjamin's letter, telling him what I had done, and entreating him, if he and Mr Playmore approved of my conduct, to keep me informed of any future discoveries which they might make at Gleninch.

After an interval—an endless interval, as it seemed to me—of ten days more, I received a second letter from my old friend; with another postscript added by Mr Playmore.

'We are advancing steadily and successfully with the putting together of the letter,' Benjamin wrote. 'The one new discovery which we have made is of serious importance to your husband. We have reconstructed certain sentences, declaring, in the plainest words, that the arsenic which Eustace procured was purchased at the request of his wife, and was in her possession at Gleninch. This, remember, is in the handwriting of the wife, and is signed by the wife—as we have also found out. Unfortunately, I am obliged to add, that the objection to taking your husband into our confidence, mentioned when I last wrote, still remains in force—in greater force, I may say, than ever. The more we make out of the letter, the more inclined we are (if we only studied our own feelings) to throw it back into the dust-heap, in mercy to the memory of the unhappy writer. I shall keep this open for a day or two. If there is more news to tell you, by that time, you will hear of it from Mr Playmore.'

Mr Playmore's postscript followed, dated three days later.

'The concluding part of the late Mrs Macallan's letter to her husband,' the lawyer wrote, 'has proved accidentally to be the first part which we have succeeded in piecing together. With the exception of a few gaps still left, here and there, the writing of the closing paragraphs has been perfectly reconstructed. I have neither the time nor the inclination to write to you on this sad subject, in any detail. In a fortnight more, at the longest, we shall, I hope, send you a copy of the letter, complete from the first line to the last. Meanwhile, it is my duty to tell you that there is one bright side to this otherwise deplorable and shocking document. Legally speaking, as well as morally speaking, it absolutely vindicates your husband's innocence. And it may be lawfully used for this purpose—if he can reconcile it to his conscience, and to the mercy due to the memory of the dead, to permit the public exposure of the letter in Court. Understand me, he cannot be tried again on what we call the criminal charge—for certain technical reasons with which I need not trouble you. But, if the facts which were involved at the criminal trial can also be shown to be involved in a civil case (and, in this case, they can), the entire matter may be made the subject of a new legal inquiry; and the verdict of a second jury, completely vindicating your husband, may be thus obtained. Keep this information to yourself for the present. Preserve the position which you have so sensibly adopted towards Eustace, until you have read the restored letter. When you have done this, my own idea is that you will shrink, in pity to *him*, from letting him see it. How he is to be kept in ignorance of what we have discovered is another question, the discussion of which must be deferred until we can consult together. Until that time comes, I can only repeat my advice,—Wait till the next news reaches you from Gleninch.'

I waited. What I suffered, what Eustace thought of me, does not matter. Nothing matters now but the facts.

In less than a fortnight more, the task of restoring the letter was completed. Excepting certain instances, in which the morsels of the torn paper had been irretrievably lost— and in which it had been necessary to complete the sense, in harmony with the writer's intention—the whole letter had been put together; and the promised copy of it was forwarded to me in Paris.

Before you, too, read that dreadful letter, do me one favour. Let me briefly remind you of the circumstances under which Eustace Macallan married his first wife.

Remember that the poor creature fell in love with him, without awakening any corresponding affection on his side. Remember that he separated himself from her, and did all he could to avoid her, when he found this out. Remember that she presented herself at his residence in London, without a word of warning; that he did his best to save her reputation; that he failed, through no fault of his own; and that he ended, rashly ended, in a moment of despair, by marrying her, to silence the scandal that must otherwise have blighted her life as a woman for the rest of her days. Bear all this in mind (it is the sworn testimony of respectable witnesses); and pray do not forget—however foolishly and blameably he may have written about her in the secret pages of his Diary—that he was proved to have done his best to conceal from his wife the aversion which the poor soul inspired in him; and that he was (in the opinion of those who could best judge him) at least a courteous and a considerate husband, if he could be no more.

And now take the letter. It asks but one favour of you; it asks to be read by the light of Christ's teaching:—'Judge not, that ye be not judged.'

CHAPTER XLVII

The Wife's Confession

'Gleninch, October 19, 18—.

'MY HUSBAND:—

I HAVE something very painful to tell you, about one of your oldest friends.

'You have never encouraged me to come to you with any confidences of mine. If you had allowed me to be as familiar with you as some wives are with their husbands, I should have spoken to you personally, instead of writing. As it is, I don't know how you might receive what I have to say to you, if I said it by word of mouth. So I write.

'The man against whom I warn you is still a guest in this house—Miserrimus Dexter. No falser or wickeder creature walks the earth. Don't throw my letter aside! I have waited to say this until I could find proof that might satisfy you. I have got the proof.

'You may remember that I ventured to express some disapproval, when you first told me you had asked this man to visit us. If you had allowed me time to explain myself, I might have been bold enough to give you a good reason for the aversion I felt towards your friend. But you would not wait. You hastily (and most unjustly) accused me of feeling prejudiced against the miserable creature on account of his deformity. No other feeling than compassion for deformed persons has ever entered my mind. I have, indeed, almost a fellow-feeling for them; being that next worst thing myself to a deformity—a plain woman. I objected to Mr Dexter as your guest, because he had asked me to be his wife in past days, and because I had reason to fear that he still regarded me (after my marriage) with a guilty and a horrible love. Was it not my duty, as a good wife, to object to his being your guest at Gleninch? And was it not your duty, as a good husband, to encourage me to say more?

'Well! Mr Dexter has been your guest for many weeks; and Mr Dexter has dared to speak to me again of his love. He has insulted me, and insulted you, by declaring that *he* adores me, and that *you* hate me. He has promised me a life of unalloyed happiness, in a foreign country with my lover. And he has prophesied for me a life of unendurable misery, at home with my husband.

'Why did I not make my complaint to you, and have this monster dismissed from the house at once and for ever?

'Are you sure you would have believed me, if I had complained, and if your bosom friend had denied all intention of insulting me? I heard you once say (when you were not aware that I was within hearing) that the vainest women were always the ugly women. You might have accused *me* of vanity. Who knows?

'But I have no desire to shelter myself under this excuse. I am a jealous unhappy creature; always doubtful of your affection for me; always fearing that another woman has got my place in your heart. Miserrimus Dexter has practised on this weakness of mine. He has declared he can prove to me (if I will permit him) that I am, in your secret heart, an object of loathing to you; that you shrink from touching me; that you curse the hour when you were foolish enough to make me your wife. For two nights and days I struggled against the temptation to let him produce his proofs. It was a terrible temptation, to a woman who was far from feeling sure of the sincerity of your affection for her; and it ended in getting the better of my resistance. I wickedly concealed

the disgust which the wretch inspired in me; I wickedly
gave him leave to explain himself; I wickedly permitted
this enemy of yours and of mine to take me into his confidence. And why? Because I loved you and you only; and
because Miserrimus Dexter's proposal did, after all, echo a
doubt of you that had long been gnawing secretly at my
heart.

'Forgive me, Eustace! This is my first sin against you. It
shall be my last.

'I will not spare myself; I will write a full confession of
what I said to him and of what he said to me. You may
make me suffer for it, when you know what I have done;
but you will at least be warned in time; you will see your
false friend in his true light.

'I said to him, "How can you prove to me that my
husband hates me in secret?"

'He answered, "I can prove it, under his own handwriting; you shall see it in his Diary."

'I said, "His Diary has a lock; and the drawer in which
he keeps it has a lock. How can you get at the Diary and
the drawer?"

'He answered, "I have my own way of getting at both of
them, without the slightest risk of being discovered by your
husband. All you have to do is to give me the opportunity
of seeing you privately. I will engage, in return, to bring the
open Diary with me to your room."

'I said, "How can I give you the opportunity? What do
you mean?"

'He pointed to the key, in the door of communication
between my room and the little study.

'He said, "With my infirmity, I may not be able to profit
by the first opportunity of visiting you here, unobserved: I
must be able to choose my own time and my own way of
getting to you secretly. Let me take the key; leaving the
door locked. When the key is missed, if *you* say it doesn't
matter—if *you* point out that the door is locked, and tell
the servants not to trouble themselves about finding the

key—there will be no disturbance in the house; and I shall
be in secure possession of a means of communication with
you which no one will suspect. Will you do this?"

'I have done it.

'Yes! I have become the accomplice of this double-faced
villain. I have degraded myself, and outraged you, by making an appointment to pry into your Diary. I know how base
my conduct is. I can make no excuse. I can only repeat that
I love you, and that I am sorely afraid you don't love me.
And Miserrimus Dexter offers to end my doubts by showing
me the most secret thoughts of your heart, in your own
writing.

'He is to be with me, for this purpose (while you are out),
some time in the course of the next two hours. I shall
decline to be satisfied with only once looking at your Diary;
and I shall make an appointment with him to bring it to me
again, at the same time to-morrow. Before then, you will
receive these lines, by the hand of my nurse. Go out as
usual, after reading them. But return privately, and unlock
the table drawer in which you keep your book. You will find
it gone. Post yourself quietly in the little study; and you will
discover the Diary (when Miserrimus Dexter leaves me), in
the hands of your friend.[1]

                                              'October 20.

'I have read your Diary.

'At last I know what you really think of me. I have read
what Miserrimus Dexter promised I should read—the

---

[1] Note by Mr Playmore:—The greatest difficulties of reconstruction
occurred in this first portion of the torn letter. In the fourth paragraph
from the beginning, we have been obliged to supply lost words in no
less than three places. In the ninth, tenth, and seventeenth paragraphs
the same proceeding was, in a greater or less degree, found to be
necessary. In all these cases, the utmost pains have been taken to supply
the deficiency in exact accordance with what appeared to be the
meaning of the writer, as indicated in the existing pieces of the manuscript.

confession of your loathing for me, in your own handwriting.

'You will not receive what I wrote to you yesterday, at the time, or in the manner, which I had proposed. Long as my letter is, I have still (after reading your Diary) some more words to add. After I have closed and sealed the envelope, and addressed it to you, I shall put it under my pillow. It will be found there when I am laid out for the grave—and then, Eustace (when it is too late for hope or help), my letter will be given to you.

'Yes: I have had enough of my life. Yes: I mean to die.

'I have already sacrificed everything but my life to my love for you. Now I know that my love is not returned, the last sacrifice left is easy. My death will set you free to marry Mrs Beauly.

'You don't know what it cost me to control my hatred of her, and to beg her to pay her visit here, without minding my illness. I could never have done it if I had not been so fond of you, and so fearful of irritating you against me by showing my jealousy. And how did you reward me? Let your Diary answer! "I tenderly embraced her, this very morning; and I hope, poor soul, she did not discover the effort that it cost me."

'Well, I have discovered it now. I know that you privately think your life with me "a purgatory." I know that you have compassionately hidden from me the "sense of shrinking that comes over you when you are obliged to submit to my caresses." I am nothing but an obstacle—an "utterly distasteful" obstacle—between you and the woman whom you love so dearly that you "adore the earth which she touches with her foot." Be it so! I will stand in your way no longer. It is no sacrifice and no merit on my part. Life is unendurable to me, now I know that the man whom I love with all my heart and soul, secretly shrinks from me whenever I touch him.

'I have got the means of death close at hand.

'The arsenic that I twice asked you to buy for me is in my dressing-case. I deceived you when I mentioned some common-place reasons for wanting it. My true reason was to try if I could not improve my ugly complexion—not from any vain feeling of mine: only to make myself look better and more lovable in your eyes. I have taken some of it for that purpose; but I have got plenty left to kill myself with. The poison will have its use at last. It might have failed to improve my complexion. It will not fail to relieve you of your ugly wife.

'Don't let me be examined after death. Show this letter to the doctor who attends me. It will tell him that I have committed suicide; it will prevent any innocent person from being suspected of poisoning me. I want nobody to be blamed or punished. I shall remove the chemist's label, and carefully empty the bottle containing the poison, so that he may not suffer on my account.

'I must wait here, and rest a little while—then take up my letter again. It is far too long already. But these are my farewell words. I may surely dwell a little on my last talk with you!

'October 21. Two o'clock in the morning.

'I sent you out of the room yesterday, when you came in to ask how I had passed the night. And I spoke of you shamefully, Eustace, after you had gone, to the hired nurse who attends on me. Forgive me. I am almost beside myself now. You know why.

'Half-past three.

'Oh, my husband, I have done the deed which will relieve you of the wife whom you hate! I have taken the poison—all of it that was left in the paper packet, which was the first that I found. If this is not enough to kill me, I have more left in the bottle.

'Ten minutes past five.

'You have just gone, after giving me my composing draught. My courage failed me at the sight of you. I thought to myself, "If he looks at me kindly, I will confess what I have done, and let him save my life." You never looked at me at all. You only looked at the medicine. I let you go, without saying a word.

'Half-past five.

'I begin to feel the first effects of the poison. The nurse is asleep at the foot of my bed. I won't call for assistance; I won't wake her. I will die.

'Half-past nine.

'The agony was beyond my endurance—I woke the nurse. I have seen the doctor.

'Nobody suspects anything. Strange to say, the pain has left me; I have evidently taken too little of the poison. I must open the bottle which contains the larger quantity. Fortunately, you are not near me—my resolution to die, or rather, my loathing of life, remains as bitterly unaltered as ever. To make sure of my courage, I have forbidden the nurse to send for you. She has just gone downstairs by my orders. I am free to get the poison out of my dressing case.

'Ten minutes to ten.

'I had just time to hide the bottle (after the nurse had left me), when you came into my room.

'I had another moment of weakness when I saw you. I determined to give myself a last chance of life. That is to say, I determined to offer you a last opportunity of treating me kindly. I asked you to get me a cup of tea. If, in paying me this little attention, you only encouraged me by one fond word or one fond look, I resolved not to take the second dose of poison.

'You obeyed my wishes, but you were not kind. You gave me my tea, Eustace, as if you were giving a drink to your dog. And then you wondered, in a languid way (thinking, I suppose, of Mrs Beauly all the time), at my dropping the cup in handing it back to you. I really could not help it; my hand *would* tremble. In my place, your hand might have trembled, too—with the arsenic under the bedclothes. You politely hoped, before you went away, that the tea would do me good—and, oh God, you could not even look at me when you said that! You looked at the broken bits of the tea-cup.

'The instant you were out of the room I took the poison—a double dose this time.

'I have a little request to make here, while I think of it.

'After removing the label from the bottle, and putting it back, clean, in my dressing-case, it struck me that I had failed to take the same precaution (in the early morning) with the empty paper packet, bearing on it the name of the other chemist. I threw it aside on the counterpane of the bed, among some other loose papers. My ill-tempered nurse complained of the litter, and crumpled them all up, and put them away somewhere. I hope the chemist will not suffer through my carelessness. Pray bear it mind to say that he is not to blame.

'Dexter—something reminds me of Miserrimus Dexter. He has put your Diary back again in the drawer, and he presses me for an answer to his proposals. Has this false wretch any conscience? If he has, even *he* will suffer—when my death answers him.

'The nurse has been in my room again. I have sent her away. I have told her I want to be alone.

'How is the time going? I cannot find my watch. Is the pain coming back again, and paralysing me? I don't feel it keenly yet.

'It may come back, though, at any moment. I have still to close my letter, and to address it to you. And, besides, I must save up my strength to hide it under the pillow, so that nobody may find it until after my death.

'Farewell, my dear. I wish I had been a prettier woman. A more loving woman (towards you) I could not be. Even now, I dread the sight of your dear face. Even now, if I allowed myself the luxury of looking at you, I don't know that you might not charm me into confessing what I have done—before it is too late to save me.

'But you are not here. Better as it is! better as it is!

'Once more, farewell! Be happier than you have been with me. I love you, Eustace—I forgive you. When you have nothing else to think about, think sometimes, as kindly as you can, of your poor ugly.

'SARA MACALLAN.'[1]

CHAPTER XLVIII

What else could I do?

AS soon as I could dry my eyes and compose my spirits, after reading the wife's pitiable and dreadful farewell, my first thought was of Eustace—my first anxiety was to prevent him from ever reading what I had read.

Yes! to this end it had come. I had devoted my life to the attainment of one object; and that object I had gained. There, on the table before me, lay the triumphant vindication of my husband's innocence; and, in mercy to him, in mercy to the memory of his dear wife, my one hope was that he might never see it! My one desire was to hide it from the public view!

I looked back at the strange circumstances under which the letter had been discovered.

[1] Note by Mr Playmore:—The lost words and phrases supplied in this concluding portion of the letter are so few in number that it is needless to mention them. The fragments which were found accidentally stuck together by the gum, and which represent the part of the letter first completely reconstructed, begin at the phrase, 'I spoke of you shamefully, Eustace'; and end with the broken sentence, 'If, in paying me this little attention, you only encouraged me by one fond word or one fond look, I resolved not to take——' With the assistance thus afforded to us, the labour of putting together the concluding half of the letter (dated 'October 20th') was trifling, compared with the almost insurmountable difficulties which we encountered in dealing with the scattered wreck of the preceding pages.

It was all my doing—as the lawyer had said. And yet, what I had done, I had, so to speak, done blindfold. The merest accident might have altered the whole course of later events. I had over and over again interfered to check Ariel, when she entreated the Master to 'tell her a story.' If she had not succeeded, in spite of my opposition, Miserrimus Dexter's last effort of memory might never have been directed to the tragedy at Gleninch. And again, if I had only remembered to move my chair, and so to give Benjamin the signal to leave off, he would never have written down the apparently senseless words which have led us to the discovery of the truth.

Looking back at events in this frame of mind, the very sight of the letter sickened and horrified me. I cursed the day which had disinterred the fragments of it from their foul tomb. Just at the time when Eustace had found his weary way back to health and strength; just at the time when we were united again and happy again—when a month or two more might make us father and mother, as well as husband and wife—that frightful record of suffering and sin had risen against us like an avenging spirit. There it faced me on the table, threatening my husband's tranquillity; nay, for all I knew (if he read it at the present critical stage of his recovery), even threatening his life!

The hour struck from the clock on the mantel-piece. It was Eustace's time for paying me his morning visit, in my own little room. He might come in at any moment; he might see the letter; he might snatch the letter out of my hand. In a frenzy of terror and loathing, I caught up the vile sheets of paper, and threw them into the fire.

It was a fortunate thing that a copy only had been sent to me. If the original letter had been in its place, I believe I should have burnt the original at that moment.

The last morsel of paper had been barely consumed by the flames when the door opened, and Eustace came in.

He glanced at the fire. The black cinders of the burnt paper were still floating at the back of the grate. He had seen the letter brought to me at the breakfast-table. Did he suspect what I had done? He said nothing—he stood gravely looking into the fire. Then he advanced and fixed his eyes on me. I suppose I was very pale. The first words he spoke were words which asked me if I felt ill.

I was determined not to deceive him, even in the merest trifle.

'I am feeling a little nervous, Eustace,' I answered. 'That is all!'

He looked at me again, as if he expected me to say something more. I remained silent. He took a letter out of the breast-pocket of his coat, and laid it on the table before me—just where the Confession had lain before I destroyed it!

'I have had a letter, too, this morning,' he said. 'And *I*, Valeria, have no secrets from *you*.'

I understood the reproach which my husband's last words conveyed; but I made no attempt to answer him.

'Do you wish me to read it?' was all I said, pointing to the envelope which he had laid on the table.

'I have already said that I have no secrets from you,' he repeated. 'The envelope is open. See for yourself what is enclosed in it.'

I took it out—not a letter, but a printed paragraph, cut from a Scotch newspaper.

'Read it,' said Eustace.

I read, as follows:—

'STRANGE DOINGS AT GLENINCH.—A romance in real life seems to be in course of progress at Mr Macallan's country-house. Private excavations are taking place—if our readers will pardon us the unsavoury allusion?—at the dust-heap, of all places in the world! Something has assuredly been discovered; but nobody knows what. This alone is certain:—For weeks past, two strangers from London (superintended by our respected fellow-citizen, Mr Playmore) have been at work night and day in the library at Gleninch, with the door locked. Will the secret ever be revealed? And will it throw any light on a mysterious and shocking event which our readers have learnt to associate with the past history of Gleninch? Perhaps when Mr Macallan returns, he may be able to answer these questions. In the mean time, we can only await events.'

I laid the newspaper slip on the table, in no very Christian frame of mind towards the persons concerned in producing it. Some reporter in search of news had evidently been prying about the grounds at Gleninch, and some busybody in the neighbourhood had in all probability sent the published paragraph to Eustace. Entirely at a loss what to do, I waited for my husband to speak. He did not keep me in suspense—he questioned me instantly.

'Do you understand what it means, Valeria?'

I answered honestly—I owned that I understood what it meant.

He waited again, as if he expected me to say more. I still kept the only refuge left to me—the refuge of silence.

'Am I to know no more than I know now?' he proceeded, after an interval. 'Are you not bound to tell me what is going on in my own house?'

It is a common remark that people, if they can think at all, think quickly in emergencies. There was but one way out of the embarrassing position in which my husband's last words had placed me. My instincts showed me the way, I suppose. At any rate, I took it.

'You have promised to trust me,' I began.

He admitted that he had promised.

'I must ask you, for your own sake, Eustace, to trust me for a little while longer. I will satisfy you, if you will only give me time.'

His face darkened. 'How much longer must I wait?' he asked.

I saw that the time had come for trying some stronger form of persuasion than words.

'Kiss me,' I said, 'before I tell you!'

He hesitated (so like a husband!). And I persisted (so like a wife!). There was no choice for him but to yield. Having given me my kiss (not over-graciously), he insisted once more on knowing how much longer I wanted him to wait.

'I want you to wait,' I answered, 'until our child is born.'

He started. My condition took him by surprise. I gently pressed his hand, and gave him a look. He returned the look (warmly enough, this time, to satisfy me). 'Say you consent,' I whispered.

He consented.

So I put off the day of reckoning once more. So I gained time to consult again with Benjamin and Mr Playmore.

While Eustace remained with me in the room, I was composed, and capable of talking to him. But, when he left me, after a time, to think over what had passed between us, and to remember how kindly he had given way to me, my heart turned pityingly to those other wives (better women, some of them, than I am); whose husbands, under similar circumstances, would have spoken hard words to them, would perhaps even have acted more cruelly still. The contrast thus suggested between their fate and mine quite overcame me. What had I done to deserve my happiness? What had *they* done, poor souls, to deserve their misery? My nerves were overwrought, I dare say, after reading the dreadful confession of Eustace's first wife. I burst out crying—and I was all the better for it afterwards!

CHAPTER XLIX

Past and Future

I WRITE from memory, unassisted by notes or diaries; and I have no distinct recollection of the length of our residence abroad. It certainly extended over a period of some months. Long after Eustace was strong enough to take the journey to London, the doctors persisted in keeping him in Paris. He had shown symptoms of weakness in one of his lungs, and his medical advisers, seeing that he prospered in the dry atmosphere of France, warned him to be careful of breathing too soon the moist air of his own country.

Thus it happened that we were still in Paris, when I received my next news from Gleninch.

This time, no letters passed on either side. To my surprise and delight, Benjamin quietly made his appearance, one morning, in our pretty French drawing-room. He was so preternaturally smart in his dress, and so incomprehensibly anxious (while my husband was in the way) to make us understand that his reasons for visiting Paris were holiday reasons only, that I at once suspected him of having crossed the Channel in a double character—say, as tourist in search of pleasure, when third persons were present: as ambassador from Mr Playmore, when he and I had the room to ourselves.

Later in the day I contrived that we should be left together, and I soon found that my anticipations had not misled me. Benjamin had set out for Paris, at Mr Playmore's express request, to consult with me as to the future, and to enlighten me as to the past. He presented me with his credentials, in the shape of a little note from the lawyer.

'There are some few points' (Mr Playmore wrote) 'which the recovery of the letter does not seem to clear up. I have done my best, with Mr Benjamin's assistance, to find the right explanation of these debatable matters, and I have treated the subject, for the sake of brevity, in the form of Questions and Answers. Will you accept me as interpreter, after the mistakes I made when you consulted me in Edinburgh? Events, I admit, have proved that I was entirely wrong in trying to prevent you from returning to Dexter— and partially wrong in suspecting Dexter of being directly, instead of indirectly, answerable for the first Mrs Eustace's death! I frankly make my confession, and leave you to tell Mr Benjamin whether you think my new Catechism worthy of examination or not.'

I thought his 'new Catechism' (as he called it) decidedly

worthy of examination. If you don't agree with this view, and if you are dying to be done with me and my narrative, pass on to the next chapter by all means!

Benjamin produced the Questions and Answers, and read them to me, at my request, in these terms:—

'Questions suggested by the letter discovered at Gleninch. First Group: Questions relating to the Diary. First Question:—In obtaining access to Mr Macallan's private journal, was Miserrimus Dexter guided by any previous knowledge of its contents?

'Answer:—It is doubtful if he had any such knowledge. The probabilities are that he noticed how carefully Mr Macallan secured his Diary from observation; that he inferred therefrom the existence of dangerous domestic secrets in the locked-up pages; and that he speculated on using those secrets for his own purpose, when he caused the false keys to be made.

'Second question:—To what motive are we to attribute Miserrimus Dexter's interference with the sheriff's officers, on the day when they seized Mr Macallan's Diary, along with his other papers?

'Answer:—In replying to this question, we must first do justice to Dexter himself. Infamously as we now know him to have acted, the man was not a downright fiend. That he secretly hated Mr Macallan, as his successful rival in the affections of the woman whom he loved—and that he did all he could to induce the unhappy lady to desert her husband—are, in this case, facts not to be denied. On the other hand, it is fairly to be doubted whether he was additionally capable of permitting the friend who trusted him to be tried for murder, through his fault, without making an effort to save the innocent man. It had naturally never occurred to Mr Macallan (being guiltless of his wife's death) to destroy his Diary and his letters, in the fear that they might be used against him. Until the prompt and secret action of the Fiscal took him by surprise, the idea of his being charged with the murder of his wife was an idea which we know, from his own statement, had never even entered his mind. But Dexter must have looked at the matter from another point of view. In his last wandering words (spoken when his mind broke down) he refers to the Diary in these terms, "The Diary will hang him; I won't have him hanged." If he could have found his opportunity of getting at it in time—or if the sheriff's officers had not been too quick for him—there can be no reasonable doubt that Dexter would have himself destroyed the Diary, fore-seeing the consequences of its production in Court. So strongly does he appear to have felt these considerations, that he even resisted the officers in the execution of their duty. His agitation when he sent for Mr Playmore to inter-fere was witnessed by that gentleman, and (it may not be amiss to add) was genuine agitation beyond dispute.

'Questions of the Second Group: relating to the Wife's Confession. First Question:—What prevented Dexter from destroying the letter, when he first discovered it under the dead woman's pillow?

'Answer:—The same motives which led him to resist the seizure of the Diary, and to give his evidence in the prisoner's favour at the Trial, induced him to preserve the letter, until the verdict was known. Looking back once more at his last words (as taken down by Mr Benjamin), we may infer that if the verdict had been Guilty, he would not have hesitated to save the innocent husband by produc-ing the wife's confession. There are degrees in all wicked-ness. Dexter was wicked enough to suppress the letter, which wounded his vanity by revealing him as an object for loathing and contempt—but he was not wicked enough deliberately to let an innocent man perish on the scaffold. He was capable of exposing the rival whom he hated to the infamy and torture of a public accusation of murder; but, in the event of an adverse verdict, he shrank before the direr cruelty of letting him be hanged. Reflect, in this connexion, on what he must have suffered, villain as he was, when he first read the wife's confession. He had calculated on undermining her affection for her husband—and whither had his calculations led him? He had driven the woman whom he loved to the last dreadful refuge of death by suicide! Give these considerations their due weight; and you will understand that some little redeeming virtue might show itself, as the result even of *this* man's remorse.

'Second Question:—What motive influenced Miserrimus Dexter's conduct, when Mrs (Valeria) Macallan informed him that she proposed re-opening the inquiry into the poisoning at Gleninch?

'Answer:—In all probability, Dexter's guilty fears suggested to him that he might have been watched, on the morning when he secretly entered the chamber in which the first Mrs Eustace lay dead. Feeling no scruples himself, to restrain him from listening at doors and looking through keyholes, he would be all the more ready to suspect other people of the same practices. With this dread in him, it would naturally occur to his mind that Mrs Valeria might meet with the person who had watched him, and might hear all that the person had discovered—unless he led her astray at the outset of her investigations. Her own jealous suspicions of Mrs Beauly offered him the chance of easily doing this. And he was all the readier to profit by the chance, being himself animated by the most hostile feeling towards that lady. He knew her, as the enemy who destroyed the domestic peace of the mistress of the house; he loved the mistress of the house—and he hated her enemy, accordingly. The preservation of his guilty secret, and the persecution of Mrs Beauly: there you have the greater and the lesser motive of his conduct, in his relations with Mrs Eustace the second!'[1]

---

[1] Note by the writer of the narrative:—Look back for a further illustration of this point of view to the scene at Benjamin's house (Chapter XXXV), where Dexter, in a moment of ungovernable agitation, betrays his own secret to Valeria.

Benjamin laid down his notes, and took off his spectacles.

'We have not thought it necessary to go farther than this,' he said. 'Is there any point you can think of that is still left unexplained?'

I reflected. There was no point of any importance left unexplained that I could remember. But there was one little matter (suggested by the recent allusions to Mrs Beauly) which I wished (if possible) to have thoroughly cleared up.

'Have you and Mr Playmore ever spoken together on the subject of my husband's former attachment to Mrs Beauly?' I asked. 'Has Mr Playmore ever told you why Eustace did not marry her, after the Trial?'

'I put that question to Mr Playmore myself,' said Benjamin. 'He answered it easily enough. Being your husband's confidential friend and adviser, he was consulted when Mr Eustace wrote to Mrs Beauly, after the Trial; and he repeated the substance of the letter, at my request. Would you like to hear what I remember of it, in my turn?'

I owned that I should like to hear it. What Benjamin thereupon told me, exactly coincided with what Miserrimus Dexter had told me—as related in the thirtieth chapter of my narrative. Mrs Beauly had been a witness of the public degradation of my husband. That was enough in itself to prevent him from marrying her. He broke off with *her* for the same reason which had led him to separate himself from *me*. Existence with a woman who knew that he had been tried for his life as a murderer, was an existence which he had not resolution enough to face. The two accounts agreed in every particular. At last my jealous curiosity was pacified; and Benjamin was free to dismiss the past from further consideration, and to approach the more critical and more interesting topic of the future.

His first inquiries related to Eustace. He asked if my husband had any suspicion of the proceedings which had taken place at Gleninch.

I told him what had happened, and how I had contrived to put off the inevitable disclosure for a time.

My old friend's face cleared up as he listened to me.

'This will be good news for Mr Playmore,' he said. 'Our excellent friend, the lawyer, is sorely afraid that our discoveries may compromise your position with your husband. On the one hand, he is naturally anxious to spare Mr Eustace the distress which he must certainly feel, if he reads his first wife's confession. On the other hand, it is impossible, in justice (as Mr Playmore puts it) to the unborn children of your marriage, to suppress a document which vindicates the memory of their father from the aspersion that the Scotch Verdict might otherwise cast on it.'

I listened attentively. In referring to our future, Benjamin had touched on a trouble which was still secretly preying on my mind.

'How does Mr Playmore propose to meet the difficulty?' I asked.

'He can only meet it in one way,' Benjamin replied. 'He proposes to seal up the original manuscript of the letter, and to add to it a plain statement of the circumstances under which it was discovered; supported by your signed attestation and mine, as witnesses to the facts. This done, he must leave it to you to take your husband into your confidence, at your own time. It will then be for Mr Eustace to decide whether he will open the enclosure—or whether he will leave it, with the seal unbroken, as an heirloom to his children, to be made public or not, at their discretion, when they are of an age to think for themselves. Do you consent to this, my dear? or would you prefer that Mr Playmore should see your husband, and act for you in the matter?'

I decided, without hesitation, to take the responsibility on myself. Where the question of guiding Eustace's decision was concerned, I considered my influence to be decidedly superior to the influence of Mr Playmore. My choice met with Benjamin's full approval. He arranged to write to Edinburgh, and relieve the lawyer's anxieties, by that day's post.

The one last thing now left to be settled, related to our
plans for returning to England. The doctors were the authorities on this subject. I promised to consult them about it,
at their next visit to Eustace.

'Have you anything more to say to me?' Benjamin inquired, as he opened his writing-case.

I thought of Miserrimus Dexter and Ariel; and I inquired
if he had heard any news of them lately. My old friend
sighed, and warned me that I had touched on a painful
subject.

'The best thing that can happen to that unhappy man, is
likely to happen,' he said. 'The one change in him is a
change that threatens paralysis. You may hear of his death
before you get back to England.'

'And Ariel?' I asked.

'Quite unaltered,' Benjamin answered. 'Perfectly happy
so long as she is with "the Master." From all I can hear of
her, poor soul, she doesn't reckon Dexter among mortal
beings. She laughs at the idea of his dying; and she waits
patiently, in the firm persuasion that he will recognise her
again.'

Benjamin's news saddened and silenced me. I left him to
his letter.

CHAPTER L

The Last of the Story

IN ten days more we returned to England, accompanied by
Benjamin.

Mrs Macallan's house in London offered us ample ac-
commodation. We gladly availed ourselves of her proposal,
when she invited us to stay with her until our child was
born, and our plans for the future were arranged.

The sad news from the asylum (for which Benjamin had prepared my mind at Paris) reached me soon after our return to England. Miserrimus Dexter's release from the burden of life had come to him, by slow degrees. A few hours before he breathed his last, he rallied for a while, and recognised Ariel at his bedside. He feebly pronounced her name, and looked at her, and asked for me. They thought of sending for me, but it was too late. Before the messenger could be despatched, he said, with a touch of his old self-importance, 'Silence all of you! my brains are weary; I am going to sleep.' He closed his eyes in slumber, and never woke again. So for this man too the end came mercifully, without grief or pain! So that strange and many-sided life—with its guilt and its misery, its fitful flashes of poetry and humour, its fantastic gaiety, cruelty, and vanity—ran its destined course, and faded out like a dream!

Alas for Ariel! She had lived for the Master—what more could she do, now the Master was gone? She could die for him.

They had mercifully allowed her to attend the funeral of Miserrimus Dexter—in the hope that the ceremony might avail to convince her of his death. The anticipation was not realized; she still persisted in denying that 'the Master' had left her. They were obliged to restrain the poor creature by force, when the coffin was lowered into the grave; and they could only remove her from the cemetery, by the same means, when the burial service was over. From that time, her life alternated, for a few weeks, between fits of raving delirium, and intervals of lethargic repose. At the annual ball given in the asylum, when the strict superintendence of the patients was in some degree relaxed, the alarm was raised, a little before midnight, that Ariel was missing. The nurse in charge had left her asleep, and had yielded to the temptation of going downstairs to look at the dancing. When the woman returned to her post, Ariel was gone. The presence of strangers, and the confusion incidental to the festival, offered her facilities for escaping which would not

have presented themselves at any other time. That night
the search for her proved to be useless. The next morning
brought with it the last touching and terrible tidings of her.
She had strayed back to the burial-ground; and she had
been found towards sunrise, dead of cold and exposure, on
Miserrimus Dexter's grave. Faithful to the last, Ariel had
followed the Master! Faithful to the last, Ariel had died on
the Master's grave!

Having written these sad words, I turn willingly to a less
painful theme.

Events had separated me from Major Fitz-David, after
the date of the dinner-party which had witnessed my
memorable meeting with Lady Clarinda. From that time, I
heard little or nothing of the Major; and I am ashamed to
say I had almost entirely forgotten him—when I was
reminded of the modern Don Juan, by the amazing appearance of wedding-cards, addressed to me at my mother-in-
law's house. The Major had settled in life at last. And, more
wonderful still, the Major had chosen as the lawful ruler of
his household and himself—'the future Queen of Song;' the
round-eyed over-dressed young lady with the strident
soprano voice!

We paid our visit of congratulation in due form; and we
really did feel for Major Fitz-David.

The ordeal of marriage had so changed my gay and gallant admirer of former times, that I hardly knew him again.
He had lost all his pretensions to youth; he had become,
hopelessly and undisguisedly, an old man. Standing behind
the chair on which his imperious young wife sat enthroned,
he looked at her submissively between every two words that
he addressed to me, as if he waited for her permission to
open his lips and speak. Whenever she interrupted him—
and she did it, over and over again, without ceremony—he
submitted with a senile docility and admiration, at once
absurd and shocking to see.

'Isn't she beautiful?' he said to me (in his wife's hearing!).

'What a figure, and what a voice! You remember her voice? It's a loss, my dear lady, an irretrievable loss, to the operatic stage! Do you know, when I think what that grand creature might have done, I sometimes ask myself if I really had any right to marry her. I feel, upon my honour I feel, as if I had committed a fraud on the public!'

As for the favoured object of this quaint mixture of admiration and regret, she was pleased to receive me graciously, as an old friend. While Eustace was talking to the Major, the bride drew me aside out of their hearing, and explained her motives for marrying, with a candour which was positively shameless.

'You see we are a large family at home, quite unprovided for!' this odious young woman whispered in my ear. 'It's all very well to talk about my being a "Queen of Song" and the rest of it. Lord bless you, I have been often enough to the opera, and I have learnt enough of my music-master, to know what it takes to make a fine singer. I haven't the patience to work at it as those foreign women do: a parcel of brazen-faced Jezebels—I hate them. No! no! between you and me, it was a great deal easier to get the money by marrying the old gentleman. Here I am, provided for—and there's all my family provided for, too,—and nothing to do but to spend the money. I am fond of my family; I'm a good daughter and sister—*I* am! See how I'm dressed; look at the furniture: I haven't played my cards badly, have I? It's a great advantage to marry an old man—you can twist him round your little finger. Happy? Oh, yes! I'm quite happy; and I hope you are, too. Where are you living now? I shall call soon, and have a long gossip with you. I always had a sort of liking for you, and (now I'm as good as you are) I want to be friends.'

I made a short and civil reply to this; determining inwardly that when she did visit me, she should get no farther than the house door. I don't scruple to say that I was thoroughly disgusted with her. When a woman sells herself to a man, that vile bargain is none the less infamous (to my mind), because it happens to be made under the sanction of the Church and the Law.

As I sit at the desk thinking, the picture of the Major and his wife vanishes from my memory—and the last scene in my story comes slowly into view.

The place is my bedroom. The persons (both, if you will be pleased to excuse them*), are myself and my son. He is already three weeks old; and he is now lying fast asleep by his mother's side. My good Uncle Starkweather is coming to London to baptise him. Mrs Macallan will be his godmother; and his godfathers will be Benjamin and Mr Playmore. I wonder whether my christening will pass off more merrily than my wedding?

The doctor has just left the house, in some little perplexity about me. He has found me reclining as usual (latterly) in my arm-chair; but, on this particular day, he has detected symptoms of exhaustion, which he finds quite unaccountable under the circumstances, and which warn him to exert his authority by sending me back to my bed.

The truth is that I have not taken the doctor into my confidence. There are two causes for those signs of exhaustion which have surprised my medical attendant—and the names of them are: Anxiety and Suspense.

On this day, I have at last summoned courage enough to perform the promise which I made to my husband in Paris. He is informed, by this time, how his wife's confession was discovered. He knows (on Mr Playmore's authority) that the letter may be made the means, if he so wills it, of publicly vindicating his innocence in a Court of Law. And, last and most important of all, he is now aware that the Confession itself has been kept a sealed secret from him, out of compassionate regard for his own peace of mind, as well as for the memory of the unhappy woman who was once his wife.

These necessary disclosures I have communicated to my

husband—not by word of mouth; when the time came, I shrank from speaking to him personally of his first wife— but by a written statement of the circumstances, taken mainly out of my letters received in Paris, from Benjamin and Mr Playmore. He has now had ample time to read all that I have written to him, and to reflect on it in the retirement of his own study. I am waiting, with the fatal letter in my hand—and my mother-in-law is waiting in the next room to me—to hear from his own lips whether he decides to break the seal or not.

The minutes pass; and still we fail to hear his footstep on the stairs. My doubts as to which way his decision may turn, affect me more and more uneasily the longer I wait. The very possession of the letter, in the present excited state of my nerves, oppresses and revolts me. I shrink from touching it, or looking at it. I move it about restlessly from place to place on the bed, and still I cannot keep it out of my mind. At last, an odd fancy strikes me. I lift up one of the baby's hands, and put the letter under it—and so associate that dreadful record of sin and misery with something innocent and pretty that seems to hallow and to purify it.

The minutes pass; the half-hour longer strikes from the clock on the chimney-piece; and at last I hear him! He knocks softly, and opens the door.

He is deadly pale: I fancy I can detect traces of tears on his cheeks. But no outward signs of agitation escape him, as he takes his seat by my side. I can see that he has waited until he could control himself—for my sake.

He takes my hand, and kisses me tenderly.

'Valeria!' he says. 'Let me once more ask you to forgive what I said, and did, in the byegone time. If I understand nothing else, my love, I understand this:—The proof of my innocence has been found; and I owe it entirely to the courage and the devotion of my wife!'

I wait a little, to enjoy the full luxury of hearing him say those words—to revel in the love and the gratitude that moisten his dear eyes as they look at me. Then, I rouse my resolution, and put the momentous question on which our future depends.

'Do you wish to see the letter, Eustace?'

Instead of answering directly, he questions me in his turn.

'Have you got the letter here?'

'Yes.'

'Sealed up?'

'Sealed up.'

He waits a little, considering what he is going to say next, before he says it.

'Let me be sure that I know exactly what it is I have to decide,' he proceeds. 'Suppose I insist on reading the letter——?'

There I interrupt him. I know it is my duty to restrain myself. But I cannot do my duty.

'My darling, don't talk of reading the letter! Pray, pray spare yourself——'

He holds up his hand for silence.

'I am not thinking of myself,' he says. 'I am thinking of my dead wife. If I give up the public vindication of my innocence, in my own lifetime—if I leave the seal of the letter unbroken—do you say, as Mr Playmore says, that I shall be acting mercifully and tenderly towards the memory of my wife?'

'Oh, Eustace, there cannot be the shadow of a doubt of it!'

'Shall I be making some little atonement for any pain that I may have thoughtlessly caused her to suffer in her lifetime?'

'Yes! yes!'

'And, Valeria—shall I please You?'

'My darling, you will enchant me!'

'Where is the letter?'

'In your son's hand, Eustace.'

He goes round to the other side of the bed, and lifts the baby's little pink hand to his lips. For a while, he waits so, in sad and secret communion with himself. I see his mother softly open the door, and watch him as I am watching him. In a moment more, our suspense is at an end. With a heavy sigh, he lays the child's hand back again on the sealed letter; and, by that one little action, says (as if in words) to his son:—'I leave it to You!'

And so it ended! Not as I thought it would end; not perhaps as you thought it would end. What do we know of our own lives? What do we know of the fulfilment of our dearest wishes? God knows—and that is best.

Must I shut up the paper? Yes. There is nothing more for you to read, or for me to say.

Except this—as a postscript. Don't bear hardly, good people, on the follies and the errors of my husband's life. Abuse *me* as much as you please. But pray think kindly of Eustace, for my sake.

THE END

APPENDIX

WILKIE COLLINS, THE GRAPHIC AND THE 'BRITISH DOMESTIC INQUISITION'

THIS short note by Edmund Yates (friend of Collins and editor of the *World*) and the longer letter by Wilkie Collins appeared in the *World* a few days after the final instalment of *The Law and the Lady* was published in the *Graphic*.

The World, 17 March, 1875, p.15

MR WILKIE COLLINS AND THE GRAPHIC

The following extraordinary paragraph appeared in the last number of the *Graphic*:

> *The Law and the Lady* by Wilkie Collins 3 vols (Chatto & Windus)
>
> We do not usually review stories which have previously appeared in our columns, as our readers are quite able to form their own opinion concerning them, but we may take the opportunity of remarking here that when an author of reputation is asked to write a story for a periodical it is the custom, not to take it 'on approval', but to accept whatever he chooses to supply. Moreover in the case of *The Law and the Lady*, the author insisted on the insertion of a clause in the agreement to the effect that his proofs were to be published without further alteration. We mention these facts in justice to ourselves, as the story is not one which we should have voluntarily selected to place before our readers.

The value of an illustrated newspaper lies in the excellence of its wood blocks, and with these the *Graphic* has been particularly happy, a double-page illustration of an English ploughing-match presented this week being a wonderful specimen of the combined efforts of the artist and the engraver. The ordinary letter-press of such a journal is usually beneath contempt. If the cuts are properly written up to, and the news of the week neatly abridged, most purchasers will be satisfied. Original writing is not required, especially when it comes in such a shape as the foregoing extract, which, as it seems to us, is a gross violation of the rules by which literary courtesy and good feeling are governed. It would be absurd indeed if a novelist of Mr. Wilkie Collins's experience and reputation were to submit the proof of his story to be hacked about by the wielder of the paste and scissors at the *Graphic* office. But that the proprietors of the journal, after availing themselves of the largely-increased circulation which the publication of *The Law and the Lady* has presumably afforded them, should attack its author, thus kicking down the ladder by which they had climbed, is conduct as ungenerous as it is ill-judged.

The World, March 24, 1875, p.21

'THE LAW AND THE LADY'
To the Editor of The World

Sir,—In your last week's number you naturally express some surprise, after reading a paragraph in the *Graphic* reflecting in disparaging and discourteous terms on a story which I publish- ed periodically in the columns of that newspaper. Wherever I go, I find that persons who take any interest in literary matters share your view. Letters have even reached me from perfect strangers, asking (to use the picturesque language of one of my correspondents) 'What the newspaper means by running down its own author?' Will you permit me to explain the mystery in your columns by means of a brief narrative of facts? It may be possible to amuse some of your readers who are my readers also, if I inform them of the curious difficulties which a writer has sometimes to contend with when addressing himself to the public.

At the express request of the proprietors of the *Graphic* I consented to permit them to publish a new work of mine, called *The Law and the Lady*, periodically, in their newspaper. The negotiations were conducted by their literary editor. Speaking as a mouthpiece of his proprietors, this gentleman's main anxiety in respect to my forthcoming work appeared to be, that it should 'give no offence to the family circle'—the sensitiveness of this same 'circle' being estimated, in the present case and in the interests of the proprietors, by the editor who was then dealing with me. As a means of quieting his fears, I informed him that I was about to write, this time (autobiographically), in the character of a young lady, and that I hoped I might be sanctioned, under those circumstances, as a perfectly harmless person by that British Domestic Inquisition, otherwise known as the family circle. On the editor's departure, considering what had passed between us—and not forgetting Swift's immortal aphorism, which declares that a nice man is a man of nasty ideas—I thought it wise to insert a clause in my agreement forbidding the alteration of any portion of my story by anybody employed in the interests of the Domestic Inquisition at the *Graphic* office, without first obtaining my consent and approbation. The agreement, thus guarded, was signed on both sides, and *The Law and the Lady* made its appearance periodically in the columns of the *Graphic* newspaper.

Towards the latter portion of the story, I had occasion to describe an attempt made by one of the male personages in the story to kiss one of the female personages—an incident, permit me to add, which, being of frequent occurrence in 'the family circle', was therefore an especially fit incident for the pages of the *Graphic*. The little scene was described (autobiographically) by the heroine of the story in these words: 'He caught my hand in his and devoured it with kisses. His lips burnt me like fire. He twisted himself suddenly in his chair, and wound his arm around my waist. In the terror and indignation of the moment, vainly struggling with him, I cried out for help.' That is all. The story is now in circulation at the libraries (in book form), and is accessible to anyone who wishes to make sure that I have correctly transferred the language used in the novel to your columns.

To my indescribable amazement, I found this passage, on its publication in the *Graphic*, clumsily altered, abridged and mutilated (without a word of warning to me), so as to make certain allusions which followed in the next number simply ridiculous. I at once wrote (with some natural indignation) to complain of this scandalous breach of courtesy, which was also a plain breach of the agreement. In reply, I received a letter from the editor, informing me that he had placed a nasty interpretation of his own on the perfectly innocent passage which I have just quoted, and that he and 'the Directors' and other 'members of the establishment'—all simmering together in a moral miasma of their own dirty raising—actually interpreted what I had written as describing '*an attempted violation of the heroine of the story*.' I have kept the letter, and I beg to assure you that I quote the writer's language word for word.

It was impossible for me, after that, to communicate directly with the person with whom I had unfortunately connected myself for the time being. In other words, it was useless to appeal to their sense of what was due to Literature, or due to a writer who had for more than twenty years held an honourable place in the public estimation. I appealed (through my lawyers) to the agreement. The omitted passages were restored, under protest, in the next number of the newspaper; and the consequent explosion of spite, which you have justly described as 'a gross violation of the rules by which literary courtesy and good feeling are governed', follows as a natural explosion of the editor's insolence and the editor's hostile feelings towards myself. It is quite needless for me to defend the perfectly innocent passage which has been so indecently misinterpreted. It has been reprinted in America, in Australia, and in Canada; it has been translated into the French, German, Italian, Russian and Dutch languages, and not a word of objection has reached me in any form. In no country but England does a writer meet with obstacles at once so contemptible and so irritating as the sort of obstacle as I have described. Your excellent article is, in this sense, a service rendered to Literature, as well as a service rendered to me.—Accept my sincere thanks, and believe me faithfully yours,

WILKIE COLLINS

London, March 20th, 1875

EXPLANATORY NOTES

2 *Note addressed to the Reader*: Collins was in the habit of writing short prefaces to his novels, often taking critics to task for their reception of earlier editions of his fiction. Here his request that the reader should bear in mind 'established truth[s] . . . that the actions of human beings are not invariably governed by the laws of pure reason' anticipates the ambiguous connotations of the novel, and its final undercutting of the notion of 'established truth'.

3 *Regnier*: a well-known actor with the Comédie-Française and an old friend of both Collins and Dickens, who planned Collins's first trip to Paris with Dickens in 1856. He collaborated with Collins on the French stage adaptation of *Armadale* in 1866 and organized the stage production of *The New Magdalen* in Paris in 1873.

7 *Chapter I*: in the manuscript of the novel and in Harper's American edition 'Part One: Paradise Lost' is inserted above the first chapter heading.

Marriage Service of the Church of England: see the end of 'the Solemnization of Matrimony' in the Book of Common Prayer (first published 1594; revised 1661). The whole of the end of the service is devoted to exhorting wifely duty and submission to her husband. The passage preceding the quotation with which the chapter opens runs: 'Saint Paul, in the aforesaid Epistle to the Ephesians, teacheth you thus; Wives, submit yourselves unto your own husbands, as unto the Lord. For the husband is the head of the wife, even as Christ is head of the Church; and he is the Saviour of the body. Therefore as the Church is subject unto Christ, so let the wives be to their own husbands in everything. And again he saith, Let the wife see that she reverence her husband . . .' (1855 edition).

Valeria: a Latin name, suggestive of strength and resolution. Collins exaggerates his tendency to use explicitly significant names in the naming of both Valeria and Miserrimus Dexter.

10 *Venus de' Medici*: the first of the references to classical sculpture and to representations of Venus (the ancient Roman goddess of beauty and love—Aphrodite in Greek mythology) as different kinds of ideal of feminine beauty in the novel. The Venus de' Medici, in the Uffizi gallery in Florence, was one of the most admired of the Venus statues in the eighteenth and nineteenth centuries. Ruskin referred to it as 'one of the purest and most elevated incarnations of woman conceivable' (*Works*, i. 433). However, the Medici Venus was also seen as representing coquettish and unstable femininity and, as Roman rather than Greek in origin, gradually came to be replaced as the ideal model of beauty by the Venus de Milo. See John Barrell, ' "The Dangerous Goddess": Masculinity, Prestige and the Aesthetic in Early Eighteenth-Century Britain', *Cultural Critique*, 12 (Spring 1989), 101–31, for further discussion of transformations in the perception of Venus statues.

11 *Cashmere tunic*: tunic made of the high quality and expensive soft wool of the Kashmir goat.

22 *Ramsgate*: as well as spending holidays there as a child, Collins stayed at the Granville Hotel in Ramsgate, *en route* to Paris, on a sailing holiday in February 1872, and lodged there again in September and October of that year to recuperate from gout. He maintained his double domestic identity during the trip, lodging with Caroline Graves at 14 Nelson Crescent for some of the time, and as 'Mr Dawson' with Martha Rudd at the other side of the bay at Wellington Crescent for the remainder. See William M. Clarke, *The Secret Life of Wilkie Collins* (London, 1988), 135–6, for details of this and other aspects of Collins's private life.

24 *dressing-case*: compartmentalized dressing-cases of the kind described here were not uncommon travel items for middle-class men.

32 *Eccentricity*: as well as retaining its general meaning the term 'eccentricity' had acquired quite specific connota-

tions by 1875. It was often seen as the early manifestation of worrying signs of mental derangement. See, for example, Henry Maudsley: 'Eccentricity is certainly not always insanity, but there can be no question that it is often the outcome of an insane temperament, and may approach very near to, or actually pass into, insanity' (*Responsibility in Mental Disease* (London, 1874), 55–6). Andrew Wynter also writes of 'persons whose unsoundness of mind is taken for mere eccentricity or for moral perversity' (*The Borderlands of Insanity* (London, 1875), 45).

46 *Lincoln's Inn Fields*: Collins himself briefly studied for the Bar at Lincoln's Inn in 1846.

Macallan or Woodville, I was his wife: Collins is correct on this legal point.

47 *Portman Square*: Collins lived at 90 Gloucester Place, Portman Square, from September 1867 until 1888, the year before his death.

48 *to the nearest stationer's to borrow a Directory*: it was common for stationers to lend reference and other books in this way.

57 *pearl powder*: face-powder made up of French chalk, oxide of bismuth, and oxide of zinc which was widely used as a cosmetic in the mid-nineteenth century. 'A Lady's toilet-table is incomplete without a box of some absorbent powder . . . We are quite within limits in stating that many tons weight of such powders are used in this country annually' (G. W. Septimus Piesse, *The Art of Perfumery* (3rd edn., 1862), 316).

73 *'Come per me Sereno'*: 'How brightly dawns this day for me', the aria from Vincenzo Bellini's opera *La Sonnambula* (1831) in which the heroine's sleepwalking trance in the final act becomes a test of her fidelity and virtue.

77 *buhl*: brass, tortoise-shell, or other material, worked into ornamental patterns for inlaying.

the Venus Milo and the Venus Callipyge: these two Greek statues represent very different notions of femininity and of female sexuality conflated into a single mythological figure. The Melos Venus (*c.*150 BC), now in the Louvre in Paris, had become the central emblem of pure classical feminine beauty; the Callipygian Venus—'she who is showing her beautiful buttocks'—the last Hellenic Aphrodite, is explicitly sexually provocative, looking over her shoulder invitingly to admire herself narcissistically.

81 *Watteau costume*: idealized peasant dress. Jean Antoine Watteau (1684–1721), French artist whose voluptuous *fêtes galantes* formed an influential part of eighteenth-century French painting.

82 *Voltaire*: (1694–1778), famous French satirist and prolific author of plays, poetry, prose romances, and philosophical works. His best-known work is *Candide* (1759).

   History of England: probably Thomas Macaulay's *History of England* (vols. i–ii, 1849; vols. iii–iv, 1855).

   Annual Register: a summary of the chief historic events of the past year, first published by John Dodsley in 1758. Collins himself owned copies of this.

87 *'Clémence . . . 1840!'*: 'Clemence. Idol of my soul. Always faithful. Alas: 2nd April, 1840.'

93 *Do you like reading Trials?*: the publication of actual trials, reported either indirectly or verbatim, dates from the late eighteenth century and was an important element in the emergence of sensation fiction. Collins specifically used a case in Maurice Méjan's collection of eighteenth-century French trials, *Recueil des causes célèbres* (1807–14) as one of the sources for *The Woman in White*. He may well have based the Macallan case in *The Law and the Lady* partly on the Lovie case in J. Hill Burton's *Narratives from Criminal Trials in Scotland* (London, 1852); a copy of this is catalogued by M. L. Bennett as being amongst the books in his library at his death. However, the case bears even closer similarities to the Madeleine Smith case of 1857; the transcript of her trial was published in volume form in the same year. See following note and the Introduction.

101 *Not Proven*: this middle finding in the Scottish legal system can be traced back to the seventeenth century, and is still available as a finding to Scottish juries to this day.

In Scottish trials the jury is made up of fifteen people (not twelve, as in England) and the outcome of trials is based on majority, rather than unanimous verdict. The Not Proven verdict in effect results in an acquittal as the case cannot be brought against the accused again, although it clearly carries a stigma. Burton comments: 'This middle finding is peculiar to Scotland. Some have held it to be a valuable institution, as leaving the stigma of suspicion where there is not sufficient evidence to convict—a stigma which never leaves its object if he is guilty, and is easily removable if any event should occur enabling him to explain suspicious facts and make his innocence apparent. On the other hand, this form has been objected to as a too accessible resting-place for jurors too unwilling to incur the responsibility of finding guilty, and unable to reconcile their consciences to a finding of not guilty.' (*Narratives from Criminal Trials in Scotland*, ii. 61.) The Not Proven verdict was used in the cases of both John Lovie and Madeleine Smith. In Burton's account, John Lovie was a farmer living near Fraserburgh who was tried for the murder of Margaret Mackessar, a servant pregnant by him, by arsenic poisoning. The case of Madeleine Smith was much more notorious and dramatic. For details of the case and its relevance to *The Law and the Lady* see Introduction, pp. xix–xx.

121 *nasty French novels next*: French fiction (such as Flaubert's *Madame Bovary*, 1857) was widely considered in England to be sexually explicit and unsuitable reading for young ladies.

123 *for the murder of his wife*: this was the end of the first volume of the first edition. In the manuscript and in Harper's American edition 'Part Two: Paradise Regained' is inserted before the begining of Chapter XV.

125 *The Indictment*: legal document served on the accused and used as the basis of the formal accusation. Published trials often included the indictment, including the published version of the Madeleine Smith trial of 1857 (which is set out in a very similar way to the Macallan trial here), although the cases in Burton's *Narratives* are

simply summarized. Collins is drawing on his own early legal training and legal contacts here.

126 *Justiciary*: the judges (not the jury).

127 *Sheriff-Substitute*: in Scotland the Sheriff is the chief judge of the county or district. The Sheriff-Substitute is his deputy, a lawyer who would act as a full-time professional judge, and who would hear cases in the first instance.

Dean of Faculty: president of the Faculty of Advocates in Scotland, equivalent to the head of the Bar in England.

Procurator-Fiscal: public prosecutor in the Sherif's court.

Lord Advocate: principal law-officer of the Crown in Scotland, equivalent to the Attorney-General in England.

141 *Symptoms of poisoning by arsenic*: arsenic poisoning, to become a hackneyed motif of crime fiction, was one of the most common methods of murder cited in Burton's *Narratives of Criminal Trials in Scotland*, in the Madeleine Smith case, and elsewhere. Collins may well have consulted a medical textbook in describing the physical symptoms described on pp.136–8. A. W. Blyth's *Poisons, Their Effects and Detection: A Manual for the Use of Analytic Chemists and Experts* (3rd edn., London, 1895), notes of the effects of acute arsenic poisoning: 'There is an acrid feeling in the throat, with nausea; vomiting soon sets in, the ejected matters being at first of the substances eaten; later they may be bilious or even bloody, or composed of a whitish liquid . . . There is coldness of the extremity with great feebleness, and the pulse is small and difficult to feel' (p. 542).

147 *killing of insects . . . killing rats*: these common domestic uses of arsenic were often used as reasons for obtaining the poison, only available from a chemist's. Both Madeleine Smith and John Lovie bought arsenic from a druggist, ostensibly for poisoning rats (Burton, *Criminal Trials*, ii. 58–9).

150 *a remedy for the defects . . . of her complexion*: see note to
     p. 171

171 *the practice of eating arsenic . . . good health*: the eating of
     arsenic by the Styrian peasantry (Styria was a region
     which bordered Austria and Hungary) was in fact re-
     ported widely in the press in the early 1850s and caused
     quite a sensation. The counsel for Madeleine Smith's
     defence used the argument that the defendant had ob-
     tained the poison for cosmetic reasons, using articles in
     Chambers's Edinburgh Journal and *Blackwood's Edinburgh
     Magazine* to argue the widespread knowledge of this
     practice. 'The Poison-Eaters' in *Chambers's Journal*
     notes: 'In some districts of lower Austria and in Styria,
     especially in those mountainous parts bordering on Hun-
     gary, there prevails the strange habit of eating arsenic.
     The peasantry in particular are given to it . . . The
     poison-eaters have a twofold aim in their dangerous en-
     joyment: one of which is to obtain a fresh, healthy ap-
     pearance, and acquire a certain degree of *embonpoint*. On
     this account, therefore, gay village lads and lasses employ
     the dangerous agent, that they might become more at-
     tractive to each other; and it is really astonishing with
     what favourable results their endeavours are attended,
     for it is just the youthful poison-eaters that are, generally
     speaking, distinguished by a blooming complexion, and
     an appearance of exuberant health.' ('The Poison-
     Eaters', *Chambers's Edinburgh Journal*, 16 (1851), p. 389)

174 *My name . . . means . . . 'most unhappy'*: Dexter's Chris-
     tian name is self-consciously explained here; his surname
     is Latin for 'right', suggesting deftness and mental agility.
     Dexter's exposition of the meaning of his name can be
     seen as a comment on Collins's allusive use of names in
     general, the significance of which he expected his readers
     to recognize. 'Dexter' is also a pun on 'writer'.

196 *he is off to the war in Spain with a red cross on his arm*: the
     Red Cross was founded in 1859 by a Swiss, Henri Du-
     nant, to care for the sick and wounded in war. The
     International Committee of the Red Cross was founded
     in 1864. The 'war in Spain' refers to the fighting which

broke out in 1873 over Carlist claims to the monarchy. The *Graphic* featured illustrations of the war during the serialization of *The Law and the Lady*.

206 *Napoleon, at the sunrise of Austerlitz*: the Battle of Austerlitz on 2 December 1803 was Napoleon's most celebrated victory over the Russians and Austrians.

the new Centaur: a mythical horse with human body, arms, and head; also, more generally, a hybrid creature; a person or thing of double nature.

209 *Ariel*: an ironic reference to the airy spirit, Prospero's servant in *The Tempest*. By extension, Dexter becomes a parody of Prospero.

227 *Wandering Jew*: a legendary figure supposedly still roaming the earth because of his blasphemy, as prophesied by Jesus—'thou shalt wander till I return'—and who became a metaphor for conditions of displacement and exile generally. The Wandering Jew was also the subject of a novel by Eugene Sue, *Le Juif errant*, published in 1845.

230 *Flying Dutchman*: the captain of a ghostly ship believed to haunt the waters round the Cape of Good Hope, and considered by sailors to be an omen of disaster. According to the legend the captain Vanderdecken was condemned to sail forever as a punishment for blasphemy. Wagner's opera based on the legend, *Die fliegende Holländer*, was first produced in 1843.

248 *Revolution of Ninety Three*: the Terror following the French Revolution of 1789.

251 *Mrs Beauly poisoned her*: the end of Chapter XXIX marks the end of the second volume.

252 *Mrs Borgia-Beauly*: a reference to Lucrezia Borgia (1480–1519), the Italian duchess of Ferrara renowned for her underhand plots, whose assassination of her previous husband was secured by her father and brother.

260 '*Prometheus Unbound*': Percy Bysshe Shelley's epic poem of 1820 based on the Greek myth of Prometheus, the god who defied Zeus's authority by bringing fire, and thus the ability to control nature, to man. For this he was

punished by Zeus by being bound to a rock and having his liver perpetually eaten by eagles. Dexter is quoting from Act IV. ll. 319–24. In his Preface to the poem Shelley celebrates Prometheus as a figure who, like Satan, dares to challenge divine authority. Like the Flying Dutchman and the Wandering Jew, they form a subtext of transgressive figures, springing from Dexter's subconscious, who indirectly allude to Valeria's quest.

266 *The Domino Noir*: comic opera of 1837 by Daniel François Auber (1782–1871), one of the principal figures in the development of comic opera in France in the early nineteenth century. 'Domino' here means a loose cloak with half-mask worn to conceal identity, especially at a masked ball. The opera, centred round disguised and substituted identities, is obviously a self-reflexive allusion to the disguised identities at work in the story, as is made clear on p. 268

281 *he has his mind under the control of his will*: the doctor's description of Dexter's intermittent insanity corresponds to the notion of *monomania*, or partial insanity, common in the mid-nineteenth century. Here the patient suffers delusion or engages in obsessive behaviour in one area only; it was not seen as affecting his moral identity. This shifts in the late nineteenth century to the degenerative model, where latent features inevitably emerge. The figure of Dexter merges these two paradigms. On the reference to his eccentricity, see the note to p. 32. The question of the legal status of the insane, in terms of both their responsibility for criminal actions and their degree of reliability as witnesses, much exercised doctors and lawyers during the nineteenth century.

284 *weekly 'Enigmas'*: puzzles or mysteries of this kind were common features of popular weekly magazines. Again the reader's process of interpretation is projected into the text.

284–5 *I found Benjamin . . . passed my lips*: the first two paragraphs of this chapter are cut from the Harper's American edition. Inserted after the sentence beginning 'You will listen to Mr Playmore' is inserted: '(I had, of course, respected Mr Playmore's confidence in me, when Benjamin and I met on my return to the hotel. Not a word relating to the lawyer's horrible suspicion of Miserrimus Dexter had passed my lips.)' (Harper's edition, p. 109.)

288 '*I have done with Gleninch . . . in store for all of us*': in the Harper's edition this reads: ' "I shall never see this place again," I said.

"Never is a long day," retorted my companion. "And time has its surprises in store for all of us." ' (Harper's edition, p. 110.)

297 *to set up an Alibi*: although the term 'alibi' was a recognized legal term at this time, Collins could not have been sure that his readership would have been familiar with it.

299 *He caught my hand in his . . . I cried out for help*: this passage was cut from the original serialization in the *Graphic*. For details, see the Note on the Text, and Appendix.

307 *Queen's Messenger*: an official of the British Foreign Office whose duty it is to carry confidential messages to any Embassy abroad.

321 *We were all monkeys before we were men, and molecules before we were monkeys!*: a satirical reference to Darwin's arguments in *On the Origin of Species by Means of Natural Selection* (1859), which had, by now, become the dominant paradigm of change and development.

365 *the eruption which had overwhelmed the town*: a reference to the volcanic eruption of Mount Vesuvius which engulfed the Roman town of Pompeii in AD 79.

377 *the fragments of the letter must be!*: Collins's use of the image of the dust-heap is possibly an indirect allusion to Dickens's *Our Mutual Friend* (1865), and its complex connections between dirt, excrement, and money, although here the dust-heap functions much more explicitly as the 'unconscious' of the household.

382 *your husband*: the rest of this chapter is cut from the Harper's edition.

410 *be pleased to excuse them*: ',in bed' follows in the first edition.

THE WORLD'S CLASSICS

A Select List

JANE AUSTEN: Emma
Edited by James Kinsley and David Lodge

J. M. BARRIE: Peter Pan in Kensington Gardens & Peter and Wendy
Edited by Peter Hollindale

WILLIAM BECKFORD: Vathek
Edited by Roger Lonsdale

JOHN BUNYAN: The Pilgrim's Progress
Edited by N. H. Keeble

THOMAS CARLYLE: The French Revolution
Edited by K. J. Fielding and David Sorensen

GEOFFREY CHAUCER: The Canterbury Tales
Translated by David Wright

CHARLES DICKENS: Christmas Books
Edited by Ruth Glancy

MARIA EDGEWORTH: Castle Rackrent
Edited by George Watson

ELIZABETH GASKELL: Cousin Phillis and Other Tales
Edited by Angus Easson

THOMAS HARDY: A Pair of Blue Eyes
Edited by Alan Manford

HOMER: The Iliad
Translated by Robert Fitzgerald
Introduction by G. S. Kirk

HENRIK IBSEN: An Enemy of the People, The Wild Duck,
Rosmersholm
Edited and Translated by James McFarlane

HENRY JAMES: The Ambassadors
Edited by Christopher Butler

JOCELIN OF BRAKELOND:
Chronicle of the Abbey of Bury St. Edmunds
Translated by Diana Greenway and Jane Sayers

BEN JONSON: Five Plays
Edited by G. A. Wilkes

LEONARDO DA VINCI: Notebooks
Edited by Irma A. Richter

HERMAN MELVILLE: The Confidence-Man
Edited by Tony Tanner

PROSPER MÉRIMÉE: Carmen and Other Stories
Translated by Nicholas Jotcham

EDGAR ALLAN POE: Selected Tales
Edited by Julian Symons

MARY SHELLEY: Frankenstein
Edited by M. K. Joseph

BRAM STOKER: Dracula
Edited by A. N. Wilson

ANTHONY TROLLOPE: The American Senator
Edited by John Halperin

OSCAR WILDE: Complete Shorter Fiction
Edited by Isobel Murray

VIRGINIA WOOLF: Mrs Dalloway
Edited by Claire Tomalin

A complete list of Oxford Paperbacks, including The World's Classics, OPUS, Past Masters, Oxford Authors, Oxford Shakespeare, and Oxford Paperback Reference, is available in the UK from the Arts and Reference Publicity Department (BH), Oxford University Press, Walton Street, Oxford OX2 6DP.

In the USA, complete lists are available from the Paperbacks Marketing Manager, Oxford University Press, 200 Madison Avenue, New York, NY 10016.

Oxford Paperbacks are available from all good bookshops. In case of difficulty, customers in the UK can order direct from Oxford University Press Bookshop, Freepost, 116 High Street, Oxford, OX1 4BR, enclosing full payment. Please add 10 per cent of published price for postage and packing.

Frankenstein

MARY SHELLEY

Adapted by Bob Blaisdell
Illustrated by Thea Kliros

DOVER PUBLICATIONS, INC.
Mineola, New York

DOVER CHILDREN'S THRIFT CLASSICS
EDITOR OF THIS VOLUME: SUSAN L. RATTINER

Bibliographical Note

This Dover edition, first published in 1997, is a new abridgment of a standard edition. The illustrations have been prepared specially for the present edition.

Library of Congress Cataloging-in-Publication Data

Shelley, Mary Wollstonecraft, 1797–1851.
    Frankenstein / Mary Shelley ; adapted by Bob Blaisdell ; illustrated by Thea Kliros.
    p.   cm. — (Dover children's thrift classics)
    "This Dover edition . . . is a new abridgment of a standard edition. The illustrations have been prepared specially for the present edition"—Bib. note.
    Summary: A monster assembled by a scientist from parts of dead bodies develops a mind of his own as he learns to loathe himself and hate his creator.
    ISBN 0-486-29930-9 (pbk.)
    [1. Monsters—Fiction. 2. Horror stories.] I. Blaisdell, Robert. II. Kliros, Thea, ill. III. Title. IV. Series.
PZ7.S54145Fu   1997
[Fic]—dc21   97-11617
                                                      CIP
                                                      AC

Manufactured in the United States of America
Dover Publications, Inc., 31 East 2nd Street, Mineola, N.Y. 11501

Contents

As I walk in the streets of Petersburg, I feel a cold northern breeze.

1. The Arctic Ocean Stranger

St. Petersburg, Russia, December 11, 17—
My dear sister Margaret,

I address this journal to you, in England, in the hope that one day you will receive it.

I am already far north of London; and as I walk in the streets of Petersburg, I feel a cold northern breeze, which has traveled from the regions toward which I am destined to go. I cannot believe that the North Pole is the home of frost and emptiness; it presents itself to my imagination as the region of beauty and delight. There, Margaret, the sun is forever visible. There snow and frost have disappeared; and, sailing over a calm sea, we may sail to a land more wonderful and beautiful than any ever seen. What may not be expected in a country of eternal light? I may there discover the power of magnetism, which attracts the needle of a compass. I shall satisfy my curiosity with the sight of a part of the world never before visited. Think of the benefit I shall bestow on all mankind by discovering near the pole a passage to those other countries.

My courage is strong; but my hopes waver, and I am often depressed. I am about to proceed on a long and difficult voyage, one that will demand all my strength. I must not only keep up the spirits of my sailors, but also sometimes my own, when theirs are failing.

1

Archangel, Russia, March 28, 17—

I have hired a vessel and am busy collecting my sailors. But there is one thing I lack. I have no friend, Margaret, with whom to share my joy. I am twenty-eight and as uneducated as many schoolboys. I greatly need a friend who would try to improve my mind.

Well, these are useless complaints; I shall certainly find no friend on the wide ocean, nor even here in Archangel, on the White Sea, among merchants and seamen.

It is impossible to describe for you the trembling, half pleasurable and half fearful, with which I am preparing to set out. I am going to unexplored regions of the Arctic Ocean, to "the land of mist and snow."

July 7, 17—

I am well advanced on my voyage. I am in good spirits; my men are bold and determined, and the floating sheets of ice that pass us do not appear to bother them. We have already reached a very high latitude; but it is the height of summer, and although it is not so warm as in England, the southern gales, which blow us toward those shores I wish to reach, give us a surprising warmth.

August 5, 17—

So strange an accident has happened that I have to write it all down, although it is very likely that you will see me before these journals can be sent to you.

Last Monday (July 31) we were nearly surrounded by ice, which closed in the ship on all sides. Our situation was somewhat dangerous, especially as we were enveloped by a very thick fog. We held fast, hoping that some change would take place.

About two o'clock the mist cleared away, and we
beheld, stretched out in every direction, vast plains of
ice, which seemed to have no end. Some of my com-
rades groaned, and I began to grow anxious, when a
strange sight suddenly attracted our attention. We saw

A being in the shape of a man sat in the sledge and guided the dogs.

a low carriage, fixed on a sledge and drawn by dogs,
pass on toward the north, at the distance of half a mile;
a being that had the shape of a man, but apparently of
gigantic stature, sat in the sledge and guided the dogs.
We watched the rapid progress of the traveler with our
telescopes until he disappeared.

This vision excited our wonder. We were, we
believed, many hundred miles from any land; but this
sighting of a man seemed to suggest that it was not so
distant as we had supposed. Shut in by the ice, however, we could not follow his track.

Before night the ice broke and freed a path for our
ship. We, however, lay to until the morning, fearing to

meet in the dark those large loose masses that float about after the breaking up of the ice. I made use of this time to rest for a few hours.

In the morning, however, as soon as it was light, I went upon the deck and found all the sailors busy on one side of the vessel, apparently talking to someone in the sea. It was, in fact, a sledge, like the one we˙ had seen before, which had drifted toward us in the night on a large piece of ice. Only one dog remained alive; but there was a human being within it whom the sailors were trying to talk into coming aboard. He was not, as the other traveler seemed to be, a native of some undiscovered island, but a European. When I appeared on deck, the shipmaster said, "Here is our captain, and he will not allow you to perish on the open sea."

On seeing me, the stranger addressed me in English, although with a foreign accent. "Before I come on board your vessel," said he, "will you have the kindness to inform me where you are going?"

You may guess my surprise on hearing such a question addressed to me from a man on the brink of death and to whom I supposed my vessel would have been salvation. I replied, however, that we were on a voyage of discovery toward the North Pole.

Upon hearing this, he appeared satisfied and agreed to come on board. Good God! Margaret, if you had seen the man who bargained in this way, your surprise would have been boundless. His arms and legs were nearly frozen, his body thin and worn out. I never saw a man in so wretched a condition. We tried to carry him into the cabin, but as soon as he left the fresh air, he fainted. We brought him back to the deck and restored him by rubbing him with brandy and forcing him to drink a small dose. As soon as he showed signs of life, we wrapped him up in blankets and placed him near the chimney of the kitchen stove. Slowly he recovered and ate a little soup.

Two days passed in this way before he was able to speak, and I often feared that his sufferings had stolen his wits. When he had in some degree recovered, I had him moved to my own cabin and attended to him as much as my duty would permit. I never saw a more interesting creature: his eyes have generally a wild expression, but there are moments when, if anyone performs an act of kindness toward him, his whole face lights up with goodness and sweetness. But he is generally sad, and sometimes he gnashes his teeth.

When my guest was a little recovered, I had great trouble keeping the men from asking him a thousand questions. The lieutenant asked why he had come so far upon the ice in so strange a vehicle.

The sufferer's face became gloomy, and he replied, "To seek the one who fled from me."

"And did the man you are chasing travel in the same way?"

"Yes."

"Then I fancy we have seen him, for the day before we picked you up, we saw some dogs drawing a sledge with a man in it, across the ice."

This aroused the stranger's attention, and he asked many questions concerning the route that the demon, as he called him, had taken. Soon after, when he was alone with me, he said, "I have, doubtless, excited your curiosity, as well as that of these good people; but you are too considerate to ask questions."

"Certainly. It would indeed be very rude of me to trouble you."

"And yet you rescued me from a strange and dangerous situation; you have kindly restored me to life."

Soon after this he asked if I thought that the breaking

up of the ice had destroyed the other sledge. I replied that the ice had not broken until nearly midnight, and the traveler might have arrived at a safe place before then.

From this moment the stranger wished to be up on deck as much as possible to watch for the sledge that we had seen; but I have persuaded him to remain in the cabin, for he is far too weak to bear the frigid air. I have promised him that someone will watch for him and give him immediate news if any such sledge should appear.

The stranger has gradually improved in health but is very silent and appears uneasy when anyone except me enters the cabin. Yet his manners are so gentle that the sailors are all interested in him. For my own part, I begin to love him as a brother, and his constant and deep grief fills me with sympathy. He must have been a fine man in his better days, being even now so attractive and good.

I said in one of my earlier entries, my dear Margaret, that I should find no friend on the wide ocean; yet I have found a man who, before his spirit had been broken by misery, I should have been happy to have had as a friend.

August 13, 17—

My guest is now much recovered from his illness and is continually on the deck, watching for the sledge. Although unhappy, he interests himself deeply in the projects of others. He has often talked with me on mine. I told him how gladly I would sacrifice my fortune, my life, my every hope, to the success of my quest. One man's life or death would be a small price to pay for the knowledge I looked for, to find a passage through the polar waters to the Pacific.

As I spoke of such willing sacrifice, a dark gloom spread over his face, and finally a groan burst from him. I paused; at length he spoke: "Unhappy man! Do you share my madness? Hear me; let me tell my tale, and you will give up such ideas."

He asked me the story of my earlier years. I spoke of my desire of finding a friend, and that a man could hardly be happy who did not enjoy such a blessing.

"I agree with you," replied the stranger. "I once had a friend, the most noble of human creatures, and am entitled, therefore, to speak of friendship. You have hope, and the world before you, and have no cause for despair. But I—I have lost everything and cannot begin life anew."

As he said this, his face expressed grief; he became silent and returned to his cabin.

August 19, 17—

The stranger said to me, "You may easily see, Captain Walton, that I have suffered terrible misfortunes. I had decided at one time that the memory of these evils should die with me, but you have changed my mind. You seek for knowledge and wisdom, as I once did; and I truly hope that the result of your wishes may not be a snake to bite you, as mine has been. I do not know that the telling of my story will be useful to you; yet I imagine that you may find a moral for your own situation. Prepare to hear of occurrences that are usually called unbelievable. I cannot doubt, however, that with your knowledge of all the details, my tale will show its truth."

I felt the greatest eagerness to hear the story and said, "Yes, I am curious. I hope as well that I may be able to help you once I know your troubles."

"I thank you," he replied, "for your sympathy, but

there is no help. I wait but for one event, and then I shall rest in peace. Nothing can change my fate; listen to my story, and you will see how unchangeable it is."

He then told me that his name was Victor Frankenstein and that he would begin his story the next day, when I should have some time.

I have decided that every night, when I am not busy with my duties, I shall write down, as nearly as possible in his own words, what he has told me during the day. Even now, as I begin my task, his full-toned voice swells in my ears; his bright eyes fix on me with all their sad sweetness; I see his thin hand moving as he talks, while the lines on his face are lit up by his soul. Strange and frightening must be his story, terrible the storm that overtook such a fine vessel on its course and wrecked it!

2. Victor Frankenstein Begins His Story

I AM SWISS by birth, from Geneva, and my family is one of the most distinguished of that country. My father was respected by all who knew him for his honesty and civic-mindedness. He passed his younger days busy with the country's affairs, which prevented his marrying early. It was not until the end of his life that he became a husband and father.

There was a large difference between the ages of my parents, but this only seemed to bring them closer. He admired and respected her virtues. He did everything to fulfill her wishes and make life easy. Caroline had suffered as a girl, tending her weak and ill father, who had been my father's best friend. He tried to shelter her, as an exotic plant is sheltered by the gardener, and to surround her with all that could please her. Her health had been shaken by what she had gone through with her father. In the two years before their marriage, my father had gradually given up all his public duties; and immediately after their wedding they traveled to Italy, where she could rebuild her strength.

From Italy they visited Germany and France. I, their eldest child, was born in Naples, Italy, and as a young child went with them on their rambles. I remained for several years their only child. Much as they were attached to each other, they gave me unbounded love.

I was their plaything and idol—their child, the innocent and helpless creature given them by heaven.

For a long time I was their only care. When I was about five years old, they passed a week on the shores of Lake Como. Their kindness often made them visit the cottages of the poor. This, to my mother, was more than a duty; it was a passion.

During one of their walks, they discovered an unusually poor cottage, with a number of half-clothed children about it. One day, when my father had gone by himself to Milan, my mother and I visited this home. There was a hardworking peasant and his wife, bent down by care and labor, feeding a skimpy meal to five hungry children. Among these there was one who attracted my mother far above all the rest. The four others were dark-eyed, hardy little urchins; this child was thin and very fair. Her hair was gold, and her eyes blue and clear.

The peasant woman, seeing that my mother had fixed eyes of wonder and admiration on this lovely girl, told her story. She was not her child, but the daughter of a Milanese nobleman. Her mother, a German, had died giving birth to her. The infant had been placed with these good people to nurse: they were better off then. They had not been long married, and their eldest child was but just born. The child's father was shortly thereafter jailed or killed; no one ever knew. In either case his property and wealth were taken over by the government; his child became an orphan. She stayed with her foster parents and bloomed in their poor home.

When my father returned from Milan, he found playing with me in the hall of our villa a child fairer than a painted angel. My mother had asked her guardians to give her up to be raised by our family. They were fond of the sweet orphan, but it would be unfair, they

I looked upon Elizabeth as mine to protect, love, and cherish.

thought, to keep her in poverty when fortune offered her such a home. The result was that Elizabeth Lavenza became a child of my parents—my more than sister— the beautiful and adored companion of all my interests and pleasures.

Everyone loved Elizabeth. On the evening before she was brought to my home, my mother had said playfully, "I have a pretty present for Victor—tomorrow he shall have it."

And when, the next day, she presented Elizabeth to me as her promised gift, I looked upon Elizabeth as mine—mine to protect, love, and cherish. We called each other "cousin." No word, no expression could describe what she meant to me—my more than sister, since till death she was to be mine only.

We were brought up together; there was not quite a year's difference in our ages. While she admired the magnificent appearance of the world around our beautiful Swiss home, I delighted in looking for its origins

and causes. The world was to me a secret that I desired
to uncover. Curiosity about the hidden laws of nature is
among the earliest feelings I remember.

On the birth of a second son, Ernest, my junior by
seven years, my parents gave up their wandering life
entirely and fixed themselves in their native country.
We had a house in Geneva and country home in Belrive,
the eastern shore of Como. We lived mostly in the country. Several years later another son, William, was born.

I cared little, in general, for my schoolmates. But I
enjoyed the closest friendship with one—Henry
Clerval, the son of a merchant in Geneva. He was tal-
ented and imaginative.

No human being could have passed a happier childhood than I. My parents were possessed by the spirit of
kindness. They were the creators of all the many
delights we enjoyed. When I mingled with other fami-
lies, I noticed how fortunate I was, and I was grateful.

I was hot-tempered, however, and passionate. My
passions led me not toward childish games but to an
eager desire to learn. Yet I was not interested in the
grammar of languages, the laws of governments, or pol-
itics. It was the secrets of heaven and earth that I
desired to learn. Meanwhile Clerval busied himself with
the stage of life; the virtues of heroes and the actions of
men were his interest.

I feel pleasure in remembering my childhood, before
bad luck colored my thoughts and changed them into
gloominess. However, in telling the story of my early
days, I also record those events that led to my misery,
for when I would try to recall the moment of birth of
that passion that later ruled my fate, I found it arose,
like a river, from small and seemingly insignificant
sources; but, swelling as it went on, it became the flood
that has swept away all my hopes and joys.

3. Frankenstein's Monster

NATURAL SCIENCE IS the study that has led to my fate; I desire, therefore, in this story, to state those facts that led to my fondness for it. I have always had a longing to penetrate the secrets of nature. In spite of the hard work and wonderful discoveries of modern scientists, I always came away from my studies unsatisfied.

The uneducated peasant looked at the forces around him and knew their practical uses. The most learned scientist knew little more. He had partially uncovered the face of nature, but her deeper mysteries remained. He might take apart matter and give it names, but final causes were utterly unknown to him. I had tried to know nature, and I had given up.

But here were books and here were men who had penetrated deeper and knew more. I took them at their word, and I became their follower.

I was, to a great degree, self-taught with regard to my favorite studies. My father was not scientific, and I was left to struggle with a child's blindness trying to slake my thirst for knowledge. I entered into the search for the elixir of life. What glory would come to the discovery if I could keep disease from human beings and make man invulnerable to any but a violent death!

Nor were these my only visions. The raising of ghosts or devils was a promise given by my favorite authors;

13

and if my magic spells were always unsuccessful, I
blamed myself rather than my instructors. And so for a
time I was busy with impossible science, guided by my
heated imagination and childish reasoning, till an accident again changed the current of my ideas.

When I was about fifteen years old, we had gone to
our house near Belrive, where we witnessed a most violent and terrible thunderstorm. It came from behind
the mountains of Jura, and the thunder burst with
frightful loudness from various quarters of the heavens. I remained, while the storm lasted, watching its
progress with curiosity and delight. As I stood at the
door, I saw a stream of fire strike an old and beautiful
oak that stood about twenty yards from our house; and
as soon as the dazzling light vanished, the oak had dis-

I saw a stream of fire strike an old and beautiful oak tree near our house.

appeared, and nothing remained but an exploded stump.

Before this I did not know the laws of electricity. At this time a man of great research in natural science was visiting us, and he explained a theory he had formed on the subject of electricity and electric shock. All that had so long had my attention suddenly became worthless. I now made myself study mathematics and the other branches of science that had secure foundations.

When I reached the age of seventeen, my parents decided that I should become a student at the University of Ingolstadt. I had before attended the schools of Geneva, but my father thought it necessary for the completion of my education that I should be experienced in other customs and manners than those of my native country. But before the time I was to leave, the first misfortune of my life occurred—a sign of my future misery.

Elizabeth had caught the scarlet fever; her illness was severe, and she was in the greatest danger. During her illness we urged my mother not to be the nurse. She had first given in to us, but when she heard that the life of her favorite was in trouble, she could no longer hold herself back. She attended Elizabeth's sickbed; her nursing defeated the danger of the fever—Elizabeth was saved, but the results of this action were fatal to her rescuer. On the third day my mother sickened.

On her deathbed this best of women retained her personal strength and kindness. She joined the hands of Elizabeth and me.

"My children," she said, "my hopes of future happiness were on the prospect of your marriage. This expectation will now be the hope of your father. Elizabeth, my love, you must supply my place to my younger children. Alas! I regret that I am taken from you; and, happy and beloved as I have been, it is hard to leave you all. But these are not good thoughts; I will try to prepare myself cheerfully for death and will hope to meet you in another world."

She died calmly, and her face expressed affection even in death. I need not describe the feelings of those whose dearest relationships are cut off by death. It is so long before the mind can tell itself that she, whom we saw every day and whose very life appeared a part of our own, can have left forever. My mother was dead, but we had still duties to perform; we had to continue our course and learn to consider ourselves lucky for the loved ones whom death has not taken.

My leaving for Ingolstadt, which had been delayed by these events, was now again decided upon. The day of my departure arrived. Clerval spent the last evening with us. He had tried to persuade his father to allow him to accompany me and to become my fellow student, but in vain. His father was a narrow-minded trader and saw idleness and ruin in the educational ambitions of his son.

When at dawn I went down to the carriage that was to take me away, they were all there—my father to bless me, Clerval to shake my hand, my Elizabeth to tell me to write often to her.

I threw myself into the carriage and started away. I, who had ever been surrounded by kind friends, was now alone. My journey to Ingolstadt was long and tiring. At length the white steeple of the town met my eyes. I got out and was brought to my room to spend the evening as I pleased.

The next morning I delivered my letters of introduction and paid a visit to some of the professors. Chance led me first to Monsieur Krempe, professor of natural science. He was an unrefined and rude man, but deeply knowledgeable of the secrets of science. He asked me several questions concerning my progress in the different branches of science. I mentioned the names of the principal authors I had studied. The professor stared. "Have you," he said, "really spent your time in studying such nonsense?"

"Yes."

"My dear sir, you must begin your studies entirely anew."

So saying, he stepped aside and wrote down a list of several books of natural science that he wanted me to read, and dismissed me after mentioning that in the beginning of the following week he intended to begin a course of general lectures on natural science and that Monsieur Waldman, a fellow professor, would lecture on chemistry on alternate days.

Although I could not agree to go hear that little conceited fellow Krempe deliver lectures, I did attend Monsieur Waldman's. This professor was very unlike his colleague. He appeared about fifty years of age, with a kind face; a few gray hairs covered his temples, but those at the back of his head were nearly black. He was short but stood straight up; and his voice was the sweetest I had ever heard.

Monsieur Waldman began his lecture with a review of the history of chemistry and the various improvements made by different men of learning. He then took a quick view of the present state of the science and explained many of its elementary terms. After having made a few experiments, he concluded the day with a short speech, which I shall never forget:

> The ancient teachers of this science [the very ones I had studied at home] promised impossibilities and performed nothing. The modern masters promise very little. They know that one metal cannot be changed into anoth-

er and that the elixir of life is a fantasy. But these scientists, who seem only to dabble in dirt and to hunch over the microscope, have indeed performed miracles. They see into the depths of nature and show how she works in her hiding places. They go up into the heavens; they have discovered how the blood circulates, and the nature of the air we breathe. They have acquired new and almost unlimited powers; they can command the thunders of heaven, mimic the earthquake, and even mock the invisible world with its own shadows.

Such were the professor's words—rather, let me say, the words of fate—that came to destroy me. As he went on, my mind was filled with one thought, one idea, one purpose. So much has been done, exclaimed the soul of Frankenstein—more, far more, will I achieve; walking in their footsteps, I will pioneer a new way, explore unknown powers, and unfold to the world the deepest mysteries of creation.

The next day I paid Monsieur Waldman a visit. His manners in private were even more mild and attractive than in public. I gave him the same account of my former studies as I had given to Monsieur Krempe. He heard with attention the little story concerning my studies and smiled at the authors' names, but without mocking me. He said that "these were men to whose untiring work modern scientists were indebted for most of the foundations of their knowledge. Their work has made ours easier. The work of men of genius is nearly always a boon to mankind." I asked him to recommend some books.

"If your wish," said Monsieur Waldman, "is to become really a man of science and not merely a petty experimentalist, I should advise you to study every branch of natural science, including mathematics."

He then took me into his laboratory and explained to me the uses of his various machines, instructing me as

*He took me into his laboratory and showed me
how to use the machines.*

to what I ought to buy and promising me the use of his
own when I should have advanced far enough in the
science. He also gave me the list of books I had requested, and I left.

Thus ended a memorable day for me; it decided my
destiny.

From this day natural science, especially chemistry,
became nearly my sole occupation. I read those works
on these subjects. I attended the lectures and became
acquainted with the scientists of the university, and I
found even in Monsieur Krempe a great deal of sound
sense and information, combined, it is true, with rudeness. In Monsieur Waldman I found a true friend.

Because I studied so hard, my progress was rapid.
Two years passed in my studies, during which time I
paid no visit to Geneva. In other studies you go as far

as others have gone before you, and there is nothing more to know; but in a scientific study there is always food for discovery and wonder. At the end of two years, I made some discoveries in the improvement of some chemical instruments, which gained me great admiration at the university. At this point, because my professors had no more to teach me, I thought of returning to my friends and my native town, but something happened that kept me there.

One of the studies that had especially attracted me was the structure of the human frame. Where, I often asked myself, did the principle of life originate? It was a bold question, the answer to which has always been shrouded in mystery. I determined from then on to apply myself to those branches of science that relate to physiology, the study of the body. Had I not had tremendous enthusiasm, this study would have been dull and almost intolerable. To examine the causes of life, we must first have the examination of death. I studied anatomy, but this was not enough; I must also observe the natural decay of the human body.

I had no supernatural horrors. To me a graveyard was merely the place that received dead bodies. Now I was led to look at the cause and progress of this decay and forced to spend days and nights in tombs. I saw how the fine form of man broke down and wasted away; I saw the worms take over our soft tissues. I paused, examining and analyzing all the details that showed the change from life to death and death to life, until from the midst of this darkness a sudden light broke in upon me—a light so brilliant and wondrous, yet so simple, that while I became dizzy with what it revealed, I was surprised that after so many men of genius who had tried to do so, I alone discovered so astonishing a secret.

Remember, I am not recording the vision of a madman. The stages of discovery were distinct and probable. After days and nights of incredible labor, I succeeded in discovering the cause of life; even more, I became myself capable of bringing to life lifeless matter. What had been the study and desire of the wisest men since the creation of the world was now within my grasp.

I see by your eagerness and the wonder and hope that your eyes express, my friend, that you expect to be informed of the secret that I know; that cannot be. Listen patiently until the end of my story, and you will understand why I will not talk about it. Learn from me, at least by example, how dangerous is knowledge and how much happier is that man who believes his native town to be the world than he who tries to become greater than his nature will allow.

When I found so astonishing a power placed within my hands, I hesitated a long time concerning the manner in which I should use it. Although I had the power to animate matter, yet to prepare a body, with all its fibers, muscles, and veins, still remained a work of unimaginable difficulty. I doubted at first whether I should try to create a being like myself or one of simpler organization; but my imagination was too excited by my first success to doubt my ability to give life to an animal as complex as man.

I prepared myself for many failures, but I never doubted that I would finally succeed. As the smallness of the parts slowed down my work, I decided to make a being of gigantic stature; that is to say, about eight feet in height. After having spent some months in collecting and arranging my materials, I began.

A new species would bless me as its creator. Many happy and excellent creatures would owe their existence to me. No father could claim the gratitude of his child so completely as I would deserve theirs. I thought that if I could animate lifeless matter, I might in time (although I now found it impossible) renew life where death had come.

During the night, I collected bones, organs, and flesh from tombs.

The moon gazed on my midnight labors while I chased nature to her hiding places. I collected bones, organs, and flesh from tombs. In a cell at the top of the house, separated from all the other apartments by a staircase, I kept my workshop of creation. The dissecting room and the slaughterhouse gave me many of my materials; and often I turned with loathing and disgust from what I was doing even as I brought my work near to completion.

The summer months passed while I was so engaged, heart and soul, in one project. My father did not scold me in his letters and took notice of my silence only by asking what I was studying. Every night I had a fever, and I became nervous; the fall of a leaf startled me, and I shunned my fellow creatures as if I had been guilty of a crime.

It was a dreary night in November when I beheld the fulfillment of my work. I collected the instruments of life around me, hoping that I might infuse a spark of being into the lifeless thing that lay at my feet. It was already one in the morning; the rain pattered against the panes, and my candle was nearly burned out when, by the glimmer of the light, I saw the dull yellow eye of the creature open; it breathed hard, and a convulsion jolted its arms and legs.

How can I describe my emotions or the wretch whom I had created? His limbs were in proportion to his body, and I had selected his features as beautiful. Great God! His yellow skin scarcely covered the work of muscles and arteries beneath; his hair was lustrous black and flowing, his teeth pearly white; but these features only formed a more horrid contrast with his watery eyes, shriveled complexion, and straight black lips.

For nearly two years I had worked hard, with the sole purpose of giving life to a lifeless body. For this I had deprived myself of rest and health. Now that I had finished, the beauty of the dream vanished, and breathless horror and disgust filled my heart. Unable to bear the sight of the being I had created, I rushed out of the room and continued a long time walking back and forth across my bedroom, unable to sleep. At last I threw myself on the bed in my clothes and slept, but I was disturbed by the wildest dreams. I started from my sleep with horror.

I beheld the wretch—the miserable monster I had created.

By the dim and yellow light of the moon, as it forced its way through the window shutters, I beheld the wretch—the miserable monster I had created. He held up the curtain of the bed; and his eyes were fixed on me. His jaws opened, and he muttered some sounds as a grin wrinkled his cheeks. He might have spoken, but I did not hear; one hand was stretched out, seemingly to stop me, but I escaped and rushed downstairs.

I hid in the courtyard belonging to the house where I lived, and I remained there the rest of the night, walking up and down, listening, fearing each sound as if it were announcing the approach of the demonical corpse to which I had so miserably given life.

Oh! No man could stand the horror of that face. I had gazed on him while unfinished; he was ugly then, but when those muscles and joints were able to move, he became unimaginably uglier.

At length morning dawned. The porter opened the gates of the court, and I ran out into the streets. I did not dare to return to my apartment, but at every turning I feared meeting the wretch. I continued walking for some time, trying, by exercise, to ease my mind. I crossed the streets without any clear idea of where I was or what I was doing.

I soon came to the inn at which the various coaches and carriages usually stopped. For some reason I paused here; but I remained some minutes with my eyes on a coach that was coming toward me from the other end of the street. As it drew nearer, I saw that it was a Swiss vehicle; it stopped just where I was standing, and as the door opened, I saw Henry Clerval, who, on seeing me, instantly sprang out. "My dear Frankenstein," exclaimed he, "how glad I am to see you! How lucky that you should be here at the very moment of my arrival!"

Nothing could equal my delight in seeing him; I grasped his hand and in a moment forgot my horror and misfortune; I felt suddenly, and for the first time during many months, calm and joyful. I welcomed my friend, and we walked toward my college.

Clerval said, "You may imagine how great the difficulty was to persuade my father that all necessary knowledge is not contained in bookkeeping. But his affection for me eventually overcame his dislike of education, and he has permitted me to come here to college."

"It gives me great delight to see you; but tell me how are my father, brothers, and Elizabeth."

"Very well and very happy, only a little worried that they hear from you so seldom. But my dear Frankenstein," he said, gazing directly into my weary eyes, "I did not before notice how very ill you appear; so thin and pale; you look as if you had not slept for several nights."

"You have guessed right; I have lately been so deeply buried in one project that I have not allowed myself enough rest, as you see; but I hope that this project is now at an end and that I am finally free."

I could not bear to think of the event of the past night. I walked quickly, and we soon arrived at my college. I then reflected that the creature I had left in my apartment might still be there, alive and walking about. I dreaded seeing this monster, but I feared still more that Henry might see him. Asking him, then, to remain a few minutes at the bottom of the stairs, I darted up toward my room. I threw the door open, as children do when they expect a ghost to stand waiting for them on the other side; but nothing appeared. I stepped in: the apartment was empty. I could hardly believe that so great a good fortune could have come to me, but when

I saw that my enemy had fled, I clapped my hands for joy and ran down to Clerval.

He at first attributed my high spirits to his arrival, but when he watched me more carefully, he saw a wildness in my eyes, and my loud, strange laughter frightened him.

"My dear Victor," he cried, "what is the matter? Do not laugh that way. How ill you are! What is the cause of all this?"

"Do not ask me," I cried, putting my hands before my eyes, for I imagined I saw the dreaded creature glide into the room. "Oh, save me! Save me!" I fell down in a fit.

4. Illness and Death

THIS WAS THE beginning of a nervous fever that confined me for several months. During all that time
Henry was my only nurse. He spared my father and
Elizabeth the news of the severity of my illness. Surely
nothing but his unbounded attention could have
restored me to life.

Slowly, but with frequent relapses, I recovered. In a
short time I became as cheerful as I had been before I
developed my passion for creating life.

"Dearest Clerval," I exclaimed, "how kind, how very
good you are to me. This whole winter, instead of pursuing your studies, as you promised yourself, you have
attended me in my sick room. How shall I ever repay
you?"

"I may speak to you on one subject, may I not?"

I trembled. One subject! What could it be? Could he
talk about something about which I dared not even
speak?

"Calm yourself," said Clerval, "I will not mention it if
it bothers you; but your father and cousin would be
very happy if they received a letter from you in your
own handwriting. They hardly know how ill you have
been and are worried at the long silence."

"Is that all, my dear Henry? Of course my first
thought is of those dear, dear friends I love!"

"If this is so, my friend, you will perhaps be glad to

see a letter that has been lying here some days for you;
it is from your cousin, I believe."

Clerval then put the following letter into my hands. It
was from my own Elizabeth:

My dearest cousin,

You have been ill, and even the constant letters from
dear kind Henry are not enough to reassure me on your
account. You are forbidden to write—to hold a pen; yet
one word from you, dear Victor, is necessary to calm
our fears.

Get well—and return to us. You will find a happy,
cheerful home and friends who love you dearly. Your
father's health is good, and he asks but to see you. How
pleased you would be to see your younger brother
Ernest. He is now sixteen and full of energy and spirit.
He looks upon studying as hateful; he spends his time
in the open air, climbing the hills or rowing on the lake.
I fear that he will become an idler unless we allow him
to do as he wishes and enter a military career in a distant country.

Little change, except the growth of the dear children,
has taken place since you left us. I must say a few
words to you, my dear cousin, of little darling William.
I wish you could see him; he is very tall for his age, with
sweet blue eyes, dark eyelashes, and curling hair. When
he smiles, two little dimples appear on each cheek.

I have written myself into a better mood, dear cousin;
but my worry about you returns upon me as I finish.
Write, dearest Victor—one line, one word will be a
blessing to us. Ten thousand thanks to Henry for his
kindness and his letters. Adieu! My cousin, take care of
yourself, and, I beg you, write!

Elizabeth
Geneva, March 18, 17—

"Dear, dear Elizabeth!" I said when I had read her letter. "I will write instantly and relieve them from worrying." I wrote, and this action greatly tired me; but my health was returning, and in another two weeks I was able to leave my chamber.

Clerval had come to the university to make himself the complete master of Oriental languages, and he easily persuaded me, fed up with science, to study with him. I felt great relief in being the fellow pupil with my friend, and found not only instruction but peace in the works of the Orientalists. When you read their writings, life appears to consist of a warm sun and a garden of roses.

Clerval had come to the university, and I studied with him.

Summer passed away in these studies, and my return to Geneva was fixed for the end of fall; but I was delayed by several events, and winter and snow arrived, making the roads impassable. I put off my journey until the spring.

The month of May had already come, and every day I expected the letter that was to fix the date of my departure. Henry proposed a walking tour in the area around Ingolstadt. I agreed with pleasure to this. We passed two weeks in these rambles; my health and spirits had long come back to me, and they gained strength from the exercise. I became the same happy creature who, a few years ago, loved and beloved by all, had no sorrow or care.

We returned to our college on a Sunday afternoon; the peasants were dancing, and everyone we met appeared happy. My own spirits were high, and I bounded along with feelings of joy.

In my chambers I found the following letter from my father:

My dear Victor,

You have probably waited for a letter to fix the date of your return to us. How, Victor, can I relate our misfortune?

William is dead! That sweet child, whose smiles delighted and warmed my heart, who was so gentle, yet so happy! Victor, he is murdered!

Last Thursday (May 7th) I, my niece, and your two brothers went to walk in Plainpalais. The evening was warm, and we walked farther than usual. It was already dusk when we thought of returning, and then we discovered that William and Ernest, who had gone on before, were not to be found. So we rested on a seat to wait for them. Soon Ernest came and asked if we had seen his brother; he said that he had been playing with him, that William had run away to hide, and that he had looked for him and afterwards waited for him a long time, but he did not return.

This account rather alarmed us, and we continued to search for him until nightfall, when Elizabeth wondered if he might have returned to the house. He was not there. We returned again, with torches, for I could not rest at the thought that my sweet boy had become lost and was exposed to all the damps of night; Elizabeth also suffered with worry. At about five in the morning I discovered my lovely boy, whom the night before I had seen blooming and active, stretched on the grass, pale and motionless; the print of the murderer's fingers was on his neck.

He was brought home, and Elizabeth fainted. When she again had her wits, she wept. Come, dearest Victor; you alone can console Elizabeth. She weeps continually. We are all unhappy, but will not that be an additional reason for you, my son, to return and be our comforter?

Your affectionate and afflicted father,
Alphonse Frankenstein
Geneva, May 12, 17—

I motioned to Clerval to take up the letter while I walked up and down the room. Tears gushed from Clerval's eyes as he read the account of my misfortune.

"I can offer you no consolation, my friend," said he. "Your disaster cannot be fixed. What do you intend to do?"

"To go instantly to Geneva; come with me, Henry, to order the horses."

It was completely dark when I arrived on the out-skirts of Geneva; the gates of the town were already shut, and I had to pass the night at Secheron, a village about a mile from the city. The sky was calm. Unable to rest, I decided to visit the spot where my poor William had been murdered. As I could not pass through the town, I had to cross the lake in a boat to arrive at Plainpalais. During this short voyage I saw the lightning playing on the summit of Mont Blanc. The storm appeared to approach rapidly. I soon felt the rain com-ing slowly in large drops.

While I watched the storm, I wandered on with a hasty step. I then noticed in the gloom a figure that

In the storm, I noticed a figure hiding behind a clump of trees.

stole from behind a clump of trees near me; I stood fixed, gazing; I could not be mistaken. A flash of lightning lit up the object and showed its shape plainly to me; its gigantic stature and the deformity of its hideous face instantly showed me that it was the wretch, the filthy demon to whom I had given life. What was he doing there? Could he be the murderer of my brother? No sooner did the idea cross my mind than I became convinced of its truth; my teeth chattered, and I was forced to lean against a tree for support.

The figure passed me quickly, and I lost it in the gloom. Nothing in human shape could have destroyed that fair child. *He* was the murderer! I could not doubt it. I thought of chasing the devil, but it would have been in vain, for another flash showed him to me hanging among the rocks of the steep Mount Salève. He soon reached the summit and disappeared.

I remained motionless. The thunder stopped, but the rain still continued. I turned over in my mind the events that until now I had wanted to forget: the whole line of my progress toward the creation, the appearance of the work of my own hands alive at my bedside, and its leaving. Two years had now nearly gone by since the night on which he first received life, and was this his first crime? Alas! I had turned loose into the world a crazed wretch who delighted in bloodshed.

Day dawned and I walked toward the town. The gates were open, and I hurried to my father's house. My first thought was to reveal what I knew of the murderer and have him pursued. But I paused when I thought about the story that I had to tell. A being whom I myself had formed and brought to life had met me at midnight among the cliffs of a forbidding mountain. I well knew that if any other had told such a story to me, I should have looked upon it as the ravings of a madman.

Besides, the strange animal would escape any chase we made, if I were even believed. Who could arrest a creature capable of climbing the steep sides of Mount Salève? I decided to remain silent.

It was about five in the morning when I entered my father's house. I told the servants not to disturb the family and went into the library to wait.

I gazed at the picture of my mother, which stood over the mantelpiece. Below this picture was a miniature of William, and my tears flowed when I looked upon it. While I was weeping, Ernest entered.

"Welcome, my dearest Victor," said he. "Ah! I wish you had come three months ago, and then you would have found us all joyous. You come to us now to share a misery that nothing can help."

Tears fell from my brother's eyes.

My father entered. I saw unhappiness on his face, but he tried to welcome me cheerfully. We were soon joined by Elizabeth. Time had altered her since I last beheld her; it had given her loveliness finer than the beauty of her youthful years.

My father, on the other hand, noticed with pain the change in my face, and tried to give me strength.

"Do you think, Victor," said he, "that I do not suffer also? No one could love a child more than I loved your brother"—tears came into his eyes as he spoke—"but is it not a duty of the survivors that they should give up adding to the unhappiness by an appearance of too much grief? It is also a duty owed to yourself, for too much sorrow prevents you getting better."

5. Frankenstein Meets His Monster

SEVERAL DAYS LATER we went to our house at Belrive. This change was good for me. The shutting of the gates regularly at ten o'clock and the impossibility of remaining on the lake after that hour had made our living within the walls of Geneva very uncomfortable to me. I was now free. Often, after the rest of the family had gone to bed for the night, I took the boat and passed many hours on the water.

Sometimes, with my sails set, I was carried by the wind; and sometimes, after rowing into the middle of the lake, I left the boat to go its own way. I was often tempted, when all was at peace around me, to plunge into the silent lake, that the waters might close over me forever. But I held back when I thought of the heroic and suffering Elizabeth, whom I tenderly loved, and whose life was bound up with mine. I thought also of my father and surviving brother; should I, by departing this world, leave them exposed and unprotected to the violence of the fiend whom I had let loose among them?

There was always room for fear so long as anything I loved remained behind. My hatred of this fiend cannot be imagined.

Ours was a house of sadness. My father's health was poor. Elizabeth was no longer that happy creature who in earlier youth wandered with me on the banks of the lake and talked of our future.

"William was killed," said she, in agony, "and the murderer has escaped. He walks about the world free, and perhaps respected."

I listened in pain to her words. I, not in deed but in effect, was the true murderer. Elizabeth saw the sadness in my face, and kindly taking my hand, she said, "My dearest friend, you must calm yourself. These events have affected me, God knows how deeply; but I am not so wretched as you are." Even as she spoke, I drew near to her, as if in terror, for fear that at that very moment the destroyer had been near to rob me of her.

Sometimes the passions of my soul drove me to seek, by exercise and by change of place, some relief from my feelings. It was during one such instance that I suddenly left my home and went off toward the near Alpine valleys to forget myself and my sorrows.

My wanderings took me toward the valley of Chamonix. I had visited it during my boyhood. Six years had passed since then: I was a wreck—but nothing had changed in those scenic views.

The weather was fine; it was about the middle of August, nearly two months since William's death. I went far into the ravine of Arve. I passed the bridge of Pellissier, where the ravine, which the river forms, opened before me, and I began to climb the mountain that overhangs it. Soon after that I entered the valley of Chamonix. The high and snow mountains were its boundaries. Immense glaciers approached the road; I heard the rumbling thunder of falling avalanches. Mont Blanc raised itself from the surrounding peaks, and its tremendous dome overlooked the valley.

At length I reached the village of Chamonix. For a short time I remained at the window in the inn watching the lightning that played above Mont Blanc and listening to the rushing of the Arve, which went its noisy way beneath.

I spent the following day roaming through the valley. The steep sides of vast mountains were before me; the icy wall of the glacier overhung me; a few pines were scattered around; and the silence was broken only by the thunder sound of the avalanche or the cracking of the ice. These scenes kept my mind from the thoughts over which I had brooded for the last month.

The next morning, the rain was pouring, and thick mists hid the tops of the mountains. But what were rain and storm to me? My mule brought me toward the top of Montanvert. The view of the tremendous and slowly moving glacier filled me with awe and joy.

The climb up was dangerously steep. In a thousand spots I was able to see the traces of the winter avalanche, where trees lay broken. The path, as I went along higher, was cut into by ravines of snow, down which stones continually rolled from above; one of them was particularly dangerous because the slightest sound, even a loud voice, might shake the air and cause a landslide of snow. I looked on the valley beneath; mists were rising from the rivers which ran through it, while rain poured from the dark sky.

It was nearly noon when I arrived at the top of the climb. For some time I sat upon the rock that overlooks the sea of ice. A mist covered both that and the mountains. Soon a breeze blew away the clouds, and I walked down into the glacier. The surface is very uneven, rising like the waves of a troubled sea, with deep gaps here and there. The field of ice is almost three miles wide, and I spent nearly two hours in crossing it. The opposite mountain is steep-cliffed rock. I stood upon it, gazing on Montanvert and Mont Blanc.

It was then that I beheld the figure of a man, at some distance, advancing toward me with great speed. He bounded over the gaps in the ice, among which I had

The figure of a man advanced toward me with great speed.

walked with care; his height and build, also, as he came, seemed to be more than that of a man.

I was troubled; a mist came over my eyes, and I felt faint. I saw, as the shape came nearer, that it was the wretch I had created. I trembled with rage and horror, deciding to wait for him and then fight with him in mortal combat. He approached; his face showed bitterness while his ugliness made him almost too horrible to look at.

"Devil," I said, "do you dare approach me? And don't you fear my vengeance? Go away, vile beast! Or rather, stay, so that I may trample you to dust!"

"I expected this greeting," said the demon. "All men hate the wretched; how, then, must I be hated, who am miserable beyond all living things! Yet you, my creator, hate and reject me, your creature, to whom you are bound by ties breakable only by the death of one of us. You propose to kill me. How dare you play in this way with life? Do your duty toward me, and I will do mine toward you and the rest of mankind. If you will go along with my conditions, I will leave them and you at peace; but if you refuse, I will kill your remaining friends."

"Hateful monster! You murderous fiend! The tortures of hell are too good for you! Wretched devil! You reproach me with creating you; come on, then, that I may kill the being I so thoughtlessly created."

I sprang at him, but he easily dodged me.

He said, "Be calm! I beg you to listen to me. Haven't I suffered enough? Life is dear to me, and I will defend it. Remember, you made me more powerful than yourself; my height is greater than yours, my muscles stronger. But I will not be tempted to fight you. I am your creature, and I will be mild and polite to my natural lord if you will also do your duty to me. Oh, Frankenstein, do not be fair to every other person and trample upon me alone, to whom your justice and affection is most due. Everywhere I see happiness, from which I alone am excluded. I was kind and good; misery made me a fiend. Make me happy, and I shall again be good."

"Go away! I will not listen to this. There can be no conversation between you and me; we are enemies. Go! Or let us fight to the death!"

"How can I persuade you to listen to me, your creature, who begs for your kindness and sympathy? Believe me, Frankenstein, I was good; my soul glowed with love; but am I not miserably alone? You, my creator, hate me; what hope can I gather from your fellow creatures, who owe me nothing? They spurn and hate me. The deserted mountains and icy glaciers are my refuge. I have wandered here many days; the caves of ice, which I do not fear, are a home to me, and the only one that mankind does not mind me having. If more people knew of me, they would do as you do and arm themselves for my destruction. Shall I not then hate them who hate me? Yet it is in your power to help me, and deliver them from my evil rage.

"Let your feelings be moved, and do not put me off. Listen to my story; when you have heard that, give me up or help me, as you shall judge that I deserve. But listen to me. The guilty are allowed, by human laws, to speak in their own defense before they are condemned.

"Frankenstein, you accuse me of murder, and yet you would destroy your own creature. Listen to me, and then, if you can, destroy the work of your hands."

"Cursed be the day, hated devil, in which you first saw light! Cursed be my hands that formed you! You have made me wretched beyond words. You have left me no power to think whether I am fair to you or not. Go! Relieve me from the sight of your detested face!"

"I relieve you this way, my creator," he said, and

placed his hands before my eyes, which I pushed away. "That is how I take from you a sight which you hate. Still you can listen to me with kindness. Hear my tale; it is long and strange, and the temperature of this place is not good for you; come to the hut upon the mountain. The sun is yet high in the heavens; before it goes down, you will have heard my story, and then you can decide. On you it rests whether I leave forever the world of men and lead a harmless life or become the murderer of your fellow creatures."

As he said this, he led the way across the ice; I followed. I decided at least to listen to his tale. We crossed the ice and climbed the opposite mountain. The air was cold, and the rain again began to fall; we went into his hut. I sat myself by the fire that my creature had lighted, and he began his story.

6. The Monster's Story

"IT IS VERY DIFFICULT to remember the first period of my life; all the events of that time appear confused. I saw, felt, heard, and smelled at the same time; and it was, indeed, a long time before I learned to tell my senses apart.

"I remember a strong light pressed upon my nerves, so that I had to shut my eyes. Darkness then came over me and troubled me, but hardly had I felt this when, by opening my eyes, the light poured in upon me again.

"I walked and went outside. I now found that I could wander wherever I liked. The light became more and more bothersome to me, and the heat tired me as I walked. I looked for a place where I could be in shade. There was a forest near Ingolstadt, and I lay by the side of a brook resting, until I felt tormented by hunger and thirst. I ate some berries which I found hanging on the trees or lying on the ground. I satisfied my thirst at the brook and then, lying down, was overcome by sleep.

"It was dark when I awoke; I felt cold also, and half frightened, finding myself so alone. Before I left your apartment, I had covered myself with some clothes, but these were not enough to keep me from the damp of night. I was a poor, helpless, miserable wretch; I knew nothing; but feeling pain come in on me from all sides, I sat down and wept.

43

"Soon a gentle light came over the heavens and gave me a feeling of pleasure. I started up and saw a radiant form rise from among the trees—the moon! I gazed with a kind of wonder. It moved slowly, but it lit up my path, and I again went out in search of berries. I was still cold when under one of the trees I found a huge cloak with which I covered myself, and I sat down upon the ground. I felt light and hunger and thirst and darkness; sounds rang in my ears, and on all sides various scents came to me; the only object that I could make out was the bright moon, and I fixed my eyes on that with pleasure.

"Several changes of day and night passed, and I began to tell my senses apart from one another. I gradually saw plainly the clear stream that supplied me with drink and the trees that shaded me with their leaves.

"I was delighted when I first discovered that a pleasant sound came from the throats of the little winged animals. Sometimes I tried to imitate the pleasant songs of the birds, but I was unable to. Sometimes I wished to express my feelings in my own way, but the sounds that broke from my mouth frightened me into silence again.

"The moon had disappeared from the night, and again, with a smaller form, showed itself while I still remained in the forest. My sensations had by this time become distinct, and every day my mind received more ideas. My eyes became accustomed to the light and to seeing objects in their right forms; I could tell insects from plants, and by degrees, one plant from another. I found that the sparrow uttered harsh songs, while those of the blackbird and thrush were sweet.

"One day, when I was cold, I found a fire that had been left by some wandering beggars, and I was overcome with delight at the warmth I drew from it. In my joy I thrust my hand into the live coals, but quickly drew it out again with a cry of pain.

"How strange, I thought, that the same cause should produce such opposite effects! I looked at the coals, and to my joy found them to be wood. I quickly collected some branches, but they were wet and would not burn. I was confused by this and sat still watching the fire. The wet wood I had placed near the heat dried and caught on fire. I thought about this and discovered the cause. When night came on and brought sleep with it, I was in the greatest fear that my fire should go out. I covered it carefully with dry wood and leaves and placed wet branches upon it; and then, spreading my cloak, I lay on the ground and sank into sleep.

"It was morning when I awoke, and my first care was to visit the fire. I uncovered it, and a gentle breeze quickly fanned it into a flame. I observed this also and made a fan of branches. When night came again I found, with pleasure, that the fire gave light as well as heat and that the discovery of this element was useful to me in my food, for I found some of the meat that the travelers had left had been roasted and tasted much better than the berries I gathered from the trees. I tried, then, to cook my food in the same manner, placing it on the live embers. I found that the berries were spoiled by this while the nuts and roots were much improved.

"Food, however, became hard to find, and I often spent the whole day searching for a few acorns. I decided to leave this place, to look for one where the few needs I had would be more easily satisfied. In leaving, however, I much regretted the loss of the fire, as I did not know how to make one.

"I wrapped myself up in my cloak and struck across the wood toward the setting sun. I passed three days in these rambles and finally discovered the open country. A great deal of snow had fallen the night before, and the fields were all white; I found my feet chilled by the cold, damp substance that covered the ground.

"It was about seven in the morning, and I longed to find food and shelter; at length I saw a small hut, which had doubtless been built for the shelter of some shepherd. This was a new sight to me, and I looked at the structure with great curiosity. Finding the door open, I entered. An old man sat in it near a fire, over which he was preparing his breakfast. He turned on hearing a noise and seeing me, shrieked loudly and ran out of the hut and across the fields. His flight somewhat surprised me. But I was enchanted by the appearance of the hut: here the snow and rain could not come; the ground was dry. I devoured the remains of the shepherd's breakfast, which was bread, cheese, and milk. Then, overcome by weariness, I lay down among some straw and fell asleep.

"It was noon when I awoke and, attracted by the warmth of the sun, which shone brightly on the white ground, I decided to begin again my travels; and, bringing along the remains of the peasant's breakfast in a bag I found, I set out across the fields for several hours, until at sunset I arrived at a village. I admired the huts, the cottages, the houses. The vegetables in the gardens and the milk and cheese that I saw placed in the windows of some of the cottages whetted my appetite.

"I entered one of these cottages, but I had hardly placed my foot within the door before the children shrieked, and one of the women fainted. The whole village was roused; some fled, some attacked me.

"Bruised by their stones, I escaped to the open country and took refuge in a low, bare shack. This shack, however, joined a cottage; after my bad experience in

"I entered one of the cottages, and the children shrieked."

the village, I dared not enter the cottage. My place of refuge was made of wood, but so low that I could barely sit upright in it. There was no floor but the earth itself, but it was dry. And although the wind poured through numerous cracks, I found it a pleasant shelter from the snow and rain, and still more from the cruelty of mankind.

"As soon as morning dawned, I crept out so that I might look at the cottage and find out if I could remain in my shelter. It was at the back of the cottage and surrounded on the sides by a pigsty and a clear pool of water. One side was open, and by that side I had crept in. I decided to live in this shack. It was a paradise compared to the forest.

"I ate my breakfast of bread, which I had stolen, and was about to go out and drink from the clear pool when I heard a step and, looking through a crack, I saw a young creature passing by with a pail on her head. The girl was young and gentle, yet she was poorly dressed, in a blue petticoat and cotton jacket. Her blonde hair was braided. I lost sight of her, and in about fifteen minutes she returned with the pail, which was now partly filled with milk. As she walked along, a young man met her. Uttering a few sounds, he took the pail from her head and brought it to the cottage himself. She followed, and they disappeared.

"Soon I saw the young man again, with some tools in his hand, crossing the field behind the cottage; and the girl was also busy, sometimes in the house and sometimes in the yard.

"On looking at my shack, I found that one of the windows of the cottage had once looked out in its direction, but the panes had been filled up with wood. In one

The young girl listened as the silver-haired old man played the guitar.

of these pieces of wood was a small crack through which I could peek. Through this crack a small room was visible; it was clean but very bare of furniture. In one corner, near a small fire, sat a silver-haired old man, leaning his head on his hands. The young girl was busy in cleaning up the cottage; but soon she took something out of a drawer, which she worked with her hands, and she sat down beside the old man, who, taking up an instrument, began to play and make sounds sweeter than the voice of the nightingale. It was a lovely sight, even to me, who had never seen anything beautiful before.

"The old man played a sweet, sad song that drew tears from the eyes of the girl; the old man took no notice of this until she sobbed. He then said a few words, and the girl, leaving her work, knelt at his feet.

"He raised her and smiled with such kindness and affection that I felt sensations of a strange and overpowering nature; they were a mixture of pain and pleasure, such as I had never before felt, either from hunger or cold, warmth or food; and I left the window unable to bear these feelings.

"Soon after this the young man returned with a load of wood. The girl met him at the door and took some of the wood into the cottage and placed it on the fire; then the young man showed her a large loaf of bread and a piece of cheese. She seemed pleased and went into the garden for some roots and plants, which she placed in water and then upon the fire. She then continued her work while the young man went into the garden and dug up roots. After he had done this for an hour, the young woman joined him, and they entered the cottage together.

"They all sat down to eat. The meal was quickly over. The young woman again cleaned up the cottage, and the old man walked in front of the cottage in the sun for a few minutes, leaning on the arm of the young man. The old man returned to the cottage, and the young man, with tools different from those he had used in the morning, went out across the fields.

"Night quickly came on, but to my wonder, I found that the cottagers had a way of keeping the light by the use of candles and I was delighted to find that the setting of the sun did not put an end to the pleasure I had in watching my human neighbors.

"In the evening the young girl and the young man were busy in tasks I did not understand; and the old man again took up the instrument which made the divine sounds that had enchanted me in the morning. As soon as he had finished, the youth began, not to play, but to say words while the others listened; I since found that he was reading aloud, but at that time I knew nothing of speaking or reading.

"The family, after having done this for a short time, put out their lights and went to bed. The cottagers arose the next morning before the sun. The young woman fixed up the cottage and prepared the food, and the youth went out.

"This day passed in the same way as the first. The young man was busy out of doors, and the girl indoors. The old man, whom I soon saw to be blind, spent his time on his instrument or in thought.

"A long period passed before I realized that this family was suffering poverty. Their food consisted entirely of the vegetables of their garden and the milk of one cow, which gave very little during the winter. Several times the younger people placed food before the old man and had none for themselves.

"This kindness moved me. I had been accustomed, during the night, to stealing a part of their food for myself, but when I found that in doing this I deprived the cottagers, I stopped and satisfied myself with berries, nuts, and roots, which I gathered from a near-by forest. I found also another way through which I was able to help them. The youth spent a great part of each day in collecting wood for the family fire, and during the night I often took his tools and brought home enough firewood for several days.

"I remember that when I did this for the first time, the young woman, upon opening the door in the morning, appeared greatly surprised to see a pile of wood. She uttered some words in a loud voice, and the youth joined her and also expressed surprise. I observed, with pleasure, that he did not go to the forest that day but spent it in repairing the cottage and gardening.

"Slowly I made a more important discovery. I found that these people had a way of telling about their experience and feelings to one another by making sounds. I noticed that the words they spoke sometimes brought pleasure or pain, smiles or sadness, in the hearers. This was a godlike talent, and I wanted to learn it. But I found it too difficult. They spoke quickly, and the words they uttered, not having any apparent connection with visible objects, meant nothing to me.

"By great study, however, and after having spent several months there, I began to see that the names were given to some of the most familiar objects of conversation; I learned and used some of the words: 'fire,' 'milk,' 'bread,' and 'wood.' I also learned the names of the cottagers themselves. The youth and the girl had each of them several names, but the old man had only one, which was 'father.' The girl was called 'sister' or 'Agatha,' and the youth 'Felix,' 'brother,' or 'son.' I cannot describe the delight I felt when I learned the ideas for these sounds and was able to pronounce them. I

made out several other words without being able as yet
to understand or use them, such as 'good,' 'dearest,'
'unhappy.'

"I spent the winter in this way. The gentle manners
and beauty of the cottagers greatly endeared them to
me; when they were unhappy, I felt depressed; when
they rejoiced, I felt joy.

Felix picked the first little white flower
from the snowy ground for his sister.

"In the midst of their poverty, Felix carried with
pleasure to his sister the first little white flower that
peeped out from beneath the snowy ground. Early in
the morning, before she had risen, he cleared away the
snow on her path to the milk house, drew water from

the well, and brought the wood from the shed, where, to his surprise, he found his wood supply always replenished by an invisible hand. In the day, I believe, he worked sometimes for a neighboring farmer, because he often went out and did not return until dinner, yet brought no wood with him. At other times he worked in the garden, but as there was little to do in the frosty season, he read to the old man and Agatha.

"This reading had puzzled me very much at first, but by degrees I discovered that he uttered many of the same sounds when he read as when he talked. I guessed, therefore, that he recognized on the paper signs for speech, and I longed to understand these also; but how was that possible when I did not even understand the sounds for which they stood as signs?

"I longed to introduce myself to the cottagers, but I knew I ought not to do so until I had first become master of their language, which might help them overlook the deformity of my face and body.

"I had admired the perfect appearances of my cottagers—their grace, beauty, and delicate complexions; but how terrified I was when I viewed myself in the water outside! At first I started back, unable to believe that it was indeed I who was reflected in the pool; and when I became convinced that I was the monster that I am, I was filled with sadness and horror.

"As the sun became warmer and the light of day longer, the snow vanished, and I looked at the bare trees and the dark earth. From this time Felix was busier, and their hunger disappeared. Their food was hearty and wholesome, and they had enough of it. Several new kinds of plants sprang up in the garden. The old man, leaning on his son, walked each day at noon if it did not rain, as I found it was called when the sky poured forth its water.

"My life in the shack was always the same. During the morning I watched the actions of the cottagers, and when they went to their various chores, I slept; I spent the remainder of the day in watching my friends. When they went to bed, if there was any moon or if the night was starlit, I went into the woods and gathered my own food and fuel for the cottage. When I returned, I cleared their path of the snow and did those chores I had seen done by Felix. These chores made them wonder about the 'good spirit' who had helped them.

"I imagined presenting myself to them. I imagined that they would be disgusted until, by my gentle manner and kind words, I should first win their favor and afterwards their love. Although my voice was very unlike the soft music of their tones, yet I pronounced such words as I understood with some ease.

"Spring came rapidly; the weather became fine and the skies cloudless. It surprised me that what before was barren and gloomy should now bloom with the most beautiful flowers and greenery. My senses were refreshed. It was on one of these days, when my cottagers were resting from their labor—the old man played on his guitar, and the children listened to him—that someone tapped at the door.

"It was a lady on horseback. She was dressed in a dark suit and covered with a black veil. Agatha asked a question, to which the stranger only replied by saying, in a sweet accent, the name of Felix. On hearing this word, Felix came up to to the lady, who, when she saw him, pulled up her veil. Her hair was shining black and strangely braided; her eyes were dark but gentle.

"Felix was delighted when he saw her. She wiped a few tears from her lovely eyes, held out her hand to him, and he kissed it. He called her his sweet Arabian. She did not seem to understand him, but smiled. He helped her down from the horse and brought her into the cottage. Some conversation took place between him and his father, and the young stranger knelt at the old man's feet and would have kissed his hand, but he raised her and hugged her.

"I soon noticed that although the stranger uttered sounds and appeared to have a language of her own, she neither understood nor was understood by the cottagers. They made many signs that I did not understand, but I saw that she brought gladness to the cottage. Soon, I found, by the hearing of the same sound, which the stranger repeated after them, that she was trying to learn their language; and the idea instantly occurred to me that I should make use of the same instructions to learn it as well. The stranger learned about twenty words at the first lesson; most of them were those that I had already acquired. As night came on, Agatha and the Arabian went to bed early. Felix kissed the hand of the stranger and said, 'Good night, sweet Safie.'

"She and I improved rapidly in the knowledge of the language, so that in two months I began to understand most of the words uttered by my cottagers. In the meantime, my nightly rambles were an extreme pleasure to me, although they were shortened by the late setting and early rising of the sun; I never went out during daylight, fearful of meeting with the same treatment I had formerly endured in the first village I entered.

"I spent my days in close attention in order to master the language more quickly. I understood and could imitate almost every word they spoke. While I improved in speech, I also learned how to read, since it was taught to the stranger, and this opened before me a wide field for wonder and delight. Lessons were impressed upon me deeply. I heard of the difference of sexes, and the birth and growth of children, how the father loved the smiles of the baby, how all the life and cares of the mother were wrapped up in the child; how the mind of youth expanded and gained knowledge; of brother, sister, and all the various relationships that bind one human being to another.

"But where were my friends and relations? No father had watched my first days, no mother had blessed me with smiles and kisses; or if they had, all my past life was now a blot, which I could not remember. From my earliest remembrance I had been as I then was in height and appearance. I had never yet seen a being resembling me or who claimed any relationship with me. What was I?"

7. The Monster's Rage

"ONE NIGHT IN the beginning of August, during my usual visit to the neighboring wood where I collected my own food and brought home firewood for the cottagers, I found on the ground a leather bag containing several pieces of clothing and some books. I eagerly picked it up and returned with it to my shack. Fortunately the books were written in the language which I had learned from my neighbors. They gave me extreme delight. I read and studied them while my friends were busy with their chores.

"As I read, I reflected on my own feelings and life. I found myself similar yet at the same time strangely unlike the beings about whom I read and watched. I was hideous and my body was gigantic. What did this mean? Who was I? What was I? Where did I come from? These questions continually came to me, but I was unable to answer them.

"Soon after my arrival in the shack, I had discovered some papers in the pocket of the coat that I had taken from your laboratory. At first I had not looked at them, but now that I was able to read, I began to study them. It was your journal of the four months that led up to my creation. You described in these papers every step you took in the progress of your work; this account was mingled with stories of your life. You doubtless remem-

57

ber these papers. Here they are. All the details are told of my creation, in language that showed your horror. I sickened as I read.

"'Hateful day when I came to life!' I exclaimed in agony. 'You cursed creator! Why did you make a monster so hideous that even *you* turned from me in disgust?' These were my thoughts.

"But when I thought about the goodness of the cottagers, I persuaded myself that when they began to know my own goodness, they would feel for me and overlook my ugliness. Could they turn from their door one, however monstrous, who asked for their kindness and friendship?

"Autumn passed in this way. With surprise and grief I saw the leaves fall, and nature again become barren and bleak. But I turned with more attention toward the cottagers. The more I saw of them, the greater became my hopes of gaining their friendship.

"The winter came on, and an entire cycle of the seasons had taken place since I awoke into life. I finally decided to enter the cottage when the blind man should be alone. I had wisdom enough to know that my ugliness was the cause of the horror of those who had seen me. My voice, although rough, had nothing terrible in it; I thought, therefore, that if in the absence of the children I could gain the good will of the old man, I might by his support be tolerated by the younger ones.

"One day, when the sun shone on the red leaves that had fallen over the ground, Safie, Agatha, and Felix went out on a long walk, and the old man, at his own wish, was left alone in the cottage. When his children had left, he took up his guitar and played several sad, sweet songs. Finally, laying aside the instrument, he sat thinking.

"My heart beat quickly; this was the hour and

moment of truth, which would satisfy my hopes or prove my fears. All was silent in and around the cottage; it was an excellent opportunity.

"I left the shack and approached the door of their cottage. I knocked. 'Who is there?' said the old man. 'Come in.'

"I entered. 'Pardon me,' said I; 'I am a traveler in need of a little rest; you would greatly help me if you would allow me to remain a few minutes before the fire.'

"'Enter,' he said, 'and I will try in what way I can to help you; but, unluckily, my children are out, and as I am blind, I am afraid I shall find it hard to provide some food for you.'

"'Do not trouble yourself, my kind host; I have food; it is warmth and rest only that I need. I am an unfortunate creature; I look around and I have no family or friend upon earth.'

"'Do not despair. To be friendless is indeed unfortunate, but the hearts of men are often full of brotherly love and kindness. Be hopeful. If you will tell me your story, I perhaps may be able to help you. I am blind, and cannot judge your face, but there is something in your words that tells me that you are honest. I am poor and living far from my homeland, but it will give me pleasure to help a human creature.'

"'Excellent man! I thank you and accept your generous offer. You raise me from the dust by this kindness; and I trust that, by your help, I shall not be driven from the society and kindness of your fellow creatures.'

"'Heaven forbid!'

"'How can I thank you, my best and only friend? From your lips I have heard the voice of kindness; I shall be forever grateful.' I sank on the chair and sobbed aloud. At that moment I heard the steps of the young cottagers. I had not a moment to lose, but seizing the hand

of the old man, I cried, 'Now is the time! Save and protect me! Do not desert me!'

"'Great God!' exclaimed the old man. 'Who are you?'

"At that instant the cottage door was opened, and
Felix, Safie, and Agatha entered. Who can describe their
horror on seeing me? Agatha fainted, and Safie rushed
out of the cottage. Felix darted forward, and tore me

Felix darted forward, tearing me from his father,
and struck me with a stick.

from his father, to whose knees I clung, and struck me
with a stick. I could have torn him limb from limb, but I
kept myself from doing so. I saw him about to attack me
again, when I left the cottage and escaped, unnoticed,
to my shack.

"Cursed, cursed creator! Why did I live?

"When night came, I left the shack and wandered in
the wood; and now, no longer worried about being
found out, I let out, in my agony, fearful howlings. Oh!

What a miserable night I passed! There were no men that existed who would pity or help; and should I feel kindness toward my enemies? No; from that moment I declared everlasting war against mankind, and more than all, against him who had created me.

"The sun rose; I heard the voices of men and knew that it was impossible to return to my shack during that day. I hid myself in thick underbrush. That night, I crept out from my hiding place and went in search of food. When I had gathered enough, I went back to the cottage. All there was at peace. I crept into my shack and awaited morning. But even after the sun mounted high in the heavens, still the cottagers did not appear. Where were they? Soon I saw, outside, Felix and another man approach.

"'We can never again live in this cottage,' said Felix. 'The life of my father is in the greatest danger, owing to the dreadful event I have told you. My wife and my sister will never recover from their horror.'

"Felix and his companion entered the cottage, in which they remained for only a few minutes, and then left. I never saw any of the family again.

"I continued for the remainder of the day in my shack. My cottagers had left and had broken the only link that held me to the world. For the first time the feelings of revenge and hatred filled my heart, and I did not try to control them. As night came on, I placed firewood and straw around the cottage, and after having destroyed the garden, I waited until the moon had gone down to begin my task.

"I lighted the dry branch of a tree and danced with fury around the cottage. I lit the straw. The wind fanned the fire, and the cottage was quickly covered in flames.

"I decided to go far away from there. The thought of you, Frankenstein, crossed my mind. I learned from your papers that you were my father, my creator; and to whom could I go to but you? Among the lessons Felix had given Safie was geography. You had mentioned Geneva as the name of your native town, and toward this place I decided to go. I possessed a map of the country.

"I traveled only at night, fearful of meeting a human being. Nature decayed around me, and the sun became heatless; rain and snow poured around me; mighty rivers were frozen; the surface of the earth was hard and bare, and I found no shelter. The nearer I approached your city, the more deeply did I feel the spirit of revenge. I arrived on the outskirts of Switzerland when the sun had recovered its warmth and the earth again began to look green.

"One morning, finding that my path lay through a deep wood, I decided to continue my journey after the sun had risen. I wound among the paths of the wood, until I came to its edge, which was bounded by a deep and rapid river. Here I paused, not exactly knowing what path to take, when I heard the sound of voices, which led me to hide myself in the shade of a tree.

"I was scarcely concealed when a young girl came running toward the spot where I was hidden, laughing, as if she ran from someone in play. She went on along the steep sides of the river, when suddenly her foot slipped, and she fell into the rapid water. I rushed from my hiding place and into the powerful current, and saved her and dragged her to shore. I was suddenly interrupted by the approach of a peasant, who was probably the person from whom she had playfully fled. On seeing me, he darted toward me and tearing the girl from my arms, hurried away toward the deeper parts of the wood. I followed, I hardly knew why; but when the man saw me draw near, he aimed a gun at me and fired.

I sank to the ground, and the gunman, with more speed, went on into the wood.

"This was then the reward of my kindness! I had saved a human being from death, and as a result I now was wounded by a bullet. The feeling of kindness and gentleness which I had had a few moments before gave way to rage. The agony of my wound, however, overcame me, and I fainted.

"For some weeks I led a miserable life in the woods, trying to cure the wound which I had received. When it did heal, I continued my journey, and two months later I reached Geneva.

"It was evening when I arrived, and I found a hiding place among the fields that surround the city. I was wondering how I should approach you when I was disturbed by a beautiful child who came running into the spot where I had chosen. Suddenly, as I gazed on him, an idea came upon me that this little creature had lived too short a time to be horrified by my ugliness. If, therefore, I could stop him and show him that I was friendly, I should not be so lonely.

"I caught the boy as he passed. As soon as he saw me, he placed his hands over his eyes and screamed. I drew his hands away, and said, 'Child, what is the meaning of this? I do not mean to hurt you; listen to me.'

"He struggled and cried, 'Let me go, monster! Ugly wretch! You wish to eat me and tear me to pieces. You are a beast. Let me go, or I will tell my papa.'

"'Boy, you will never see your father again; you must come with me.'

"'Hideous monster! Let me go. My papa is an important man! He is Mister Frankenstein—he will punish you. You dare not keep me.'

"'Frankenstein! You belong then to the family of my

"The child struggled and I grasped his throat to silence him."

enemy—toward whom I have sworn eternal revenge;
you shall be my first victim.'

"The child struggled and called me names; I grasped
his throat to silence him, and in a moment he lay dead
at my feet.

"I gazed on my victim, and my heart swelled with triumph; clapping my hands, I exclaimed, 'I, too, can create misery; my enemy can be hurt; this death will bring
despair to him, and a thousand other miseries shall tor-
ment and destroy him.'

"For some days I haunted the spot where these
scenes had taken place, sometimes wishing to see you,
sometimes deciding to leave the world and its miseries
forever. At length I wandered toward these mountains
and have climbed over them, consumed by a burning
passion that you alone can satisfy. We may not part
until you have promised to do what I ask. I am alone and
miserable; mankind will not accept me; but a female
creature as ugly and horrible as I am would accept me.
My companion must be of the same type and have the
same defects. This being you must create."

8. The Monster's Bride

THE MONSTER FINISHED speaking and fixed his gaze upon me, awaiting my reply. As I remained silent, he continued, "You must create a female for me with whom I can live. I demand it of you, and you must not refuse."

"I do refuse," I said, "and no torture shall ever make me agree to do it. Shall I create another like yourself, so that your joint wickedness might destroy the world? Go away! I have answered you; you may torture me, but I will never consent."

"You are in the wrong," replied the fiend, "and instead of threatening, I am content to reason with you. I am wicked because I am miserable.

"Am I not shunned and hated by all mankind? If I cannot gain love, I will cause fear. Beware; I will work at your destruction. What I ask of you is reasonable; I demand a creature of another sex, but as hideous as I; this is little enough, but it shall content me. It is true, we shall be monsters, cut off from all the world; but on that account we shall be more attached to each other. Our lives will not be happy, but they will be harmless and free from the misery I now feel. Oh! My creator, make me happy; let me give thanks to you! Let me see that you have some feeling for me; do not deny me my request!"

I was moved. I thought there was some justice in his argument. His story and the feelings he now expressed proved him to be a creature of fine sensations, and did I not as his maker owe him all the portion of happiness that it was in my power to give him?

He saw my change of feeling and went on. "If you agree, neither you nor any other human being shall ever see us again; I will go to the vast wilds of South

"Am I not shunned and hated by all mankind? Do not deny me my request!"

America. My food is not that of man; I do not destroy animals for my appetite; acorns and berries give me enough. My companion will be the same. We shall make our bed of dried leaves; the sun will shine on us as on mankind and will ripen our food. The picture I present to you is peaceful and human, and you must feel that you could deny it only out of cruelty."

His words had a strange effect upon me. I felt sorry for him and sometimes felt a wish to help him, but when I looked at him, when I saw the disgusting beast who moved and talked, my heart sickened and my feelings changed to those of horror and hatred. I tried to control these feelings.

After a long pause I decided that justice due to him and my fellow humans demanded of me that I should go along with his request. I said, "I consent to your demand, on your promise that you will leave Europe forever, and every other place where men live, as soon as I shall deliver into your hands a female who will go with you in your exile."

"I swear," he cried, "by the sun and by the blue sky of heaven and by the fire of love that burns in my heart, that if you grant my prayer, you shall never see me again. Return to your home and begin your work; I shall watch your progress; when you are ready, I shall appear."

Saying this, he quickly left me, fearful, perhaps, of my changing my mind. I saw him go down the mountain with greater speed than the flight of an eagle.

His story had taken the whole day, and the sun was upon the edge of the horizon when he left. Morning dawned before I arrived at the village of Chamonix; I took no rest but returned immediately to Geneva.

Day after day, week after week passed away on my return to Geneva. I found that I could not make a female without again devoting several months to study and calculations. I had heard of some discoveries made by an English scientist, the knowledge of which would be helpful to my work, and I decided to ask my father for permission to visit England.

I did not want to work on this creature while in my father's house. I knew that a thousand fearful accidents might occur, the slightest of which would horrify everyone. I must leave all those people I loved while working.

Once begun, the project would quickly be carried out, and then I might return to my family in peace and happiness. My promise fulfilled, the monster would go away forever.

My father, however, insisted that I go with a companion, my friend Clerval. This interfered with my plans, yet I agreed. To England, therefore, I was bound, and it was understood that my marriage with Elizabeth should take place immediately on my return.

It was at the end of September that I left Switzerland with Clerval. Alas, how great was the contrast between our feelings! He was alive to every new scene, joyful when he saw the beauties of the setting sun, while I, a miserable wretch, was haunted by a promise that kept me from enjoying anything.

At length we arrived in London. After passing several months in this wonderful and famous city, we received a letter from a person in Scotland who had formerly been our visitor at Geneva. He mentioned the beauties of his native country and asked us to journey as far north as Perth, where he lived. Clerval eagerly accepted this invitation, and I agreed to go along.

I packed up my chemical instruments and the materials I had collected, deciding to finish my work in some out-of-the-way nook in the northern highlands of Scotland.

We left London on the 27th of March. I was not sorry. I had not worked to fulfill my promise for some time, and I feared the effects of the demon's disappointment. He might remain in Switzerland and avenge himself on my relatives. This idea tormented me. I waited for letters with impatience; if they were delayed, I was overcome by a thousand fears. Sometimes I thought that the fiend followed me and might punish my tardiness by murdering my friend Clerval. Because of this I told

Clerval that I wished to make the tour of Scotland alone. "You go and enjoy yourself," I said. "I may be gone for a month or two; but do not interfere with my travels, I beg you. Leave me at peace for a short while, and when I return, I hope it will be with a lighter heart."

Having parted from my friend, I decided to visit some remote spot of Scotland to finish my work alone. I did not doubt that the monster followed me and would know when I had finished.

I crossed the northern highlands and chose one of the most distant of the Orkney Islands as the scene of my labors. It was a place fitted for such work, being hardly more than a rock whose high sides were beaten upon by the waves. The soil was barren, with hardly enough pasture for the few cows and barely enough oatmeal for its natives, which consisted of five people. Vegetables and bread, and even fresh water, had to be brought from the mainland, which was about five miles away.

On the whole island there were but three miserable huts, and one of these was empty when I arrived. This I rented. It contained but two rooms, and these were poor. The thatch roof had fallen in, the walls were unplastered, and the door was off its hinges. I ordered it to be repaired, bought some furniture, and moved in.

In this hut I devoted the morning to labor; but in the evening, when the weather permitted, I walked on the stony beach of the sea to listen to the waves as they roared and dashed at my feet. I thought of Switzerland; it was far different from this lonely and barren landscape.

As I went on with my work, it became every day more horrible and disgusting to me. Sometimes I could not get myself to enter my laboratory for several days, and at other times I worked day and night in order to complete my work. It was, indeed, a filthy job. My heart was often sickened at the work of my hands.

I grew restless and nervous. Every moment I feared to meet the demon. In the meantime I worked on, and my labor was already far along. I looked toward its completion with hope.

I sat one evening in my laboratory; the sun had set, and the moon was just rising from the sea. Three years before, I had been working in just this way and had created a fiend whose barbarity had filled my heart with remorse. I was now about to form another being whose character I also did not know; she might become ten thousand times more evil than her mate and delight, for its own sake, in murder and violence. He had sworn to leave civilization and hide himself away, but she had not; and she, who in all probability was to become a thinking and reasoning animal, might refuse to go along with an agreement made before her creation. They might even hate each other; the creature who already lived hated his own ugliness, and might he not have a greater horror of it when it came before his eyes in the female form? She also might turn with disgust from him to the superior beauty of man; she might leave him, and he might be alone again, more angry than ever for having been spurned by one of his own kind.

Even if they were to leave Europe and live in the new world, one of the first results of their love would be children, and a race of devils would be born upon the earth who might terrorize mankind. Had I a right, for my own benefit, to put his curse upon future generations?

I trembled and my heart failed within me when, on looking up, I saw by the light of the moon the demon at the window. A ghastly grin wrinkled his lips as he gazed on me. Yes, he had followed me in my travels; he had

I saw the demon at the window, and a ghastly grin wrinkled his lips.

waited in forests, hid himself in caves, or taken refuge in the heaths; and he now came to check on my progress and claim the fulfillment of my promise.

As I looked on him, I thought I had to have been mad to promise to create another being like him, and I suddenly tore to pieces the monster on which I was working. The wretch saw me destroy the creature on whose future life he depended for happiness, and with a howl he ran off.

I left the room and, locking the door, made a vow never to begin again my labors. Several hours passed as I sat in the next room at the window gazing on the sea; it was almost motionless, for the winds were hushed. A few fishing boats alone specked the water, and now and then the gentle breeze brought the sound of voices as the fishermen called to one another.

In a few minutes I heard the creaking of my door. soon I heard the sound of footsteps along the passage; the door opened, and the wretch whom I dreaded appeared. Shutting the door, he approached me and said, "You have destroyed the work which you began. do you dare to break your promise? I have suffered hard and long; I left Switzerland with you; I crept along after you through Europe and across England. Do you dare to destroy my hopes?"

"Leave me!" I cried. "I do break my promise; I will never create another like you, equal in monstrousness."

"Remember that I have power; you believe yourself miserable, but I can make you so wretched that the light of day will be hateful to you. You are my creator, but I am your master; obey!"

"Your threats cannot move me to do an act of wickedness. Shall I, in cold blood, set loose upon the earth a demon whose delight is death and violence? Go away!"

"Shall each man," cried he, "find a wife, and each beast have his mate, and I be alone? I had feelings of affection, and they were met by hatred and scorn. Are you to be happy while I grovel in wretchedness? You can frustrate my other passions, but revenge remains! I may die, but first you shall curse the sun that gazes on your misery. Beware, for I am fearless and therefore powerful. I will watch with the cunning of a snake, that I may sting with its venom. You shall be sorry!"

"Devil, stop these words. I have declared my decision to you, and I am no coward to bend to your threats. Leave me; there is no changing my mind."

"Then I shall go; but remember, I shall be with you on your wedding night."

I started and exclaimed, "Villain! Before you threaten my life, be sure that you are yourself safe."

I would have grabbed him, but he escaped and fled the house. In a few minutes I saw him in his boat, which shot across the waters and was soon beyond my sight.

The night passed away, and the sun rose from the ocean; my feelings grew calmer. I left the house, the horrid scene of last night's dispute, and walked on the beach. I saw a fishing boat land close to me, and one of the men brought me a packet; it contained letters from Geneva, and one from Clerval asking me to leave my deserted island and to meet him at Perth so that we might go on southward together. This letter brought me back to life, and I decided to leave the island at the end of two days.

Yet before I left, there was a task to do; I must pack up my chemical instruments. The next morning, I unlocked the door of my laboratory. The remains of the half-finished creature, whom I had destroyed, lay scattered on the floor. With trembling hands, I brought the instruments out of the room, but then I realized that I ought not to leave the remains of my work to horrify the peasants; and so I put them into a basket, with a large number of stones, determined to throw them into the sea that very night.

Between two and three in the morning, the moon rose; and I then, putting my basket aboard a little rowboat, sailed out about four miles from the shore and cast my basket into the sea. I listened to the gurgling sound as it sank and then sailed away from the spot. I heard only the sound of the boat as it cut through the waves; this murmur lulled me, and in a short time I slept soundly.

I do not know how long I remained in this sleep, but when I awoke I found that the sun had already climbed into the sky. I steered my course toward the land. I saw boats near the shore and found myself suddenly trans-

ported back to the neighborhood of civilized man.
Several people crowded toward the spot where I landed. They seemed very surprised at my appearance.

"My good friends," said I, "will you be so kind as to
tell me the name of this town and tell me where I am?"

"In the town of Tervalon, where a murder was committed last night," said an elderly, well-dressed man.

I was introduced to the elderly man, who was the
mayor. A fisherman, he told me, had reported that he
had been out fishing the night before with his son and
brother-in-law, James Cahill, when they landed at a
creek about two miles below. The fisherman walked on

By the light of the lantern, they found the body of a dead man.

first, and his companions followed him. As he was walking along the sands, he struck his foot against something and fell on the ground. His companions came up to help him, and by the light of their lantern they found that he had fallen on the body of a man who was, to all appearances, dead. The first guess was that it was the corpse of some person who had been drowned and was thrown on shore by the waves, but on examination they found that the clothes were not wet and even that the body was not yet cold. They instantly carried it to the cottage of an old woman near the spot and tried to restore it to life. It appeared to be a handsome man, about twenty-five years old. He had apparently been strangled, for there was no sign of any violence except the mark of fingers on his neck.

When the mark of the fingers was mentioned, I remembered the murder of my brother and felt myself trembling. The mayor asked if I would go into the room where the body lay for burial. I entered the room and was led up to the coffin. When I saw the lifeless form of Henry Clerval stretched before me, I gasped for breath and collapsed.

9. Frankenstein's Wedding

FOR THE NEXT two months I lay in a fever, on the point of death. At this time my father traveled from Geneva to my side. In my first words to him, I said, "Are you, then, safe—and Elizabeth—and Ernest?"

My father calmed me with news of their welfare and said, "You traveled to England to find happiness, but death seems to follow you. And poor Clerval—"

The name of my poor murdered friend brought tears to my eyes, and we wept for several minutes.

My father was my good angel, however, and I gradually recovered my health. I was allowed to return to my native country.

It was necessary, indeed, that I should return without delay to Geneva so that I might watch over the lives of those I loved and lie in wait for the murderer.

On our voyage by ship, I passed through, in my memory, my whole life—my quiet happiness while living with my family in Geneva, the death of my mother, and my departure for Ingolstadt. I remembered, shuddering, the madness that hurried me on to the creation of my hideous enemy, and I called to mind the night in which he first lived. I wept bitterly.

The voyage came to an end. We landed and went on to Paris. A few days before we left Paris on our way to Switzerland, I received the following letter from Elizabeth:

My dear Victor,

It gave me the greatest pleasure to receive a letter from my uncle dated at Paris; you are no longer at a far distance, and I may hope to see you in less than two weeks. My poor cousin, how much you must have suffered! I expect to see you looking even more ill than when you left Geneva. This winter has been passed most miserably, yet I hope to find that peace is in your heart.

You well know, Victor, that our marriage had been the favorite plan of your parents ever since our childhood. We were told this when young and taught to look forward to it as an event that would certainly take place. We were fond playmates during childhood and, I believe, dear and valued friends to each other as we grew older. But as brother and sister often have a fondness toward each other without wanting to be married, may not such also be our case? tell me, dearest Victor. Answer me, I beg you, with simple truth—do you not love another?

You have traveled; you have spent several years of your life at Ingolstadt; and I confess to you, my friend, that when I saw you last autumn so unhappy, I could not help supposing that you might regret our engagement and believe yourself bound in honor to fulfill the wishes of your parents. I confess to you, my friend, that I love you and that in my airy dreams of the future you have been my constant friend and companion. But it is your happiness I want as well as my own when I declare to you that our marriage would make me miserable unless it were of your own free choice.

Do not let this letter disturb you; do not answer tomorrow or the next day or even until you come if it will give you pain. My uncle will send me news of your health, and if I see but one smile on your lips when we meet, I shall need no other happiness.

Elizabeth
Geneva, May 18, 17—

This letter revived in my memory what I had before forgotten, the threat of the fiend: *"I shall be with you on your wedding night!"* On that night would the demon try to destroy me and tear me from any little happiness that promised to relieve my sufferings. On that night he had determined to kill me. Well, so be it; a deadly struggle would take place: if he were victorious, I should be at peace and his power over me be at an end; if he were defeated, I should be a free man.

I wrote to Elizabeth. My letter was calm and affectionate. "I fear, my beloved girl," I said, "little happiness remains for us on earth; yet all that I may one day enjoy is centered in you. Chase away your fears; to you alone do I dedicate my life."

In about a week after the arrival of Elizabeth's letter, we returned to Geneva. The sweet girl welcomed me with warm affection, yet tears were in her eyes as she saw how illness had touched me.

Soon after our arrival my father spoke of my marriage to Elizabeth, asking when it would be. When I looked confused, he asked, "What, have you fallen in love with someone else?"

I replied, "I love Elizabeth and look forward to our union with delight. Let the day therefore be fixed; and I will dedicate myself to the happiness of my cousin."

I therefore arranged with my father that if my cousin would agree, the ceremony should take place in ten days.

Great God! If for one instant I had thought what might be the hellish intention of my fiendish enemy, I would rather have run away forever from my native country and wandered a friendless outcast over the earth than have consented to this marriage. But the monster had blinded me to his real intentions; and when I thought that I had prepared only my own death, I brought on that of a far dearer victim.

Preparations were made for the event, congratulatory visits were made, and all wore smiles. It was agreed that immediately after our weddings we should proceed to Villa Lavenza and spend our first days of happiness beside the beautiful lake near which it stood.

In the meantime I took every precaution to defend myself in case the fiend should openly attack me. I carried pistols and a dagger with me constantly and was ever on the watch to prevent him from taking me by surprise.

Elizabeth seemed happy; my calmness helped greatly to relieve her worries. But on the day that was to fulfill my wishes and my fate, she was sad, and a feeling of dread came over her; and perhaps she also thought of

After the wedding, Elizabeth and I began our journey by water.

"a terrible secret" that I had promised to reveal to her on the following day.

After the wedding a large party gathered at my father's, but it was agreed that Elizabeth and I should begin our journey by water, sleeping that night at Evian and continuing our voyage on the following day. The day was fair, the wind was with us; everything smiled on our wedding voyage.

Those were the last moments of my life during which I enjoyed a feeling of happiness. We passed rapidly along. I took the hand of Elizabeth.

"You are sorrowful, my love," I said. "Ah! If you knew what I have suffered and what I may yet suffer, you would try to let us enjoy the freedom from sadness that this one day at least permits us to have."

"Be happy, dear Victor," replied Elizabeth. "There is, I hope, nothing to worry you; and be assured that if I do not seem joyous, my heart is contented. What a divine day it is! How happy and peaceful all nature appears!"

The wind, which had up to now carried us along with swiftness, sank at sunset to a light breeze; the soft air just ruffled the water and caused a pleasant motion among the trees as we approached the shore. The sun sank beneath the horizon as we landed, and as I touched the shore, I felt those cares and fears come back to me which soon were to cling to me forever.

It was eight o'clock when we landed; we walked for a short time on the shore and then retired to the inn. The wind, which had fallen in the south, now rose in the west. The moon had reached her summit in the sky and was beginning to go down; the clouds swept across it swifter than the flight of the vulture. Suddenly a heavy rain came down.

I had been calm during the day, but as soon as night came, a thousand fears arose in my mind. I was anxious and watchful; my right hand grasped a pistol hidden in my shirt. Every sound terrified me, but I decided that I would not shrink from the fight until my own life or that of my enemy was over.

Elizabeth asked, "What is it that bothers you, my dear Victor? What is it you fear?"

"Oh! Peace, peace, my love," I replied. "After this night, all will be safe; but this night is dreadful, very dreadful."

I passed an hour in this state of mind. Suddenly I thought about how fearful the fight that I expected would be to my wife, and I asked her to go to bed, resolving not to join her until I had discovered and conquered my enemy.

She left me, and I continued some time walking up and down the passages of the house and inspecting every corner that might be a hiding place. But I discovered no trace of him and was beginning to think that some lucky chance had kept him away, when suddenly I heard a shrill and dreadful scream. It came from the bedroom. As I heard it, the whole truth rushed into my mind. I rushed into the room.

Great God! Why did I not then die! Why am I here to tell the story of the destruction of the purest creature on earth? She was there, lifeless, thrown across the bed, her head hanging down and her pale features covered by her hair. Could I see this and live? Alas!

While I still hung over her, I happened to look up. With a feeling of horror, I saw at the open window that most hideous and hated creature. A grin was on the face of the monster; he seemed to jeer, as with his fiendish finger he pointed toward the corpse of my wife. I rushed toward the window and, drawing the pistol from my shirt, I fired; but he escaped and, running with the swiftness of lightning, he plunged into the lake.

The firing of my pistol brought a crowd into the room. I pointed to the spot where he had disappeared,

I rushed toward the window and fired the pistol.

and we followed the track with boats. After passing several hours, we returned hopeless, most of my companions believing it to have been my imagination about there being a monster.

I was bewildered, in a cloud of wonder and horror. The death of William, the murder of Clerval, and lastly of my wife; even at that moment I did not know if my only remaining friends were safe from the evil of that fiend; my father even now might be writhing under his grasp, and Ernest might be dead at his feet. I started up and resolved to return to Geneva with all possible speed.

Nothing is so painful to the human mind as a great and sudden change. The sun might shine or the clouds might go down: but nothing could appear to me as it had done the day before. A fiend had snatched from me every hope of future happiness; no creature had ever been so miserable as I was. One by one my friends were taken away. I was left alone. I must now tell, in a few words, what remains of my hideous story.

10. Frankenstein Pursues the Monster

I ARRIVED AT Geneva. My father and Ernest yet lived, but the old man had lost the charm and delight of his later years—his Elizabeth. He was unable to rise from his bed, and in a few days he died in my arms.

I was possessed by a maddening rage when I thought of the monster I had created, the miserable demon I had sent abroad into the world for my destruction. I prayed that I might have him within my grasp to bring revenge on his cursed head.

Uncertain how to track the fiend, I wandered for many hours. As night approached, I found myself at the entrance of the cemetery where William, Elizabeth, and my father were buried. I entered it and went to the tomb that marked their graves. Everything was silent except the leaves of the trees, which were shaking in the wind. The night was dark. I knelt on the grass and kissed the earth and cried out, "I swear to chase down the demon who caused this misery, until he or I shall die in mortal combat."

Through the stillness of night, I was answered by a loud and fiendish laugh. A well-known and hated voice whispered, "I am satisfied, miserable wretch! You have determined to live and suffer, and I am satisfied."

I darted toward the spot from which the voice came, but the devil escaped me. Suddenly the moon arose and shone full upon his ghastly body as he fled.

I went after him; and for many months this has been my task. Guided by a slight clue, I followed the windings of the Rhone. On the Mediterranean we both boarded a vessel bound for the Black Sea, but somehow he escaped me. Amidst the wilds of Tartary and Russia, although he still kept out of my reach, I constantly followed in his track. Sometimes the peasants, scared by this horrid monster, informed me of his path; sometimes he himself, who feared that I might despair and die if I lost all trace of him, left some mark to guide me. When the snows came down, I saw and followed the print of his huge step on the white plain.

When I could, I followed the courses of the rivers; but the demon generally avoided these, as it was here that the population collected.

What his feelings were I cannot know. Sometimes, indeed, he left marks in writing on the bark of trees or cut in stone that guided me and brought out my fury. "My power over you is not yet over," he wrote. "Follow me; I seek the everlasting ice of the north, where you will feel the misery of cold and frost, to which I am unfeeling. You will find near where you are a dead rabbit; eat it and gain your strength. You will need it. Come after me; we have yet to fight for our lives, but many hard and miserable hours must you suffer until that period shall arrive."

As I continued my journey northward, the snows thickened and the rivers were covered with ice. Another message he left was in these words: "Prepare for the worst! Wrap yourself in furs and provide yourself with food, for we shall soon enter upon a journey where your sufferings will satisfy my hatred."

Some weeks before this period I had obtained a sledge and dogs and thus traveled across the snows with speed. I was able to gain on him, so much so that when I first saw the ocean he was but one day's journey ahead of me, and I hoped to cut him off before he should reach the shore. I pressed on, and in two days arrived at a wretched seaside village. I asked the natives about the fiend, and they told me a gigantic monster had arrived the night before, armed with a gun and many pistols. He had carried off their store of winter food and, placing it in a sledge, he had stolen their dogs to draw it and had gone on his way.

He had escaped me, and I now faced an almost endless journey across the ice plains and mountainous icebergs, amidst cold that few of the natives could long endure, and which I could not hope to survive. I exchanged my land sledge for one made for the ice-covered ocean, bought a stock of food, and departed from land. I cannot guess how many days have passed since then. Huge and rugged mountains of ice often barred my passage, and I often heard the thunder of the sea beneath. But again the frost came and made the paths of the sea safe.

Once, after the poor dogs that pulled the sledge had climbed to the top of a sloping iceberg, I looked out and suddenly my eye caught a dark speck on the plain of ice ahead. I strained my sight to find out what it could be and uttered a wild cry of excitement when I made out a sledge and the hulking shape of the fiend.

I gave my dogs a good portion of food and then continued my route. The sledge was still visible, and I never again lost sight of it. I gained on it, and after nearly two days' journey, I beheld my enemy at no more than a mile away, my heart bounding within me.

But now, when I appeared almost within grasp of my foe, I lost all trace of him. A ground sea was heard; it thundered as the waters rolled and swelled beneath me. I drove on, but in vain. The wind arose; the sea

The sea had surrounded the piece of ice I was left upon.

roared; and with the shock of an earthquake, it split and cracked open the ice in front of me. In a few minutes the sea had surrounded the piece of ice I was left upon.

Many hours passed; then I saw your ship. I had no idea that ships ever came so far north and was astounded by the sight. I quickly destroyed part of my sledge to construct oars, and with great effort I was able to enter the sea and row my ice raft in the direction of your ship.

Oh, Walton, my friend, must I die and the monster yet live? If I do, swear to me that he shall not escape, that you will seek him out and kill him. Once his words had power over my heart; but do not trust him, and plunge your sword straight into his heart.

11. Walton and the Monster

August 26, 17—

Dearest sister,

You have read this strange and amazing story; and is it not horrifying? Sometimes, in painful agony, he could not continue his tale; at other times, his broken voice could barely utter the words. His tale is told with an appearance of truth, yet I must say that the letters of Felix and Safie, which he showed me, and our sighting of the monster from the ship, brought to me a stronger belief in the truth of his story than his claims to it. Such a monster, then, really exists! Sometimes I tried to gain from Frankenstein the details of how he created the monster, but on this point he refused to tell me anything.

"Are you mad, my friend?" he asked. "Would you create for yourself and the world a demonical enemy? Peace, peace! Learn from my miseries."

Thus a week passed away, while I listened to the strangest tale ever told. Shortly afterward our ship was surrounded by icebergs that allowed of no escape and threatened at every moment to crush us. Finally the ice began to move, and we heard roarings like thunder as the ice cracked in every direction.

My unfortunate guest, meanwhile, was so ill he was confined to his bed.

When the ice cracked behind us and allowed us a passage toward the south, I made the decision to bring my men and the ship back to England.

"Do you, then, really return to England?" asked Victor Frankenstein from his bed.

"Alas!" I told him. "Yes, I cannot lead them further into danger."

"Do so, if you will; but I will not. I must pursue the fiend to the end of my life." Saying this, he tried to spring from the bed, but instead he fell back and fainted.

It was hours before he recovered, and when he did, he called me to come near. "My strength is gone," he said. "I feel that I shall soon die, and that he, my enemy, will live. During these last few days I have been thinking about my life. In a fit of madness, I created a creature and was bound to try to give him happiness. This was my duty; but there was another duty higher than that. That was my duty to my fellow human beings. I was right to refuse to create a mate for the monster. He was wicked; he destroyed my loved ones. I do not even now know where his thirst for vengeance may end. The task of his destruction was mine, but I have failed. Now that you are returning to England, you will have little chance of meeting with him. Farewell, Walton!" He sank into silence. About half an hour later he tried to speak but was unable; he pressed my hand, and his eyes closed forever.

Margaret, what comment can I make on the death of this extraordinary man?

Wait! I hear something. It is midnight; the breeze is blowing. There is a sound of a human voice; it comes from the room where Frankenstein lies dead. I must get up and go look. Good night, my sister.

Reaching out one huge hand, the creature hung over the coffin.

Great God! What a scene has just taken place! I hardly know whether I shall be able to write it down! Yet the tale which I have set down would not be complete without this final event.

I entered the room where Frankenstein lay. Over him hung a creature which I cannot find words to describe—gigantic, monstrous, ugly. As he hung over the coffin, his face was hidden by long locks of ragged hair; but one huge hand, in color and texture like that of a mummy, was reaching out. When he heard the sound of my approach, he sprang toward the window. Never did I see so disgusting and ugly a face. I shut my eyes and called on him to remain.

He paused, looking on me with wonder, and turned toward the lifeless form of his creator.

"In his murder my crimes are done with," he said. "Oh, Frankenstein! What does it matter that I now ask you to pardon me? I destroyed you by destroying all you loved. Alas, he is dead, he cannot answer me."

I approached this giant; I dared not again raise my eyes to his face, there was something so hideous and unearthly in it. "Your sorrow," I said, "is worthless. If you had listened to your conscience, Frankenstein would yet have lived."

"Do you think that I did not then feel agony and sadness? He," the monster continued, pointing to his creator, "he did not suffer in his death one thousandth of the anguish that was mine. Do you think that the groans of Clerval were music to my ears? My heart was made to be awakened by love and kindness, and it was broken by misery and became violent and full of hatred.

"After the murder of Clerval, I returned to Switzerland. I hated myself. But when I found out that he, my creator, dared to hope for happiness from which I was forever barred, then I was filled with a thirst for vengeance. I remembered the threat I had made and decided that I would carry it out. Yet when she died— then I was not miserable. I had cast off all feeling. Evil from then on became my good. The completion of my demonical plan became my passion. And now it is ended; there is my last victim!"

"Wretch!" I said. "You throw a torch into a building, and when it burns up, you sit among the ruins and cry over its destruction. Hypocritical fiend! It is not pity for him that you feel; you are sorry only because the victim is no longer in your power."

"Oh, it is not so—not so," interrupted the creature. "I am content to suffer alone. Once my imagination had dreams of goodness, of fame, of enjoyment. Once I dreamed of meeting with beings who, pardoning my outward form, would love me for the excellent qualities I was capable of showing. I cannot believe that I am the same creature whose thoughts were once filled with beauty and goodness. But it is so; the fallen angel becomes a devil. Yet even Satan had friends and companions; I am alone.

"You, who call Frankenstein your friend, seem to have a knowledge of my crimes and his misfortunes. But in the details he gave you of them he could not sum up the hours and months of misery I suffered. For while I destroyed his hopes, I did not satisfy my own desires. I wanted love and fellowship, and I was rejected. Yes, it is true that I am a wretch. I have murdered the lovely and the helpless; I have strangled the innocent as they slept and grasped to death the throat of those who never injured me or any other living thing. I have brought my creator to misery. There he lies in death. You hate me, but your hatred cannot equal that with which I regard myself.

"I shall leave your ship on the ice raft that brought

me here and shall seek the northernmost point of the world; I shall gather material for my funeral fire and burn this miserable body to ashes. Stained by crimes and torn by sadness, where can I find rest but in death? Farewell! I leave you, the last human these eyes will ever see."

He turned to the figure on the bed and exclaimed, "Farewell, Frankenstein! Destroyed as you were, my agony was still worse than yours. But soon I shall die, and what I now feel will be no longer felt. I shall climb atop my funeral pyre of torturing flames. My ashes will be swept into the sea by the winds. My spirit will sleep in peace. Farewell."

He sprang from the cabin window as he said this, upon the ice raft that lay close to the ship. He was soon carried away by the waves and was lost in darkness and distance.